The French Gardener

**Center Point
Large Print**

**This Large Print Book carries the
Seal of Approval of N.A.V.H.**

The French Gardener

SANTA MONTEFIORE

CENTER POINT PUBLISHING
THORNDIKE, MAINE

To my sister-in-law, Sarah,
with love

This Center Point Large Print edition
is published in the year 2009 by arrangement with
Simon & Schuster, Inc.

Originally published in Great Britain in 2008
by Hodder and Stoughton.

Copyright © 2008 by Santa Montefiore.

The text of this Large Print edition is unabridged.
In other aspects, this book may vary
from the original edition.
Printed in the United States of America.
Set in 16-point Times New Roman type.

ISBN: 978-1-60285-494-9

Library of Congress Cataloging-in-Publication Data

Montefiore, Santa, 1970–
    The French gardener / Santa Montefiore.
        p. cm.
    ISBN 978-1-60285-494-9 (lib. bdg. : alk. paper)
    1. Country life—England—Fiction. 2. Country homes—England—Fiction.
        3. Gardening—Fiction. 4. Gardens—Fiction.
        5. Triangles (Interpersonal relations)—Fiction. 6. Large type books. I. Title.
    PR6113.O544F74 2009
    823´.92—dc22
    2009012827

Acknowledgments

The idea of a magical garden did not live for me until I went to see Georgia Langton in Dorset. Not only is she a gifted gardener, but one of England's most charming eccentrics. She inspired me and fired me up with ideas so that the book was pure pleasure to write from beginning to end. I thank her profusely and assure the reader that any technical errors found in the text are entirely my own.

Once again Sue Johnson-Hill was on hand in Bordeaux to answer my questions with enthusiasm and patience. I thank her for coming to my aid a second time!

I'm extremely grateful to my father for giving me a deep understanding of life and an appreciation of nature. I could not imagine my hero without his wise example.

My mother is a fountain of knowledge, a sensitive editor and a shrewd sounding board for me to bounce ideas off. She has given me so much of her time and enthusiasm and for that I'm enormously grateful.

The book wouldn't be suitable for publication without a thorough pruning from my UK editor, Susan Fletcher. She is a superb editor and a great connoisseur of good writing. She has the patience and attention to detail that I do not. I value her advice and thank her for taking the trouble to make sure the book is as good as it can possibly be.

My agent, Sheila Crowley, has the unique ability of making me feel like I'm her only author. She's tireless, cheerful, yet formidable when a heavy gun is required. I thank her for being there to fight in my corner and for her encouragement when I'm tearing my hair out and getting nothing written!

I'm extremely proud to be published in the United States, and to have such an enthusiastic, energetic and professional team at Simon & Schuster. I'd like to thank them all, but especially Trish Todd, my editor, for having such confidence in my writing. Her belief in my ability means a great deal to me and gives me enormous encouragement to continue writing.

I also thank Kate Rock again, and again, for without her help I would never have got published to start with; Eleni Fostiropoulos and my fantastic team at Hodder; my fellow author, Elizabeth Buchan, for generously sharing ideas; and my old school friend, Cosima Townley, for introducing me to Miss Fitz, thus inspiring me to include a ferret of my own.

I thank my darling children, Lily and Sasha for their inspiration and their love.

My greatest debt of gratitude, as always, goes to my husband, Sebag. He's indefatigable with thoughts and ideas, constant in his support and wise in his advice. His paw prints are all over this book!

Prologue

Hartington House
Summer 2004

It was nearly dusk when she reached the cottage, a cardboard box held tightly against her chest. The sun hung low in the sky, turning the clouds pink like tufts of cotton candy. Long shadows fell across grass already damp with dew. The air smelled sweet, of fertile soil and thriving flowers. Tiny dragonflies hovered in the still, humid air, their wings glinting in the light. The cottage was quaint, symmetrical, with a tall roof that dwarfed the walls below it. It might once have been a barn, or grain shed, positioned as it was in the middle of a field. The roof tiles were brown and covered in moss, the chimney leaning a little to the left. The top of the roof sagged slightly, as if it had grown tired with age. Roses tumbled over the door where the paint had already started to peel. It looked sadly neglected, forgotten at the bottom of the garden by the river, hidden in a small copse. A fat pigeon settled down for the night, cooing lazily in the gutter, and a couple of squirrels scurried up a chestnut tree and crouched in the crook of a branch to watch her with suspicious black eyes.

She stood awhile, contemplating the gentle flow of the river Hart as it ran down the valley to the

7

sea. She remembered fishing with nets and throwing sticks into the water from the little stone bridge. Nothing had changed. Cows still mooed in the field downriver and the distant sound of a tractor rattled up the track behind the hedge. She blinked through the mist of nostalgia and put the key in the lock.

The door opened with a whine, as if in protest. She entered the hall, noticing at once the lingering scent of orange blossom. When she saw the sitting room, cluttered with photographs, trinkets and books, she assumed someone was living there. As far as she knew, the agent hadn't yet sold the estate, which included the cottage. It had been on the market now for over ten months. "Hello," she called out. "Is anyone there?" No reply. She frowned a little nervously and closed the front door behind her. She put the box down on the floor of the hall. The air was warm and musty, smelling of old memories and tears. Her eyes stung with tears of her own.

She went into the kitchen where the table was laid with china cups and a teapot, the chairs pulled out. The remains of a tea for two. She put her hand on the back of one of the chairs to steady herself. In all the years she had lived in the big house, she had never entered the cottage. It had always been locked and she had never been curious. Judging by the layer of dust that covered the kitchen table, no one else had been there either.

She heard a noise upstairs, like a footstep. "Hello," she called again, suddenly afraid. "Is anyone here?"

Still no reply. She returned to the hall and picked up the box. Her attention was once more drawn upstairs. She turned to face the light that flooded the landing. It seemed not of this world. Her fear dissolved in its magnificence and a silent call came from deep inside her heart.

Tentatively, she began to climb the stairs. At the top of the landing, on the left, was an empty room. She put the box down in there, then stood back a moment not wanting to leave it. Inside the box was something of enormous value. She found it almost impossible to part with, but knew it was the right thing to do. Even if it was never found, she could rest in the certainty that she had done her very best. She didn't like to keep secrets from her own family, but this was one that she would take to her grave.

A bedroom across the landing drew her away from the box. It smelled familiar, of cut grass and the same sweet scent of orange blossom she had noticed in the hall. She sat on the bed, in the shaft of sunlight that streamed through the thick covering of mildew that had stained the window green. It was warm upon her face, amber—the color of wistfulness. She closed her eyes, sensing the presence of someone close, and listened. Once again her eyes stung with tears. She knew if she opened them the moment would be lost.

"Don't go," she said in the silence of her mind. "Please don't leave me." Then she leaned back and waited for a response.

Autumn

I

The yellow leaves of the weeping willow in autumn

Hartington House, Dorset
October 2005

Gus crept up to his mother's study door and put his ear to the crack. He inhaled the familiar smell of Marlboro Lights and felt his frustration mount at the sound of her husky voice speaking on the telephone. He knew she was talking to his teacher, Mr. Marlow. He assumed, correctly, that she wasn't on his side. Gus was a problem no one wanted to take the trouble to solve. "I don't believe it!" she exclaimed. "I'm so sorry, Mr. Marlow. It won't happen again. It really won't. His father will be down tonight from London. I'll make sure he talks to him . . . You're right, it's absolutely not on to bite another child . . . I'll find him and send him straight back to school." Then her tone softened and Gus heard her chair scrape across the wooden floorboards as she stood up. "I know he *can* be a bit aggressive, but we only moved from London a couple of months ago. It's been difficult for him. He's left all his friends behind. He's only seven. He'll settle in. Just give him time, Mr. Marlow? Please. He's a good boy, really."

Gus didn't hang around to hear more. He tiptoed back down the corridor and out the garden door onto the terrace. The lawn was a rich, wet green, sparkling in the pale morning light. He took a deep breath and watched mist rise into the air. He shoved his hands into his trouser pockets and shivered. He'd left his coat at school. Swallowing his resentment, he wandered across the terrace and up the thyme walk lined with shaggy round topiary balls. His shoulders hunched, his feet kicking out in front of him, his eyes searched for some small creature upon which to vent his anger.

At the end of the thyme walk was a field full of sheep belonging to their neighbor Jeremy Fitzherbert. Among the sheep was a disheveled old donkey called Charlie. Gus enjoyed nothing more than bullying the beast, chasing him around the field with a stick until his braying grew hoarse and desperate. He climbed the fence. Sensing danger, Charlie pricked his ears. He spotted the little boy jumping down and his eyes widened with fear. He stood frozen to the ground, nostrils flaring, heart turning over like a rusty engine.

Gus felt a jolt of excitement. He forgot about biting Adam Hudson in the playground, about running out of the school gates and up the High Street, about his mother's angry voice and his own clawing sense of isolation. He forgot about everything except the sudden rush of blood as he set off in pursuit of the donkey.

"You a scaredy cat?" he hissed as he approached the terrified animal. "Whoooa!" He lunged at him, delighting in the clumsy way the donkey stumbled back before cantering stiffly off towards the woods at the top of the field, braying in panic. What a shame he hadn't brought the stick. It was more fun when he hit him.

Bored of that game, Gus continued into the woods, leaving Charlie trembling in the corner of the field, surrounded by sheep. The ground was soggy, strewn with twigs and brown leaves amongst which a shiny pheasant scraped the earth for food. The sun shone weakly through the leaves, illuminating the spiders' webs that adorned the surrounding shrubbery with lace. Gus picked up a twig and began to swipe the webs, squashing the fleeing spiders under foot. The pleasure was fleeting, and he was left with the emptiness of believing, albeit subconsciously, that he was of no value to anyone.

Miranda Claybourne put down the telephone and remained at the window, staring out over the orchard. The ground was littered with apples and the last of the plums. She had sensed her son's presence at the door, but now he had gone. Of all the days Gus had to choose to play truant, he had chosen Deadline Day. She stubbed out her cigarette, reassuring herself that a lapse in her struggle to quit was absolutely okay; three puffs hardly

15

counted. She didn't have time to go looking for him, and anyway, she wouldn't know where to start, the grounds were so large and, she observed with a sinking feeling, desperately overgrown and wet. The thought of tramping about in gumboots was intolerable for a city girl used to Jimmy Choos and concrete. On top of everything she had her monthly column for *Red* to finish. So far, the only advantage of living in the country was not having to brush her hair and apply makeup for the school run. Gus and his five-year-old sister, Storm, cycled up the drive every morning, leaving their bikes by the gate to take the school bus that conveniently stopped for them at eight. In London she had had to get up early in order to make herself presentable to the other mums in four-by-fours and oversized sunglasses who carried off a seemingly effortless glamour in Gucci, their smooth hair colored and cut to perfection at Richard Ward. In Hartington she imagined that barely anyone would have heard of Gucci or Richard Ward, which had seemed charmingly quaint on arrival, but was now simply quaint. She complained wittily in her column, which chronicled her struggle to adapt to country life, and turned her resentment into hilarity. Along with the wet, dreary weather, somehow wetter and drearier in the countryside than in London, the quaintness of Hartington was almost intolerable. There was nothing to do but laugh.

Unlike her husband, Miranda hadn't wanted to

move out of London. The very thought of being farther than a whiff of perfume from Harvey Nichols made her break into a cold sweat. Eating at the local pub rather than at the Ivy or Le Caprice was almost enough to confine her permanently to her own kitchen table. How she missed her Pilates classes in Notting Hill, lunches at the Wolseley with her girlfriends, stopping in at Ralph Lauren for a little self-indulgence before returning home. But they had had no choice. Gus had been kicked out of school for being aggressive, and moving him to a quiet country school seemed the sensible option. He had a whole year to go before they could pack him off to boarding school where the problem of Gus would be taken out of their hands. For Miranda and David Claybourne, one year of Gus's bad behavior was an incredibly long time.

Oh God, what am I going to do? I really don't have time for this, she muttered to herself, throwing her cigarette into the wastepaper bin and covering it with a few scrunched-up pieces of newspaper so she wouldn't be reminded of her lack of willpower. She wished she had hired another nanny instead of insisting she do it all single-handedly. That was the trouble with being a working mother: the guilt. It went in tandem with exhaustion, trying to be everything to everyone while retaining a little for oneself. David had suggested she hire a cook and a gardener, that way she'd have more time to write. Living in the country wasn't like London where one could order a home delivery of sushi or a Chinese take-away from Mr. Wing; here she had to get in her car and go into town, which required planning. She didn't have time to plan meals. The only good thing was Mr. Tit the milkman who arrived every morning with the papers and milk in his white van marked with the license plate: COW 1. He made her laugh during the bleakest hour of the day, when it was still dark and damp outside and she was struggling to get the children ready for school. As for the garden, it was a proper garden, not a patio with a few potted plants, but acres and acres of land. It wasn't so easy to find help in the country. London was full of foreigners begging for work; in Dorset there didn't seem to be any foreigners at all. It was all so alien and unnerving. She didn't belong. David had fallen in love with the house on sight because it appealed to his aspirations of grandeur. She had accepted it halfheartedly, longing for Notting Hill and asphalt, slightly guilty for not appreciating such a big house in so idyllic a set-ting. But what on earth was one to do in the coun-tryside?

As a freelance journalist she was always under pressure. They didn't need the money: David worked in the City and earned more than most people could spend in a lifetime, but writing was in her blood and she couldn't have stopped even if she had wanted to. She dreamed of one day writing a novel, a great big love story like *Anna Karenina* or *Gone with the Wind*. However, she had yet to come up with a good plot. Until she did, she was stuck with writing articles for magazines and newspapers, which at least fulfilled her need to express herself and gave her a vital foothold in London. Miranda busied herself at her computer so she didn't have to listen to the small voice of despair whispering inside her head. She put off her chores, hoping they'd go away, that David would admit it had all been a terrible mistake and take them back to where they belonged. After all, the countryside hadn't changed Gus. But David's enjoyment of the country rested on the fact that he could return to the city on Sunday and swank about having spent the weekend at his country estate. She was stuck down here indefinitely.

She considered her husband: handsome, debonair David Claybourne. Always in control, always strong and capable, cruising effortlessly through life as if he'd done it all before, loads of times. Now that they had moved she rarely saw him. At first he had returned home on Thursdays, staying until Sunday night. Now he arrived late on Friday and left after lunch on Sunday. He was tired, wanting to spend the weekend sitting in front of the television watching golf. If she didn't know him so well she would suspect he was having an affair—but David was much too concerned about what other people thought to stray.

She returned to her desk and dialed her husband's number at Goldman Sachs. Apart from wanting to share her anxiety about Gus, she just wanted to hear his voice. "Darling, it's me," she said when he picked up the telephone.

"Now, what's going on down there, sweetheart? Everything all right?" He sounded buoyant. She was immediately reassured.

"It's Gus, he's run off."

David heaved an impatient sigh. "Not again!" She suddenly felt bad for having ruined his day.

"You're going to have to give him a good talking to tonight," she said. "He'll listen to you."

"A good hiding is what he deserves."

"It's against the law. You can tell that kind of law was made by people with no children."

"Did you speak to Mr. Marlow?"

"Yes. He's not very happy. God forbid Gus gets kicked out of this school, too!" She began to toy with a pencil.

"He won't. They're more tolerant in the country. Besides, he'll grow out of it. He's just adjusting to his new surroundings."

"I hope you're right."

"You sound down, darling."

"I'm just really up against it. I've got to finish my column and I can't get to my desk I've got so many domestic chores to see to. Now Gus has run off, I won't have time to write. I'm tearing my hair out!"

"And such pretty hair!" he quipped. "Look, if you took the trouble to hire help you'd have time for the important things." He was baffled by his wife's uncharacteristic ineptitude. She had commanded the builders for eight months like a formidable colonel, but recently she had lost momentum. "You should have listened to me and hired a nanny. Jayne might have come with us had we made her an offer she couldn't refuse. Your dreams of being the domestic goddess haven't quite materialized, have they? We were fools to let her go. She was the only one Gus responded to. You're the mistress of an estate now, Miranda. Get organized down there, for God's sake, before you drive us both mad." David clearly believed their son's problems were his wife's responsibility.

"He'll come back when he's hungry," she retorted casually, hurt that he was blaming her once again. "Then I'll send him back to school." She put down the telephone and returned to her desk, glancing bleakly at the ironic title of her column: "My Bucolic Dream."

Gus sat under a tree and felt his stomach rumble. He wanted to go home and sit by the fire in the playroom and watch *Lord of the Rings* on DVD. He longed for Jayne's cottage pie and apple crumble with custard. Slowly his anger ebbed away, cooled by the damp wind that now penetrated his bones. He rubbed his hands together and

21

blew hot air into them. Even if he had had the vocabulary he wouldn't have been able to explain his actions, even to himself. He didn't know why he was poisoned with frustration and anger. He felt rejected. Lashing out made him feel better. Suddenly a large bubble expanded in his belly, rose up his windpipe and escaped his throat in a large, uncontrollable sob. His tears shocked and appalled him but he was unable to stop.

"You all right, lad?" Gus swiveled around, swallowing his weeping with a gulp. He hadn't heard the man approach. Beside him panted two black sheepdogs. "You're David Claybourne's boy, aren't you?" said Jeremy Fitzherbert. Gus nodded. Jeremy introduced himself and his thin, weathered face creased into a smile. One of the dogs leaned against his brown corduroy trousers which were tucked into green Wellington boots. A tweed cap covered thinning brown hair. His eyes were small and bright and very blue. He patted the dog's head with one gloved hand, a long stick in the other. The very stick Gus had used to torment the donkey. "Shouldn't you be at school? Come on, let me take you home."

Gus reluctantly got to his feet. One of the dogs made a rush for him. Gus recoiled. "Oh, it's a wanting-to-jump-up dog!" said Jeremy with a chuckle. "Don't worry, he doesn't bite. The thin one's Mr. Ben, the fat one's Wolfgang." Jeremy patted Mr. Ben fondly. Gus wiped his face with his sleeve and followed Jeremy down the path.

22

The sheep were gathered into a tight formation, ready to be shepherded. Charlie the donkey remained in the far corner of the field, watching them warily. "Charlie!" Jeremy called, delving into his pocket for a carrot. "Come on, old boy!" Charlie didn't move. "What's up with him?" Jeremy muttered to himself. Gus dropped his eyes and shoved his hands into his pockets. "Donkeys." Jeremy sighed, shaking his head. "I'll go and take a look at him later. He's an old codger. You know he's over ninety?"

"Really," Gus replied, looking up from beneath his dark fringe. Jeremy noticed something hard in those pale blue eyes and frowned. He didn't know how to talk to someone Gus's age, so he strode on across the field and up the thyme walk without uttering another word. Gus trudged silently behind him, wondering how he was going to get that stick back.

Once at the garden door Gus slunk in, tossing Jeremy a hasty look, more of dismissal than of gratitude. "Is your mother in? I'd like to see her," said Jeremy, lingering on the terrace.

Gus hesitated and bit his lip. He seemed to gather himself before he was able to contemplate facing his mother. "Mu-um!" he shouted at last.

Miranda's hands froze over the keys of her laptop at the sound of her son's voice. She felt a rush of relief. She hurried into the hall to find Gus, hands in pockets, feet shuffling, face grubby with mud and tears. Her heart buckled. "Darling, I've been so worried. Where have you been?" She kneeled to pull him into her arms but he stiffened. He was as cold as a corpse. "You can't just run off like that. It's not safe." Then she noticed Jeremy hovering at the door. "Oh, I'm sorry, I didn't see you," she said, getting up.

"I'm Jeremy Fitzherbert, your neighbor." He took off his glove to shake her hand. "We've waved at each other from a distance but never been properly introduced."

"Oh yes, you've met my husband, David." His hand was rough and warm. He noticed her manicured nails and the large sapphire and diamond ring on the third finger of her left hand. She smelled of lime. "I'm Miranda. Thank you for bringing him home. I've been out of my mind worrying about him."

"He was in the woods," said Jeremy. "No harm can come to him there, I assure you. Unless he gets caught in a fox trap."

"Fox trap?" Her eyes widened.

Jeremy shrugged. "They eat my chickens. Even go for the odd sheep if they're feeling particularly adventurous. I think Gus is far too astute to wind up in one of those." Miranda turned to her son, but he had disappeared.

"I'm used to London parks, not the countryside. This is all rather new to me," she said, an edge to her voice. Jeremy took in the long brown hair tied into a ponytail and the pale blue eyes, made of the same hard crystal as her son's. She was a beautiful woman with high, angular cheekbones and a strong jaw, though rather too thin for his taste. "Do you have a wife, Mr. Fitzherbert?"

"Jeremy, please," he insisted with a grin. "No, I'm a poor bachelor. In fact, I'm a charity case, Miranda. Every kind-hearted female I know is intent on finding me a bride, but who wants to be a farmer's wife these days?" He smiled diffidently, his eyes twinkling with humor.

"Oh, I'm sure there's someone out there for you. You've got plenty of time. No biological clock to push *you* into marriage before you're ready." She smiled. She didn't want to give him the impression that she was discontented. "The reason I ask whether you have a wife is that I'm looking for a cook. Oh, and a gardener. It's the sort of thing a woman might know. You don't happen to know anyone, do you? Or how I might go about it? You see, I'm extremely busy; I'm a writer. I just can't go scouring the countryside for help."

Jeremy nodded knowingly. She'd probably had an army of Filipinos in London. "The best thing to do is post a notice in Cate's Cake Shop in town. She's got a large clientele. Why don't you offer someone that cottage by the river? It's empty, isn't it?"

"That pile of rubble! I couldn't imagine anyone wanting to live there. It's a ruin."

Jeremy laughed. "Oh, it has a certain charm. It wouldn't take too much to resurrect it. If you offer the cottage you're more likely to find someone to work on the estate. I don't know of anyone locally. You'll have to bring someone in. A cottage is a good incentive."

"Perhaps you're right."

"I'll ask around."

"Thank you." She looked at him standing outside in the cold and rashly offered him a cup of coffee, regretting it even as she spoke.

"I've got to take a look at Charlie," he said, declining her offer.

"Charlie?"

"The donkey. A friendly animal. He's cowering in the corner of the field. Not like him at all. Hope the lad's okay. Found him crying in the woods. I have a horse, Whisper, if he'd like a ride sometime. Let me know. I'm in the book."

"Thank you," Miranda replied, closing the door behind him. She looked at her watch. What on earth was she going to give Gus for lunch?

She found her son sitting on the banquette in the kitchen, playing with his Game Boy. When she entered he glared at her sulkily. "Now, darling," she said, endeavoring to sound stern. "What's all this about biting another little boy at school? How do you think you're going to make friends if you bite them?"

"Don't want any friends," he replied, without taking his eyes off the game.

"Why did you bite him?"

"He started it."

"I don't care who started it. You can't go around bullying people. Do you want to be kicked out and go to boarding school early?"

"No," he replied hastily, looking up. He didn't want to go to boarding school at all. "Are you going to make me go back to school today?"

"No," she replied, reluctantly changing her mind. She didn't have the heart to send him back. "I've got to go into town and post a notice in the cake shop. You can hang out here, if you like. I'll put some fish cakes in the oven."

"Can I watch *Lord of the Rings*?" Gus had discarded his sulk like a coat that was no longer necessary.

"If you promise not to bully other children."

"I promise," he said lightly, climbing down from the bench.

Miranda gave him a hug. "I love you," she gushed, repeating the three words that always made up for the lack of time she gave her son. Gus didn't reply but hurried off to the playroom. Miranda went to telephone the school to inform them that Gus had been found but wouldn't be returning on account of a stomachache and to arrange for an older child to look out for Storm on the school bus. She would send Gus to meet her at the end of the lane. It was the least he could do.

• • •

Jeremy whistled for his dogs and walked back to the field. Charlie was still standing in the corner. "Come on, old boy," he said, taking off his glove and pulling out the carrot. He liked to feel that velvet muzzle near to his skin. It took a few moments for the donkey to realize that Jeremy was alone. When he did he tossed his head and galloped across the field. He snorted at Jeremy and nuzzled his soft nose into his hand, taking the carrot carefully so as not to bite his master's fingers. Jeremy rubbed the short fur between the animal's eyes and smiled at him affectionately. "What's the matter with you, Charlie? Why were you standing over there in the corner? It's not like you to decline the offer of a carrot." Jeremy set off up the field towards the woods. Charlie followed. He wanted more than anything to go with him, to the safety of Manor Farm where he used to live with Whisper. But Jeremy simply patted him again and closed the gate behind him, leaving Charlie at the mercy of the horrid little boy who chased him with a stick.

II

Wild winds whistling around the house at night like playful spirits

Miranda drove down the narrow, winding lane into town. Hartington was a charming, old-fashioned settlement dating back to the sixteenth century built on the river Hart. The bridge at the top of the town was said to have been constructed especially for Queen Elizabeth I so that her carriage did not get stuck in the mud as she traveled to the castle, now a ruin, that was a five-minute walk from the other side of town. The people of Hartington were proud of their heritage and there was a fete every June in celebration of its royal visitor.

The high street was barely wide enough for a car. The small shops gave the impression of leaning in like trees along hedgerows making the road look even narrower. There was Troy's hair salon, Cate's Cake Shop, a gift shop, antique shop, delicatessen and a bookshop. Then the street opened into a large green which boasted a pond with ducks and a cricket pitch. Along one side stood the town hall, a classical sandstone building with imposing pillars and tall green doors, and the Duck and Dapple Inn with dark Tudor beams and small windows. Along the other side was Hartington Primary School where young Adam Hudson still smarted from his bite, and Mr. Marlow still fumed at the audacity of Gus Claybourne's running off. St. Hilda's Church and the rectory dominated the green where the Reverend Freda Beeley held services and prayer meetings and old Colonel Pike complained weekly about the fact that the vicar was a woman.

Since moving to Hartington House, Miranda had ventured into town on the odd occasion that she needed something, like a gift for her mother-in-law's birthday or a can of baked beans. She hadn't bothered to speak to the locals although it was plain from the way they looked at her that they all knew who she was. After all, she had moved into Hartington House, the big estate on the other side of the river. Surrounded by winding lanes and hills, the house was hidden away like a secret, detached from the town that seemed not to have moved with the times. In London, people didn't stop to chat in the street and neighbors who had lived in the same building for years were unacquainted. Miranda recoiled at the thought of everyone knowing things about her and judging her. Of being invited to coffee mornings at the town hall or having to go to church and shake hands with people she had no desire to meet. It was bad enough that the children were at school and would start bringing their new friends home, though, judging by Gus's recent attempts at striking up friendships she doubted he'd find anyone to invite. As she parked her jeep at the top of the street, in the car park behind the gift shop, she shuddered at the thought of having to butter up the lady who owned the cake shop. The last thing she needed was to get sucked into local life. Indeed, the word "community" made her stomach churn, conjuring up images of provincial women in headscarves sitting around cups of tea discussing fund-raising for the new church roof. *Well,* she resolved, *I'll stick up my notice, smile sweetly and shoot off.*

Cate Sharpe was perched at a round table chatting to Henrietta Moon who owned the gift shop. Cate's brown hair was cut into a severe bob, framing a thin, pale face with bitter chocolate eyes and a small mouth above a weak chin. "You know, Henrietta," she said, letting her vowels slip lazily. "You shouldn't drink hot chocolate if you're trying to lose weight. If I had a weight battle like you, I'd drink coffee. It gets the metabolism going." Henrietta smiled, a defense mechanism she had adopted in childhood. She shook her head so that her long chestnut hair fell over her face, and took a deep breath.

"I've given up dieting," she explained. It wasn't true, but it was easier to pretend she didn't care. "Life is too short."

Cate put her hand on Henrietta's in a motherly way, although Henrietta was thirty-eight, only seven years younger than Cate. "Look, you know I think the world of you, but if you don't do some-

31

thing about it your life will be a hell of a lot shorter. You're a pretty woman. If you lost the odd stone you'd have more chance of finding a man. I hate to say it," she added smugly, "but men are put off by large women. That amount of flesh just isn't attractive. I can say that to you, can't I, because I'm your friend and you know I have your best interests at heart." Henrietta simply nodded and gulped down a mouthful of chocolate. "Quiet today, isn't it?" Henrietta nodded again. "Can't be easy, though, working opposite a cake shop!" Cate laughed. Cate, who owned a cake shop and never gained an ounce. Cate, who was always impeccably dressed in little skirts with nipped-in waists and tidy cardigans, whose white apron embroidered in pretty pink with the name of the shop never carried a single stain. Cate, whom no one liked, not even her own husband. Henrietta's eyes glazed as Cate rattled on about herself.

Henrietta's mouth watered as she surveyed the cakes on the counter. It was so cold outside—a cake would add some insulation. However, Cate sat between her and the counter like Cerberus, destroying any hope of wicked indulgence. At that moment the door opened and in walked Miranda Claybourne. Both Cate and Henrietta recognized her immediately: the snooty Londoner who had moved into Hartington House.

"Good morning," said Miranda, smiling graciously. She pushed her Chanel sunglasses to the top of her head and strode across the black and white tiled floor. The place was very pink. Pink walls, pink blinds, pink baskets of delicious looking cakes all neatly lined up in rows. Finding no one behind the counter she turned to the two women. "Do you know where she's gone?"

"You mean me," said Cate, getting up. "I'm Cate."

"Miranda Claybourne," Miranda replied, extending her hand. "I've just moved down here and need to hire some help. Jeremy Fitzherbert, our neighbor, says you're the person to talk to. Apparently this is the heart of Hartington." She chuckled at her own pun.

Cate was flattered. She proffered Miranda a hand limp and moist like dough.

"Well, I know everyone and this place is usually buzzing. I have a notice board over there." She pointed to the wall by the door where a corkboard was littered with small pieces of paper. "Can I offer you a coffee?" Cate was damned if she was going to let the new arrival get away. Miranda was reluctant but there was something in Cate's demeanor that suggested she'd take offense if Miranda declined.

"I'd love to," she said, thinking momentarily of Gus alone at home before slipping out of her Prada coat and taking a seat at the round table. Cate brought over a pink cupcake and a cup of coffee and placed them in front of their guest. Henrietta gazed at the cake longingly.

"Gorgeous coat!" Cate said, sitting down. "Oh, this is Henrietta," she added as an afterthought. "She owns the gift shop."

"We have met," said Henrietta, who would never expect a woman like Miranda Claybourne to remember her. "You've been into my shop."

"Oh, yes," Miranda replied, recalling the hurried purchase of a scented candle and some notepaper. "Of course we have."

Henrietta lowered her eyes; she'd never seen anyone more glamorous in her life.

"So?" Cate persisted. "How's it going?"

"Great," Miranda replied, reluctant to talk about herself. There wasn't much positive to say and she didn't want to offend them.

"What sort of help do you require?" Henrietta asked. Miranda noticed what beautiful skin she had, like smooth toffee. She must have been in her late thirties and yet she hadn't a single line. She wanted to ask what products she used on her face, but didn't want to strike up a friendship. Miranda took a sip of coffee. It was delicious; she needn't have lamented the absence of a Caffè Nero after all.

"Well, I need someone to cook and clean, and a gardener. The garden's a mess."

"You know that garden used to be a showpiece," said Henrietta.

"Really? You could have fooled me."

"Oh yes," agreed Cate. "The Lightlys created the

most beautiful gardens. I can't imagine that you're very into gardens, being a Londoner."

"Ava Lightly was very green-thumbed," Henrietta added hastily, worried Cate might have caused offense. She had a rather unpleasant manner when confronted by strangers, like a wary animal marking her territory with a mixture of sweetness and spite. "But she left a couple of years ago. It doesn't take long for a garden to grow wild if it's not taken care of."

"Well, I'm not at all green-thumbed," said Miranda, glancing at her prettily polished nails and inwardly grimacing at the thought of having to manicure them herself. "It depresses me to look out onto a mess." Henrietta's mouth watered as Miranda bit into the cake. "Do you make these yourself?"

Cate nodded and protruded her lips so that her chin disappeared completely. "You won't find better coffee or cake anywhere in Dorset. I hope you'll become a regular. Once you've bitten there's no going back."

"I can see why," said Miranda, wondering how such a scrawny woman was capable of making such rich and succulent cakes without eating them herself.

"I'll ask around as well," Henrietta offered help-fully. "I get a wide variety of people coming into my shop. Hartington attracts people from all around and you never know." She smiled and

Miranda found herself warming to her. She had the sweet, self-deprecating smile of a woman unaware of her prettiness.

The door opened again, letting in a cold gust of wind. "Look at you!" cried a man with a wide grin and a smooth, handsome face. "Keeping her all to yourself? Etta, you're a shocker! Cate, your secrecy doesn't surprise me at all. From you I expect the worst."

"This is Troy," said Henrietta, her face opening into a beaming smile. "He's opposite if you need your hair done. Not that you do, of course, it's perfect."

He turned to Miranda, hands on the waist of his low-cut jeans. "You've been here how long and you haven't even bothered to say hello? We're all terribly hurt, you know." He pouted. Miranda's spirits rose at the sight of Troy's infectious grin. "Cate, love of my life, I need a cake. It's bloody cold out there and I've got old Mrs. Rattle-Bag coming in for her blue rinse at twelve."

"You're so rude, Troy," Henrietta gasped with a giggle. "She's not called that at all, and Troy's really Peter," she added to Miranda.

"May I?" said Troy, not waiting for a response. "Make that a coffee, too!" He settled his clear hazel eyes on Miranda and appraised her shamelessly. "You're the most glamorous thing to set foot in Hartington in years. The last time I saw such glamour was in the woods above Hartington, a fox, if I recall, wearing a stunning coat all her own. I can see the Prada label on yours, by the way, and I'm loving your leather boots, *so* this season." He sniffed with admiration, drawing in the sugar-scented air through dilated nostrils, then added conspiratorially, "You're beautiful as well. What's your husband like?" Miranda nearly spat her coffee all over his suede jacket. "Is he gorgeous, too?"

"God, I couldn't say. Beauty's in the eye of the beholder," Miranda replied, laughing in astonishment. "*I* think he's handsome."

"You're posh, too. I love posh. If you have a title I'll give you a free haircut!"

"I don't, I'm afraid. Simple Mrs. Claybourne."

"But Mrs. Claybourne of Hartington House. That's terribly grand. Beautiful and grand, that's a heady combination. Enough to turn a gay man straight!"

"She's looking for help," Henrietta informed him. "A cook . . ."

"I can cook," he volunteered, without taking his eyes off her.

"And a gardener."

He dropped his shoulders playfully. "There I'm no help at all. Every green thing I touch dies. It's a good job my cat's not green or that would be the end of her! It would be a shame to kill off what were once the most beautiful gardens in Dorset." Henrietta noticed Cate had gone very quiet. She was making the coffee, her back turned. She threw an anxious glance at Troy, who turned his attention to the counter. "How's my coffee, sweetheart?"

"Just coming," Cate replied. The atmosphere had suddenly cooled, as it did according to Cate's moods. It had been careless of them to ignore her.

Miranda, sensing the shift, glanced at her watch. "Goodness, I must get going. It's been very nice to meet you all."

"Likewise," said Henrietta truthfully. "We'll find you your gardener, don't worry."

"Going already?" Troy gasped. "We've only just met. I've had all of ten minutes in your company. Don't you like my cologne?"

"I like it," said Miranda, shaking her head in amusement. "It suits you."

"You mean it's sweet."

"Yes, but nice sweet."

"The relief is overwhelming." He shot her a devilish smile. "Do bring Mr. Claybourne in for a trim sometime. I'd love to meet him." He wiggled his eyebrows suggestively.

"I don't know," she replied. "I might not get him back." She stood up and shrugged on her coat. The girls watched her enviously. It was black and fitted, with wide fur-lined lapels and shoulders sharp enough to graze the air she walked through. "Thank you for my coffee and cake," she said to Cate. "I really haven't tasted better. Not even in London." Cate perked up. "May I stick this on your board?" She took a typed piece of paper out of her bag.

"I'll make sure they all read it," said Cate, but she needn't have bothered; the note was so big there was no way anyone could miss it.

"Well," gushed Troy when Miranda disappeared into the street. "She's quite a looker. 'Thank you for my coffee and cake,'" he said, imitating her accent. "I love it!"

"She was rather cool to start with but she warmed up. I don't think she knows what to make of you, Troy," Henrietta teased.

"She's perfectly nice but I think she's a little stuck-up, don't you? A typical Londoner, they always think they're better than the rest of us," said Cate silkily, bringing over Troy's coffee and cake. "She's one of those women used to lots of servants running around after her. She's clearly lost without a housekeeper and a cook and a gardener and God knows what else. She bowled in here without any pleasantries as if this were the post office. It's taken her, what? Two months to come and introduce herself. Too grand for Hartington. Probably thinks we're all very provincial. She's pretty though," she added with a little sniff. "In a rather ordinary way."

"I think you're being harsh," said Troy. Everyone knew that Cate rarely had anything nice to say about anyone. "She wasn't too grand for your coffee."

"That showed her, didn't it? She won't find a better coffee in London."

"I should get back to the shop. I've left Clare there all on her own," said Henrietta, referring to her sister.

"I shouldn't worry, it's not as if you're busy," said Cate. "Would you like a cake to take back with you?"

"A cake?" repeated Henrietta, confused. Hadn't Cate berated her for eating too much not five minutes ago?

"For Clare, silly," said Cate, popping one into a bag. Henrietta took the bag and left, feeling thoroughly humiliated.

Miranda returned home to find Gus sitting in front of the fire watching *Lord of the Rings*. He was eating a packet of chips and drinking a can of Coca-Cola. "Don't you have any homework to do?" she asked.

Gus shrugged. "I left my bag at school."

Miranda sighed. "Well, you'd better bring it back on Monday or you'll be in trouble again. Your father's coming home tonight. He's not happy about what you did today."

"I didn't mean it," said Gus, stuffing his mouth with a handful of chips. "I didn't start it."

"I don't want to listen. I've got to work. Your sister will be home soon so you'll have to turn that off. She's frightened of those ghastly creatures."

"Orcs," Gus corrected.

"Whatever. Make sure you turn it off."

"But Mum . . ."

"Off!"

Miranda returned to her desk. She could still taste that delicious cake and her head buzzed from the coffee. The people she had just met would pepper her column rather nicely. Troy was marvelously fruity and Henrietta voluptuous and sweet and totally dominated by Cate who was toxic, in spite of her magical recipes. They'd make a nice little trio. The trick was to build characters that featured monthly, then she could write the book, sell the film rights and watch the world turn into a giant oyster. Her fingers began to tap swiftly over the keyboard.

After a while she heard the front door open and close and the soft footsteps of her five-year-old daughter, Storm. "Darling," she shouted, a little frustrated that Storm had come home just as she was getting into her characters. Storm appeared at the door looking glum. Her brown hair was swept off her face and her cheeks were pink from the cold. "Did you have a good day at school?"

"No. Gus is a bully," she said.

Miranda stopped typing and looked at her daughter. "A bully?"

"Madeleine doesn't want to come for a playdate because she's frightened of Gus."

"I know. He bit a little boy today."

"I saw the bite mark, it was bleeding."

"I'm sure he showed it off like a war wound!" said Miranda with irritation. No doubt the mother would be on the telephone to complain.

"He pulls the legs off spiders."

"Jolly good thing, too, they're horrid."

"They're God's creatures." Storm's eyes sparkled with tears.

"Darling, who on earth have you been talking to?"

"Mrs. Roberts says all creatures are special. Gus kills everything."

"Come here, sweetie," she said, pulling her daughter into her arms.

"I don't like Gus."

"You're not alone," said Miranda with a sigh. "Why don't you go and play in your bedroom? He's watching *Lord of the Rings*." Storm pulled away. "Do you have any homework?"

"Yes."

"I'll come up in a minute and help you with it." But Storm knew that the minute would extend into an hour and she'd end up having to do it on her own. Her mother was always too busy.

Storm sat in her pink bedroom. The wallpaper matched the curtains, depicting little pink cherubs dancing among flowers. Even the lightbulbs were pink, casting the room in a soft rosy glow. The bookshelves were laden with cuddly toys and books. She had pretty jewelry boxes where she kept trinkets and hair slides, glittery butterflies and bracelets. She had pink notebooks in which she pretended to write with pink pencils, and a Win Green gingerbread playhouse made from embroidered pink cotton full of the pink cushions she collected in every shade and size. It was there that she hid now with her reading book from school. She felt sad and alone. She pulled her favorite pink cushion to her chest and hugged it close, drying her tears on the corner. What was the point of a beautiful room if she had no friends to show it off to?

Miranda finished her column and e-mailed it off with a sigh of relief. She had forgotten about her daughter's homework. She wandered into the kitchen to pour herself a glass of wine, picking a carrot out of the fridge to quell the urge to smoke. It was time for the children's tea. All she could think of was eggy bread. Gus had already had fish cakes for lunch. As she stared blankly into the fridge the telephone rang. Sticking the handset between her cheek and shoulder she pulled out a couple of eggs. "Yes?" she said, expecting it to be her husband.

"Hi, it's Jeremy here."

"Oh, hi."

"You know you were looking for a gardener?"

"Yes," she replied, brightening.

"I've found someone who might do. He's called Mr. Underwood. He's quite old and rather eccentric, but he loves gardening."

"How did you find him?"

"He used to work on the farm."

"And now?"

"He's semiretired. He could do a few days a week for you."

"How old is he?"

Jeremy hesitated. "Midsixties."

"Will he be up to it? There's a lot to be done over here."

"Just give him a go. He's a good man."

Storm padded in, dressed in a pink fairy outfit complete with glittering crown, wings and wand. "Mummy, I'm hungry," she whined, her large eyes red rimmed from crying. Miranda frowned, hesitating a moment.

"Okay, I'll see him," she agreed hastily. "Can he come tomorrow morning? I know it's Saturday but . . ."

"I'll send him over."

"Good. Thanks, Jeremy." She hung up and turned to her daughter. "I'm making you eggy bread, darling. Are you all right?"

"Eggy bread?" exclaimed Gus, hovering in the doorway. "I hate eggy bread."

"Gus, you're in no position to complain about anything today. It's either that or spaghetti."

"Spaghetti," said Gus.

Storm screwed up her nose. "I like eggy bread."

"I'm not a restaurant. It's spaghetti for both of you." She couldn't face a tantrum from Gus, and

Storm wouldn't complain. Storm scowled. "You can have as much ketchup as you like," Miranda added to appease her. "I really don't have the energy to fight with you today."

She watched her children eat, taking pleasure from her glass of wine. David was coming home tonight. She'd bathe and change into something nice. Cook him calves' liver with baked potatoes and red wine sauce. She wanted to impress him, encourage him to spend more time at home. She craved his company. It was boring on her own in the country.

III

Misty mornings that hold within them the promise of a beautiful day

David Claybourne arrived at Hartington House at eight. Gus, in blue gingham pajamas, was waiting in the kitchen with his mother. Storm was tucked up in bed with her toy rabbit and favorite pink cushion, dreaming of bringing her new friends home to play.

When she heard the front door open Miranda told Gus to stay in the kitchen while she went to talk to his father. They lingered in the hall for what seemed like a long time, their voices low. Gus shuffled on the banquette, having drunk his glass of milk, and felt his spirit grow heavy with antici-

45

pation. He yawned and began to scratch lines into the pine with a spoon.

Finally his parents walked into the kitchen, looking serious. His father didn't greet him, but pulled out a chair and sat down. His mother handed her husband a glass of wine, before pouring one for herself. "Your mother tells me that you bit a child and ran away from school today." Gus stared at his father without blinking. He was determined not to show weakness. Aragorn never showed weakness. "This has got to stop. Your behavior is unacceptable." Gus said nothing. "As a punishment you'll not watch any television for a week." Gus's mouth opened in silent protest. He was too stunned to complain. "You've driven us both to the end of our tether. And I warn you, Gus, that if you continue to bully other children and disrupt classes we'll be left no choice but to put you into boarding school early. Do you understand?" Gus fought a rebellious tear as it broke ranks and balanced on his eyelashes. He nodded. "What do you have to say for yourself?"

"I didn't start it," Gus whispered. The tear fell onto his cheek, and he brushed it off with his sleeve.

"I don't wish to hear the ins-and-outs of your playground antics. I've had enough. Now off to bed."

Gus slunk down from the bench and walked slowly past his parents. Neither made a move to kiss him good night. Once in his bedroom he closed the door behind him, flung himself onto the bed and howled into the pillow.

"I should go up and see him," said Miranda anxiously. "He's only little."

"No, Miranda," David replied firmly. "This is the problem. You're too indulgent. You didn't send him back to school but let him watch DVDs all afternoon. No wonder he doesn't learn. What kind of message are you sending out? Let him cry himself to sleep. He's not going to learn if you go pandering to him all the time. Harden your heart. It's not fair on Gus to let him grow into a monster. It's our responsibility to teach him how to behave."

"But I don't know how to." Miranda took a swig of wine and sank into a chair.

"Don't be ridiculous. It's not rocket science. Now, have you started looking for help?"

"Yes," she replied, brightening. "I've posted a notice in the cake shop in town. According to our neighbor, Jeremy Fitzherbert, that's the nerve center of Hartington. He's sending someone to see me tomorrow. A gardener called Mr. Underwood."

"Appropriate name," he replied, nodding his approval. David was a man who liked to see things done.

"He's rather old."

"I never judge a person before meeting him."

"I suppose he'll have loads of experience."

"And a cook? Speaking of which, something smells good."

"Calves' liver," she replied. "Your favorite."

"You might become a domestic goddess after all." He drained his glass and stood up. "Right, I'm going to have a bath."

Miranda watched her husband leave the room. He hadn't even asked her about herself, nor had he noticed the cashmere dress she was wearing. She had gone to such trouble, washed her hair and applied makeup. She began to make the wine sauce. The onions made her eyes water. She suddenly felt exhausted. The last year had been unrelenting. What with Gus being asked to leave school the previous Christmas and having to homeschool him with a tutor while they found a house, redecorated and moved, all in time for the start of the September term. She could still hear him whimpering upstairs. "Damn!" she swore as she cut her finger. "Oh, I can't stay down here while Gus cries his eyes out in his room," she hissed, opening one of the drawers and pulling out a Spider-Man Band-Aid. She wrapped it over the wound and set off up the stairs.

Gus was sobbing noisily. Miranda entered his room, which smelled of old biscuits, and sat down on his bed. He stopped crying when he felt her presence and lifted his head off the pillow. She looked at him in bewilderment and placed her hand on his head where his dark hair had grown sticky around his hairline. "Gus," she whispered. "It's over now. Daddy's not angry anymore." Gus's face seemed to implode and he began to sob again. "Darling, it's all right. We're not cross anymore." Then more insistently, "Gus, pull yourself together." Gus continued to sob. Miranda grabbed him under his arms and pulled him onto her knee so that she could hug him. He buried his face in her neck the way he had done as a small child. "What is it, darling?" she asked, holding him tightly.

"I don't know," he replied at last, his voice hoarse and his breathing ragged. "I don't want to go to boarding school."

There was nothing more she could do. She held him until he calmed down, then put him back into his bed, kissed his forehead and turned off the lights. He went to sleep quickly, his pale face suddenly sweet and innocent in repose. She gazed at him for a while, asking herself why she had such a troubled child. She didn't imagine for a moment that it had anything to do with her.

David finished his bath and changed into a pair of chinos and a blue Ralph Lauren shirt. He was handsome, with shiny black hair, tanned skin and navy eyes framed by long eyelashes that would have looked too feminine on a less masculine face. David was strong and muscular from taking the time to work out every morning in the gym beneath his office. He was also vain. He dressed well, wore expensive aftershave, and worried constantly about hair loss. He was a man of self-confidence, having made a lot of money in the

City, married a beautiful woman and bought a large country house while investing in a small pied-à-terre in Kensington. David had it all: the perfect family in Dorset and the perfect mistress in London. Two separate lives. Everything was as it should be. He felt he was only doing what every man had a right to do. He loved his wife; he didn't love his mistress. But his wife could hardly expect him to remain celibate all week. Surely that was the deal. She gets the house in the country, he gets laid in London; no one gets hurt.

Downstairs, Miranda finished cooking the liver. She laid the table for two and waited for her husband to appear. Lighting a candle now seemed too theatrical, so she blew it out and put it away. It was all very unfair, she thought to herself. She cooked, washed up, kept the house clean, did the laundry, drove to Sainsbury's once a week to do the shopping, looked after the children, on top of which she had her career. David just had the career. He didn't have to think of anyone but himself. "Sod it," she muttered and poured a third glass of wine. "It's as if he doesn't see me anymore."

David was in a good mood when he appeared in the kitchen. Miranda was light-headed. He helped himself to dinner, then sat down.

"Darling, you've gone to so much trouble tonight." He looked her over appreciatively. "I have a very beautiful wife."

Her spirits leapt like a rekindled flame. "Thank

you. Tell me about London, then I can live vicariously through you!"

"The same as when you left it, only colder," he replied. She swallowed her disappointment and pressed for more details.

"Who have you been hanging out with?"

"Usual crowd, when I have time. I've been in the office until ten every night this week. I'm shattered."

"How's Blythe?" She had bumped into her old school friend at Gus's judo class in Chelsea. After years of not seeing one another they had grown close again as Miranda supported her through an acrimonious divorce. "I keep trying to call her but I just get her answering machine. That's what happens when you move to the country, all your friends forget about you!"

"She hasn't forgotten about you. She's been busy with lawyers and accountants, as you can imagine. In fact, I've been giving her a little advice," he replied pompously, holding his fork in midair. "I told her she needs to manage her divorce like a business. She's her own biggest client. She's got to cut the best deal possible. It's no good expecting the lawyer to sort it all out for her. He doesn't know what she wants. He's only thinking in terms of how much money he can get her and, as a percentage, how much he can get for himself. He might be the best in town, but she's still got to tell him what she wants. I told her to write a list. This is the last-chance saloon. Once she's closed the door, that's it. There'll be no going back to ask for the things she didn't bother to mention. He'll get away with everything and she'll be left regretting her procrastination."

"Did she listen to you?"

"I think so. The trouble is she's overemotional, can't see the forest for the trees. At the moment she just wants out. I told her money is important, at least for the sake of her son. She knows what's good for her. I'm happy to help. I never liked her husband anyway. A real ass!"

"It's shocking how many of our friends are divorcing," Miranda sighed. "Once we get sorted we should invite Blythe and Rafael for the weekend. He's a dear little boy and might be a good influence on Gus. Typical, isn't it? We meet again after years, discover we're neighbors, then I move down here. The boys were just getting to know each other."

"So long as Gus doesn't bite Rafael."

"Let's give it some time. Gus will settle." Her face darkened a moment. The problem with Gus wasn't going to go away.

"Do you think he should see someone?" she asked tentatively.

"A shrink?" David was appalled.

"Well, a child psychologist."

"Over my dead body am I letting someone interfere with my son. There's nothing wrong with Gus.

Nothing that boarding school won't put right."

"But he doesn't go for nearly another year—and he doesn't want to go."

"It's a stage. He'll grow out of it. You've just got to stay on top of it, Miranda. You're the one around all week. It's up to you."

"I suppose you're going to tell me to run my family like a business. That Gus is my biggest client." She let out a shallow laugh.

"No darling, *he's* the business," David corrected, quite seriously. "*I'm* your biggest client."

After watching the news they both went to bed. David sat up reading *The Economist* while Miranda, drunk and exhausted, curled into a ball with a pillow over her eyes to block out the light, used to having the bed to herself. They didn't make love. David made no advances and Miranda, while affronted that he didn't desire her after a week apart, was rather relieved.

The following morning, Storm entertained herself playing in her bedroom, while Gus, banned from television, wandered into the woods to set traps for unsuspecting animals. David read the papers over breakfast of eggs, bacon and toast, which Miranda cooked. She prepared to interview the gardener. "Do you want to see him with me?" she asked David, who, without taking his eyes from the *Telegraph*, replied that it was her department. "You're Minister of Domestic Policy," he said.

"And who are you?" she asked, irritated by his lack of interest.

"I'm prime minister," he replied. "If you want a second opinion I'll gladly give it. Otherwise, darling, I trust your judgment implicitly."

Miranda sent David off to sample Cate's coffee and waited in her study. She was tired of having to do everything herself. She recalled the army of builders and decorators she had marched down to Hartington to transform the house into her dream home. David had let her decorate it as she wished—her good taste was one of the reasons he had married her—and dutifully paid the bills without resistance. As minister of domestic policy, she was expected to build a home for him and their children. It didn't occur to him to step down from his high office and help. It struck her that there was nothing they shared anymore. Even the children fell under her jurisdiction while he was the prime minister puppeteer, holding all the strings.

As she pondered the state of her marriage the doorbell rang and she hurried across the hall. She took a deep breath and prayed that Mr. Underwood would be the perfect gardener and added, while she was on the line to the Lord, that a cook and a housekeeper might follow. She opened the door to find a gnomelike man dressed in a brown jacket and trousers with a tweed cap set on an abundant crown of curly gray hair. When he saw her he hastily took off the cap and held it against his waistcoat.

"I'm Mr. Underwood, come about the gardening job," he said in a broad Dorset accent. Miranda didn't extend her hand; he looked as though he wouldn't know what to do with it.

"Do come inside, Mr. Underwood," she replied, stepping aside to let him pass into the hall. A gust of damp wind blew in with him. "Gosh, it is wet today," she exclaimed, closing the door behind him. "I hate drizzle."

"Global warming," he said dolefully. "One day it's as hot as summer, the next it's as cold as Siberia! These days you don't know what to expect."

"Please come into my study, Mr. Underwood." He followed her, casting his eyes over the flag-stone floor and freshly painted cream walls. There was a large, empty fireplace where logs should have been burning and a pretty rug where one would expect a couple of sleeping dogs. When the Lightlys had owned Hartington there was always a fire in the grate and a cheery flower arrangement on the wide refectory table in the hall. The round table that now took its place looked lonely with only a lifeless sculpture positioned on top.

"Just moved in then?" he asked. Miranda noticed he spoke deliberately and slowly, clearly a man in no hurry.

"Yes. Do you know the house?"

"Aye. This was once the most beautiful garden in Dorset."

"Really," she said, showing him to an armchair. He noticed she hadn't lit the fire in her study either, but it smelled of smoke, which was encouraging.

"Mrs. Lightly was a gifted lady."

"So I'm told."

"You should light the fires in this house. I could bring logs in for you if you like."

"Thank you. You see, we need someone like you." Although, as he put his stumpy finger up his nose and wiggled it about, she wasn't quite so sure.

"Got an itchy nose," he explained, giving his finger another wiggle.

"Thank you, Mr. Underwood. Now tell me, I gather you worked for Jeremy Fitzherbert?"

He withdrew his finger and wiped it on his jacket. "I worked on the farm for over forty years. Ploughing, sowing, but what I enjoy most is gardens. Have you seen the toadstools in the woods?" His eyes shone like hematite.

Miranda shook her head. "Toadstools?"

"Aye. There'll be a fair few up there. It's a wet autumn. D'you know that the mushroom itself is only the fruit of the mushroom plant?"

"No, I didn't."

"It's only when the plant growing in the ground becomes strong enough to produce seeds that mushrooms appear."

"Really?" She tried to sound interested. This wasn't going quite as well as she had thought.

"There are a lot of edible toadstools but most people don't know that. They eat only mushrooms. Mrs. Underwood cooks a good toadstool soup. She knows which ones to eat and which ones not to eat." Miranda noticed Mr. Underwood's large belly. He was clearly well fed. She narrowed her eyes thoughtfully.

"This is a large property, Mr. Underwood."

"Mrs. Lightly did it all on her own," he said, nodding slowly with admiration.

"Didn't she have anyone to help her?"

"Only Hector. It was her passion."

"Well, it's been left to go wild for a year at least. There's a lot of work to be done. I'm not sure that you're strong enough to do it on your own."

He looked affronted. "Not strong enough!" he gasped, insulted. He jumped up, took off his jacket and stood, flexing his muscles in his shirtsleeves. "Look at this. Hard as rock it is. Hard as solid rock."

"Thank you, Mr. Underwood."

"You're as old as you feel, m'lady. Inside here I'm a strapping lad."

"I'm sure you are, Mr. Underwood. Mrs. Underwood is very lucky to have you. Tell me, how well does she cook?"

He rubbed his belly. "The little wife? She's a good woman. No one can cook like Mrs. Underwood."

Miranda decided to take a gamble. Desperation compelled her to be impulsive. "We're looking for a cook," she said. Mr. Underwood's weathered face widened into a smile and his round cheeks shone pink.

"Look no further, m'lady. Mrs. Underwood will feed you all up good and proper. Used to cook for Mrs. Lightly when she had visitors."

"So she knows the place?"

"Aye, she does."

"Would she have the time?"

He nodded eagerly. "Aye, she's got time all right. Little nippers are grown up now with nippers of their own." Miranda's mind was racing.

"I'd like to meet Mrs. Underwood," she said firmly. "Perhaps she could come up tomorrow and cook Sunday lunch for the four of us. As for you, Mr. Underwood, let me speak plainly. This place is a mess and you clearly know a thing or two about gardens. Perhaps you could start sweeping leaves and chopping logs so we can light our fires and I'll keep looking for someone"—she hesitated, anxious to find the right word so as not to offend him—"to work with you on the landscaping side. I think this place requires two pairs of hands, don't you?"

Mr. Underwood nodded slowly. He didn't quite understand what she meant by landscaping. However, he loved chopping logs and lighting fires, and was already envisaging vast mountains of leaves.

"I'll pay you eight pounds hour and you do as much as you're able."

"That's as good to me as plum pudding, m'lady," he replied, clearly pleased.

"Call me Mrs. Claybourne," she added.

"Mrs. Claybourne, m'lady."

She sighed and let it go. "You can start on Monday and don't forget to tell Mrs. Underwood to come up tomorrow, if she can—perhaps she could call me to discuss details."

David returned from Cate's Cake Shop in a good mood. He strode into the kitchen where Miranda was roasting a chicken and grabbed her around the waist, kissing her neck behind her ponytail. "You were right about that coffee. It's given me a real buzz. Charming people, too. I can't think why we never explored before. It's a quaint place."

"Do you like it?" She turned to face him, leaning back against the Aga.

"I had a little chat with the locals, gave them a bit of advice about their businesses." He smiled mischievously.

"Oh, David, you didn't?"

"Of course I didn't. What do you take me for, a pompous ass?"

"I should hope not!"

"I chatted to Cate, who's definitely hot for me. Colonel Pike—asked him a bit about the war. They all knew who I was. Of course, I can't remember them all by name, but they were suitably deferential. I think I'm going to enjoy being lord of the manor. Should spend a little more time down here. It's like living fifty years ago. Can't think why we didn't move out sooner."

"That Cate's a snake in the grass. Watch out for her."

"Saw your notice up on the board. Sweet!"

"It's not sweet. It's practical. You'll see, it'll do the trick."

"Let's hope so. The lady of the manor shouldn't be getting her fingers dirty in the garden and cleaning the house. I want my wife to have the smooth hands of a duchess."

"Lucky my work is all at the computer then, isn't it?"

"How did your meeting with Mr. Underwood go?"

"He'll do, for the moment. We still need a proper gardener. He can do odd jobs, raking leaves, mowing, logs, that sort of thing. His wife is coming to cook lunch tomorrow. She used to cook for the previous owners."

"I'm impressed, darling." He lifted her chin. "I never thought you'd pull it all together."

"I've been so busy . . ." He silenced her with a kiss.

"Shhh. Don't forget your biggest client!"

IV

The crab-apple tree laden with fruit

Miranda awoke in the middle of the night. David lay on his stomach, fast asleep. She watched him for a moment, his back rising and falling in the silvery light of the moon that entered through the gap in the curtains. Lying there beside her he looked like a stranger, remote and out of reach. She could almost feel the heat of his body and yet he was so very far away. They seemed not to connect anymore, as if the miles that separated them had distanced them spiritually, too. She listened to the wind whistling over the roof of the house and felt an ache of loneliness, an ache she usually suppressed by being busy. After a while she climbed out of bed, slipped into her dressing gown and padded into her walk-in closet. She closed the door and turned on the light. Decorated like a boutique with shelves and drawers in mahogany, it was the room she had particularly looked forward to: an entire room dedicated to her clothes. Now the dresses and suits which hung neatly on wooden hangers divided by season and occasion seemed redundant. She laughed bitterly. What occasion? She had nothing to go to down here. She had no friends. Even her friends in London were beginning to forget she existed.

One by one she pulled the dresses out, gazing at them longingly. She was talking to herself. *You, darling little Dolce number. With the Celine handbag and Jimmy Choo shoes, you cut a dash at the charity ball at the Dorchester and at David's fortieth birthday party. Together we turned every head in the room. And you, Tulah trouser suit with your pretty shoulders and long trousers, with those Louboutin heels and Anya Hindmarch handbag, you carried me through those girls' lunches in Knightsbridge and committee meetings for Haven Breast Cancer. And you, little black Prada dress, a must-have for any woman worth her fashion credentials, now you sit like a ghost from my old life with boxes and boxes of exquisite shoes and barely used handbags. In London I always felt glamorous. I always had confidence. But down here, in Hartington, I'm disappearing. I don't know who I am anymore. I'm losing my sense of self.*

With increasing regret she opened each shoe box and took out the shoes, holding them up and turning them around in her hands as a jewelry expert might look at diamonds in the light. She was only thirty-three and yet she felt life was over. Glancing at her reflection in the mirror she was struck by how stringy she looked. She didn't have the youthful bloom she was once envied for; there were blue-gray shadows under her eyes and her skin was pale and sallow. She had to get a grip. Sort herself out. Go running, meet people, invite friends for the weekend. She couldn't allow herself to wallow in self-pity, that wouldn't keep David interested. The thought of hitting Ralph Lauren for a stylish country wardrobe made her spirits rise before she realized she had no one to leave the children with. If only she could get away for a day, Bond Street would surely resuscitate her. Those who think money doesn't buy happiness just don't know where to shop, she remembered with a wry smile, turning off the light and returning to bed. David slept on, oblivious of his wife's unhappiness.

The following morning Gus wandered around to the front of the house and saw an old Fiat parked on the gravel. He looked at it curiously. It was rusting, muddy and the pale gray paint was peeling. In the backseat sat a springer spaniel breathing fog on the windows. He tapped his knuckle against the glass. The dog wagged his tail. Gus wondered who the dog belonged to. When he walked away the animal began to bark. "Shut up, you silly mutt!" he shouted.

"Who are you calling a silly mutt? Not my Ranger, I hope." Gus was stunned to see a strange woman standing at the front door of his home, her hands on wide hips, who fixed him with narrowed eyes. "You'll be young Gus, then," she said, nodding thoughtfully. Her jaw was as square as a spade. The boy knew instinctively that this was a woman one didn't confront. "I hear you have quite a bite on you." Gus wondered how she knew. She looked at his bewildered face and softened. "Let's give Ranger a run around. He'll be misting up the windows of my car." She strode down the steps towards the vehicle. "Open it then, lad, it's not locked." Gus did as he was told and Ranger jumped out, wagging his tail excitedly and springing up to greet his mistress.

"Who are you?" said Gus, watching her pat the animal fondly with capable, pink hands.

"I'm Mrs. Underwood. I'll be cooking your lunch today, young master Gus. Roast leg of lamb, potatoes from my own garden, beans, peas and carrots. You look like you need some color in those cheeks of yours." Gus rubbed them with his hand. "Growing lads like you need vegetables. Off you go, Ranger, and have a run around!" The dog did as he was told and galloped off into the field that led down to the river. "That used to be a beautiful meadow of wildflowers." She sighed and shook her head. "Mrs. Lightly would have a seizure if she saw what has become of it."

Gus followed her back into the house, leaving Ranger to run about the property, which he seemed to know. The aroma of cooking meat filled the hall and Gus's stomach rumbled. "I'd have thought a family like you would be at church," said Mrs. Underwood, walking down the corridor towards the kitchen. "I'd be there if I weren't here. Can't say I'm a great fan of Rev. Beeley. I like a man to represent God. A man I can look up to. After all, Jesus wasn't a woman, was he? If he'd been a she, no one would have taken a blind bit of notice." Gus half-listened to her chatter, curious to see what she was cooking.

Miranda was perched on a stool in the kitchen, reading the papers. The smell of cooking had drawn her there, too. She was in a good mood. It felt right having Mrs. Underwood stooping over the Aga. She was as a cook should be: big, fat and enthusiastic, though Miranda couldn't help but spare a thought for her husband who was half her size in all but belly. "Giving Ranger a run around," said Mrs. Underwood, washing her hands in the sink. "He'll be in the river by now."

"Smells good, doesn't it, Gus?" said Miranda. "Mrs. Underwood is cooking for us today. And Mr. Underwood is going to help in the garden."

"He might be old but he's as strong as an ox, Miranda," said Mrs. Underwood. Miranda noticed that she had been called by her Christian name right from the first while Miranda called her Mrs. It didn't seem right, but there was nothing she could do. Mrs. Underwood was clearly a woman used to doing things her own way and Miranda was young enough to be her daughter.

"Where's Dad?"

"In the sitting room. Now don't go and bother him, he's reading the papers."

"Can I watch *Lord of the Rings*?" he asked.

"No, darling. You know Daddy said you can't watch it for a week. Why don't you go outside? It's not raining."

"There's nothing to do."

"Nothing to do?" Mrs. Underwood gasped. "In the countryside?"

"Where's Storm?" he asked despondently.

"In the playroom."

Gus put his hands in his pockets and wandered out.

Mrs. Underwood had to bite her tongue. She didn't know Miranda well enough to tell her how to entertain her children. With all that land there was plenty to do. Poor London kids, she thought, they need to be taught how to have fun in the countryside. By the look of their mother, who had gone back to reading the papers, she wasn't going to be the one to do it.

Gus couldn't face sitting in the playroom. Storm wasn't interested in doing the things he liked and he couldn't watch television. Instead, he went out the front door to kick the gravel, looking for something to destroy. He found a stick on the ground. It wasn't large enough to torment the donkey, but it was the perfect size to throw for a dog. He headed across the field towards the river, scanning the countryside for Ranger. He hadn't explored that side of the garden. The field didn't look like much and was overgrown with weeds. The other side was more exciting with the field full of sheep, Charlie, and the woods beyond. But Ranger had gone this way. Mrs. Underwood said he liked the river.

After a while he came to the river. It was about twenty feet wide, straddled by a gray stone bridge. A path had once run down the field, over the bridge and on to the little cottage that nestled among a cluster of chestnut trees. Gus could tell no one lived there. The windows were dark and dusty. Distracted by a noise in the water, he turned his attention to the river. His spirits rose when he saw Ranger climbing up the bank and shaking his black and white coat until it stuck up in pointy tufts. "Ranger!" he shouted. The dog bounded up, his tail whirring like the propeller of a helicopter. He let him sniff the stick then threw it as far as he could. Ranger was used to the game and galloped after it. Gus patted him when he returned with the stick in his mouth, dropping it at the boy's feet. He threw it again and again.

What finally brought the game to an end was Gus's curiosity about the little abandoned cottage. There was something compelling about those blind windows and neglected walls where ivy was slowly creeping over the bricks like a patient octopus. He left the stick on the ground and approached it. The door was locked, the pale blue paint chipped and peeling. He rubbed a window with his sleeve and peered inside. To his surprise the room was full of furniture. There were a sofa and two armchairs in front of a fireplace that gaped like the mouth of a corpse. Pictures hung on walls decorated with stripy yellow paper. If it hadn't been for the damp patch that darkened one corner it would have almost looked inhabited. He wandered around trying all the windows until he came to one that was broken and swinging on its hinges. He seized the opportunity and climbed inside.

His heart pounding with excitement at this new discovery, he forgot the injustice of being punished for a fight he didn't start and began to explore. The rooms were small and gloomy. He wished he'd brought a torch. There were papers on the desk in the sitting room, a wastepaper bin full of rubbish, books on the shelves against the wall, logs in the basket beside the fire. Everything was as if the occupier had gone out one day and never returned.

Gus explored every room. There was a modest kitchen with a rough table on which two teacups were placed alongside a teapot, milk jug and an empty plate. The little cottage was like a shrine and although Gus was only a boy, he sensed he was walking over someone else's sadness. It was as if the air was damp with tears.

After a while his rumbling stomach reminded him of Mrs. Underwood's roast lamb. He climbed back out the way he had come and called Ranger. The dog was waiting outside, lying against the wall of the cottage, strangely subdued. "Come on, you silly mutt, it's lunchtime." The dog made no move to follow. Gus tried to tempt him with the stick, but still he did not come. "Well, I'm not missing out for you. Stay if you want to, but I'm going home." He set off over the bridge and through the field. It wasn't until he was back at the house that the dog appeared, galloping over the long grass towards him.

"Where have you been?" Miranda asked when she saw her son's sweaty red face and sparkling eyes.

"Nowhere," he replied secretively. He wasn't going to share the cottage with anyone. "Just mucking around outside."

"Good. It's lunchtime. Go and call your sister. We'll eat in the dining room." Storm was watching *Fifi and the Flowertots* on television. Gus would have been furious had he not made such an exciting discovery down by the river. Storm waited for him to complain and was surprised when he didn't. Reluctantly she turned off the television and followed him through the house to the dining room.

David had spent the morning reading the papers and watching golf on television. It hadn't occurred to him that his wife might welcome his company. They were growing used to being apart. Besides, after a busy working week he needed time on his own to unwind. The smell of roast lamb wafted through the house mingling with the wood smoke

69

from the fire Mrs. Underwood had insisted on lighting in the hall. Mr. Underwood had filled the basket with logs the day before from the barn that stood beside the walled vegetable garden. The Lightlys had clearly enjoyed fires, for the barn was full of neatly chopped wood. As David walked across the hall to the dining room he felt rather smug: He was the proud owner of a proper country house.

"Something smells good," he exclaimed, finding his family already at the dining room table. He peered over the sideboard where the roast leg of lamb was placed, ready to be carved.

"I think we've found our cook," said Miranda.

"I'll reserve judgment until I've tasted it," said David, pulling out his chair and sitting down. "I think we should use this room more often," he added, casting his eyes over his wife's tasteful decoration. Mrs. Underwood entered carrying a tray of vegetable dishes. David made a move to help her.

"Oh no you don't, Mr. Claybourne, I can manage it. God didn't make me big and strong to let others do my work for me." Miranda was slightly put out at hearing her husband David referred to as mister. Mrs. Underwood balanced the tray on the corner of the sideboard and unloaded the vegetables. Gus had never seen so many. "These potatoes are from my own garden, they taste like potatoes should." There were beans, peas and carrots, sprinkled with parsley and butter. She began to carve. The meat was tender and rose pink in the middle. David's mouth watered.

The first bite confirmed what Miranda already knew. Mrs. Underwood would be a fine addition to the family. "I don't think I've tasted better," said David, as the lamb melted on his tongue.

"It's organic Dorset lamb," said Mrs. Underwood proudly. "There's a farmers' market in Hartington every Saturday morning."

"Really?" said Miranda.

"I'm surprised you don't know about it." She placed the gravy on the table.

"I don't go into town much."

"You will. Once you've settled in you'll get to know it and its people. The best way to become part of the community is to go to church. The Lightlys always sat in the front pew. There wasn't a person in town who didn't like them." Miranda cringed at the idea of playing lady of the manor, but it added another piece to David's picture-perfect country life.

"I think it's a terrific idea. It's about time we got to know the locals."

"Do you?" said Miranda, screwing up her nose. She envisaged those ghastly coffee mornings with stay-at-home mums and meetings in the church hall to discuss the flower rota. "Darling, we never went to church in London."

"More reason why we should start now. Gus and

Storm should have a religious education. It'll do them good to become part of the fabric of the place. Help them settle in." Miranda read between the lines and looked at Gus, busily tucking into his vegetables. Gus usually hated vegetables.

"I'll leave you to it, then," said Mrs. Underwood, making towards the door. "There's steam pudding for dessert. Let me know when you're ready."

"You're hired," David called after her.

"I know," she replied with a chuckle. "It's good to be back."

"Mrs. Underwood?" said Miranda.

The older woman stopped in the doorway. "Yes?"

"What's your first name?"

She straightened. "Mrs. Underwood," she replied curtly. "Everyone calls me Mrs. Underwood."

"Oh," Miranda replied, feeling foolish.

"Let me know when you're ready for pudding," she repeated with a smile. "Syrup sponge was Mr. Lightly's favorite."

After lunch David's satisfied gaze rested on his wife. There was nothing like a belly full of good food to make him feel horny. He ran his hands through his hair and leaned back in his chair. "How would you children like to watch a video for a while?" Miranda frowned. Hadn't he forbidden Gus to watch television? "Mummy and I would like a siesta." Her frown melted into a smile. Gus jumped down from his chair.

"Make sure you watch something that Storm will enjoy," Miranda shouted as they bolted for the playroom. David took his wife's hand.

"How about it, Mrs. Claybourne?"

"How about it indeed," she replied, squeezing his hand. She felt the warm sensation of their reconnection.

"Well done, darling. You've found a cook and a gardener. There's a fire blazing in the hall and the children are happy. Now you can make me happy." He stood up and led her out of the room.

"I don't think Mr. Underwood is a proper gardener," she murmured as they walked into the hall.

"He'll do for the time being. He can light fires and burn leaves. Besides, it's autumn. There's not a lot one can do in autumn."

"Everyone keeps telling me this used to be the most beautiful garden in England. I'm beginning to feel we're committing a terrible sin not looking after it."

"It's only a garden, darling." He led her upstairs and into the master bedroom. "Now let's get down to the important business before I have to catch that train to London."

Gus and Storm sat in front of the television watching *Nanny McPhee*. They had already seen it before, loads of times, but it was the only DVD that they both enjoyed. Storm noticed Gus had been rather quiet over lunch, as if he was keeping a delicious secret. He fidgeted on the sofa, his gaze drawn outside by an invisible magnet. After a while he announced that he was bored of the movie and was going outside. "Can I come, too?" Storm asked, not because she wanted to play with him, but because he reeked of something mysterious.

"No," he replied. "I want to play on my own."

"That's not very nice," she complained. "You're a poo!"

"You're a baby." He stood up and marched out of the room.

Storm gave him a minute, then followed him.

Gus noticed Mrs. Underwood's car had gone, taking Ranger with it. He was disappointed. The dog had been good company. The perfect company, in fact, for a boy who liked to play on his own. He wasn't stupid like Charlie. Gus ran off through the field to the little bridge. The clouds had cleared and the sun shone, catching the ripples in the river and making them sparkle. The air was sweet with the smell of wet earth and foliage, and the breeze had turned unexpectedly warm. He hurried across to his secret cottage, and climbed inside.

Storm watched from a distance. She had never been to that side of the garden. There was something wild and enchanting about it as the light glittered magically on the raindrops quivering on the grass and leaves. She saw her brother disappear inside the cottage and stood awhile looking about. The stone bridge delighted her, reminding her of the bridge in *Winnie-the-Pooh*. She leaned over and gazed onto the water. Below, she could see pebbles and rocks hidden among the weeds. She wondered whether there were fish and decided she'd ask her mother for a net so she could catch one. Then she turned her attention back to the cottage. Gus had been in there a long time. She knew he'd be cross if he discovered she had followed him. She bit her nails and gazed longingly at the cottage, half hoping that Gus would appear. But he didn't. She wondered what he was doing in there. Slowly, she began to walk towards it.

She peered through the window to the left of the front door. It had already been rubbed clean by Gus's sleeve so she could see inside. She gasped as she took in the room. Someone obviously lived there. With an accelerating heart she tiptoed around to the window on the other side of the front door. Pulling away the long tentacles of ivy so she could see in, she thought perhaps this was Snow White's house or Goldilocks's and imagined the seven dwarves were out with their spades or the three bears were sleeping upstairs.

Suddenly Gus appeared around the corner. "What are you doing here?" he demanded "This is my house!"

"No it isn't," she retorted, withdrawing from the window.

"I told you I wanted to play on my own."

"But I've got no one to play with." Gus's rejection was like a slap on the face. Storm's cheeks burned and her eyes glittered with tears.

"Tough!"

"I want to go inside."

"You can't."

"Why not?"

"Because only boys can climb in and besides, you don't know the password."

"What's a password?"

"You see, you don't even know what it is."

"You're mean."

"Go and cry to Mummy then."

Storm began to sob. Gus watched her impassively. "You're not my brother!" she said. "I hate you!" And she turned and ran along the riverbank, ignoring the little stone bridge that would lead her home.

V

The little stone bridge at sunset. The amber light playing upon the smooth surface of the river.

Gus watched her go then returned to the cottage. He was furious that she had discovered his secret but felt a niggling worry that she hadn't returned over the bridge, but had continued up the river into unknown territory. In London their mother had never let them out of her sight. In the park, if they had so much as disappeared behind a bush she would have called them back, her voice tight with panic. Now Storm was wandering about on her own. Gus felt guilty. If anything happened it would be his fault. The worry didn't niggle for long. He began to explore upstairs where two bedrooms and a bathroom nestled beneath the eaves. The sun shone in through the windows and caught the flakes of dust stirred up by his footsteps, making them sparkle like glitter. It was quiet and warm, the air charged with something magical. Gus forgot all about Storm and stepped inside the first bedroom.

Storm hurried along the riverbank, sobbing loudly. She hated Gus, she hated the countryside, she hated her new school and she hated the new house. She wanted to go back to London, to her old bedroom, to her school where she had lots of friends, to all that was cozy and familiar. After a while she came to a fence. On the other side was a field full of cows. Afraid of the possible presence of a bull, she leaned on the gate and rested her head on her arms, her woolly coat soaking up her tears like a sponge.

Suddenly she was aware of being watched. She heard the squelch of hooves in the mud and a gentle snorting as the shiny black cows warily approached her. If she were Gus she would have tried to frighten them, but Storm was frightened herself. She raised her eyes but dared not move. They formed a semicircle on the other side of the gate, jostling each other forward, their large eyes bright and curious. Storm was sure they could knock down the gate if they wanted to.

"Put out your hand," came a voice beside her. She was surprised to see a stranger lean on the fence and extend his hand towards the cows. He smiled at her and his weathered brown face creased about the eyes where the crows'-feet were already long and deep. He had the kind of smile that warmed a person from the inside and Storm immediately felt better, as if the lonely hole in her heart had been temporarily plugged. She remembered her mother telling her not to talk to strangers. But this man was nice, not at all like the horrid men she had been warned about.

Storm copied the man and stuck out her hand. At first the cows didn't move any closer, just observed the extended hands, snorting their hot steamy breath into the damp October air. Storm waited, excited now that she was no longer alone. She noticed the man's hand was rough and dry, the skin on his palm etched with hundreds of lines like a road map. At last the cows began to edge their way towards them, slowly at first and then with growing confidence. Storm began to tremble as one of the cows stretched its neck and brought its wet nose closer. "Don't be afraid," said the man. He had a funny accent. "They're Aberdeen Angus cows, very gentle creatures. They are afraid of *you*." He put his hand closer to hers and the cow blew onto their skin. "You see. She likes you." With the back of his fingers he stroked the cow's nose. The cow put out her tongue and licked Storm's hand.

"Her tongue is all rough," she said, giggling with pleasure.

"That's because it's got to grab hold of the grass. If it were smooth the grass would slip through." The rest of the herd now saw that the two humans were friendly and surged forward, wanting their own turn. "We have some new friends," he said and laughed. He was surprised that the child had suddenly made him happy. A while ago he had been sitting on the riverbank, head in his hands, the unhappiest he had been in twenty-six years.

"What is your name?" he asked.

"Storm."

"Storm is an unusual name. My name is Jean-Paul." He studied her flushed face, grubby where her tears had fallen, and felt a wave of compassion. A child her age shouldn't be wandering the fields on her own. "Do you live near here?"

"Hartington House," she replied, repeating the name her mother had taught her. Jean-Paul blanched and for a moment he was lost for words. "It's the other side of the river," Storm continued. But Jean-Paul knew that. He raised his eyes as if he could see over the trees to where the house nestled in the neglected gardens.

"I think I should take you home," he suggested quietly. Storm nodded, disappointed. She didn't want to go home. She wanted to stay with the cows. Jean-Paul sensed her disappointment. "You can come back another time. The cows will always be pleased to see you. They know you now."

"My brother doesn't want to play with me," she said. "He's mean."

"Do you have any other brothers or sisters?"

Storm shook her head sadly. "Just Gus."

"How long have you lived here?"

"Not long," she replied. "We used to live in London."

"I bet you did not have such a big garden in London."

"We didn't have a garden at all, but we had the park."

Jean-Paul shrugged. "But a garden is more magical than a park. Gardens are full of secret places."

"Gus's house is secret."

"You need to ask your father to build you a playhouse of your own."

"He's busy," she said, lowering her eyes so that her eyelashes almost brushed her cheek.

"Then you should make a house in the hollow tree."

"The hollow tree?"

"The hollow tree in the wild garden." The child had clearly never heard of the wild garden either. "Come, I'll show you."

They approached the little stone bridge. Jean-Paul cast his eyes at the cottage and his face turned gray. "That's Gus's secret house," said Storm, pointing at it. Jean-Paul said nothing. His heart had broken all over again. She had gone. Why had he bothered coming back? What had he expected to find? He should have let ivy grow over his memories as it was growing over their cottage. He should have moved on. But he loved with all his heart. If he suffocated his love he would surely die with it.

"Come, Storm. I'll show you the hollow tree." He walked over the bridge without glancing back at the cottage. The wild gardens, once full of purply-blue camassias and buttercups, cowslips and fluffy dandelions, had been neglected. Instead of being cut down for winter, the grasses were long and out of control. How he had loved to walk through them on those balmy spring evenings on his way to the cottage. Now it had been starved of love.

"You see that tree over there." His voice was hoarse with emotion. He pointed to a large oak that dominated the garden. "It's hollow."

"What does hollow mean?"

"No inside. It is like a shell. You can climb in it and make it into a camp." He took a deep breath. "It's been done before," he added quietly. Storm's curiosity was aroused, but Jean-Paul began to walk towards the house. "Shouldn't we let your mother know that you are back?"

"She's busy," said Storm. Jean-Paul frowned. He ran his hand through his dark hair, now graying at the temples, and looked at the little girl inquisitively. "I doubt she is too busy to notice that you have been gone. How old are you, Storm?"

"Nearly six," she replied proudly.

"You are very grown up. But even grown-ups look out for each other. Let's go and tell her you are back, just in case, eh?" His natural instinct was to hold her hand. How often he had walked those gardens holding the hands of small children, teaching them the magic and mystery of nature. But he knew it wouldn't be appropriate with this little girl. Instead, he put his hands in his jacket pockets and continued to walk towards the front of the house.

It was just as he remembered it: the soft gray stone walls and tiled slate roof; the tall, elegant chimneys where doves used to settle and coo; the three dormer windows with their little square panes of glass where the children had peered out and waved. The symmetrical harmony of the design and the peaceful way it melted into the surrounding trees and shrubbery as if they had all been created at the same time and grown old together.

Jean-Paul rang the bell. Storm stood beside him, waiting for her mother to appear. She didn't imagine she would have been worried; Mummy had been asleep. After a while, the door opened to reveal Miranda in a brown velour tracksuit, hair pulled back into a ponytail, cheeks glowing. She looked at the strange man and then at Storm and felt a sudden pang of guilt. "Are you all right, darling?" she said, crouching down to look at her daughter. She could see from Storm's grubby face that she had been crying. "What happened?" She directed her question at the stranger.

"I found her down by the river. She was alone." Miranda noticed the man's French accent. She couldn't fail to notice, too, how attractive he was. "My name is Jean-Paul."

"Please come in," she said. "Thank you so much for bringing her home."

"I don't want to trouble you," he said, his face solemn.

"You're not troubling me at all. Please, I'd like to thank you." Miranda wished she wasn't so scruffy. It was very unlike her to be seen without makeup and she was sure her tracksuit had a stain on the thigh. She couldn't bear to look. "I can't imagine what she was doing down by the river. Goodness, my children are running wild. Our neighbor, Jeremy Fitzherbert, only brought Gus back from the woods a couple of days ago. They're used to London parks and small gardens." Jean-Paul followed Miranda down the corridor to the kitchen. He noticed at once how different the house was on the inside and felt the dramatic change in vibration, as if a cold draft ran through the hall lowering the temperature in spite of the fire in the grate. Storm skipped beside Jean-Paul. He was her new friend.

"I thought you were watching a video," said Miranda to Storm, taking two cups from the painted cream dresser and placing them on the black granite worktop. "Would you like tea or coffee, Jean-Paul?"

"Coffee, please," Jean-Paul replied, perching on a stool.

"We saw some cows," said Storm. "One licked my hand." Storm held it up, grinning proudly.

"God! How horrible. You'd better wash it at once. I hope you haven't put your fingers in your mouth." She shuffled Storm to the sink, turned on the tap and lifted her up. Storm grabbed the soap and put her hands under the water.

"Her tongue is rough so she can eat the grass," the child continued.

"That's right, give them a good wash," Miranda encouraged, more concerned about germs than the nature of the cow's tongue. When she had finished, Miranda put Storm down and began to make the coffee. She noticed Jean-Paul looking at her with a bemused expression on his face. His mouth was sensual, uneven and twisted into a small smile. His eyes were warm, toffee-brown and deep-set, surrounded by long dark lashes. What struck her most was not the color, though it was rich and velvety, but their expression. They were filled with compassion as if he had a deep understanding of the world.

"We've just moved here," she said, pouring ground coffee into the machine. "We're still adjusting."

"Change takes time. But this is a beautiful place. You will be very happy here." The way he spoke sounded almost prophetic.

"What brings a Frenchman to Hartington?"

"That is a good question. I don't really know myself."

"You don't look like a tourist."

"I am not."

Storm pulled a stool over to where Jean-Paul was perched and climbed up. "Jean-Paul is going to build me a little house in a tree," she said, smiling up at him.

"She was sad she didn't have a secret house, like her brother," said Jean-Paul.

"Gus won't play with her, that's the trouble. He's nearly eight. Storm's too little for him. Do you have children?"

"No, I never married," he said.

What a waste of an attractive man, she thought.

"Gus will be going to boarding school next year," she continued.

"Boarding school? He is very little."

"Believe me, if anyone needs boarding school, it's Gus." She chuckled, opened the fridge and took out a carton of milk. "Besides, I work. The sooner they're both packed off to boarding school the better."

"What do you do?"

"I'm a journalist. A frustrated novelist, actually. I like to think that when the children go to boarding school I'll have the time to write a book."

He looked down at Storm. "Little Storm will go, too?"

"When she's eight and a half. I've got you for a while longer, haven't I, darling?" said Miranda, smiling at her daughter. But Storm only had eyes for the handsome Frenchman.

"What do you do, Jean-Paul?" She poured coffee into his cup and handed it to him.

He hesitated while he took a sip. Then he looked at her steadily and replied, "I garden."

Miranda was astonished at the coincidence. "You're a gardener?"

He gave a wry smile. "Yes, why not?" He shrugged in the way Frenchmen do, lifting his shoulders and raising the palms of his hands to the sky. "I garden."

"I'm sorry, it's just that I've been frantically looking for someone to do our garden. Everyone keeps telling me that the previous owners were brilliant gardeners and that this was the most beautiful garden in the country. I'm now feeling guilty that I'm letting it go. As if it's a great crime or something."

He stared into his coffee cup. "Did you know the people who lived here before you?"

Miranda shook her head. "No. Old people, I think. Lightly or something. They moved away."

"I see."

"You're not . . . I mean . . . you wouldn't consider . . ."

"I will bring this garden back to life," he said.

Miranda looked pleased. "My husband will think I'm mad. I don't even know you."

She couldn't have known why he suddenly offered himself. That it wasn't a wondrous coincidence but a promise made over two decades before.

"Trust me, I am more than qualified. This is no ordinary garden."

"We have a cottage just over the river. It's in need of repair. It wouldn't take long. We'd be happy for you to live there rent free."

He turned to Storm. "Gus's secret house, no?"

"It's very dirty," Storm piped up. "It's all dusty. I've looked inside."

"We'd clean it out, of course. It's a charming place. I bet it's an idyll in the summertime."

"It will do," he replied. He stood up and walked over to the window. "It would be a shame to let it go," he said gravely. "After all the work that has gone into it." *After all the love that has gone into it*.

He drained his cup. "I must go," he said. "I have

some things to sort out in France. I will return at the end of the month and I will give you a year."

"That gives us enough time to prepare your cottage."

"You never told me your name," he said, walking into the corridor.

"Miranda Claybourne."

"I ask of you one thing, Mrs. Claybourne." His gaze was so intense she felt her stomach lurch.

"Yes, what is it?"

"That you take my advice without question. I promise, you will be more than satisfied."

"Of course," she replied, blushing again. His charisma was alarming.

"You don't trust me now, but you will." He turned to Storm, who was following them into the hall. "There is magic in the garden," he said, crouching to her level.

"Magic?" she gasped, eyes wide with excitement.

His voice was a whisper. "Magic, and I am the only one who knows how to use it."

"Can I help you?" she whispered back.

"I cannot do it without you." He grinned at her. Miranda caught her breath at the sight of his smile. It transformed his entire face, giving it an air of mischief. "You will see what happens to the garden when we look after it. The more love we put into it, the more love it gives back."

"Mummy, Mummy, I want to help find the magic!" Miranda laughed. "I'd like to find the magic, too," she said, shaking his hand. He took hers and raised it to his lips. Her stomach flipped over like a pancake. She watched him disappear into the darkness. That was the oddest job interview she had ever conducted. They hadn't even discussed his wages. She bit her lip, feeling excited but uneasy; she hadn't found him, he had found her.

With a light step she returned to the kitchen to make the children's tea.

"He's nice," said Storm, jumping after her with excitement.

"Yes, he is," Miranda replied, picking up his empty coffee cup. "He's very nice. Although, God knows how I'm going to break this to your father. I know nothing about him. I have no references. He could be . . ." She shook her head. "No, I've got good gut instinct. He's honest. After all, he brought you home, didn't he?"

"I was frightened of the cows," said Storm.

"Were you, darling? Is that why you had been crying?"

"He taught me how to put my hand out."

"Where did you find him?"

"By the river."

"What was he doing there?" Miranda loaded their cups into the dishwasher.

"I don't know."

"What were *you* doing there?"

"Gus wouldn't play with me."

"You mustn't run off on your own."

"When will I see Jean-Paul again?"

"Well, he's going to be our gardener. We have to clean out the little cottage." Miranda frowned at her daughter. "Why did he say it was Gus's secret house?"

"Because Gus says it's his."

"Ah, so that's where he's been running off to."

"He won't play with me."

"That's because you're smaller than him and you're a girl. Little boys don't like playing with girls."

"He doesn't play with boys either."

"He should."

"No one likes him."

Miranda pulled out a loaf of bread. "You can have sandwiches for tea," she said, ignoring Storm's comment. Miranda didn't like to think of Gus being unpopular. Not only because it hurt her, but because it highlighted the fact that her son had a problem. A problem she was too frightened to deal with.

At that moment Gus burst in. He was relieved to see his sister alive.

"Mummy's going to clean out the cottage," said Storm triumphantly.

"What cottage?" said Gus, making furious eyes at his sister.

"*Your* cottage," Storm replied.

"The little cottage by the river," his mother added. "We have to clean it out for the new gardener."

"He's my friend," said Storm.

"What gardener?" Gus asked, feeling cornered. Everyone knew but him.

"A nice Frenchman is going to do the garden for us and he's going to live in the cottage."

"But it's my secret place!" Gus protested.

"You'll have to find another," said Miranda. Storm smirked at her brother, thinking of the hollow tree. That was *her* secret place and she wasn't going to share it with Gus.

That evening Miranda called David on his mobile phone to explain about Jean-Paul. To her surprise he accepted the news without question. He was short with her and distracted, which was just as well; had she told him any other time, he might have taken more interest.

David turned to his mistress with a sigh. "That was Miranda," he said, tossing his mobile on the bed. "She's found a gardener."

Blythe ran her fingers across his chest. "Lady Chatterley," she giggled. "Beware!"

"I don't think my wife has it in her."

"Oh, I think there's a little of Lady Chatterley in all of us."

"She's too much of a snob," he said.

"Have you seen him?"

"I doubt he's competition. He's a gardener, for Christ's sake!"

"She might like a bit of rough."

"Miranda?"

"I'm joking." She kissed him. "Oh Romeo, I've really got you going, haven't I?"

"And now I will punish you!"

He climbed on top of her and spread her legs with his knees. He had enjoyed his wife after lunch and now he was enjoying his mistress. The thing about sex was that the more he had the more he wanted. He pressed his mouth against hers and parted her lips, sliding his tongue inside to silence her. She lay like a starfish, open for him to take as he pleased. Her own husband had never been so masterful. Aroused by the thought of the two women in his life, both beautiful, both his, David entered her for the second time with triumph. He was the king of his world.

VI

Our cottage in summer when the sweet scent of honeysuckle is carried up on the breeze

Cate's Cake Shop was busy for a Monday morning. Colonel Pike sat in the corner by the window reading *The Times*, a cup of coffee steaming on the table beside a hot buttered crumpet. Every now and then his mustache would twitch at something he found offensive and he'd mutter under his breath. The Reverend Freda Beeley was enjoying tea with a couple of her choir members, Jack Tinton and Malcolm Shawditch, discussing their plans for Christmas and the carol concert to raise money to repair the church spire. Two elderly ladies sat gossiping about their friend Joan Halesham who had left her husband of sixty-two years for her old school sweetheart. "Sixty-two years!" exclaimed Dorothy Dipwood. "What's the point of exchanging one old codger for another? After eighty they're all the same, aren't they? Especially when one's as blind as Joan." William van den Bos, an avid collector of Napoleona who owned the bookshop, was at the table nearest the cakes, tucking into a large slice of lemon drizzle and talking to a man who had telephoned claiming to own Napoleon's chamber pot. "I'm extremely interested in the chamber pot," said William, dapper in a three-piece tweed suit, complete with gold dress-watch and monocle. "But I must be sure it's the real thing. I've been offered three penises by three different collectors in the last month. One simply can't be too careful."

Henrietta hadn't yet opened her gift shop and was sitting with Troy, whose first appointment of the day had been canceled. "She always does this to me," he complained. "And she asked me to come in half an hour early. Bitch!" But what interested them more than anything else was the attractive Frenchman who had sat alone in the shop the day before. "He barely uttered a word," said Cate, perching tidily at Henrietta and Troy's table. "But what he did say was delivered in such a sexy French accent I almost forgot I was married and declared myself available and ready to elope at a moment's notice."

"It was only by chance that I saw him popping in here. I was on my way to lunch when I realized I had forgotten to feed Cindy. If I hadn't gone back for the cat I would have missed him." Troy sighed melodramatically. "Is that luck or is it fate? You don't see many men as attractive as him in Hartington. We're hardly the Riviera, are we? I was positively drooling!"

"What was he like?" Henrietta asked.

"Gorgeous," said Cate.

"Gay?" asked Troy hopefully.

"Single?" laughed Henrietta.

"Frenchmen like skinny women," said Cate, screwing up her freckled nose in mock sympathy. Henrietta took another bite of brioche. "Definitely not gay. Sorry, you two."

"Did he have that smug married look?" Troy interjected icily. Cate ignored the jibe. Troy always stuck up for Henrietta.

"No. He looked single, actually," she replied, lifting her chin. "But he didn't smile. He looked serious and sad. I treated him to coffee. His face brightened a little after that. You know my coffee! He was clearly a tourist. He asked about Hartington House. Wanted to know who lived there. I think he thought the gardens were open to the public. He seemed very disappointed when I told him the gardens were all overgrown and a posh new family from London had moved in. I felt sorry for him."

"Did you tell him to go and see the castle?" Troy lowered his voice and leaned into the table conspiratorially. "Seeing Jack and Mary Tinton in fancy dress would have cheered him up. They're a hoot!"

"What do you mean, fancy dress?" Henrietta glanced over at Jack Tinton. He looked like any other fifty-year-old in jeans and corduroy jacket.

"They've just taken it upon themselves to dress up as Elizabethan characters and walk about the place for tourists. They charge a pound to have their photograph taken. Can you imagine paying a pound to be photographed with those two clots! The castle pays them five pounds an hour. They rake it in. If you want a laugh, go up there on a weekend and watch them prance around in long skirts and breeches. It's better than pantomime."

"Better than the castle, too," said Cate drily. "Why anyone wants to pay good money to wander around a pile of old stones is beyond me. Go to Hampton Court or the Tower of London, now that's proper history. Not an old ruin that claims to have had Elizabeth the First as a visitor."

"Bah!" exclaimed the colonel from the corner. He folded his paper and stood up crossly. "Nothing good about the world these days." The vicar and her two companions stopped talking and looked up at him in surprise. "Dirty hospitals, congestion, underpaid, overworked, ill-educated, foulmouthed, thugs, graffiti, gang warfare, exposed midriffs, skinny models, obesity, poverty, terrorism, war, murder, abduction, rape." He snorted in fury. "I tell you, nothing good about the world. Bloody lucky my number's nearly up. Can't be doing with it all." He moved stiffly across the room. Only the two old ladies continued chatting as if he wasn't in the room. He threw some change on the counter and shuffled out, replaced by a gust of damp wind.

"Ah, so that's why he hangs around after church," said the Reverend Beeley, chuckling good-naturedly. "At his age, it's hardly worth going home."

Cate put the change in the till and returned to her chair, smoothing down her white apron.

"I wonder if he'll come back," sighed Henrietta. There were precious few attractive single men in Hartington.

"He's in every morning. Takes the same table and grumbles about the same things. Negative people are so trying!" Cate complained, clamping her small mouth in displeasure.

"No, I mean the Frenchman. Do you think he'll be back?" said Henrietta.

"Who can say? Just passing through, I should imagine. He was delicious, though. His eyes were the softest brown I've ever seen. He gave me quite a look when he left." Cate always had to bring the conversation around to herself. "You know that lazy, bedroom look."

"How old was he?"

"Early fifties," said Cate. "He might come back." She nodded knowingly. "A man like that appreciates good coffee."

They all turned as the door opened, letting in another gust of cold air. "Told you," said Cate triumphantly. "They always come back." She stood up and greeted Miranda as if she were an old friend. "What can I get you?"

"A coffee with hot milk on the side, please," said Miranda. She turned to the notice board and ripped off the piece of paper advertising the two job vacancies.

"Found someone, have you?" said Cate.

"Yes," replied Miranda cagily. "As a matter of fact, I have."

"A cook *and* a gardener? That's quick," said Troy.

"Not in this town. Everyone passes through my cake shop."

Miranda didn't have the heart to tell her that neither Mrs. Underwood nor Jean-Paul had seen her notice board.

She greeted Troy and Henrietta with a polite smile—she didn't want to encourage them—and went to sit by the window beside the Reverend Beeley's table. No sooner had her bottom touched the wood than the vicar leaned over, heaving her large bosom across the gap between their chairs. A pair of spectacles on a beaded chain swung over the ledge like a helpless mountaineer. "Hello," she said in a fruity voice. "I'm Rev. Beeley, your vicar. I gather you're new in town."

"Yes." Miranda realized that she had been stupid to think there was such a thing as a quiet coffee in Cate's Cake Shop.

"As the vicar of Hartington I'd like to welcome you. I'd be delighted to welcome you to church, too, if you feel the desire to attend our services. You should have received the parish magazine. It lists all our services and special events. I do hope you'll come."

"Thank you," Miranda replied, pulling a tight smile and wondering if she could claim to be Jewish. Admitting she was agnostic wouldn't be good enough for the zealous Rev. Beeley.

"It is a pleasure. The Lightlys were very devout. They attended every Sunday. The church really came to life when Mrs. Lightly arranged the flowers. She had a magic touch. Her gardens were the most beautiful . . ."

"So I've been told," Miranda interjected briskly. She was fed up hearing about the Lightlys' beautiful gardens. If it weren't for the miraculous arrival of Jean-Paul she would shout at them all to shut up. In fact, she felt quite smug, as if she were guarding a delicious secret. "If they had the most beautiful gardens in England, why did they move?"

"I suppose they didn't want to rattle about in a big house. The children had grown up and moved away, except the youngest who inherited her mother's green thumb. Then, what with Phillip's illness . . ." The vicar broke off with a sigh and shook her head mournfully.

"Phillip?"

"Mr. Lightly. He's much older than his wife. He suffered a stroke." She hissed the phrase as if it were a heavily guarded secret. "She looks after him herself. She's a good woman."

"Where did they move to?"

"I don't know. They left quietly. They didn't want a fuss." The vicar inhaled, lowering her lids over bulging brown eyes. "A most respectable couple. An example to us all."

Cate brought Miranda her coffee. "I met your husband on Saturday," she said, watching Miranda pour hot milk into the cup.

"He enjoyed your coffee."

"Of course. He was very friendly, talking to everyone in here, making lots of new friends. He's very charming." Miranda half-expected her to finish with the words: not like you. Cate hovered a moment, waiting for Miranda to continue the conversation, then moved away with a little sniff. Miranda didn't mind if she was offended: she didn't want everyone knowing her business.

She turned her thoughts to her children, hoping

99

Gus was behaving himself at school. Storm had been in a bright mood that morning, chattering away about the magic in the garden that Jean-Paul was going to show her. Miranda had found her in her playhouse talking to her cushions, telling them all about a special friend she had found by the river. Miranda was surprised he had made such a big impression. Storm talked of nothing else but Jean-Paul, the magic, some sort of tree and returning to see the cows. "They know me now," she had told her mother. "They'll recognize me when I go back. Jean-Paul said so." Miranda recalled the kind expression in Jean-Paul's eyes, the deep crows'-feet that cut into his brown skin. The way his smile had illuminated his face like a beautiful dawn. He didn't look like a gardener. Mr. Underwood looked like a gardener, but Jean-Paul looked like a film star.

Miranda paid for her coffee and left, striding purposefully into the bright, sunny street. She pulled her Chanel sunglasses out of her handbag and walked up the road towards the car park. The air was crisp, the shadows inky blue from the rainfall in the night. She felt a spring in her step. Was it the coffee or the knowledge that Jean-Paul was returning by the end of the month?

"She didn't even say thank you!" Cate exclaimed when Miranda had gone. Troy looked at Henrietta and frowned.

"For her coffee?" he said.

"No, for finding her a gardener and a cook!"

"You don't know that you did," said Troy.

Henrietta watched him in awe; she would never have dared talk to Cate like that. Cate who was always right. Cate who knew everything.

"Of course I did. Thanks to the notice on *my* board. How very rude!" She cleared away the cup and milk jug from Miranda's table with an impatient huff. "I told you she was snooty. Can't think what that delightful husband is doing married to her." She walked past Troy and leaned over. "Forget the Frenchman, darling. Miranda's husband is gorgeous and if she continues to walk around with a face like a boot, he'll soon be free." She tossed Henrietta a look. "Lose a stone and you can have him, too!" Troy put a hand on his friend's and waited for Cate to disappear into the small kitchen behind the counter.

"Don't listen to her, Etta. She's in one of her moods. I love you just the way you are. If I were straight, I'd marry you in an instant."

"Thank you," said Henrietta, her eyes glistening with gratitude.

"Imagine the bruises poor Nigel suffers from having to lie on her night after night. You'd be delicious to lie on. Soft and warm. No bruises from protruding bones." Henrietta blushed. "Some man is going to be very lucky indeed to find you."

"I don't think I'll ever find anyone," Henrietta sniffed. "I'm fat and dull."

"Fat and dull!" Troy exclaimed. "Listen to your-self! You're neither fat nor dull. You're lovely and sweet, with no side. You shouldn't let her treat you like that." He patted her hand again. "Come on, let's get out of here before she comes back. She's a poisonous old thing with a hairy face." Henrietta looked confused. "Haven't you noticed? She's got a face as furry as my cat's underbelly. She's chucking up after every meal. You don't think she stays that thin naturally, do you? She's got more problems than you've got insecurities."

"She must have a lot then!"

"Riddled, darling. Positively riddled. Why don't you come in at five and I'll give you a blow dry. Nothing like a hairdo to lift the spirits."

"But I've got nowhere to go."

"Yes, you have. You're having dinner with me."

"Thank you, Troy. Really, you're a good friend," she said, kissing his cheek.

"That's what friends are for. Remember, you're not the only one looking for a man. We're in it together and thank heavens we're not in competi-tion. I'd lose out to a treasure like you!"

Miranda walked down the path towards the river. The sun shone enthusiastically upon the wild grasses and weeds, catching the droplets of rain that had fallen during the night and turning them into diamonds. The wind had blown wildly in the early hours of the morning and yet orange and brown leaves clung to the branches, not yet ready to relinquish the last remains of summer. A couple of squirrels played in the oak tree that dominated that side of the house, its trunk as wide and stout as the vicar's. The way was trodden by deer and her own inquisitive children so that it formed a damp path through the field to the river. She had been there once or twice but it hadn't held the enchantment it did today. Perhaps it was the sunshine, the bright blue sky and the sense of belonging that had so far eluded her.

She stood a moment on the stone bridge, gazing down into the clear water below. She could see weeds and stones and the occasional fish that floated lazily across the sunbeams. She imagined her children playing there, throwing sticks into the water. Then she glanced over to Gus's secret house. She hadn't looked at it properly before. The estate agent had simply mentioned a cottage in need of repair, and, as she had no immediate use for it, she had thought nothing more about it. The cottage stood neglected in a small copse of chestnut trees. There was no driveway. Perhaps there had once been a track from the main house through the field and over the bridge. Now there was just grass. There was something wonderfully romantic about its isolation. It was a secret hideaway that time had left behind.

Miranda turned the key in the lock. It was a rusty old thing, but it opened with a low squeak, like the irritable yawning of an old man disturbed in sleep. Inside, the hall was tiled with dark stone slabs, the staircase narrow with a little landing where it turned the corner. She went into the sitting room. The room was full of furniture, yet the air smelled damp. No one had lit a fire in a long time. The bookshelves were heavy with books stacked in tidy rows from floor to ceiling. She ran her hand along the top of one. It wasn't as neglected as she had presumed. There was only a light coating of dust. The books were a mixture of old and contemporary, from Dickens to Sebastian Faulks. To her surprise there was a shelf of French novels.

She took in the whole room. The empty stone fireplace framed by a wooden mantelpiece that was clearly very old and beautifully carved, the pale yellow striped wallpaper tarnished by years of wood smoke. She noticed it was peeling in one corner from a leak. The carpet was worn and stained and clearly needed changing and the rug had been eaten by moths. However, there wasn't a great deal to do. The sofa was intact, the armchairs, too; the glass coffee table just needed a good wipe. She walked over to the chest of drawers, a pretty antique walnut, and opened the drawers. The house had an inhabited feel about it. If it hadn't been so dirty she would have been happy to curl up on the sofa with one of the books. With a cheery fire and a glass of wine it would be cozier than her own more formal drawing room.

She explored the kitchen. It would need new appliances but the crockery was complete. She noticed the table laid for two and thought how odd it was that the cups and plates were still there, as if the inhabitants had been spirited away in the middle of tea. She resisted the temptation to clear them away. She'd get her rubber gloves on, hire some help, and do it all at once. The children could help her. It would be fun for them.

The floorboards creaked beneath her feet as she climbed the stairs. There were two bedrooms and a bathroom. The bathroom was very old-fashioned and needed to be completely gutted. The iron bath was stained, its enamel worn away, and the taps were tarnished. One of the bedrooms was completely empty except for a box that sat in the middle of the floor, as if it had been forgotten. Before she had a moment to look inside, a rattle from the bedroom next door distracted her. Her heart jumped. Surely she was the only person in the cottage.

For a second she thought it might be Gus. Her irritation mounted as she stepped across the landing to the other bedroom. A mischievous squirrel startled her as it shot back out the window, carelessly left ajar by her son, no doubt. She put her hand on her chest and took a deep breath, relieved that it wasn't an intruder or, worse, a ghost. She looked around. There was a large iron bed, made up with sheets and quilted bedspread in a pale green flowered material. Two bedside tables with tall pillar lamps, the shades stained with yellow patches. A faded trunk at the end of the bed, a cherrywood chest of drawers with a Queen Anne mirror on top, a prettily painted pine wardrobe against the wall. Pale linen curtains hung from large wooden poles, their linings torn and discolored. The carpet was dirty but intact. She wondered why the Lightlys hadn't bothered to take all this furniture with them. Perhaps they had downscaled and hadn't the room. She opened the window wider and looked out over the field. She could see down the river to the field of cows—Storm's cows. Her spirits soared, stirred by the strange magic of the room and the glory of the view.

Her mind returned to the box in the spare room. She closed the window to keep the squirrel out, then went to open it. There was only one thing inside: a faded green scrapbook. It was thick with flowers and leaves pressed between its pages. On the front the title was written in large looped handwriting: *Rainbows and Roses*. Miranda knelt on the floor and flicked through it. It was a diary of poems, rec- ollections and essays, clearly something that was not meant to have been left behind, nor seen by the eyes of a stranger. The mystery intrigued her. The writing was feminine. The paper smelled sweet, like cut grass in early spring. She sat back against the wall and turned to the first page where four sen- tences stood alone, heavy with sorrow.

I thought the days would assuage my longing, but they only fan the fire and make me yearn for you more. With all my body and all my soul. I shall grow old loving you and one day I shall die loving you. For now I live on the memory of you here in our cottage. It is all I have left.

VII

Every rainbow I see reminds me of you

Hartington House
October 1979

Ava Lightly's voice could be heard from deep within the herbaceous border. Although she was obscured by dead lupins and the large viburnum she was busily cutting back, her enthusiastic singing stirred the crisp morning air and sent the dogs into an excited frolic on the grass. Ava was dressed in purple dungarees and a short-sleeved T-shirt, her streaky blond hair roughly secured on the top of her head with a pencil. Her hands were rough from gardening, her nails short and ragged, yet her cheeks glowed with health and her pale green eyes sparkled like a spring meadow in rain. She was happiest outside, whatever the weather, and rarely felt the cold although she was a slender woman with no fat to insulate her. She was often seen with bare arms in midwinter when everyone else was wrapped up in gloves and hats and heavy coats. At thirty-seven she retained the bloom of youth, borne of an inner contentment which shone through her skin as if her heart were made of sunshine. Her face was handsome rather than pretty, her features irregular: her nose a little too long and very straight, her mouth large and sensual, out of place on such a small face. Yet, if the features weren't beautiful in isolation, they were made so by the sensitive, cheerful expression that held them together. Her eccentric nature made her compelling. No one loved her more than her husband, Phillip Lightly, and their three small children, Archie, Angus and Poppy.

"Hey, Shrub!" called her husband, striding across the lawn. Bernie, the fluffy Saint Bernard and Tarquin, the young Labrador, stopped rolling about on the grass and galloped up to him, crashing into his legs, almost knocking him to the ground. He patted them affectionately and shooed them away with a flick of his hand. He was fifteen years older than his wife, six feet four with a straight back and wide shoulders. His face was gentle and handsome, with a long nose, high cheekbones and a strong jawline. He spent most of the time in his study writing the definitive history of wine, or abroad, visiting vineyards. However, he wasn't inclined to solitude as so many writers are. He enjoyed shooting parties and dinners that extended into the small hours of the morning, discussing history and politics over glasses of port and the odd cigar. He took pleasure from socializing with the people of Hartington after church on Sundays and invited the town to an annual wine and cheese party at the house in the summer. He was affable and well liked for his dry, English sense of humor which more often than not included clever puns whose meaning eluded the very audience he meant to entertain. Ava always laughed, even though she had heard them all before. With round glasses perched on an aristocratic nose, his fine bones and high forehead, Phillip Lightly cut a distinguished figure as he strode confidently towards the herbaceous border.

He waited awhile, enjoying his wife's tuneful singing, then he called her again by the nickname he had given her in the early days of their courtship. "Shrub, darling!"

"Oh, hello there, you!" she replied, scrambling out. There were leaves caught in her hair and a smear of mud down one cheek. She wiped her nose with the back of her hand.

"You haven't forgotten Jean-Paul, have you?" The surprise on her face confirmed that she had. He smiled indulgently. Ava was famously vague, her mind absorbed by the trees and flowers of her beloved garden. "Well," he sighed, glancing at his watch. "He'll be at the station in half an hour."

"Oh God! I'd completely forgotten. I've done nothing about the cottage."

"He's young, he'll be happy in a sleeping bag," said Phillip, folding his arms against the cold. Despite his cashmere sweater and scarf, he was shivering. "Look, I'll pick him up, but then it's over to you, Shrub."

"Thank you." She wrapped her arms around his neck. He stepped back, aware that she was covered in mud and dead leaves, but her affection won him over and he wound his arms around her, lifting her off the ground, breathing in the scent of damp grass that clung to her hair. "You're a darling," she laughed into his neck.

"You're freezing," he replied. "I'd like to wrap you in a blanket and give you a cup of hot chocolate."

"Is that all?"

"For now, yes. Got to go and collect your apprentice."

"Is this really a good idea?" she asked, pulling away. "You know I like to do the gardens on my own and Hector helps with the weeding and mowing when I need him. I don't like to be hovered over. I'm a solitary creature. Hector and I really don't need anyone else."

"We've been through this before. Besides, it's too late to go back on it now. We're doing his father a great favor and besides, that's what old Etonians do: we help one another out. After all he has done for me I'm keen to have the opportunity to pay him back. Thanks to Henri, doors have opened the entire length and breadth of France."

"All right," she conceded with a sigh. "But I don't know what he expects . . ."

"You're very gifted, Shrub. He'll learn a lot from you. If he's going to inherit the château he's got to know about running an estate."

"Can't he just hire people to do it for him?"

"That's not the point. Henri wants him out of the city and in the English countryside for a while. He's been allowed to do as he pleases in Paris."

"So, he's a playboy?"

"Henri doesn't know anyone else he can ask. He's worried Jean-Paul will drift. He wants to inspire him. Wants him to take responsibility. One day he'll inherit the château and vineyard. It's a big responsibility."

"I'm surprised he does what his father tells him. He's not a child."

"No, but his father holds the purse strings."

"Is that so important? Why doesn't he run off and do his own thing?"

"Les Lucioles is not an ordinary château. It's magnificent. Any boy worth his salt would do all he could not to lose it."

"I see." She felt very unenthusiastic about it all.

"Besides, it'll be good for the boys to have a young man about the place to rag around with. I'm an old father."

"I keep you young," she protested.

"That's true," he chuckled. "But I don't rag around much and I don't speak French. The children could do with a little home tuition." Ava smiled at him sheepishly. She spoke fluent French, having been sent to finishing school in Switzerland at sixteen.

"You make me feel guilty for not having spoken French to them from birth."

"I'd never expect that of you, Shrub. I expect you to get up in the morning, the rest is a surprise!"

She smacked him playfully. "You beast!"

"You haven't called me that for a while." He kissed her forehead.

"I don't know what you're talking about." She kissed him back, leaving him with a wide, loving smile.

She watched him stride back across the lawn towards the house, his shoulders hunched against the cold, his gait charmingly gangly. Then her eyes fell upon a pair of pigeons perched on the gutter just beneath the sloping roof. They were fat and contented. She felt the same. How lucky she was to have everything she could possibly want: a husband who loved her, three happy children, the most beautiful house in England, and her beloved gardens. The birds sat on the roof like icing on a delicious cake.

She cast her eyes about the garden. It was only just beginning to turn. She liked it like that. The expanse of green gave her a sense of serenity. The trees were still frothy, but their leaves were curling at the corners and some were a pretty shade of yellow. Birdsong still rang out across the lawns, punctuated by the odd cough of a pheasant and the husky coo of a pigeon. She liked the sparrows that nested under the gutters in springtime and had planted evergreen shrubs near the house to encourage other birds to make their homes there, too. In midwinter she let the ivy grow up the ash and sycamore trees so that the birds that remained could find shelter from the cold and predators. She had taught the children to nurture them. Poppy used the birdbath as a paddling pool in mid-summer, but in winter she put food out, slowly taming the little creatures so that some of them ate out of her hand when Bernie and Tarquin weren't around to frighten them away.

She was still working in the border when Phillip returned an hour later with Jean-Paul. Bernie and Tarquin shot around to the front of the house, barking loudly. She climbed out and wiped the sweat from her forehead as the scrunching of wheels on gravel came to an abrupt stop. She heard the opening and closing of doors, then her husband's voice greeting the dogs as if they were people. She hastened through the gate nestled in the yew hedge that hid the gardens from the front of the house. Phillip was opening the boot of his old Mercedes. No sooner had he opened it than the two dogs jumped in. Jean-Paul looked on in amazement as the dogs planted muddy paws all over his leather case. Phillip made no move to extract them. He just chuckled at the familiar sight, paying no heed to Jean-Paul's discomfort. Ava watched him from the gate. He was the handsomest young man she had ever seen.

"Hello, I'm Ava," she said, wiping her hand on her dungarees before offering it to Jean-Paul. To her surprise he brought it to his mouth with a formal bow.

"It is a pleasure to meet you," he said, looking her straight in the eye. His eyes were soft like brown suede, his gaze intense. She would have replied to him in French, but his English was perfect, although strongly accented, containing within it all that was romantic and sensual about his country. She felt something flutter inside her stomach.

"Did you have a pleasant flight?" she asked, suddenly aware of her disheveled appearance.

"I arrived in London a few days ago. I wanted to see a little culture before I came down here," he replied, his eyes wandering over the house. He thrust his hands into his pockets and hunched his shoulders. Phillip carried his case inside.

"Why don't you come in and have something to drink," said Ava, following her husband in through the porch. "You'll have to stay in the house for a week or so while I get the cottage ready for you. I'm afraid I've been slow in getting organized."

"So unlike you, Ava," Phillip added without a hint of sarcasm. "My wife is an example of efficiency. She runs this place like the captain of a ship. I'm a mere crewman, in awe of her self-discipline." Ava rolled her eyes.

Jean-Paul was not at all what she had expected. First, he didn't look like a gardener. He was beautifully dressed in a soft tweed jacket, blue shirt and pressed jeans. Around his neck he wore a faded cashmere scarf. His hair was thick, the color of chestnuts, and artfully arranged to look as though he hadn't bothered. His nose was long and aquiline, his mouth asymmetrical and sensitive. His hands were clean, nails short and tidy, not the hands of a man used to digging. On his feet were brown Gucci loafers. She hoped he had gardening boots. It would be a shame to ruin those elegant shoes.

They sat on stools in the kitchen while Ava prepared lunch. She had gathered leeks and sprouts from her kitchen garden and bought trout from the fishmonger in town. She grew herbs against the garden wall in an old water trough and had made basil butter and broad bean hummus to eat with homemade rosemary bread. She adored the smell of healthy cooking and gained great satisfaction from watching her children grow strong on her own produce.

On first meeting Ava, one would never imagine she was shy. She rose to the occasion, telling witty stories, making people laugh, barely drawing breath between anecdotes, only to disappear afterward into blissful solitude in her garden, depleted after having given so much of herself. Phillip knew she entertained in order to hide her shyness and he loved her for it. It was a secret that only he was aware of. He was touched by the way she performed before collapsing once the curtain came down. He was the only man permitted backstage, a privilege he relished. Now she began to chatter away to Jean-Paul, who looked at her with an arrogant expression on his beautifully chiseled face, as if she were an eccentric relative to be tolerated. He smiled politely, but not with his eyes. He listened while she cooked, his gaze sleepy until they all moved to the table for lunch and they fell hungrily on the feast she laid before him. Like all men, he became enlivened at the sight of a hearty meal.

"So, Jean-Paul," she said, passing him the dish of steaming vegetables. "I hear your family has a beautiful garden in France?"

"Yes," he replied, picking up the spoon and helping himself to carrots. "My mother loves gardens. Especially English gardens. We have a château near Bordeaux. It is very old. I admire what my mother has done with the gardens. One day I will create a beautiful garden of my own."

"So what do you hope to learn here?"

He shrugged. "Papa says that yours is the best he has ever seen."

"I wish I had met him. He popped in once, about eight years ago when I was away visiting my mother. I would like to have shown him around personally. I'm surprised Phillip showed him the estate beyond his wine cellar."

"Darling, there is nothing nicer than walking around your gardens in springtime with a glass of chilled white wine," responded Phillip with a chuckle.

"He says you have a great talent," Jean-Paul continued. Ava was flattered in spite of the uneasy twist in her gut that predicted a terrible clash of personalities. As attractive as he was, she simply couldn't see them working together.

"Have you left a girl behind in Paris?" Phillip asked with a grin.

Jean-Paul smirked and raised one eyebrow. "A few," he replied.

"Oh dear," said Ava, bristling at his arrogance. "I hope you don't suffer from a broken heart."

"I have never suffered in love," he said.

"Yet. There is plenty of time for heartbreak. You're young."

He nodded in agreement. "My heart will break when my mother dies. That is inevitable." She looked at him quizzically. It was a strange comment to make for a man of his age.

"You are obviously close."

"Of course. I am her only child. I am spoiled and indulged. My mother is an incredible woman. I admire her."

"I hope our sons feel that way when they are

your age," she said, though she wasn't sure whether she really did.

"You have three children, yes?"

"Two boys and a girl. You'll meet them later today when they come home from school."

"It must be nice to have siblings."

"I think they enjoy it. They fight a fair bit. No one really likes to share."

"That is true. I have never had to."

"Your English is perfect. Where did you learn to speak it so well?" Ava asked.

"I grew up with an English nanny."

"An English nanny?" Ava repeated. "Good gracious. Was she a tyrant?"

"What was she called?" asked Phillip.

Jean-Paul gave the most enchanting smile. "Nanny," he replied and laughed heartily.

"Nanny?" she repeated, disarmed by his sudden, unexpected humor.

"I never knew her real name. She was just Nanny." He looked bashful. "She left when I was twenty-one!"

Later, while Jean-Paul was unpacking in his attic bedroom, Ava confronted her husband in his study. "It's never going to work," she protested. "You can tell he's never done a day's labor in his life. He might dream of creating an English garden of his own, but I bet he's never got down on all fours in the mud. What on earth is his father thinking, sending him here? If he was eighteen and fresh out of school I would understand. But he must be in his late twenties. Doesn't he have a mind of his own? What am I going to do with him for a year? He's going to be bored stiff in Hartington. I can't imagine him picking up girls in the Duck and Dapple. It's hardly buzzing. He should be in London with other young people, not with me and the children. God, it's a disaster!"

Phillip put his hand on her shoulder and smiled. "Don't worry, Shrub, it'll work out. A bit of hard labor will do him good. You'll have an extra pair of hands and you can create all those wonderful gardens you've been longing to make but couldn't do on your own. The wildflower meadow and orchard, the cottage garden you keep going on about. Put him to work. Plant it all up. Create your dream."

"He's more suited to a yacht in St. Tropez than to a lawn mower here in Hartington."

"Give him a chance."

"I can't see him in the cottage."

"He'll be fine. Stop worrying."

"He's just not what I expected."

"What did you expect?"

She turned away and walked over to the window. Gray clouds were gathering. "I don't know." She sighed. "Someone less smooth. With rough hands and dirty fingernails like mine. In boots and grubby trousers. Not a dapper city swinger in cashmere and Gucci loafers, for God's sake." She shook her head at the absurdity of it. "He'll last a week!"

Phillip chuckled. "I think you'll inject him with enthusiasm and he'll stay forever."

"I hope to God he doesn't. I don't think *I'll* last more than a week!"

Ava picked the children up at 3:30. She parked her yellow car on the green and stepped out of it just as it was beginning to drizzle. Toddy Finton was there with her ferret, Mr. Frisby, sitting obediently on her shoulder. She had twin boys in the same class as Angus. "Hi, Ava," she said, her cheeks pink from having spent the morning hacking across the countryside on her chestnut mare.

"Hi, Toddy. How's Mr. Frisby?" She stroked him under the chin and he lifted his head sleepily.

"A bit dozy. It's the weather."

"It makes Tarquin snuggle up in front of the Aga. Bernie just lies outside, enjoying the cold. Like me, I suppose."

"Can I send the boys over to you this weekend? They tell me they've built a camp in a hollow tree."

Ava smiled. "The oak, the perfect place for a camp. I'm going to grow a wildflower meadow there. Cowslips, violets, dandelions, red and white campion. I've got someone to help me. A young man from France."

Toddy raised her eyebrows. "Is he gorgeous?"

"Yes, but much too young and arrogant for my taste. Actually, I think he'll be bored and go home. Still, I'll use him while he's here."

"You always wanted another pair of hands."

"Not a pair of smooth, manicured, never-done-a-day's-work hands."

"I love the idea of a wild garden. It'll be pretty in spring and lovely to look out over from your bedroom window."

"That's the idea."

Toddy pulled Mr. Frisby down from her shoulder and cradled him like a baby. She had wanted more children but Mr. Frisby was the baby she couldn't have. She stroked his tummy lovingly and kissed his little nose. "Why don't you bring them over tomorrow?" Ava suggested, then narrowed her eyes, scheming. "In fact, you could do me a favor."

"What's that then?"

"Take Jean-Paul out for a ride."

"Is he any good?"

"I'm sure. He looks the sort of man who makes it his business to be good at everything."

"I see."

"Then I can get into the cottage. I'd completely forgotten he was coming. It's a total mess. You can all come to lunch. I'd be rather relieved to have your company, actually. I don't know what to talk to Jean-Paul about and Phillip isn't much help. I don't think Jean-Paul gets his sense of humor!"

"He's not the only one," said Toddy, with a grin.

"Well, I'm lost for words."

"You?" Toddy feigned astonishment.

"Don't joke, Toddy. For once, I'm dumb and I feel like a clumsy old clot."

"You are funny! I'd love to come and check him out. He might do for one of my cousins, they're all in their early twenties and very pretty."

"Good. That'll be a diversion. He considers himself something of a stud, I think."

"That's the French for you."

She recalled the way he bent over to kiss her hand, looking up as he bowed, fixing her with those soft brown eyes. "Yes, they can be quite charming, can't they," she added drily. "Charming but arrogant. Mark my words; he'll be gone in a week!"

VIII

The cough of a pheasant, the coo of the pigeons, the crisp sunny days of October

Archie, Angus and Poppy stared at the stranger, mute with shyness. Archie was eight, tall like his father with his mother's straight nose and green eyes. Angus was six, with the build of a little rugby player. He had dark hair and pale blue eyes, a wide, infectious smile and creamy, freckled skin.

Both boys were handsome in their mother's uncon-ventional way. Those features, so off-kilter on her face, suited their boyish faces perfectly. Poppy was only four, but strong in both personality and opinion. She always said exactly what she thought. With long dark hair, blue eyes, fine features and her father's classical face, she was the beauty her mother was not. Yet, she was very much her mother's little girl, adoring fauna and flora and never feeling the cold. It could be said that she had inherited the best of both parents.

"Jean-Paul is going to be living with us for a while. He's going to help me design the most beau-tiful gardens in England," Ava explained, feeling a fraud. She didn't believe him capable of designing so much as a cabbage patch. Archie stared at his feet. Angus stifled a giggle. Finally Poppy spoke.

"You speak funny," she said, screwing up her nose.

"I'm from France," he replied.

"Are you going to play with us?" she asked.

Jean-Paul shrugged. "I don't know. What do you like to play?" The boys looked at their sister in alarm. The last thing they wanted was a grown-up crashing in on their games.

"I like planting vegetables."

"I like planting vegetables, too," he agreed.

"I have a marrow this big!" she exclaimed, holding her hands apart. "He's called Monty and he's in bed with a cold." Jean-Paul looked quizzi-cally at Ava.

"I'm afraid he's avoided the saucepan by becoming a friend. He gets taken out in the carriage and to show-and-tell on Fridays, if he's good." Jean-Paul's face melted into a wide smile that infected the children. Poppy ran out to fetch Monty and the boys grinned up at him, their shyness evaporating in the warmth of the Frenchman's charm. Ava was intrigued by how easily he was able to switch it on and off, one moment arrogant, the next charming and friendly.

Poppy returned with a very large dark green marrow. Ava decided it wouldn't be appropriate to repeat the quip her husband had made on learning that his daughter took it to bed: "That's setting her up for an awful disappointment when she's older." Jean-Paul took Monty and weighed him in his hands.

"He's very heavy for a baby," he said to Poppy.

"He's not a baby," she replied stridently. "He's a marrow!"

"But of course. A baby marrow." Jean-Paul looked a little alarmed. Poppy took the marrow back and cuddled it.

"He's shy. You frightened him," she accused.

"Shall we show Jean-Paul around the garden?" Ava suggested hastily. "You can show him your hollow tree," she said to the boys. Angus looked delighted, Archie less so. He wasn't sure he wanted a grown-up, a *strange* grown-up, coming to their secret camp.

"Come on, Angus," he said to his brother, tearing off before the adults had a chance to follow.

"They have much spirit," said Jean-Paul, folding his arms.

"Why don't you put on some boots and a coat? It's been rather wet lately." Jean-Paul returned with a pair of leather boots and sheepskin coat. "You don't expect to garden in those, do you?" she asked.

"Of course."

"But they'll be ruined."

He shrugged and pulled a face as if he didn't care. "I can buy a new pair."

"Gracious no! Go into the cloakroom and see if there's a pair that fits you. No point wasting good boots when you don't have to. As for the sheepskin, that's beautiful, too. Don't you have a scruffier coat?"

"No."

Ava sighed and bit her tongue. She didn't think her husband would thank her if Jean-Paul left before he had even stayed the night. She took a deep breath, gathered her patience and told him that they would go into town and buy him boots at least. "Tell me one thing, Jean-Paul," she began, knowing that now probably wasn't the best time to ask him, but unable to wait. "How much gardening have you done?"

He shook his head and grinned. She felt her annoyance fizzle away, disarmed once again by his improbable smile. "None."

"None at all?" She was aghast.

"I have watched my mother in the garden all my life. But I have little practical experience."

"Do you *want* to learn?"

"Of course. The gardens at Les Lucioles are also my inheritance."

"I don't have the time for someone who doesn't want to be here."

"A year has four seasons. We are now in autumn. I will leave at the end of the summer taking away everything that you have taught me. I will be very rich."

"And I get a spare pair of hands," she said, wondering who would gain more from this unlikely partnership.

"I hope so," he replied, his face breaking into a smile again. "I hope to leave you with something special, too."

They walked out to the terrace. Made of York stone and cobbles and surrounded by vast urns of plants and clumps of alchemilla mollis, it extended up a stone path planted with thyme and lined with balls of yew, now as ragged as dogs' coats that have been allowed to grow wild. The stones were dark and damp from dew, the grass glistening in the orangey-pink light of late afternoon. At the end of the thyme walk, beyond the old dovecote where a family of pigeons now resided, they could see a field of cows. In the woods beyond were beech and hazel trees, beginning to turn yellow and scatter the ground with leaves. The air was smoky from the fire Hector had lit in the hall and a chilly breeze swept in off the sea a few miles south of Hartington. Jean-Paul put his hands in his pockets and gazed around him. "It's very beautiful," he said in a quiet voice.

"Thank you," Ava replied. "I like it."

In that milky evening light it acquired a melancholy beauty. The summer was over, the foliage dying, the evenings drawing in, the air colder and damp, the sky streaked with crimson and gold, intensifying as the sun sank lower into the pale blue sky. She loved autumn more than summer because of its sadness. There was something so touching about the wistfulness of it, like old age from the ripe perspective of youth.

Poppy followed them down the thyme walk to the dovecote, chattering away to Monty as if he were a child. She skipped through the hedges in nothing more than a short skirt, Wellington boots and thin shirt, her ponytail flying out behind her as she weaved in and out. Bernie and Tarquin had heard the children's voices from Phillip's study and galloped out to join them, sniffing the grass and cocking their legs against the hedge. Ava was surprised to see Jean-Paul transfixed by the dovecote. It was a round stone building painted white, with a pretty wooden roof sweeping up into a point like a Chinese hat. Old and neglected, it looked as sad as autumn. "Pigeons live there now," she said. "We've never done anything to it."

"And you mustn't," he said, placing his hand against the wall in a caress. "It's enchanting just the way it is."

"These surrounding maples will turn the most astonishing red in November. Can you see they're just beginning?" She plucked a leaf and handed it to him. He twirled it between his fingers. They turned left and strolled past a copse of towering larches, their leaves the color of butter. There was a long wall lining the lawn where Ava had planted an herbaceous border. "I've been busily cutting it back," she told him. "Putting it to bed for the winter."

"There is much to do, eh?" he mused.

"Much to do."

Poppy was keen to show him the vegetable garden, hidden behind a charming old wall where roses grew in summer among honeysuckle and jasmine. The door was stiff. Poppy pushed as hard as she could, but it wouldn't budge. Jean-Paul leaned against it with his shoulder. "Is this your favorite part of the garden?" he asked her.

"Monty's favorite, because all his friends live here."

"I cannot wait to meet them."

"They might have gone away. Mummy says we have to wait until next year. They come back in spring."

"Then I will have to wait for spring. I hope Monty doesn't get sad."

"Oh no," she whispered secretively. "He's only a marrow."

The door swung open, leading into a large square garden, divided by gravel paths and box-lined borders where an abundance of vegetables grew. The walls were heavy with the remains of dying clematis, roses, wisteria and honeysuckle, the ground beneath them spilling over with hellebores and yellow senecio. The dogs rushed in, squeezing between Ava's legs and the doorpost.

She didn't know what to make of Jean-Paul. On the one hand he was arrogant and aloof. On the other he was sweet with Poppy and the dogs, and when he smiled it was as if the arrogant Jean-Paul were but a figment of the imagination. He wasn't enthusiastic about the gardens and yet was clearly moved by the beauty of the evening light on the dovecote and the melancholy hues of autumn. He seemed as reluctant to be with them as Ava was reluctant to have him. They eyed each other nervously, clearly uneasy about the months of collaboration that stretched before them. She knew instinctively that a piece of the puzzle was missing. Henri hadn't been honest with Phillip and she felt resentful for that. Why send a young man to Dorset who obviously didn't want to come?

"We harvest quite a crop in here," she said, watching her daughter skipping up the gravel path towards the patch where marrows had grown all summer. She led him under the tunnel of apple trees where ripe red fruit was strewn all over the ground. Jean-Paul bent down and picked one up, taking a large bite. "It's sweet," he said, bending down again to find one for her.

"The best are those already nibbled by insects," said Ava. "They have the nose for the tastiest fruit."

"I hope I don't bite into a wasp!"

"You'll know all about it if you do. Though, I don't think there are many wasps left now. Hector is good at finding their nests and destroying them." He handed her an apple. She bit into it, savoring the juiciness of the flesh. When Poppy skipped up he handed one to her. She licked it as if it were a lollipop.

"Yummy!" she exclaimed before bounding off again.

They left the vegetable garden and wandered through the archway in the hedge to the front of the house. In the center of the field an old oak tree stood like a galleon in the middle of a sea of grass. "This is where I want to plant a wild garden," she said, imagining it full of color in spring. "Beyond is the river Hart and your cottage."

"Can I see it?"

"I'd rather not show it to you until I have cleaned it. I'm ashamed." He looked at her, his eyes twinkling with amusement.

"Why would you be ashamed? I am only a gardener."

She couldn't help but smile back at him. "You're not a gardener yet," she replied drily. "I've never seen a gardener in cashmere."

"Don't judge people by how they look." He gazed over to the tree where two pink faces peeped out of the hole in the trunk. "There is the hollow tree," he said, striding across the grass. "It's magical!" Ava watched him go, a frown lining her brow. There was something very curious about him; she couldn't quite put her finger on what it was.

Archie and Angus disappeared inside the tree when they saw the grown-ups approaching. Poppy ran in front, shouting at the boys to let her in. "They're coming, they're coming!" she cried, her voice sending a couple of partridges into the sky. Poppy climbed in through the opening cut into the bark. The two boys peeped out from the darkness of the trunk. Jean-Paul patted the tree as if it were an animal. "This is a beautiful old oak," he said.

"I love it!" Ava exclaimed. "An old friend. Imagine what this tree has seen in its lifetime."

"It was probably here before the house."

"For certain."

"What would human beings have done without trees, eh?" He stood back to take in its glorious height. "No trees, no fuel. No fuel, no smelting. So, no bronze or iron age. No wood, no ships, no travel overseas. No empires. Perhaps no civilization at all."

"We'd still be living in caves," said Ava with a smile.

"I think your children would be all right," he chuckled, bending down to look in on them. They sat in the dark like three little pirates. "Is there room for me?"

"No, go away!" they shouted, squealing with pleasure. "Help! Help! It's Captain Hook!"

Ava left the children in the tree and took Jean-Paul to the orchard. There were plum trees, apple trees, pear trees and peach trees; a banqueting hall for wasps and bees. The sun hung low in the sky like a glowing ember, glinting through the trees, casting long shadows over the grass. A pigeon sat watching them from the rooftop, its feathers gold in the soft light, and a gray squirrel scampered across the branches. The grass was already glittering with dew, the air moist and cool. They wandered through the trees in silence, listening to the whispering sounds of nature.

"I love evening and morning the best," said Jean-Paul, his expression settled once again into solemnity. "I love the transience of it. The moment you appreciate it, it is gone." He snapped his fingers.

"Come. Let me show you where I want to create the new garden. A special garden. A cottage garden full of roses and campanula and daisies. I want tulips and daffodils in spring. I want a magical garden full of color and scent. Somewhere I can sit in peace and quiet. An abundance of flowers." Jean-Paul nodded as if he were qualified to advise her.

They arrived at an area of lawn enclosed on two sides by yew hedge. In the middle stood a solitary mountain ash. They stood at one end, watching the sun blinking through the branches of the yellow larches beyond, enflaming the tip of the dovecote. It was a large space, big enough to create something dramatic. "It has a good feeling in here," said Jean-Paul.

"Doesn't it," Ava agreed. "I've been wanting to do something with this for so long. We never go in here. The children play on the other side of the house or on the lawn by the herbaceous border. This is hidden away, like a secret."

"It will be a secret garden."

"I hope so. A surprise garden. Come on," she said with a smile. "Time for tea, I think, don't you? The children will be getting hungry now."

That night Ava lay in bed with her book, *An Enchanted April*. But while her eyes scanned the pages, her mind was not on the words. Phillip lay beside her, his reading glasses perched on the bridge of his nose. He always had at least four books on the go, placed in different parts of the house so he never found himself with nothing to read.

"Darling," Ava began, allowing her book to rest against her knees. "I can't make Jean-Paul out."

Phillip replied without taking his eyes off the page. "What is there to make out?"

"I don't know. Something isn't right. It's like the puzzle is missing one of its pieces."

"I don't follow."

"Well. This afternoon I showed him around the gardens. On the one hand he's not really interested in plants. Not as a gardener should be. But on the other he's moved by the beauty of it. He loved the silly old dovecote and the oak tree. He took real interest in them."

"What's wrong with that?" He sighed, endeavoring to be patient.

"Oh, I don't know what makes him tick."

"You've known him a day."

"Go back to your book. You just don't see it, do you?"

"I don't think there is anything to see. He's not interested in plants but appreciates the beauty of the garden. I would say that is a point in the young man's favor, wouldn't you?"

She lifted her book off her knee. "Don't worry, darling. I'm trying to find a missing piece to the puzzle. Go back to your book." He smiled and began to read again. "After all, I'm the one who's got to work with him and find him things to do. It's all very well paying Henri back for helping you with your research, but I'm the one with the responsibility. Henri's done nothing for me." She looked at him but his face was impassive. "Oh, I'll shut up. Just remember my reservations when it all goes up in smoke and Henri closes all those doors the length and breadth of France!"

IX

The sweet smell of ripe apples.
The last of the plums.

The following morning Toddy kept her word and took Jean-Paul riding, leaving the twins with Archie, Angus and Poppy, playing around the hollow tree. Mr. Frisby slept in the porch, curled up in an old jersey. Phillip had gone shooting for the weekend in Gloucestershire, taking Tarquin with him. Ava was left alone with Bernie and the children, baffled that anyone would want to kill for sport.

She took the opportunity to tidy the cottage. The last resident had been Phillip's bachelor brother who had used it as a weekend home. He had finally married and bought a house near Sherborne and Phillip had tried to rent it out. He put in a new kitchen and gave it a fresh coat of paint, but it proved unpopular as there was no driveway. People had to park their car up at the house, walk across the field and over the bridge, which was a big inconvenience for both parties. None of the potential residents had been suitable, until now.

Despite that, Ava had always liked the cottage. It

was picturesque, nestling in isolation beneath leafy chestnut trees. Symmetrical with a big mossy roof and small windows, it was like a house in a fairy tale. To Ava it was a secret cottage, shrouded in romance and so pretty, with pink and white roses that scaled the walls and tumbled over the front door in summer. Outside, the river flowed slowly beneath the stone bridge and on to the sea.

She made the iron bed with clean sheets and threw the bedspread into a corner to take back to the house to wash. She hoovered the carpets and polished the furniture, scrubbed the floor in the kitchen and hall. She threw open the windows to let autumn imbue the rooms with the sweet scent of damp grass. Satisfied with a job well done she stood awhile to admire it. A few logs in the grate, a boisterous fire, a good book and some classical music and it would feel just like home. She smiled with pleasure, then left with the bedspread.

Toddy returned with Jean-Paul in time for lunch. The children had played all morning in the tree, running into the hall with muddy boots and red cheeks. Jean-Paul disappeared upstairs to change. Toddy rummaged about in the boot of her Land Rover for a pair of slippers. Mr. Frisby awoke and scampered over the gravel to take up position around her neck like a pretty white stole. She let out a bellow of laughter as he nibbled her earlobe. "Did you miss me?" she asked, nuzzling him fondly.

Ava had roasted a couple of chickens. She stood

by the Aga making gravy while the children jostled each other over the sink, fighting to wash their hands. Toddy returned and helped herself to a glass of apple juice from the fridge. Her black hair was short and spiky from having been trapped under her riding hat, her face flushed from the wind, her eyes shining from her morning with Jean-Paul. She sidled up to Ava. "He's rather dishy!" she whispered with a smirk. "Fine figure of a man on a horse! He reminds me of a polo player I had in the Argentine before I married. He'd be fun to roll around with in the hay."

"Curb your excitement. The last thing his ego needs is someone like you fancying him. Though, I dare say he's probably worked it out already."

"There's no harm in a little window-shopping. I'm not intending to buy. That said, I wouldn't mind taking him on approval." She leaned back against the Aga to warm her bottom.

"Why don't you introduce him to one of your cousins?"

"Not a bad idea. He's going to be bored stiff in Hartington."

"He can always spend the weekends in London. Cruise the King's Road, go to the Feathers Ball at the Hammersmith Palais. Isn't that what young people do these days?"

"He's a bit old for the Feathers Ball, Ava!"

"Well, Tramp then, or Annabel's. I wouldn't know, I don't like London."

"He doesn't look like your average gardener, does he?"

"Do you see what I mean? He's too neat and tidy."

"I never trust a man who's neat and tidy. I once had a Spaniard who folded his clothes on the chair before making love. By the time he'd finished piling them up like a Benetton shop assistant I'd gone off the boil."

"You do pick them, Toddy!"

"Jean-Paul better be a closet mess or I'll stop fancying him!" She chuckled throatily.

At that moment Jean-Paul appeared in the doorway. He had changed into jeans and loafers, a pale blue shirt neatly tucked in to show off a leather cowboy belt. Toddy gave Ava a look, which she chose to ignore. "Right, children, to the table, please. Lunch is up." The children clambered onto the banquette. "Jean-Paul, help yourself to a drink. You'd better get to know your way around if you're going to be here for a while. Drinks are in the fridge or in the larder out there," she instructed, pointing to a door leading off the kitchen. "Glasses up there, in the cupboard. Did you have a good morning?"

"Fantastic!" he exclaimed. "We rode up on the hill, so high we could see the sea."

"We galloped over Planchett's plateau," Toddy added, putting down her glass so she could help dish up. "Big Red went like the clappers!"

"He's a strong horse. I had to use all my strength to stop him running away with me."

"I knew you could handle him," said Toddy. "I wasn't worried."

"I was, a little," he admitted with a grin.

Both women wavered a moment, spoons in the air, disarmed by the allure of his smile. Hastily, Ava dug her spoon into the dish of steaming peas.

Bernie wandered in, panting from having chased a pheasant across the lawn. His glistening chops were heavy with saliva. He went straight up to Jean-Paul and nudged him with his nose. Ava grabbed the towel which hung beside the Aga for this very purpose and hurried to mop up Bernie's wet mouth. She expected Jean-Paul to edge away, appalled at the sight of those slimy gums threatening to end up on his jeans, but he didn't. He bent down and swept back the dog's ears with both hands, looking him straight in the eye. Bernie, who wasn't used to people gazing at him so intensely, lowered his head bashfully. Jean-Paul took the towel from Ava's hands and wiped Bernie's chops himself, without comment. Ava didn't risk catching Toddy's eye. She could feel her friend staring at him from the butcher's table, spoon in midair, clearly remembering the Argentine polo player.

Jean-Paul handed out the plates, helped the children to ketchup and gravy and was now busy carving chicken for the three adults. The children were sitting quietly, eating their food. "Jean-Paul, you're a natural!" gushed Toddy, taking a plate and helping herself to some slices of chicken. "If you get bored over here you can always come and help out at Bucksley Farm."

"This household is very English," he replied, smiling at Ava. "If it continues like this, I think boredom will be the least of my problems!"

"I've finished the cottage," Ava said, finally sitting down with her lunch.

"Ah, good," he replied.

"I'll take you there this afternoon. Then you're independent. You can come and go as you wish. It'll be your home for as long as you are here."

"You are very generous."

"Don't thank me until you've seen it. It's rather rustic, I warn you."

"I have no problem with rustic."

"That's good."

"And you can come out riding with me whenever you want," Toddy interjected slyly. Then, responding to a warning look from Ava, she added: "I have some cousins your age who live nearby. The girls are especially pretty. They'd be good company for you. If you prefer, you can ride out with them."

"I have a lot of choices," he replied, taking a mouthful of chicken. "Ava is a marvelous cook!" He nodded appreciatively. "Everything you prepare is delicious. I don't think I want to go and live in the cottage after all!"

Ava was flattered. "You can have lunch and dinner with us whenever you like." Though, she doubted he'd do either once he had settled into the cottage.

After lunch they all walked through the field to the river to show Jean-Paul his new home. The children left their camp to play on the bridge, throwing twigs into the water. The air was damp, the sky gray on the horizon, bad weather was coming in off the sea. It would rain later.

"I haven't done anything about firewood, Jean-Paul, but the barn near the house is full of logs. Take as many as you need, there's a cart you can fill and pull down here. If you wait until Monday, Hector will help you."

"I can do it myself. Don't worry."

"It's going to pour," said Toddy, thinking of her horses out in the field.

"I suggest you stay in the house tonight and move into the cottage tomorrow. You don't have so much as a bottle of milk in the fridge, so you'd better eat with me. You can take my car into town on Monday and buy everything you need. Fred the milkman comes during the week with dairy products and the papers, Ned the breadman comes three days a week to deliver bread and buns. I have an account with both. Please feel free to order whatever you require."

• • •

At the sight of the cottage Jean-Paul's face widened into a broad smile. "It is adorable," he said, striding towards it. "I will be happy here, for sure."

Toddy nudged Ava. "Won't be going home then," she hissed with a chuckle.

"Or to live with you," Ava replied. "Bad luck!"

They joined him as the first drops of rain began to fall. Ava fished in her trouser pocket for the key. "It's rather old and rusty, but it works." The door opened with a whine and they walked inside. The children remained outside, watching the rain create patterns on the water.

Inside it was warmer. The air was perfumed with wood polish, wax and pine-scented floor cleaner. Upstairs the windows were still open. A draft hurtled down the stairs. They took off their boots. Ava ran upstairs to shut out the rain, Jean-Paul and Toddy went into the sitting room. Bernie lay outside against the door, watching the children.

As Ava closed the window, she caught sight of the children on the bridge. Archie and the twins were ragging around, while Poppy and Angus were pointing at something in the water. Suddenly the sky opened, throwing out buckets of rain. They squealed like startled mice and scampered off in the direction of the hollow tree. Then, in the midst of the rain, the clouds parted and the sun unexpectedly shone through, setting the sky alight with the most beautiful rainbow. The sunshine flooded her spirit with joy and she was at once gripped with the need to share it. She ran downstairs.

"Hurry, outside!" she yelled, her voice quivering with excitement.

Toddy and Jean-Paul appeared in the hall. "What's going on?" Toddy demanded, her thoughts turning immediately to her children. She had a vision of them drowning in the river.

"A rainbow!" Ava replied, opening the door. "You've got to see it." She struggled into her boots and dashed outside. Bernie leapt to his feet, catching her sense of exhilaration.

Ava could feel the rain dripping down her neck but she didn't mind. It was worth it. She had never seen a rainbow so clear that she could pick out every color, even the elusive pink which sits between green and turquoise and is usually so blurred as to be hidden altogether.

She looked at Jean-Paul, and caught him looking at her. She smiled, masking the unease she felt beneath the intensity of his stare.

Ava folded her arms and for once she shivered in her shirtsleeves.

"Wow! That's impressive!" Toddy exclaimed, wrapping her coat tightly about her. "Can we go back inside now?"

"You go. Take Jean-Paul with you. I want to stay out until it goes," Ava replied.

Toddy hurried back to the cottage and Jean-Paul was left no option but to follow.

Ava walked over to the bridge where she stood in the rain, now falling in a light drizzle. She was glad to be alone. She wished Toddy would go home and Jean-Paul would disappear. The sooner he moved into the cottage the better. She wasn't good at being around people all the time. She was beginning to feel trapped, unable to breathe. There on the bridge, alone with the elements, she felt better. She could hear the gentle trickle of the stream and the wind rustling through the trees, but no voices. It was quiet.

Finally, the rainbow faded. The clouds closed to hide the sun, like curtains on a magnificent stage. Ava was once again faced with having to perform. Toddy and Jean-Paul emerged and she turned to smile at them. "I think a cup of tea would warm us all up, don't you, Ava?" said Toddy stridently, setting off towards the house.

"I wonder where the children ran off to?"

"They'll be soaking wet, I should imagine," said Toddy. "We should put them all in a hot bath!"

"I bet they hid in the hollow tree. They're probably as dry as little moles." She was right. They saw the grown-ups approaching and peeped out excitedly.

"My God! They're packed in there like sardines," Toddy exclaimed. "Are they all alive?" Poppy spilled out and ran to her mother.

"Did you see the rainbow?" she cried. "It was enormous!" Ava took her hand. It was cold and wet.

"Did you see pink?"

"Yes!" And she listed the colors one by one. "Pink and green go together, don't they, Mummy?"

"You're right, darling. Pink and green go together. They are my favorite colors." She turned to Jean-Paul. "Next time, look out for pink. It's there, but you have to really look for it."

"Like beauty," he said. "Beauty is in everything if you really look for it."

"That's open to debate," interjected Toddy. "I look for it every morning in the mirror but it still eludes me."

"I think your children see it every time they look at you," said Jean-Paul. Toddy looked embarrassed. "Your own beauty is not yours to find," he continued.

Ava walked on, holding her daughter's hand. She was certain that Jean-Paul had found his own beauty in the mirror a long time ago.

That night Ava laid two places for dinner at the kitchen table. She busied herself cooking a lasagna so that she didn't have to look at them. Those two placements made her feel anxious, as if she were on a first date. It was years since she had eaten alone with a strange man. It didn't feel right. Had Jean-Paul been plain or gauche, it wouldn't have mattered. The fact was, he was handsome. Worse, he was *predatory*. Her stomach twisted with nerves. What on earth was she going to talk about? She decided not to have pudding. That way dinner would be short and she could leave him in the sitting room watching *Dallas* and go to bed. She contemplated keeping Archie up, but that might look odd. She didn't want to behave like an inexperienced twenty-year-old. Good God, she was a married mother of thirty-seven. Finally, she put the place settings on trays and decided they could both eat in front of the telly.

To her surprise, Jean-Paul left straight after he had eaten. He said he was tired, and thanked her for a magical day. "I have already learned a lot," he told her. Then with a smile that made Ava regret her churlishness, he added, "I have learned to look out for pink. Next time I see a rainbow I will look harder." With that, he took her hand and brought it to his lips in the same formal way with which he had greeted her the day before.

X

The taste of warm wine, the smell of burning fields, the last of summer sunshine

The following day Ava took the children to church. Jean-Paul moved into the cottage. She didn't see him all day. Hidden away on the other side of the river he kept to himself, though he did borrow her old Morris Minor to drive into town. He said he wanted to take a look around. Explore the neighborhood. Ava didn't think he'd be too impressed. It was a universe away from Paris.

She didn't have time to miss Phillip. Besides, she was used to his long absences. In an old pair of jeans and shirt, her hair piled on top of her head and held in place with a pen, she pottered about the garden while the children played on the lawn. It was a warm October day. Unusually warm. The sun shone brightly as if it were June, the temperature rising to sixty-eight degrees. Poppy discarded her clothes and ran about in her pants. The boys dragged all the terrace cushions out of the shed and made a castle on the grass, which they destroyed by jumping on it before rebuilding, only to do the same all over again. With her secateurs and wheelbarrow, Ava was as contented as a bee in summer, humming quietly to herself in the bushes.

Bernie lay under an apple tree, sleeping through the whoops of laughter echoing across the lawn. He awoke a few minutes before Phillip's car could be heard coming up the drive. Ears pricked, he sat up, then galloped down the lawn to the archway cut into the hedge and bounded to the front of the house. The children followed excitedly, pursued by Ava wielding a trowel.

By the time Ava reached him, Phillip was holding Poppy in his arms, patting Bernie and listening to his sons' breathless chatter. He saw her standing in the archway, laughing at him. "Hello, Shrub!"

"Hello there, you!" she replied, looking at him coquettishly.

"I've brought back a brace of pheasants."

"Wonderful. Jean-Paul has moved into the cottage."

"Well, ask him to join us. More the merrier." Ava was disappointed. She had hoped they could enjoy a quiet dinner together.

"I haven't seen him all day. I think we should leave him in peace," she replied. No sooner had she uttered those words than Jean-Paul came striding up the field in a pair of brand-new Wellington boots.

"Jean-Paul!" Phillip greeted him warmly. "I see you have moved into the château!"

Jean-Paul grinned. "I had to buy boots to get there. That little shop by the church has everything," he replied. Ava's heart sank. She knew Phillip would ask him for dinner and that he would accept.

"Would you like to join us for dinner?" he asked. "I've brought back a brace of pheasants. Ava's a splendid cook." Poppy wriggled down and followed her brothers back onto the lawn. "We could almost eat outside."

"I would love to, thank you," Jean-Paul replied.

Ava bit her tongue. Infuriated by her husband's lack of sensitivity, she turned on her heel and followed the children, leaving Jean-Paul and Phillip talking like two old friends.

That night Phillip confronted her in the bedroom. "What's wrong, Shrub? You've been in a sulk all evening."

"I'm fine," she replied, walking into the bathroom to run a bath. Phillip followed her.

"You barely said a word all dinner."

"I'm just tired. I've been entertaining people all weekend." She poured oil into the water, filling the room with the scent of gardenia.

"Jean-Paul?"

"Toddy came yesterday with the boys. I thought it would be nice for us to have dinner together. I didn't want to see anyone else. I'm tired of performing. I just want to relax and not have to make an effort."

He put his arms around her. "I'm sorry," he said, breathing into her neck. He kissed the tender skin below her hairline. "I didn't think."

"Next time," she replied with a sigh.

He swung her around and curled a stray piece of hair behind her ear. "Is he very hard work?"

"Jean-Paul? No. He's perfectly nice. He's even nicer when he's in the cottage and out of my hair."

"You're doing me a huge favor having him here. I really appreciate it. Henri will be grateful."

"I know. Grateful and helpful. You'd better reward me."

"I'll reward you in plants."

"I showed Jean-Paul the place I want to plant a cottage garden. He was interested."

"Really?" Phillip wasn't sure whether or not she was being sarcastic.

"Oh yes, he took it all in. If he had had a pen and pad he would have taken notes."

"Good."

She looked at him askance. "He doesn't have a clue, Phillip. I'm going to be dragging him around like an unwanted sack."

"That's rather harsh. Get him to do all the dirty work for you. Like digging and clearing up."

"I will. He won't like it and he'll leave to the sound of doors slamming the length and breadth of France." She laughed.

"That's better. You were horribly sullen."

"You'd better treat me a little better then, or I'll have a permanent potato face."

"I will. I hate the potato face." He went back into the bedroom. "Everyone sends their love, by the way. They all missed you." Ava ignored him and sank into the bath, feeling her irritation ebb away.

The following day Ava introduced Jean-Paul to Hector. She was relieved to see he was dressed appropriately in a pair of faded jeans and country shirt in muted colors. He had rolled up the sleeves to reveal brown arms glistening with a light covering of hair. On his feet were his new Wellington boots.

Hector was in his sixties, dressed in the same tweed cap and waistcoat he had worn for as long as Ava had known him. His face was gnarled like an old tree, his eyes bright as new conkers. He spoke with a strong Dorset drawl, curling his Rs as tight as pigs' tails. "Could do with a little help in the garden," he said, unsmiling. Hector rarely smiled. "Especially as them leaves are coming down quicker than I can rake them up." Jean-Paul was dismayed to be handed a rake and taken off to sweep. By the look on his face Ava was certain he had been expecting to do more interesting things. His obvious disappointment made her feel bad in spite of her happiness at being left alone to do the herbaceous border. It amused her to think of those two endeavoring to hold a conversation. She couldn't imagine what they had in common. If Jean-Paul managed to understand half of what Hector said it would be a miracle.

Jean-Paul spent all day clearing the grounds. Raking leaves, mowing the grass with the old Dennis mower, cutting down a dead pear tree, generally clearing away the debris of a plentiful summer. He had stopped only to eat the sandwiches he had made himself and drink a can of beer from Ava's fridge. He looked done in.

"I think it would be a good idea to work with Hector this week. Get to know the place a bit," Ava suggested.

Jean-Paul was not amused. His face clouded but

he made no complaint. "*Bon*," he said briskly. "If that is what you want."

"I do," she replied. "It's not all creative."

"So I see."

"You'll get very fit."

"I'm already fit." He spat the words, flashing his eyes at her angrily from under his eyelashes. "I'm going to light the bonfire. I was wondering whether the children are home. They might like to help me."

"I'm going to pick them up now. They'd love to help."

"Good. I will wait."

"Have a cup of tea in the kitchen. You've worked hard all day. Have a rest."

He shook his head. "No. I have a few more loads to take to the fire."

"I'll send the children up with marshmallows."

"Marshmallows?"

"You don't know what they are?" He shook his head. "Then it will be a surprise. They'll love showing you." His features softened. She smiled at him, but he did not return the smile.

She drove to school, debating her actions, justifying the jobs she had made Jean-Paul do with Hector. He wasn't here on holiday. It wasn't meant to be a picnic. What did he expect? At least the weather was good. If he was sulky in sunshine, what in God's name was he going to be like in rain and snow? She consoled herself that he would soon be gone. He wouldn't last until winter. She'd never know what he was like in snow and he would never see the wonder of her garden in summer.

The children were thrilled at the prospect of showing Jean-Paul how to roast marshmallows. Poppy waved a picture of a sunflower in front of her face. "Darling, not while I'm driving. I don't care whether you're Gauguin or Matisse. Let's get home alive, shall we?"

The boys compared stickers they had swapped in the playground. "Robert told me that we can write to Asterix and they'll send us a whole box of stickers," said Angus.

"A whole box?" replied Archie breathlessly, looking down at his handful of Esso tigers.

Ava listened to them in amusement. This week stickers, last week conkers, next week something else.

Back at home they ran to the vegetable garden where Hector and Jean-Paul were standing in front of an enormous mountain of leaves and cardboard boxes. The sky had clouded over and it was getting cold. Ava followed with the bag of marshmallows.

"I want to show him!" cried Poppy, skipping up to her mother. "Please, can I!"

Ava opened the packet and handed her daughter a pink marshmallow and stick. "All right, but let me help you," she said, taking her hand.

Jean-Paul had regained his color. He no longer

looked angry. He watched the boys take a handful of marshmallows each and give one to him.

"You have to put it on a stick," said Archie importantly. "Otherwise you'll burn your fingers."

"Thank you," said Jean-Paul. "I would not want to burn my fingers."

"I burned my finger once," volunteered Angus, holding it up. "But Mummy put a bandage on it and it got better."

"Your mother is very clever," said Jean-Paul seriously.

"Watch!" Poppy shouted, holding her marshmallow in a bright yellow flame until it caught a little flame of its own. "See!" she hissed excitedly, standing stone still as if she held a poisonous snake on the end of her stick.

"Right, you can take it out now," said Ava.

"Blow, Mummy!" Ava brought it to her mouth and blew. It had melted into a sticky sugary ball. "Can I eat it now?" she asked. Ava tested it on her lips, blew again, then handed it to her daughter. Poppy pulled it off and popped the marshmallow into her mouth. She smiled in delight. "Yummy!" she exclaimed.

"Have a go," Ava said to Jean-Paul. "Consider this your initiation into the garden. If you pass this, you can be a member of our club, can't he, Hector?"

Hector nodded. He leaned on his pitchfork, watching the children contentedly.

Jean-Paul held his marshmallow over the fire while the boys shouted instructions at him. The Frenchman indulged them, doing as he was told, asking questions to make them feel important. Ava noticed how sweet he was with the children and how much they enjoyed having him around, especially the boys. He was someone new to show off to. Inside him there was a boyishness they were drawn to.

The marshmallow event drew them all together. The sun went down behind the garden wall, setting the tops of the trees ablaze with a bright golden light. The sky darkened, the air grew moist, the wind turned cold. But they were hot in front of the fire. The mountain diminished into a low mound of embers, glowing like molten copper each time a gust of wind swept over them. They ate all the marshmallows.

Then Jean-Paul suggested they play a game. "If this is my initiation into *your* club, then you have to be initiated into mine," he said seriously.

Ava watched in astonishment as he began to dance around the fire making whooping noises with his hand over his mouth. His unbuttoned shirt blew about his body illuminating his skin in the firelight. He lifted his feet and jumped about, pretending to be a Red Indian. The children joined in, following Jean-Paul closely, copying his erratic movements, their small figures casting eerie shadows on the garden wall. Ava roared with laughter, and even Hector smiled, revealing small yellow teeth and gaping black holes where there were none. Inspired by the exhibition, Ava clapped her hands, wishing she had a drum so she could join in.

That evening, Ava was sorry Jean-Paul did not come for dinner. She had seen an unexpected side of him. They had parted in the vegetable garden. She with the children, he alone. She thought of him in the cottage, beside the fire, eating in front of the television then going to bed, and wondered whether he would be lonely. She resolved to lend him her car any time he wanted so he could go into town, and she'd remind Toddy to introduce him to her cousins. He'd appreciate the company of girls his age.

"How did it go today with Jean-Paul?" Phillip asked over dinner. Ava had made a special effort to cook partridges with breadcrumbs, bread sauce and gravy. She had steamed red cabbage to which she had added a little ginger, and had boiled carrots with honey. She had lit a candle on the table and dimmed the lights. Phillip opened a bottle of Bordeaux and poured two glasses. "Was he helpful?"

Ava smiled contentedly. "He was. In fact, he was a pleasure to have around. We roasted marshmallows in the bonfire and they all danced around it like Red Indians."

"Not Hector, I hope. Wouldn't do his heart any good at all."

"Certainly not! Jean-Paul led the children. It was very funny. Poppy following as best she could, the boys thinking they were incredibly clever, kicking their legs out and spinning around. No wonder they're quiet upstairs, I should imagine they're exhausted!"

"Was he any good in the garden?"

"He helped Hector. I didn't see much of him all day. I think he was pretty pissed off he had to rake leaves, but it's not all about planting roses."

"He'll get used to it. He'll reap the rewards of his labor in spring."

"If he's still here."

The next few days she saw little of Jean-Paul. He worked with Hector while she busied herself in the borders. She asked him for dinner, but he refused, claiming he was having dinner at the pub. She dared not ask who with. It was none of her business. She wandered around the garden, trying to work out how she was going to plant her cottage garden, trying to imagine it, but nothing came. Perhaps the project was simply too ambitious. She should concentrate on the wild garden around the hollow tree instead. On Wednesday, when he had declined her third invitation for dinner, she realized she was being unfair. He had come to help her, she couldn't send him off to work with Hector all day. That wasn't keeping her side of the bargain. He had proved he was willing to work hard.

It was late. The sun had set, the sky was a deep navy studded with stars and there was a misty moon. She walked across the field towards the river. She wasn't going to apologize, but she was going to ask his advice on the cottage garden. Perhaps he did have ideas. She hadn't given him a chance.

The bridge looked silver in the moonlight, straddling the river that trickled gently in the silence. She loved the night. It was like being wrapped in velvet. Her spirits rose as she approached the cottage and she walked with a bounce in her step. The lights were on, the smell of smoke scenting the damp air with nostalgia. She stood a moment gazing at the little house, lit up as if by spotlight, enjoying the romance of it. Then she knocked on the door.

Jean-Paul's face blanched with surprise when he saw her. She wore a T-shirt under her purple dungarees and seemed not to feel the cold. He shivered as the wind swept into the hall. "Come in," he said, standing aside. She took off her boots and walked into the sitting room. There was a fire in the grate, a box of paints and glass of murky water on the coffee table. Jean-Michel Jarre resounded from the tape recorder. She hadn't imagined he could paint.

He didn't offer her a drink, but stood in the doorway waiting for her to speak. She walked over to the fire. "I've come to ask your advice," she said, suddenly losing confidence. He had bathed, his hair was still wet. His blue shirt, the sleeves rolled up, hung over his Levis.

"Advice?" He looked unconvinced. "Why would you want to do that? You clearly don't think I have anything to offer."

"That is not true," she protested.

"Oh come on, Ava!" he exclaimed, striding into the room and flopping onto the sofa. He put his hands behind his head and stretched out his legs. "You've sent me off with Hector. How do you know what I can do and what I can't do?"

"I don't," she conceded. "Let's be honest, shall we? You coming here was not my idea. It was Phillip's. I didn't want you. I didn't need any help. I'm more than capable of doing it on my own."

"Then why are you here asking my advice?"

"Because I am at a loss and perhaps you can help me. You said yourself not to judge people. I judged you. I'm hoping I was wrong."

"How can I help you?"

"The cottage garden."

"Ah." He sat forward, put his elbows on his knees and rubbed his chin thoughtfully. Ava felt a surge of relief. Her white flag had been accepted. "The cottage garden," he repeated.

"Yes," she said. "I've tried, but I can't picture it."

"As it happens, I have had some thoughts."

"You have?" He reached over the arm of the sofa and pulled out a large ring-bound block of artists' paper.

"I didn't know you painted."

"I have painted something for you," he said.

He placed the book on her knee. She gazed at it, speechless with admiration. There, in vibrant colors and bold, confident strokes, was a picture of her cottage garden. A grassy path snaked across it, bordered on both sides by flowers and shrubs, glistening on a bright summer's day. In the middle was the mountain ash, encircled by a pretty round bench in French gray. It was perfect. She could not have dreamed a more beautiful garden.

XI

The melancholy cry of a lone gull hovering on the wind

Hartington House, 2005

It was then that I realized M.F. wasn't so very different from me. We were two artistic people, yearning to create something beautiful.

Miranda's eyes stung with tears. Folded in half and stuck to the page was the picture of the cottage garden. The colors were as vibrant as the day they had been painted. She ran her fingers across the paper, over pink roses and white lilies, and imagined the dawning of love. For a moment she felt a wave of melancholy at the emptiness in her own heart. But it came and went before she allowed herself to analyze it. If she filled her days with her work and the practical chores of running the house she wouldn't feel the ache, like stuffing a hole with cardboard. She focused all her attention on the picture. That bench was still circling the mountain ash. She wondered whether they had sat there, creating the gardens together, their affection growing with each plant they sowed. Suddenly she was gripped with enthusiasm. Perhaps Jean-Paul could resurrect that garden, breathe life back into it and she could live awhile, vicariously.

Although there were no names in the scrapbook she assumed the book belonged to the previous owner, Mrs. Lightly. Little was written about the physical aspects of M.F. Much was written about his nature: one moment smiling and joyous, the next sullen and petulant. A creative young man, swathed in frustration. She wondered why Mrs. Lightly had left the book in the cottage. As it was weighted with so much significance, it was unlikely that she would forget it. Or perhaps she felt the affair was best left in the past. Miranda could imagine the old woman chuckling at the absurdity of her girlish crush and leaving the book behind deliberately.

It wasn't written as a love story, with a beginning, middle and end, but as a series of memories. Miranda wanted to submerge herself in them and take her time. She flicked through the pages, pausing occasionally to dwell on pressed leaves and flowers and the sentences written beside them in Mrs. Lightly's pretty looped writing. She was aware that she was meant to be getting the cottage ready for Jean-Paul. She didn't have the time to linger over someone else's love affair. However, the book was compelling, like a whole world compressed into a hundred pages. The love story held such allure. She knew if she allowed herself to read on, she would lose herself completely. She closed the book reluctantly. There were things to be done in the house. Mrs. Underwood was coming at midday to discuss the details of her employment. Mr. Underwood required direction. She had to find out who the local builders were, not to mention the domestic chores she had to undertake until she found a housekeeper to do them for her. She left the cottage with the scrapbook tucked under her arm, a spring in her step.

As she made her way up the field towards the house she saw Mrs. Underwood's car on the gravel. Ranger was cocking his leg on one of the tires while Mrs. Underwood waited on the step, arms crossed over the buttress of her expansive bosom, her face sagging in repose.

"Hello!" Miranda shouted, quickening her pace. "I'm so sorry, I've been delayed. Got to sort out that cottage for the gardener." She checked herself, remembering the woman's husband. "The *landscape* gardener." Mrs. Underwood nodded. "I haven't seen Mr. Underwood yet, I assume he's in the garden."

"Oh aye, keeping himself busy, I should imagine. Hard to keep that man down." Miranda unlocked the door. Mrs. Underwood sighed. "Sign of the times. In my day, no one locked their doors. We were in and out of each other's houses all day long. It's not like it was."

"Well, you didn't have microwaves and e-mail, mobile phones and satellite telly, did you? So, it's not all bad."

Mrs. Underwood looked appalled. "What do you need all that rubbish for? They don't save time, just give you more time to fill up. Everyone's running around like headless chickens. In my day we all had time for a chat." Miranda thought it best not to argue. People like Mrs. Underwood were content to sit in the past and lament the wicked ways of the modern world.

Miranda hid the scrapbook in her study, then took Mrs. Underwood into the kitchen to discuss wages and hours. She noticed Mr. Underwood had filled the log baskets and lit the fires while she had been out. The air smelled of burning wood. Mrs. Underwood commented on it proudly. "Mrs. Lightly always had the fires lit. Not that she ever felt the cold. Oh no, Mrs. Lightly wore short sleeves even in snow and I never saw her shiver." Now Miranda's curiosity had been aroused, she wanted to know more about the woman in the scrapbook.

"Let's have a cup of tea, Mrs. Underwood," she suggested, pulling out a stool. "What will you have? Earl Grey?"

"Allow me, Miranda."

"You sit down, Mrs. Underwood."

"I insist. I can't sit like a pudding being waited on by my employer. It's not right." She took the kettle from Miranda and held it under the tap. "Besides, I've got to get to know the kitchen. It's changed since Mrs. Lightly was here."

Miranda sat on the stool. "What was Mrs. Lightly like?" she asked. "I've heard all about her beautiful gardens, but nothing about her."

Mrs. Underwood paused a moment. "She was an original. God broke the mold when He made her. Mr. Lightly was very English. Tall as a tree, with a big friendly smile. Everyone liked Mr. Lightly. He was the sort of man who always had time to talk. Mrs. Lightly, she was an eccentric. She'd come alive like a fire, telling funny stories and entertaining everyone, then she'd suddenly run out of fuel, make her excuses and leave. You always knew when she'd had enough. Those that didn't would find themselves talking to the walls. She'd be out in her garden, alone on that bench, enjoying the silence. She liked to be on her own best of all, though that's not to say she didn't love her children and Mr. Lightly. Besides them, I'd say she *liked* and *tolerated*, but she wasn't a sociable person like Mr. Lightly. Mr. Lightly liked having guests in the house. You'd never imagine for a moment that she didn't like entertaining. But she didn't. I could tell. She was happier when she had the house to herself."

"What did she look like?"

Mrs. Underwood plugged the kettle in and took two cups down from the cupboard. "She wasn't beautiful like you, Miranda. She was handsome, I'd say. Her features were so alive, her expression so kind and sensitive that she became beautiful the better you got to know her. Some people are like that, aren't they? Mrs. Lightly wasn't vain. She didn't plaster her face with makeup or do her hair all fancy. It was long and curly. She'd twist it up on the top of her head and stick a pencil through it, then spend all afternoon looking for her pencil." She chuckled again. "She was scatty. The house was full of clutter because she never put anything away. She had a wonderful sense of humor. Everything had a funny side, even the bad times. Though I don't imagine her finding a funny side to Mr. Lightly's sickness. After that I didn't see much of them. They stopped entertaining and withdrew. She looked after him herself." She shook her head, popping two teabags into the pot. "That's love, isn't it? If my old man got sick I'd do the same for him. They drive you up the wall, but you love them. Wouldn't want to be without them."

Miranda instinctively knew not to mention the scrapbook. Mrs. Lightly's secret love was probably known only to the two of them. "The cottage," she began carefully. "Who lived there?"

"Oh, I don't know." Mrs. Underwood looked puzzled. "I think it's been a ruin for years."

"It's adorable."

"Mr. Lightly's brother used it as a weekend cottage, but that was before I knew them. I think Mr. Lightly tried to rent it out after his brother moved away. But it's very impractical being in the middle of a field."

"Did you always cook for them?"

"Not in the early days. They had an old cook called Mrs. Marley. She was famous for chocolate walnut cake, but a person can't live on that alone, can they? When Mrs. Marley retired I came to do the odd weekend. They had a lot of literary types down here from London. They'd play charades after dinner, I'd hear them whooping with laughter from the kitchen. Mr. Lightly was a famous writer, you know. I once read his name in the papers. He won all sorts of prizes. He was a very modest man, though."

"What did he write about?"

"Wine. He spent a lot of time researching in France. He'd leave Ava alone in the house for weeks on end while he traveled to vineyards. Their cellar was quite something, I tell you. Full of dusty bottles as old as me!"

"Ah, that would account for all those French books in the cottage."

"Mr. Lightly loved books. His study was full of them. Piled up on the floors and tables, spilling out into the hall. His study was where yours is now. I'm glad to see you've filled them."

"There's nothing more depressing than empty bookcases."

"Mr. Lightly didn't have enough space. Probably why he had to use the cottage. I've only ever read one book."

"Oh? Which one?"

"*The Secret Garden*. Mrs. Lightly gave it to me. It took me weeks to finish. I'm ever such a slow reader. I prefer to sew. If I'm not cooking and growing my own vegetables, I'm doing my needlepoint. I sit by the fire with my feet up doing my needlepoint while Mr. Underwood watches the telly. That's the way I like it, Mr. Underwood in his armchair, me in mine, feet up, watching the telly. Oh the things they have on these days, it's a wonder people leave the house!"

They drank their tea, agreed to the hours and wages of Mrs. Underwood's employment and Miranda handed her a key. "That'll suit me perfectly," said Mrs. Underwood, putting her cup down on the sideboard. "If you're still looking for a housekeeper, I know a lady who could do it. Fatima, she's Muslim. Mother of Jemal who owns the convenience shop in town. She's looking to do something now her granddaughter's gone to university. She's a good woman and hard-working, I should imagine. Jemal will open on a Sunday if you ask him."

"How do I get in touch with her?"

"I'll be seeing her this afternoon. I've got to go and buy some ketchup. My grandchildren are coming on Sunday and little Kevin won't eat anything unless it's covered in ketchup. Such a pity! I'll give Fatima your number and tell her to call you."

"Thank you. She sounds ideal. By the way, who's the local builder? I need to get that cottage ready and it's in a right state!"

"That'll be Derek Heath and his boys Nick and Steve. You'd better give him a call right away if you want to get them before Christmas. They're very booked up. Hard to pin down."

"Are they reliable?"

"Reliable? Gold dust, that's what they are, gold dust! You can bring your fancy builders down from London but nothing compares to the local boys. Half the price, too. They're honest, hard-working lads and they get the job done." She smiled wickedly and winked. "Easy on the eye, too. I'd have thrown my cap at Derek if I hadn't been married to Mr. Underwood. I'll be happy to take them cups of tea." She jotted the number down for Miranda. "Tell them it's urgent, they'll sort something out. They know the house well. Used to do the odd thing for Mrs. Lightly."

Once Mrs. Underwood had gone, Miranda telephoned Derek Heath on his mobile. To her surprise he said he could start in a week—the job he had booked had been canceled. "You're lucky," he said in his country drawl. "Or perhaps it's fate. I'm not a believer myself, but my wife is and she'd say it was definitely meant to be." Miranda put down the receiver and thought of Jean-Paul. Was he fate, too?

At five o'clock, Henrietta left Clare in charge of the shop to nip across the street to Troy's for her cut and blow-dry. She had felt low all day. Little by little, Cate's bitchiness had worn her down. Humor wasn't much of a shield against Cate's carefully aimed arrows. "It makes her feel better to pull you down," said Troy, settling her into the chair. "I'm going to give you long layers, darling. It'll lift you. You need a lift in more ways than one. That Cate's a miserable old cow. You know what they say? Happy people are nice people, unhappy people are nasty people. Cate is clearly unhappy. She might make the best coffee in Dorset but she's as bitter as a bar of Green & Black's."

"I'm not happy in my skin, Troy. I'd feel better if I had less of it!" She gave a weak laugh.

"There's too much pressure on women these days to be thin. Thin doesn't mean happy."

"But it means married."

"Not necessarily. There are plenty of men out there who like fulsome women. You're not fat. Fat is Rev. Beeley."

"She also happens to be five foot tall."

"A gnome, darling. Which is why she's unmarried. No one wants to marry a gnome."

"A Womble?"

"Seen any lately?"

"Haven't been to Wimbledon Common for years."

"You're a proper height and a gorgeous, voluptuous shape. You should celebrate your size, not hide under clothes made for women four sizes larger than you. I'm going to give you a killer hairdo."

"What's the point? There aren't any single men in Hartington."

"I bet there's somebody here, right under your nose."

"You?" She gazed at him longingly.

"If only," he sighed. "But I'd make you even more miserable. You need a man to make love to you, not to put you on a pedestal and worship you while he makes eyes at the postman."

"Not our Tony?"

"Not specifically, no. There has to be someone in Hartington. Isn't that what happens in romantic novels? The heroine always ends up with the local man she'd never noticed before."

"I've looked at every man who walks down the street. Perhaps I'm not destined for marriage. I'm destined to envy other women with prams and pushchairs, fridges scattered with school drawings and timetables. I'd make a good wife. I'd cook him delicious dinners, run him hot baths, massage his feet after a busy day, organize his life like a secretary. I'd give him roly-poly children and a bit of roly-poly myself. I'd make him happy. But all the good I have to give is turning sour in my belly. If I don't find someone soon I'll ferment into vinegar and won't be of any worth to anyone."

"You talk a lot of nonsense, Etta. You've got plenty of time."

"But I don't want to be an old mother." She clutched her belly. "I want to have children while I'm young enough to run in the mothers' race."

"You'll always be young enough to make the picnic."

"But what's the fun in making a picnic on a Zimmer frame?" She watched pieces of her hair drop to the floor like feathers.

"It'll happen and when it does I'll be more than a little jealous." He watched her smile. "God made me gay to torment me."

"He made you handsome to torment me," she giggled.

"At least we can laugh about it. That makes it bearable."

"Just. There comes a point, though, when laughing isn't enough." They gazed at each other in the mirror, across the insurmountable space that separated them, suddenly serious. He bent down and planted a kiss on her exposed neck.

"I do love you, though," he said, frowning.

"I know. And I love you. You're my friend. Hell would be a place without you."

Derek Heath began on the cottage the following week with the help of his two sons. Their radio, an old machine splattered with layers of paint, was positioned on the windowsill as they ripped out the kitchen units and retiled the floor to the sound of Queen's *We Will Rock You*. Derek's older brother, Arthur, came out of retirement to help. Dressed in immaculate white coveralls, he mended the leak in the sitting room and repapered the walls. Mrs. Underwood brought them trays of tea and biscuits, lingering to chat longer than was necessary. Mr. Underwood joined her, finding jobs to do by the river to justify his presence. The moment Storm and Gus finished school they left their bikes on the gravel and hurried to the cottage to watch. Derek patted them affectionately, remembering his own boys as children, musing at the rapid passing of time. He gave Gus small tasks while Storm helped pour the tea and hand round biscuits. Miranda watched them tear out Mrs. Lightly's memories and felt a moment's regret. This was "their" cottage. It was where she had left the scrapbook. She couldn't help but feel ashamed of her callous disregard for the woman's past.

Fatima came for an interview. She was a big-featured woman with brown skin and small brown eyes, her head covered in a scarf. Her lips were full and when she smiled the gaps between her teeth were large and black. She was short and round in the middle, like a honeypot, her feet clad in sandals and white socks. Before Miranda could explain what she wanted Fatima silenced her with an extravagant sweep of her hand. "I know how rich people like their houses cleaned," she declared in a thick Moroccan accent. "You won't be disappointed. Fatima clean your house until it shine." She flashed Miranda a wide smile, a gold filling catching the light. "Fatima know." She was decisive. Miranda was left no option but to hire her. "You have made the right decision," she exclaimed portentously. "You will not regret it." Miranda returned to her desk to write an article for *Eve* magazine on the joys of self-employment, and wondered how all those other self-employed mothers managed to get anything done!

David arrived on Friday night exhausted and in an ill temper. However, the fish pie Mrs. Underwood had left for dinner transformed his mood so that when he tucked into the apple and blackberry crumble he was almost jolly. "Darling," he said, taking her hand. "Things are looking up!"

"I think so," she agreed. "It feels like home."

"The fires are lit, dinner is delicious. Gus hasn't played truant all week." He sat back in his chair. "This is the life." He patted his stomach. "Now I'm going to have a bath and turn on the telly. See if there's anything worth watching." He left Miranda feeling a mixture of pride and resentment. The house was perfect but he hadn't asked about her, or about the children. He simply assumed that Gus had behaved himself because she hadn't told him otherwise. She drained her wineglass and looked at the dishes David had left on the table. Before she indulged in self-pity she remembered the scrapbook smoldering in her study. The mere thought of it caused a frisson of excitement to career up her spine. She wouldn't tell David. It would be her secret. The thought of holding something back gave her a sense of superiority over her husband. A sliver of control. She'd load the dishwasher and wash up, watch television with him and share his bed but, on Sunday night, when he left, she would have the scrapbook to curl up with and someone else's love to feast upon.

XII

The pink light of sunset setting the sky aflame

At the end of October the cottage was finished and Jean-Paul returned to Hartington. Miranda had woken in a good mood, deliberated over what to wear, finally deciding on a pair of Rock & Republic skinny jeans tucked into boots, an Anne Fontaine white shirt and an extravagant spray of Jo

Malone Lime, Basil & Mandarin scent. She had taken time to wash and blow-dry her hair, leaving it long and shiny down her back. Not that she wanted to look as though she'd taken trouble; after all, he was only the gardener.

He arrived in late afternoon. Gus and Storm were on half term, hanging around the bridge, waiting for the enigmatic Frenchman to appear. Gus pretended he wasn't interested, throwing sticks into the water, but in fact was curious and putout that Storm had already met him.

When Miranda opened the door her heart stalled a moment; he was even more handsome than she remembered, in a felt hat, sheepskin coat and faded Levis. He stepped into the hall and took off his hat. His graying hair was tousled and he ran a hand through it, casting his eyes about the place, searching for ghosts in the shadows.

"The children are waiting for you at the cottage," she said. "I've filled your fridge so I can offer you a cup of tea down there."

"Good, then let's go."

Miranda followed him onto the gravel. The sky was a deep navy, turning to pink and gold just above the tree line. The air was damp, the ground wet from a heavy shower that morning. Brown and red leaves gathered on the grass, blown about by the wind, and a couple of gray squirrels chased each other up the oak tree. Jean-Paul watched them and, for an instant, was sure he saw three little faces peering out like Red Indians in a tepee. He hesitated, Miranda's nervous chatter muffled against the sudden eruption of children's laughter. He squinted and strained his ears, but the laughter blended with the wind and the little faces were swallowed by the dusk. It was just the evening light filtering old memories; the oak tree was dark and empty and silent.

They continued down the path to the bridge where Storm and Gus waited. When she saw him, Storm broke into a run, eager to show off to Gus. "Mummy! Mummy!" she cried. "I'm going to make magic in the garden!" Jean-Paul's face relaxed into an affectionate smile, the sight of the children putting right all that was wrong about the place. "We've tidied the cottage for you," she said proudly, springing beside him like a kangaroo. Gus remained on the bridge watching Jean-Paul warily from behind a curtain of dark hair. Jean-Paul was Storm's friend.

Jean-Paul sensed Gus's suspicion as if it were a miasma of smoke around him. He nodded affably then proceeded towards the cottage. He knew not to force his friendship. The child would come when he was ready. Miranda opened the door with the same rusty key that Ava had used a lifetime ago. They had both been young then; neither knowing that they would forge a love so strong that in all the years that followed she would remain at the very center of his heart like a thorny rose—

beautiful but inflicting pain. The house was the same, the gardens remained, though neglected, their cottage barely touched: yet Ava had been the breath that had brought it all to life. Without her, the place was dead.

He stepped inside. There was a smell of fresh paint and polish—and the unexpected scent of orange blossom? He was aware that Miranda was expecting a reaction but he wanted to be alone to retrace their every moment together. The afternoons they had made love on the sofa in front of the fire, the mornings they had crept beneath the sheets to hold each other for a few stolen moments, the terrible day they had sat staring at each other across the kitchen table knowing it had to come to an end, as inevitably as a tree losing its leaves in autumn.

He took off his coat and almost stumbled into the kitchen where Miranda put the kettle on to make tea. Storm opened a packet of digestive biscuits. Gus crept in out of the dusk. Jean-Paul looked around the room and saw that everything had changed. There were new units, a smart black Aga, gray floor tiles where there had been wood. Miranda looked at him anxiously. "Do you like it?" Storm brought him a biscuit and he was once again wrenched away from the past. The little girl's bashful smile soothed the cracks in his heart.

"I like it," he replied.

Miranda's shoulders dropped with relief. "I'm so

pleased," she said, taking cups down from the cupboard. "I did a big shop for you. I didn't know what you'd want so I bought a bit of everything. You can borrow my car if you like and check out the town. Sainsbury's is a few miles out the other side, past the castle. I must take the children to the castle. I haven't had time yet." Jean-Paul remembered her using that excuse before. Time. He glanced at Gus standing shiftily in the corner and felt his loneliness; it leaked out of every pore.

"Will you show me where I will sleep?" he asked Gus. The little boy shrugged and left the room.

"I'll show you!" Storm squeaked, hurrying out after her brother.

"But you gave him a biscuit," retorted Gus angrily, grabbing her shirt.

"Let me tell you a secret," Jean-Paul said calmly. Both children turned to stare at him with wide, curious eyes. "Come upstairs," he added, striding past them. Once in the bedroom he opened the window. "I think you will find there is a family of squirrels who think that this is their house."

"I know," said Gus, sitting on the bed. "I've seen them."

"You have?"

"This was my secret camp," he said grumpily.

"I think you can do better than this," said Jean-Paul. "How about a camp in a tree?"

"A tree house?" said Gus, unconvinced.

"A tree house built in the branches so that in

178

summer no one knows you are there. A tree house that has an upstairs and a downstairs."

"There isn't one of those here," Gus scoffed.

"Not yet, but we will build it."

"Can you do that?"

"Not on my own. But you and Storm will help me."

"Mummy says you're the gardener," said Gus.

"Isn't a tree part of the garden, too?"

"The hollow tree!" Storm cried. "But that's going to be *my* secret camp."

Jean-Paul shook his head and sat on the bed beside Gus. "Come here, Storm," he said, beckoning her over. She stood before him, her bottom lip sticking out sulkily. "Do you remember I told you about the magic in the garden?"

"Yes."

"The magic only works when we all act together. Do you understand?" Storm frowned, Gus looked skeptical. "What is the point of being at different ends of the garden? There is only so much that we can do on our own. Imagine what incredible things we can create together?"

"Can we build the tree house tomorrow?" Storm asked.

"I don't see why not," said Jean-Paul. *We will breathe life back into the garden and the sound of children's laughter will once again ring out from the old oak tree. I cannot bring the love back but I can create new love. That is how I will remember her.*

Downstairs, Miranda had made the tea. She took it into the sitting room on a tray and lit the fire. She was pleased with the cottage. It was cozy and clean. The carpet had been replaced, the walls repapered and new curtains hung, breaking on the floor in generous folds. She had kept all the books and ornaments. He wouldn't know that they had belonged to Phillip Lightly. She hoped the children weren't bothering him. For a man who had no children of his own he was very sweet and patient with them. She wondered why such a handsome man had never married. Perhaps he had suffered a terrible loss or tragedy that had prevented him from sharing his life with someone. He had the air of a man used to being on his own.

After a while all three came downstairs. Jean-Paul sat beside the fire, in the armchair that Miranda had had recovered in green ticking. She gave him a cup of tea and sat opposite him. She had a tendency to chatter when nervous and made a deliberate effort not to overdo it. After all, she kept telling herself, he was just the gardener.

"The children are on half term this week. I hope they don't get in your way," she said.

"Jean-Paul is going to build us a tree house," said Gus, trying not to sound too excited in case it didn't happen. He was used to his father making promises he didn't keep. "If he's not too busy," he added. Jean-Paul looked at him intently. Like "time," the word "busy" bothered him.

"Your tree house is at the very top of my list of priorities," he said seriously. "What is a garden without a tree house? What is a garden without magic? We have to build a tree house for the magic to work." Storm giggled. Gus stared at Jean-Paul, not knowing what to make of him. He had never come across an adult who put *his* desires first. Jean-Paul turned his attention to Miranda. "I will walk around the garden tomorrow and see what we can salvage, what needs to be cut back, what needs to be replanted. Already I can see the wild garden needs to be replanted so that it flowers in the spring."

"Whatever you suggest." Miranda didn't want to know the details. She just wanted it done.

"Is there a vegetable garden?" he asked, blinking away the sudden vision of Archie, Angus and Poppy dancing around the bonfire that autumn evening after roasting marshmallows on the flames.

"Yes, it's a mess."

He turned to the children. "How would you like to help me plant the vegetable garden in the spring?"

"Me, me!" Storm volunteered immediately. "What shall we plant?"

Jean-Paul rubbed his chin in thought. "Marrows, pumpkins, rhubarb, raspberries, strawberries, potatoes, carrots . . ."

"You're going to plant all those?" said Gus.

"Of course. With your help. After all, you're going to eat them."

Gus screwed up his nose. "I hate rhubarb."

"You won't hate our rhubarb."

"I think that's a wonderful idea," enthused Miranda. "You'll meet Mrs. Underwood. She cooks for us. There's nothing she likes more than fresh vegetables. There's a farmers' market in town on a Saturday, though I'm ashamed to say I haven't been yet. I've barely had a moment."

"Then, what we don't eat we will sell." Gus's eyes lit up. "And you, Gus, can take a cut of the money." Jean-Paul looked at Miranda for approval. She nodded. She could tell Gus was warming to Jean-Paul, in spite of himself. He was an independent child. He didn't need attention like his sister, or at least he didn't want to look as if he needed it. She put that down to his age. He was just beginning to flex his wings. He had never been one of those needy children who wanted his parents around. She watched him assessing the new arrival with a mixture of curiosity and admiration. There was something compelling about Jean-Paul, like the Pied Piper of Hamelin with his magic flute.

They finished tea and Miranda felt it wasn't fair to linger longer than necessary. "I'm sure you want to unpack and settle in," she said, standing up. "We'll see you tomorrow."

"I will assess the garden and let you know what

182

is needed. Then we have work to do, no?" He spoke to the children.

"Our tree house," said Storm happily. Gus said nothing. His head was buzzing with conflicting thoughts. He followed his mother outside where a bright moon turned the river silver, yearning to give in to excitement but too afraid. The number of times his hopes had been reduced to disappointment were too many to count.

Jean-Paul stood in the doorway, watching them go, remembering the sight of Ava on the bridge watching the rainbow. Alone, in France, he'd search for the pink in every rainbow, as if she were a pot of gold at the foot, but he had never found it. Years had passed, rainbows had come and gone, pink had always eluded him. He wondered whether it really did exist, hidden there between green and blue, or whether it was a colorful figment of Ava's lively imagination.

Where is she now? He was too afraid to inquire. He didn't think he would have the will to go on if she had stopped loving him. There were many possibilities too horrendous to contemplate. He wasn't ready for those. Time might have dulled her memory of him, the years stolen the intensity of feeling she once had. He had come back for her, but she had gone. Perhaps that was a sign. If she still loved him she would have waited. She would have kept their garden alive, not let it shrivel and die in the hands of strangers. There was no use searching for her, she obviously didn't want to be found. She would only repeat what she had said to him in that kitchen twenty-six years ago and he never wanted to hear those words again.

He returned to the sitting room and began to move slowly about picking up ornaments, turning them over in his hands. To the uninitiated those objects meant nothing at all; to Jean-Paul they were small tokens of love that Ava had given to him over the year he had lived there. A little enamel box in the shape of a bouquet of flowers, a china frog, a heart box containing a dried rosebud, a set of eight wooden apples, a crystal tree. He had left them there hoping she would change her mind; she never did and so they remained. He was surprised and heartened to find them there, along with all his books neatly arranged in the bookshelves. He hoped she might have kept them to remember him by, but with a sinking heart, he realized that she had left them behind with her memories, to die like the flowers in her gardens.

XIII

The morning light through the leaves of the chestnut trees

When Jean-Paul awoke it took him a moment to orientate himself. He opened his eyes to the familiar sight of the bedroom ceiling and heard the twittering birds in the chestnut trees outside, heralding the dawn. He could see the sky through the gap in the curtains, slowly turning a pale shade of gray. He lay there with nothing but a memory. A memory so strong he could smell the scent of damp grass in her hair, feel the softness of her skin, run his fingers down the smoothness of her face, hold her slim body against his and kiss her lips. Then the memory faded, turning cold beside him. Their cottage remained but her love no longer warmed it.

Why had he come? What did he hope to achieve? Surely it would be better to return to his château? He sat up and rubbed his eyes. How could he return now, without her? His whole life had been gradually moving towards this point. He had dreamed it, planned it, fantasized about it. He hadn't considered what came after. He got up and walked into the bathroom. His reflection stared back at him unhappily, his eyes raw, the shadows dark beneath them. He looked old. *Oh*

God, if nothing comes after, I can't go on. I can't live in nothing.

He dressed, made himself a cup of strong coffee and left the cottage. He was eager to get outside, to look around the garden, to find her there beneath the rotting foliage and make her flower again. It was a crisp morning. His breath rose on the air like smoke. The scent of damp earth was sweet on the breeze and those squirrels, intrepid and mischievous, watched him walk over the bridge then made a dash for his bedroom window, only to find he had outwitted them and closed it.

He stood a moment in the middle of the field that had once been Ava's wildflower garden. The oak tree dominated it like a small fortress. He would build the children their house and they would play in it as Archie, Angus and Poppy had done. He crouched down and ran his hands through the wet weeds that grew in abundance. He'd have to start again. Mow it all down and replant it so that in March it would dazzle with crocuses, cowslips, daffodils and buttercups. Ava had loved to see the summer flowers when she opened her bedroom curtains in the morning. He looked towards the house. It was bewildering to witness it belonging to another family, strangers using the rooms that had once been Ava's and Phillip's. Miranda had redecorated. She had even ripped out the kitchen and replaced it. The house was far more splendid than when it had belonged to Ava and yet it had no soul.

It was a beautiful show house; but it didn't live.

He strode across the gravel to the archway in the hedge. There was now a smart black gate, its hinges oiled to perfection. The walled vegetable garden was, as he expected, neglected and overrun with weeds. The old brick wall was intact, but the borders were heaped high with dead flowers and bushes, the climbing roses falling away from the wall and drooping sadly. The box that lined the vegetable patches was in need of a dramatic haircut. It wouldn't take long to tidy it all up and replant. They'd have vegetables in spring. He was heartened to see the apple trees, the ground beneath them scattered with decaying fruit. He bent down and searched for one that was edible, then took a bite. The taste made him smile with gratitude that some things never change.

He wandered along the stone pathways that led through the vegetable patches. He was uplifted to see the arched frame that straddled the path still in one piece though no sweet peas had flourished there that summer. He'd grow runner beans there with Ava's favorite pink and white sweet peas and the children would help pick them as Poppy had loved to do. He found Hector's old toolbox in one of the greenhouses, Ava's gardening gloves and instruments beneath a table strewn with empty pots and seed packets. It would be a challenge to sort the place out, but he knew he could do it. He'd do it for her.

The herbaceous border was as overgrown and ignored as the rest of the grounds but he found a wheelbarrow full of dead branches at the far end, indicating that someone had already started weeding. He didn't imagine that was Miranda. She had the hands of a woman who had never done a day's digging—as clean and manicured as his had once been. He looked down at his fingernails, short and ragged, his palms rough and lined like the bark of a tree. No one would ever imagine the smooth, insouciant man he had once been. He had shed that skin in this very garden. Finally, he came to the dovecote. How often he had used it in his paintings. In the pink light of dusk, the pale liquid light of morning and in the silvery light of a full moon.

Ava had been surprised to see that he painted. She hadn't imagined him to be artistic. She had written him off as a shallow, spoiled young man who drifted aimlessly through life without a care in the world. But he had been far from aimless; his longings were bullied into hiding by his controlling father. At Hartington he had been able to set them free. To paint without guilt. To create and be admired for it. *You gave me so much, Ava.*

It wasn't long before the children found him. Gus was prepared for disappointment, his face long and sullen, his fringe hiding the spark of hope in his eyes lest it serve only to humiliate him. Storm ran ahead enthusiastically, too young to have been crushed by her parents' lack of interest. Jean-Paul greeted them with a smile, their presence in the garden banishing his sorrow like sunshine breaking through cloud. "I am glad you are up," he said, putting his hands on his hips. "I thought I would have to start without you. Are you ready? We have lots of work to do." He led them off to the greenhouse where they picked up the tools Jean-Paul selected, then proceeded towards the hollow tree.

"It's completely hollow," Storm cried, poking her head out at Gus. Her brother forgot his resentment and climbed in, as enthralled as she was.

"It's a real den," he said, gazing around at the husk of bark that formed a perfect playhouse. "We should find something to put on the ground. Something soft," he said.

"Like hay," she volunteered.

"Yes, like hay. Jean-Paul!" Gus shouted, sticking his head out. "Where can we find hay to line the floor?"

"You won't find hay at this time of year. But wood shavings will do and I know just the place. We need wood for the tree house and a ladder. Come with me!"

They pulled their supplies in a cart across the field to the tree. Jean-Paul left the children in their den while he returned for the ladder, where Ava had always kept it in one of the greenhouses. When he got back, Miranda had emerged from her study and was watching the children while they excitedly told her about their project. She had never seen them so animated. Not even *Lord of the Rings* had put so wide a smile on her son's face. When she saw Jean-Paul, she thrust her hands into her coat pockets and grinned. He smelled her lime scent on the breeze. She would be good-looking if she didn't have the pinched look of a woman starved of affection. "I see you've been busy," she said, hugging her sheepskin around her. His eyes were drawn to her feet. She followed his gaze and grinned. "You can take the girl out of London but not London out of the girl!" She laughed, knowing her open-toed Gina heels looked ridiculous in the countryside.

"If they are going to help me in the garden, I have to bribe them with a house. From here they will be able to see the church spire of Hartington. I've looked around the garden. There is much to do. Who has been weeding in the border?"

"Oh, that's Mr. Underwood. I've just hired him. He's helping out. You know, clearing up the leaves." She didn't quite know what he did. "He'll be here somewhere."

"He can help me then. I need more than one pair of hands. It is a big job. We need to get things cut back and replanted. Is there a nursery nearby?"

"Yes. A big one by the golf club. You can't miss it. It's rather good, so I'm told. Take my car."

Jean-Paul leaned the ladder against the tree and scaled it, a plank of wood and baler twine under his arm. In spite of the cold he worked in shirt-sleeves and jeans. He was slim-hipped and lithe, moving from branch to branch as if trees were his natural habitat.

"Gus, pass me the hammer," he instructed, pulling a nail out of his breast pocket and placing it between his lips. Gus scrambled out of the tree. He climbed the ladder with the hammer and passed it to Jean-Paul. "Right, come up here and hold this plank still." Gus glanced at his mother. She was looking up at him, her face suddenly serious.

Fueled by his mother's attention and Jean-Paul's confidence in him, Gus did everything he was told with eagerness. Jean-Paul didn't treat him like a little boy, but as an equal, as capable of assisting as any man. He ran up and down the ladder with tools and twine, passed him small planks of wood and sticks. He watched the Frenchman build a platform around the branches. Once that was secure, he built the walls, leaving gaps for two windows and a door. He made a proper roof using two boards of plywood he had found in the barn, and a sturdy beam. For the door he used an old cupboard that he knew had been Poppy's; it fitted perfectly. Gus didn't mind that it was pink. Phillip had hated throwing things away, keeping the oddest assort-ment of objects from curtain poles to an old wood burner in a shed attached to the back of the barn. Miranda was surprised Jean-Paul had found it. She didn't even know it existed.

She looked at her watch, aware that she should have been writing, but Jean-Paul was compelling. She'd get to her computer after the children had gone to bed and then she would answer all the e-mails requesting articles and changes to the ones she had already submitted. Right now, she was enjoying watching the Frenchman entertain her children.

"We will leave the ladder here for the moment," Jean-Paul told Gus. "Until we build our own steps. For that we need the right size wood. You can come with me and choose it. There must be a timber yard here somewhere."

"Mr. Fitzherbert will know," said Gus. "He's our neighbor."

"Then we will ask him," said Jean-Paul, climbing down the ladder. Gus remained on a branch, gazing over the treetops to where the spire of St. Hilda's soared into the sky. "Look! It's Mr. Underwood," he exclaimed, waving. "Mr. Underwood. I'm in a tree!"

Mr. Underwood gazed up at the tree house. "It's a palace!" he gasped, taking off his cap in homage.

"This is Jean-Paul, the landscape gardener," said Miranda, hoping Jean-Paul would have the sense not to correct her.

"Pleased to meet you," said Mr. Underwood. "I've been doing a bit of clearing up," he informed him importantly. "There's a lot of work to be done in the garden. I'm glad there'll be the two of us."

Jean-Paul looked at the elderly man and recognized his need to feel useful.

"I'm glad to be of help," he said with a smile. Mr. Underwood puffed out his chest and nodded. "We have two more helpers. Gus and Storm," he added with a wink.

Mr. Underwood nodded again, his lips curling into a grin. "They can look out for fryers up there."

"Fryers?"

"Rabbits," said Mr. Underwood. "I'll get my gun out and kill the buggers. Put them in the pan and fry them. That's all they're good for." Jean-Paul remembered watching rabbits at dusk with Ava and her children. Poppy used to leave bowls of carrots for them, delighting when she found them empty in the morning.

Jean-Paul clicked his tongue. "We'll secure the vegetable gardens so they can't get in. I'd prefer to befriend them than make them my dinner," he said with a chuckle.

"I'd like one as a pet," said Storm.

Jean-Paul patted her head. "You'll soon be sharing your den with them," he said. "Them and the squirrels."

Miranda returned to the silence of her study with reluctance, sat at her desk and switched on her computer. After a while she was absorbed by her e-mails and finally by her article, her fingers tapping swiftly over the keys.

That afternoon Jean-Paul took Gus and Storm to buy seeds. Gus helped fill their basket and chose the vegetable seeds with Storm, taking the packets down from the stand as if they were sweets. The seeds he couldn't purchase there he'd get sent from Les Lucioles.

On the way back they stopped at Jeremy Fitzherbert's farm. Jean-Paul remembered it well. Jeremy's father, Ian, had run the farm back then. Jeremy had been in his twenties. He had helped out during the harvest, rouging and manning the dryer. Jean-Paul doubted he would remember *him*. They had never been introduced.

Jeremy was in the workshop with his manager, discussing the need to replace the old Massey Ferguson tractor. When he saw the children standing in the doorway, he broke off his conversation and approached. Mr. Ben trotted up to Gus and sniffed his boots, his thick tail wagging with excitement. They smelled of Ranger. "Hi there," Jeremy exclaimed.

"My name is Jean-Paul. I'm working for Miranda Claybourne up at the house."

"Ah." Jeremy nodded. "These two helping you, are they?"

"They are. I couldn't do without them," he replied, smiling. Jeremy was warmed by the Frenchman's grin.

"What can I do for you?" he asked.

"I need timber to make a ladder for the children's

tree house. I thought you might know where to buy some."

"Buy some? Good Lord. You don't need to buy it. I have a barn full of timber. We're constantly felling trees. Come, I'll show you." The two men walked through the farm followed by the children and Mr. Ben. It was exactly as Jean-Paul remembered it. The dryer was the same, scattered with wheat from the harvest. The barns were still peeling their green paint, the corrugated iron roof thick with moss and leaves. He remembered bringing the children to play on the mountains of wheat in the summer with Ava. Ian hadn't minded the mess they made, patiently sweeping the ground once they'd left. He'd have done anything for Ava Lightly.

Jeremy's barn was full of timber, logs and hay bales. "As you see, we've got more than we need."

"If you can spare some, we'd be grateful."

"You'd be doing me a favor." He looked at Jean-Paul, an unlikely figure in Hartington. "How are you finding it down there?"

"I only arrived yesterday."

"Oh," Jeremy replied, wondering what Miranda had hired him to do. "They're nice people, the Claybournes."

"Yes." Jean-Paul rubbed his chin. Suddenly he felt compelled to ask about Ava. "Did you know the previous owners?" He tried to control the tremor in his voice.

"Yes. Ava Lightly was a wonderful gardener. Do you know them?"

Jean-Paul shook his head. "I am the gardener now."

"Ah," said Jeremy, grinning sympathetically. "You're taking on quite a legacy."

"I know." He pulled a face as if the mere thought of the project defeated him. "Do you know why they moved?"

"Phillip had a stroke. I think the house became too much for them."

"Do you know where they moved to?"

"No idea, I'm afraid. They went very quiet for a few years and then were gone without any fuss or fanfare. The town would have liked to say good-bye. They were very popular around here." He hesitated a moment then added, "And devoted to each other."

Jean-Paul turned away, pretending to be looking for the children. He did not want Jeremy to see the pain those words had caused him. He gritted his teeth and tried to pull himself together, but a lump of grief had lodged itself in his throat. In an effort to dissemble he bent down to pat the dog. Mr. Ben buried his wet nose in his hand. Jeremy remained oblivious of the blow he had dealt. Jean-Paul rested his forehead against Mr. Ben's for a moment to play for time. "Beautiful animal," he said.

"Mr. Ben's rather special," Jeremy replied with a chuckle. "Wolfgang's a little long in the tooth these days. Spends most of the day asleep."

Jean-Paul called the children and arranged to return later with a suitable vehicle to transport the timber. "It's good to meet you," said Jeremy. "I'd love to come and see what you're up to sometime. Those gardens were quite something once."

"Any time," Jean-Paul replied.

"If you need help, I've strong hands on the farm and would be happy to lend you a few men."

"Are those your cows down by the river?" he asked.

"Yes. Aberdeen Angus."

"Storm's new friends." He looked down at the little girl. "You haven't forgotten them, have you?"

"No," she replied. "They have rough tongues. They're nice."

"I have horses. I've told Miranda, but if you and the children want to ride, let me know. Whisper's very docile."

"That would be fun," Jean-Paul replied.

"Good." Jeremy watched them climb into Miranda's jeep. "I hope to see more of you, then." He waved as they drove out of the farm.

There was something intriguing about Jean-Paul. He didn't look like a gardener. He was too handsome for a start. He shook his head and smiled. His presence in Hartington was sure to set the cat among the pigeons.

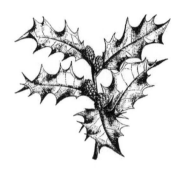

Winter

XIV

A rainbow requires both rain and sunshine

Hartington House, 1979

So began our project together. Darling Phillip was as thrilled as I; Henri would be pleased his son was getting involved and doors would continue to open the length and breadth of France. He returned to his study and buried himself in research. We were left to create our cottage garden. I didn't show Phillip the painting. It was so personal, so intimate, coming from the very core of M.F. that I didn't feel it was right to share it with anyone. He had painted it for me and I was surprised and touched that he had taken the trouble to understand what moved me. That was the first secret I had ever kept from my husband. It would be the first of many secrets, creeping into our marriage like poison ivy.

Ava and Jean-Paul set about digging the borders in the cottage garden according to Jean-Paul's painting. They marked out the path with sticks so that it meandered like a stream, wide enough for two people to walk together comfortably. The borders were to be edged with stones to allow the plants to spill over. Hector helped in his quiet, solemn way and Ian Fitzherbert let them use his small tractor and trailer to carry away unwanted earth. It was a sunny day, the sky a deep primary blue without a cloud to be seen anywhere. They worked in their shirtsleeves, Ava in her purple dungarees, her hair held up with a pen, Jean-Paul in low-slung jeans and shirt although the air was crisp and cold. They toiled all day, laughing and chatting like old friends.

They ate sandwiches for lunch, eager not to delay their work unnecessarily. They sat on a rug while Hector returned to fetch his lunch box from the greenhouse. Ava had never expected to enjoy Jean-Paul's company. She had resented his presence in her garden and been suspicious of his good looks, as if being handsome made him less profound. She had been wrong.

"How can your father disapprove of your painting?" she asked, biting into a turkey sandwich.

Jean-Paul shrugged. "He wants me to be a reflection of himself. I am his only son. His only child. He is a very ambitious, controlling man. I have never liked him."

"That's sad. Not to like your own father."

"I am used to it." He shrugged again.

"He should be proud you paint so beautifully."

"He is not proud. Besides, I don't paint well

enough." He shook his head resignedly. "I do it for myself. I will never be good enough to do it professionally."

"Why not?"

He flashed her an enchanting smile and for an instant gazed at her with eyes full of affection. "Because I am realistic, Ava. I don't live in a world of dreams. I know I am not good enough. Papa knows that, too."

"Just because you won't make money doesn't mean it's not a worthwhile thing to do."

"I know that."

"So, what does your father expect of you?"

"To run the vineyard. To make good wine. To uphold the family name. To inherit the château and produce a son to pass it all on as he has done."

"Couldn't you just tell him to bugger off? You're not a child."

Jean-Paul put down his sandwich and suddenly looked troubled. "I don't want to hurt my mother. I am all she has." He held her a moment with his eyes. "She has no marriage. My father has a mistress in Paris. *Maman* lives in Bordeaux. Les Lucioles means everything to her. It would break her heart if Papa disinherited me."

"I don't understand. You're doing what he wants because of a château?"

"It is not just any château. It is special. Perhaps one day you will see it, then you will understand. It is as magical to me as Hartington House is to you."

"It must be very magical then."

"I agreed to come here because *Maman* asked me to. It is not just about the château, it is about my mother and doing what is right. She loves her home, too, and has put her heart into it. The love she should be investing in my father she invests in me and Les Lucioles."

"You're in the middle of something bigger than you," she acknowledged.

"Yes."

"Some people make their lives so complicated."

"I don't think they mean to."

"Perhaps not. I'm grateful for my simple life. It might not be spicy but it's tranquil. I'd sacrifice a lot for tranquility."

"You and Phillip are lucky. You have a good marriage."

"I know." She smiled tenderly. "He's a good egg."

"A good egg?" Jean-Paul laughed incredulously.

"Oh, you've never heard that expression?" He shook his head. "A good egg, as eggs run, but who likes runny eggs? Do you get it?" They laughed together. Hearing it with the ears of a foreigner made Ava realize what a very silly expression it was.

That afternoon, when the children returned from school, they came to watch their mother in the garden. Phillip strode out, in a green Barbour and wellies, to take the dogs for a walk. Bernie and Tarquin rolled about on the grass in excitement, their barking biting into the damp air. "Don't forget your parents are coming for the weekend, Shrub," he reminded her, as he set off towards the dovecote.

"Phillip thinks I have no memory for things other than plants," she told Jean-Paul with a chuckle. "He thinks I inhabit another world. 'Planet Ava'!"

"I'd like to live on Planet Ava," he said, taking a swig of beer.

"I don't think you would. It's a lonely planet really."

"I like to be alone, too."

"Good. I won't worry about you in the cottage then. I was about to invite all Toddy's cousins over to meet you."

"There's alone and lonely," he said with a grin. "I like to be alone, but I don't like to be lonely, so if they are pretty, I would be happy to meet them." He stood up and laughed, holding out his hand to Ava. He pulled her up.

"All right, Mr. Frenchman!" she said. "I'll call Toddy. But if they're pigs don't blame me. I know the French have very high standards when it comes to women."

"Perhaps. But the English have something that the French don't have."

"What's that?"

"A sense of humor."

She laughed. "I'm so glad it's not all about manicures and silk underwear."

"But imagine the power of that combination—silk underwear *and* a sense of humor? A woman like that would be something, no?"

"I can't say I've given the matter much thought. Now, back to the garden, you! Save your sexy thoughts for when you're lonely in the cottage."

Archie, Angus and Poppy helped load the cart with the turf that Ava and Jean-Paul cut with their spades, rolling it up like long carpets. When they grew bored of that game they searched for insects in the newly exposed soil, squeaking in delight when they found a fat worm or centipede. Ava had taught them to love all creatures, explaining their purpose in the garden and how they lived, so that the children respected them as living beings and not as playthings to abuse. "Look, Mummy! Here's a really juicy worm," cried Archie, placing it carefully on a leaf and carrying it to his mother.

"He's delicious," she agreed, stopping to look. "Now darling, find a nice place for him. With any luck a bird will find him later. He'll make a feast for a hungry pigeon." Once he had shown his siblings, Archie did as he was told and settled the worm in the mud. Angus climbed onto the tractor and made purring noises, turning the steering wheel left and right while Poppy pretended the rolls of turf were Swiss rolls on their way to the bakery. The garden rang with their laughter. It was just another day at Hartington House. For Jean-Paul it was a new and exciting world. He had no experience of a united and loving family.

That evening Ava invited Jean-Paul to stay for dinner. They sat in the drawing room, by the fire, having bathed and changed out of their muddy clothes. The children were in bed, exhausted after so much fresh air. Phillip came downstairs in a smoking jacket and slippers, having read them *The Velveteen Rabbit*, and opened a bottle of wine. "Your garden's beginning to take shape," he said, bringing in a tray of glasses. Ava sat on the sofa, her hair tied in a loose ponytail so that wisps floated about her face and neck. She wore wide trousers under a long Moroccan housecoat and a pair of crimson sequined slippers. Her cheeks glowed from having worked in the cold all day and her eyes sparkled with happiness. It had been a perfect day.

"We'll plant it up next," she said, grinning at Jean-Paul. "Our reward will come in spring. It's going to look marvelous!" Jean-Paul lay sprawled in an armchair, his hair damp from the bath and sticking up in points.

"I never thought digging a garden would be fun," he admitted.

"This is only the beginning. Digging is the boring bit," said Ava. "The planting is the fun part. Watching the gardens grow is the icing on the cake."

"What are you going to plant?" Phillip asked, handing them both glasses of wine, then taking a seat himself.

"I've drawn a sketch," she said, pulling a roughly folded piece of paper from her coat pocket. "I want an explosion of color. I want it stuffed full of shrubs and plants." She looked at Jean-Paul, knowing that he knew she was thinking of his painting. "I thought buddleia, geraniums, roses, polyanthus, campanula, lavender, delphiniums, lupins, daisies. Goodness, I haven't held back."

"It sounds marvelously chaotic. Rather like you, Shrub." Phillip chuckled in his good-natured way.

"We've bitten off quite a lot more than we can chew, but I think we can do it. Jean-Paul and Hector are prepared to work like slaves."

"I'm a good egg!" Jean-Paul said and laughed.

"A good egg, as eggs run," Ava added with a grin. "We'll send you back to France an Englishman."

"I raise my glass to that," added Phillip.

"Mummy." Poppy was standing in the doorway in her white nightie, holding her marrow in a blanket. "He can't sleep," she said, hugging it close.

"Oh dear," said Phillip, playing along. "Have you tried rocking him a little?"

"Yes," she said earnestly. "But he keeps waking up. He keeps waking *me* up."

"Come here," said Ava gently, opening her arms. "I think you need a cuddle, darling. It's not fun being kept awake by that naughty Monty, is it?" Poppy shook her head. She never doubted she'd be received with love, whatever the time of night.

"I'm very tired," she said, shuffling over to her mother. Ava pulled the little girl onto her lap and wrapped her arms around her, kissing her temple. "Daddy, if I love Monty like the little boy loved the velveteen rabbit, will he become real?"

"Ah," said Phillip with a frown. "I'm not sure the nursery magic extends to vegetables. That's a question for the vegetable fairy."

"I so want him to be real," she sighed.

"If you want him to be real, darling, he will be. He'll be whatever you want him to be. You just have to use your imagination," said Ava.

"But I want everyone else to see that he's real."

"We do," Jean-Paul interjected, leaning forward and resting his elbows on his knees. "To me, he's been real since I was introduced to him." Poppy hid her smile behind the blanket, disguising her delight by pretending to be sleepy.

"You see," said Ava, kissing her again.

"I think you should take him back to bed," said Phillip. "He'll only be grumpy in the morning if he doesn't get his sleep." Ava lifted Poppy off her lap and led her out of the drawing room. The child caught Jean-Paul's eye and smiled shyly.

The rest of the week was taken up with planting all the flowers and shrubs. They followed Ava's plan, placing each pot in its place on top of the soil, before planting it. Jean-Paul listened as she explained her reasons for positioning them as she did, patiently teaching him the names and preferred conditions of each. At the end of the day the children watered them with small watering cans of their own. By the end of the week they had finished planting. As if by magic gray clouds gathered above them and it began to rain. The children ran about with their mouths open, catching the drops on protruding tongues, while Ava and Jean-Paul laughed in astonishment at their good fortune. Hector drove the tractor back to Ian Fitzherbert's farm, shaking his head at the family's eccentricity.

Ava asked Toddy to bring her cousins for lunch on Sunday to meet Jean-Paul. Toddy was delighted, guaranteeing two, if not three, twentyish girls for him to choose from. "They're jolly pretty," she assured her. "Especially Lizzie. God, if I were only ten years younger I'd throw myself at Jean-Paul." Ava's parents, Donald and Verity, arrived on Friday night with Heinz, a small red sausage dog whose sharp yap and short scurrying legs terrified Bernie almost as much as Mr. Frisby.

Verity was similar to her daughter—a handsome woman with kind green eyes and strong bone structure who never felt the cold, but her strident

210

nature had been mercifully diluted in Ava. With gray hair swept up into a beehive, her head looked out of proportion with her short body, but not even her daughter had the courage to tell her the look was outdated and unbecoming. Her husband had ceased to notice long ago; it was her personality that demanded attention and no one could ignore that. She spoke her mind, as old people do, and knew best, as grandmothers do. But she loved her grandchildren, always bringing presents and telling them stories which she'd invent as she went along, holding them in her thrall with colorful descriptions and eccentric characters which included their own toys magically brought to life.

"Did you know that Daisy Hopeton has left her husband and four children to run off with a South African who owns a vineyard in Constantia?" said Verity over dinner. Ava's appalled reaction was very satisfactory. "I know," continued Verity, shaking her beehive. "It's ghastly. Poor Michael doesn't know whether he's coming or going. Having to bring up those four children on his own. Why, Oliver's only Archie's age."

"That's terrible," gasped Ava, who had been a childhood friend of Daisy's. "How can a woman leave four children?"

"Quite," Phillip agreed. "It's disgraceful."

"Disgraceful," Donald repeated. He'd listened to nothing else all the way from Hampshire and was now bored of the subject. Verity was fired up with the story and had been on the telephone spreading it around to all her friends.

"From the horse's mother's mouth," Verity confirmed when Phillip asked how she'd heard. "As you can imagine, she's beside herself. One doesn't expect one's own child to let one down in such a public way. For a South African! She's run off to the other side of the world. Why she didn't take her children with her, I can't imagine. What sort of woman leaves her children? It's unthinkable!"

"She must have been dreadfully unhappy," said Ava, trying to find something nice to say.

"Nonsense, darling! You bite the bullet and get on with it. One can't expect to be happy all the time. That's the trouble with your generation, you didn't live through the war. You expect to be happy, as if it's a right. It's not a right. It's a bonus. The cherry on the cake. Daisy's a mother and she owes it to those children to bring them up. They're going to have to live with the knowledge that they were abandoned. Imagine what a terrible scar. Those poor darlings. My heart bleeds for them. *Bleeds* for them," she repeated with emphasis. "Darling, this soup is frightfully good. What is it?"

"Parsnip and ginger. I'm so glad you like it," said Ava, still reeling from the scandal.

"Perhaps if you'd remained friends with Daisy, she wouldn't have got into this mess," continued Verity. "You'd have been a good example to her. Such a pity!" Donald looked at Phillip and rolled his eyes.

The following day Ava showed her mother around the garden. Jean-Paul appeared for work even though it was Saturday. "I want to water those plants," he explained. "And the children want to build a bonfire."

"I'm Ava's mother," said Verity. It didn't occur to her to shake his hand; after all, he was just the gardener. So when Jean-Paul took hers and raised it to his lips, murmuring "*Enchanté*," Verity didn't know whether to be shocked or flattered.

"They're keeping you busy," she said, trying not to look flustered.

"I am not an idle man. I like to be busy."

"Well, there's no shortage of things to do in this garden, is there?"

"Where are the children?" Ava asked.

"They are in the hollow tree. They are playing pirates." He ran a hand through his hair, leaving it sticking up in thick, glossy tufts.

"Have they got my Heinz?"

"Yes, they have, *madame*. I believe he's a shark."

"Then what are Bernie and Tarquin?" Ava asked with a smile.

"Sea monsters."

"Where are you from?" Verity asked.

"Bordeaux," he replied.

"They produce gardeners there, do they?"

"Indeed," Jean-Paul replied.

She frowned at him, unsure where to place him on

the human food chain. "What do your parents do?"

The corners of Jean-Paul's mouth twitched with amusement. "They work in the iron and steel industry," he replied. Ava looked on in bewilderment.

"Really?" Verity exclaimed, unimpressed.

"Yes, my mother irons and my father steals." With that he sauntered off.

"Good gracious, he's rude," commented Verity, watching him go in amazement. "Did you hear what he said? His father steals! Don't tell me he's your gardener?"

"Mummy, he's teasing! Remember I told you about Phillip's French friend Henri de la Grandière? Jean-Paul is his son. He's come to work for a year to gain experience."

"I remember you said something about it. Still, he's jolly rude. If he wasn't so easy on the eye, I'd be offended."

"I've asked Toddy for lunch tomorrow with some of her cousins. I thought I should introduce him to girls his own age."

"That's very good of you, darling. I'm sure that's beyond the call of duty. Mind you, one never really knows how to treat someone in his position. He's neither staff nor guest."

"Friend," interjected Ava.

"If you say so, though I like things to be clearly defined. Trouble brews when the lines are blurred. When people don't know where they stand."

"Mother, you're very out of date."

"Well, yes. I suppose I am. But I am right, you know."

On Sunday Toddy arrived for lunch with Mr. Frisby, the twins, and the two pretty young cousins, Lizzie and Samantha. The boys ran off to the bonfire which they could see smoking over the wall of the vegetable garden. The girls hovered with Toddy, breathless with excitement. Ava welcomed them warmly, showing them into the drawing room where Verity was holding court on the sofa with Phillip and Donald. They were certainly pretty. Blondes, with blue eyes accentuated by the heavy-handed use of blue eyeliner. Both were bosomy girls, though Lizzie was the slimmer of the two, in a pair of tight jeans with a pink sweater inscribed with the words "Light My Fire." Her lips shimmered with pink gloss and her wrists jangled with dozens of bracelets. Samantha was rounder with rosy cheeks, permed hair and red nail varnish. She wore a blue shirt over a long fishtail skirt. They stood in a cloud of Anaïs Anaïs scent which made Ava want to sneeze. She watched them shake hands with her mother. They were polite, though a little too gushing, their faces sweet but fleshy with pale shiny skin and vacuous expressions like lovely cows. By the look on Donald's face as he stood to introduce himself, he thought them ravishingly beautiful.

"Where is he?" Toddy hissed, taking Mr. Frisby off her shoulder to cradle him and scratch his tummy.

"He's out with the children," Ava replied.

"Let's take the girls outside," Toddy suggested. "Much less awkward than meeting in here."

"Good idea," said Ava. "Come on Lizzie, Samantha. Let's go and see the bonfire."

"Do you have to go?" Donald was beginning to enjoy himself. He was about to follow when his wife grabbed him by the belt.

"No, darling. You're an old man. They're here to meet Jean-Paul. Sit down and act your age."

"I thought it would be jolly to watch the grand-children."

"No, you didn't." She smiled as he sat beside her and crossed his arms. "You read her sweater and took her at her word. I think it's for the Frenchman's benefit and, by the look of him, he'll have no trouble lighting her fire."

XV

The cold crisp mornings of winter.
The scent of burning leaves.
The sight of our breath rising
on the air.

Ava watched the two girls flirt and giggle with Jean-Paul. He stood, leaning on a pitchfork, his shirt roughly tucked into jeans that emphasized his slim hips and long legs. He had rolled up his sleeves, baring brown forearms and hands already rough from laboring in the garden. He gazed at them arrogantly, his mouth curling in amusement, clearly enjoying their attention. Ava stood with Toddy, pretending to be watching the children, but she could see him in her peripheral vision. Lizzie and Samantha leaned towards him, their body language leaving no doubt that they found him attractive. Ava was fascinated by this flirtatious dance and was reminded of her first meeting with Phillip. It felt like a long time ago. In the company of these two young creatures she felt old and dowdy—a partridge beside birds of paradise.

"Are you thinking what I'm thinking?" said Toddy, letting Mr. Frisby jump off her shoulder to run about the vegetable patches.

"I doubt it, Toddy," Ava replied drily.

"Lizzie and Samantha make me feel uncomfortably grown up."

"Yes, I know what you mean," she agreed with a sigh.

"I never thought I'd be this old. They've got their whole lives ahead of them. Courtship, marriage, children. They can still pick their man. They still have choices. It makes me sad to think I'll never flirt like that again, or make love for the first time."

"We have new things to look forward to," said Ava, not quite certain what those things were.

"Like extramarital affairs and divorce."

"Don't be so cynical, Toddy."

"I'm not married to Mr. Wonderful. Sometimes I'd rather like to have another round. People shouldn't stay married for so long. In the old days we died at thirty. Now we live so long, it's like two lifetimes. I think one should be able to call it quits halfway through and enjoy another marriage when it starts to grow humdrum. Do you know what I mean?"

"Sort of." Ava laughed affectionately.

"I won't leave him, you know that. Just enjoy thinking about it sometimes. You know, if I was honest, I wouldn't mind an affair. If I could guarantee it would remain a secret. That no one would ever know or get hurt."

"Anyone in mind?"

"No. That's the other hurdle, of course. There's no one in Hartington. But I do miss the buzz of those first, intoxicating encounters. My marriage is a bit too comfortable, like a trusty old slipper I can't be bothered to wear anymore. The desire's gone. Do you and Phillip roll about a lot?"

"Toddy, you can't ask me that!" Ava was embarrassed.

"Come on. Is it the same for all of us? Are we all in the same boat?"

Ava crossed her arms. "I'm sorry, Toddy. Phillip and I have a very healthy marriage."

"Oh." Toddy sounded disappointed. "No affair for you, then?"

"No."

"Well, there's always a silver lining. At least we won't be fighting over the same man!"

"That is true," Ava agreed. "I'm pleased to say that I'm happy with the one I've got."

Ava went inside to check on Mrs. Marley, the cook. A scrawny little woman with gray hair tied into a neat bun and a kindly smile that she bestowed on everyone indiscriminately, she was at the sink straining the summer peas and broad beans that Ava had picked and frozen. "Can I send Phillip in to carry?" Ava asked. Mrs. Marley smiled at her through the cloud of steam.

"That would be good, Mrs. L., if you wouldn't mind. These beans are a treat. I had one or two to taste."

"Would you like to take a bag home for your dinner?"

"Oh, Mrs. L., would you mind?" She went pink with delight.

"Not at all. I've got so many."

"Stanley will be so pleased. He loves his food."

"The way to a man's heart is through his stomach, Mrs. Marley."

"That's the way to keep them, too," she added with a grin. "Sadly, that's not the way with children, is it? Feed them up and watch them go. My Nigel's nearly fifteen now. He'll go without his tea to have fish 'n' chips with his girl. Never thought he'd prefer a girl to meat 'n' two veg at home."

"He's a long way off leaving, Mrs. Marley. Your Susie's only little."

"My Susie." She smiled tenderly at the thought of her. "She's a little 'un. At least I've got little Susie."

"Time flies, though, doesn't it?" Ava hesitated a moment. "I want to freeze them so they never grow up. I'd like to freeze myself. I don't want to grow up either."

Mrs. Marley laughed and handed her a pair of oven gloves. "Trouble is, Mrs. L., you never feel grown-up inside. It's a shock to look at myself in the mirror every morning, it really is. I used to have jet-black hair. It was my crowning glory. Now I'm as gray as a pigeon!"

As Ava was leaving the kitchen, a dish of crisp roast potatoes in her hands, she was met by Jean-Paul. "Can I help?" he asked.

"Thank you," she replied. "But it's in hand. You go and entertain those girls." She grinned at him mischievously.

"You don't think I'm interested, do you?"

"Why ever not? They're pretty enough."

"They are too young and inexperienced for my taste. I like a woman who has lived. Those girls are nice, but they are as unripe as a pair of green apples on a tree."

"Really, Jean-Paul," she protested, feeling her cheeks turn hot.

"I prefer the apple to have fallen off the tree."

"Those bruised and browning fruit ravaged by bees?" She walked past him down the corridor towards the dining room. But the way he had looked at her remained in the crimson hue of her cheeks.

"Yes. Those are the best. They taste sweeter. The green ones are a little sour."

Ava walked into the dining room with a bounce in her step and a wide smile on her face. She had felt old and dowdy next to Lizzie and Samantha, but now she felt attractive, something she hadn't considered in a long time. Her looks had never been high on her list of priorities. Of course, Jean-Paul was teasing. She was married and there was no chemistry between them anyway. But a little flattery never did any harm.

Jean-Paul was placed between Lizzie and Samantha. Toddy kept an eye from the other end of the table where she sat between Phillip and Donald. The three young people were laughing and joking together. Toddy was pleased. She was fond of her cousins and particularly fond of Ava. She relished the idea of returning a few favors by taking Jean-Paul off her hands. If Lizzie and Samantha introduced him to their crowd, Ava would be grateful. After all, what was she going to do with him when they weren't gardening? The poor man had to have young people his own age to socialize with. She knew how Ava hated to feel caged in by anyone but Phillip.

Ava looked at her children. Having larked about during the main course, they were silent as they tucked into Mrs. Marley's blackberry and apple crumble with custard. Poppy was struggling to serve herself another dollop of custard. Ava sensed she was being watched and turned to find Jean-Paul gazing at her wistfully. She frowned. He snapped out of his trance and nodded towards Poppy. Ava pulled a face to indicate that there was nothing to do but leave her to it. She felt a moment's confusion. His gaze had been full of tenderness.

Jean-Paul went to Poppy's aid before the jug tipped its contents over the table. Ava turned to talk to her father, making a conscious effort not to look at Jean-Paul. His flirting was charming, but she wasn't going to swoon like those gushing girls, both silent now that he had left them. Besides, flirtation wasn't appropriate at the lunch table in front of her husband, nor was it appropriate given that Jean-Paul was her employee.

After lunch Verity announced that it was time to leave. "The A303 will be a nightmare on a Sunday afternoon if we don't hit it early." Donald was just settling into the sofa beside Samantha, where he had longed to be since she had arrived, when Verity sent him to find Heinz. "The last I heard he was playing pirates at the hollow tree," she told him.

"No, darling, I gave him his lunch in the back of the car, then let him have a wander. Why don't you go and call him? He answers to you."

"If he's at the other end of the garden he won't hear me." She shook her head at his futile attempts to chat up a girl young enough to be his daughter. "Really, old men are so sad!" she hissed to Ava as she strode into the hall. "Have you seen Heinz?"

"I'll help you look," Ava volunteered. Jean-Paul remained in the drawing room talking to Lizzie on the club fender. Samantha tried to concentrate on Donald's questions, but her eyes kept drifting over to her sister.

"Poor Daddy," said Ava. "Samantha's longing to talk to Jean-Paul, but she's stuck."

"Serves her right, silly girl," Verity sniffed. "Shouldn't have that silly slogan on her shirt."

"That's Lizzie, Mummy."

"They both look the same to me. Too much eye

makeup and not enough up top and I don't mean hair." She touched her beehive affectionately. "Fortunately, that dreadful lip gloss has been licked off during lunch. Young girls wear too much blue eyeliner these days. It's dreadful. That crumble was delicious, by the way. Was that one of yours?"

"No, Mrs. Marley made it."

"She's a gem, isn't she? Always cheerful. I do love cheerful people. Delicious roast potatoes. Very crisp. What's her secret?"

"Oil infused with herbs from the garden."

"Ah, that explains it. You wouldn't make up a little doggie bag for me, would you? I'd love to take some home, for your father's lunch tomorrow. You know how he loves potatoes, especially yours."

"Why don't I make you a basket, put some carrots and broad beans in, too?"

"Darling, you're wonderful. To think you're mine. I wouldn't believe it if you didn't look so like me." She cast her daughter a sidelong glance. "Before you grimace, let me just say that I have jolly good bones and have aged well. You know where you're going, looking at me, and it isn't a bad place. Can't think why your father has to drool over those young things. It's quite unbecoming and very foolish. They only laugh at him."

"It makes him feel young," Ava replied kindly. "Actually, they don't mind. I think they're flattered—an intelligent, gentle man like Daddy taking time to ask them about themselves. They should be grateful. It's not like they've got an awful lot to say, have they?"

Ava and Verity walked around the garden calling for Heinz but the little dog remained elusive. Donald heard them shouting for him and relaxed. It would be a while before they found the damn animal. It hadn't been his idea to buy a sausage dog small enough to get lost down any rabbit or badger hole. He would have bought a big dog like Bernie. At least one didn't have to watch where one put one's feet all the time!

After ten minutes Ava appeared in the doorway, red-faced and out of breath. "We need help," she exclaimed. The room fell silent. "We've lost Heinz. He's nowhere to be found."

"Good God!" Donald huffed, pushing himself up. "Sorry, Samantha. You're now going to have to race over the grass in those pretty shoes of yours."

"I don't mind," she replied. "I'd like to see what Jean-Paul has done in the garden!" Samantha giggled. "I know nothing about flowers. Maybe he can show us around."

"With any luck he'll be stuck down a hole and that'll be that!" Donald continued under his breath. "Never liked the damned thing." He turned to Jean-Paul. "Come on. You must know every corner of the place by now."

Jean-Paul shrugged. "I'm getting there. It's a big estate. Let's get the children to help. If we make it into a game they'll enjoy it."

"And with any luck they're small enough to check out all the rabbit holes," added Phillip, conjuring up such a funny image in his mind that he chuckled.

"Good idea," said Ava, hurrying through the hall to shout across the field to the hollow tree. At their mother's summons the children tumbled out like bees from a hive, flying across the grass, yelling for Heinz.

Verity was getting frantic. Heinz was her baby. "If he's dead, I'll never forgive myself," she wailed, wringing her hands. By now her beehive was coming apart, sticking out around her head like a furry dandelion clock. Her face suddenly looked gaunt, framed by such a large spray of hair.

"If he's lost I'll open a bottle of Dom Perignon," muttered Donald to Phillip. It was beginning to get dark.

Toddy turned her thoughts to Mr. Frisby. She hadn't seen him since before lunch. Not that she worried. He always came back. Mr. Frisby knew which side his bread was buttered. She went around to the front of the house to check in the boot of the Land Rover. There, snuggled up among old blankets and Toddy's riding boots, were Heinz and Mr. Frisby, both exhausted from their morning's activity in the hollow tree. "Oh Lord," she sighed, guilty that her pet had abducted Verity's. "How am I going to break this to Verity?" She needn't have worried, Verity was so relieved her darling Heinz was alive and well that she thanked Toddy profusely, pressing a bewildered Heinz to her bosom.

Donald was disappointed they had to leave so soon, though Samantha had turned her attention on Jean-Paul and there was no distracting her from the Frenchman's charm. She said good-bye to Donald, then hurried off to Jean-Paul's cottage with Lizzie, telling Toddy that Jean-Paul would drive them home later in Ava's car.

After tea Toddy gathered her children and said her own good-byes. The twins were sparkly-eyed and covered in mud from having played outside all afternoon. Once in the back of the Land Rover they grew quiet, not bothering to stifle their yawns.

Ava bathed hers and put them to bed, reading them a shorter story than usual because it was late and they were all tired. Poppy insisted on a long hug, wrapping her arms around her mother's neck and nuzzling her sleepily. Ava closed her eyes and savored the warm body pressed against hers, aware that every day her daughter grew a little bigger and a little closer to rejecting her embraces.

That night she lay in bed with Phillip, enjoying their usual postmortem of the day. "Toddy asked me if we still 'rolled about a bit,'" said Ava. Her husband looked suitably horrified.

"What did you say?"

"That it's something I never discuss."

"I'm happy to hear it."

"But I did say that we have a very healthy marriage."

"Well done." He grinned boyishly. "We do, don't we, Shrub?"

"Yes, darling, very healthy."

He leaned forward and kissed her neck. "You smell of damp grass."

"I can't. I've had a bath."

"You always do. It's in your blood. You know it's not like normal blood, it's green."

"You're silly." She considered telling him what Jean-Paul had said. But it sounded so arrogant, assuming a young man was flirting with her. She was so much older and she wasn't pretty. She had hands like sandpaper and unruly hair; she didn't wear makeup and fashionable clothes. She was probably as far from Jean-Paul's tastes as it was possible to get. "I think those girls hit it off with Jean-Paul," she said instead.

"I think Donald hit it off with Samantha," he replied, chortling at the recollection.

"Mummy was furious. I don't see any harm in enjoying the company of a girl. It makes him feel young. It's not like he's flirting in an embarrassing way." There was a pause as her mind turned back to Jean-Paul. "They're in the cottage," she continued. "I hope they're having fun."

"I wouldn't look too closely if I were you. Those girls have definitely been over the guns a few times."

"Do you think?"

"Oh yes," he replied knowingly. "They'll give Jean-Paul a run for his money!" He turned to embrace his wife. "So, we roll about a bit, do we?" He breathed into her neck and the bristles on his face tickled her skin. She wrapped her arms around him and returned his kiss. He was warm and soft and comfortingly familiar. How could Toddy refer to her husband as an old slipper? If she tired of making love to Phillip she'd be tired of life.

"Mummy," came a small voice from the doorway. Both parents sprang apart as if scalded. "I can't sleep." It was Angus, in his blue airplane pajamas, hugging his toy rabbit. Phillip sighed resignedly, kissed his wife and left the bed to sleep in his dressing room. There wasn't room for the three of them to sleep together comfortably. Ava watched him go with regret, then patted the bed.

"Come on, darling. Mummy will look after you." Angus crawled beneath the blankets, closed his eyes and fell asleep immediately. Ava lay on her side holding her child's hand, stroking the soft skin with her thumb. Her heart flooded with tenderness before she closed her eyes and fell asleep.

XVI

*The intrepid robin on my windowsill.
Morning trips to break the water on
the birdbath.*

November brought shorter days and cold winds. At night the gales moaned around the house like mischievous ghosts bent on frightening the children into their parents' bed. It hardly rained. The air was dry, the sky cerulean, the light bright and crisp upon the red leaves of the sweet gum trees. Jean-Paul and Ava busied themselves planting the wild garden. As the days moved towards Christmas they grew together like trees, barely aware of their intensifying friendship. They began to anticipate each other's actions, to understand without having to explain, and they laughed all the time. Having thought that they had nothing in common, they realized that they had a great deal. Above all, they were both enchanted by the magic of the garden and the secret world of the flora and fauna that inhabited it.

When the children returned from school Ava didn't like to work unless she was doing something that included them. Time with her children was precious. Ava knew they liked to have Jean-Paul around. He took time with them and played games that were always creative and original. They'd watch birds, drawing them in notebooks their mother gave them, writing their habits in their large, childish scrawl. Poppy collected feathers and stuck them onto the pages along with leaves of interest. She would have stuck creatures in there too had her mother not explained that they were living animals to be treated with respect. "Just because they are small, doesn't mean they don't feel as we do. If you were to look down on us from a great height we would be as small as them, but we feel pain, don't we?" So Poppy carried around a shoe box in which she collected worms and slugs to look at closely before setting them back in the earth.

Jean-Paul helped the children sketch. He taught them how to observe and put down on paper what they saw. Angus, although only six, had a natural talent, taking his sketches back to the house to color in at the kitchen table. Ava framed the best and hung them in her bedroom.

One afternoon in early December they went on an expedition to the woods. The cows had been let out into the field beyond the thyme walk. The children liked to tame them, putting out their hands so the animals could lick their skin with their rough tongues. Ian Fitzherbert had taken the time to explain why they had tongues like that and how they had five stomachs in order to make milk. The children considered all animals their friends, even the hairy spiders that Ava secretly loathed. Every time Archie collected one for his jar, she was tempted to scream, but she knew she'd only teach her children to fear them. So she smiled proudly and told him how clever he was and how deliciously juicy they were with their fat little bodies and swift legs as they scurried about the glass. She showed them webs, especially after a rainfall when they sparkled with gems, or in winter when the frost made them glitter. She reminded herself that spiders were ugly by no fault of their own. How could she love gardens if she didn't love all who lived in them?

That evening they carried baskets to fill with "treasure" from the woodland floor. Poppy searched for feathers, many from the pheasants and partridges Ian Fitzherbert reared, but also those of pigeons and smaller birds. The boys preferred more substantial things, like conkers, but they had gathered those in October, polishing them and tying them to string for their games. Now there wasn't much to collect except mushrooms. Ava wasn't sure which were edible and which were poisonous so she forbade the boys to touch them, encouraging them to find other things like unusual leaves, or spent cartridges from shoots.

As they busied themselves among the trees and bushes, Jean-Paul and Ava walked together up the path that cut through the middle of the wood. They didn't feel the need to talk. They watched the children, praised their efforts when they ran up to show what they had found, but otherwise they walked in the comfortable silence of old friends. The light was mellow as the sun hung low in the western sky, hitting the tops of the trees and turning them golden. It was chilly down there in the shadow, but Ava wore only a T-shirt and her face glowed with warmth. They watched the changing colors of sunset, moved by the melancholy of the dying day. Finally they reached the edge of the wood. Jean-Paul stopped walking.

"There is great beauty in the tragedy of sunset," he said.

"It's because it's transient," she replied, gazing across the field. "You can enjoy it for a moment only and then it is gone, like a rainbow."

"I suppose it is human nature to want what we cannot have."

Ava pretended not to notice the significance of his words.

"I love this time of year," she said brightly, walking on. "The weather is crisp yet there are still leaves on the trees, turning into wondrous colors. Midwinter makes me sad. Nothing grows, everything is dead."

"I admire you," he said suddenly.

Ava laughed. "Whatever for? I don't think there's much in me to admire."

"You have a loving family. Your children are happy. Your home has a magical warmth to it. And you, Ava, you have an inner beauty that grows the more I get to know you."

"Really, Jean-Paul, that's very sweet. I've never thought I have an inner beauty."

"You do. You have a quality I have never seen before. You are contradictory. You seem very confident and yet I sense that inside you are not as you appear. You are a great storyteller, a good entertainer, and yet you prefer to be alone. You pretend you like spiders but I can see that they frighten you. You are a good woman. For that I admire you the most."

"Thank you," she said briskly. "I'll tell Phillip. He'll be pleased someone admires me."

"I don't think he would be pleased to know another man is falling in love with his wife."

Ava was silenced.

"You don't have to answer. I know that you are married and that you love your husband."

"Then why tell me?" she asked crossly. This declaration would spoil what had been an enjoyable friendship.

"Because one day you might surprise me and tell me that you feel the same way."

She thrust her hands into her pockets. "I'm far too old for you," she said, trying to make light of it, not daring to look at his face. "You're my employee. You're not allowed to fall in love with your boss."

"I cannot help myself."

"You're French, you fall in love with everyone."

"You are wrong. I have never lost my heart to anyone."

"Please, Jean-Paul, save your flirting for Lizzie and Samantha. They are more your age and they are free to love you back."

"Don't you see? I feel nothing for those girls. They are nice enough. But you are wise and creative and original. There is no beauty for me in faces that show nothing but their youth. I enjoy every line on your face, Ava, every expression, because it is always changing. Their faces are blank by comparison. They haven't lived. You are an old soul. You have lived many lives, and so have I. I feel I have been looking for you all my life, Ava. That the hole in my heart is your shape exactly. It keeps me awake at night."

They walked on, the silence now awkward between them.

"I'm sorry if I have made you sad," he said at last. "That was never my intention."

She looked at him. His face was drawn into a frown and his eyes seemed to have sunk into shadow. She felt a wave of compassion.

"I'm sorry, too," she replied, realizing that this wasn't a silly joke. As a friend, he deserved to have his feelings treated with respect. "I'm sorry that I can't love you back," she added softly.

"Do you want me to leave?"

"Not if you want to stay."

"I want to stay. I wish I hadn't said it now. I wish I hadn't destroyed our friendship."

"Oh, Jean-Paul, how could you?" Impulsively, she hugged him. He wrapped his arms around her and hugged her back. She caught her breath. It felt so natural to be there. She pulled away, unbalanced. "We still have so much to do in the garden. I need you."

They continued to walk along the side of the wood. The sun sank lower until it was a mere orange glow on the horizon. The children ran out of the woods, their baskets full. Archie held a spider in cupped hands and Poppy had tucked feathers into her hairband. Angus had collected snails and a giant mushroom, in spite of his mother's instructions. "We'll show it to Mrs. Marley," Ava said, taking his basket from him. "She'll know if we can eat it. In the meantime, don't lick your fingers. I don't want you to get a tummy ache." For the rest of the way home the children remained close. Ava chatted about the garden, trying to put Jean-Paul's words out of her mind. But they hung between them like neon signs, impossible to ignore.

Back at the house, Jean-Paul lingered a moment on the gravel. "Do you want to come in for a cup of tea?" she asked, taking off her boots.

"No. Thank you. I'll get back to the cottage. I feel like painting."

Ava understood. When she felt melancholy she

liked to sit alone in the garden. "I'll see you tomorrow then."

"Good night," he said, resting his eyes on her for a moment longer than was natural. She watched him walk towards the field, his footsteps scrunching heavily on the stones. She closed the door. Once in the light, outside looked pitch-black.

That night she sat in the sitting room with Phillip, trying to read. The fire glowed in the grate and Crystal Gayle sang out from the gramophone. After a while she realized she had read the same page twice. Her eyes scanned the words but her mind was playing over and over her conversation with Jean-Paul. It was a shock to discover that he felt something more than friendship. She would have written off his confession as a natural rite of passage for a Frenchman had she not seen the depth of feeling in his eyes. He had not been playing a game. He really had fallen in love with her. She turned the page, dismissing it as a fever from which he would soon recover. She glanced at Phillip, sitting in the armchair, his reading glasses on his nose. He sensed her gaze and raised his eyes. "What are you looking at, Shrub?"

"You," she replied with a smile.

"Do you see anything you like?"

"I see someone I love," she said truthfully.

"I'm so pleased. Anything less and I'd be very disappointed."

"Silly!" He returned to his book.

She shook Jean-Paul from her mind and returned to hers. However, Jean-Paul's confession had made a small chink in her heart, by way of her vanity. A chink that, though tiny, weakened the whole.

I admit that I was flattered by his confession and more than a little excited. A man as handsome as M.F. finding me attractive, it was something that had never crossed my mind. I had never entertained even the smallest idea of love. He was like a beautiful animal to be admired from afar, to befriend, but not to covet for oneself. As alarming as I found our conversation in the woods, I kept it to myself. I didn't share it with Phillip. Perhaps, somewhere in the darkest corners of my heart I was falling for him, too, I just didn't know it. I should have sent him back to France and avoided the pain that was to follow. But how could I have known? I didn't anticipate the danger I was sailing into, like a merry vessel in calm water coasting towards an unseen waterfall that would threaten to destroy everything I loved. For now I enjoyed the attention from the safety of my marital bed.

Miranda began to cry. Alone in her study, curled up in the armchair beside the fire, she ran her fingers over the red leaf of a sweet gum tree stuck on the page with glue. She had been married for eight years, but she had never felt a love as intense as Ava's.

XVII

The sound of roaring fires and the taste of roasted chestnuts

Hartington House, 2005

David didn't seem the least bit curious about Jean-Paul. The garden was Miranda's department, like decoration and general maintenance; he trusted her judgment. Mrs. Underwood was a treasure and her husband, although eccentric, kept the home fires burning and the paths free of leaves. Of Fatima, who worked two mornings a week, he had no opinion. He had no desire to meet the housekeeper.

The first weekend after Jean-Paul had moved into the cottage David didn't notice much difference, except for the tree house which kept the children occupied right up until bath time. Gus had shown it off proudly, demanding that he climb the ladder and take a look inside the house which boasted a toy cooker, table and two chairs. Storm showed him the hollow tree camp, although he was too big to enter himself. He wondered what sort of gardener would go to the trouble of building such an exquisite playhouse. They didn't ask to watch DVDs and Gus left his PlayStation in his bedroom. He also noticed the children played together without quarreling. That was a miracle in itself. His curiosity was aroused, but, as Jean-Paul did not come up to the house, David felt no compulsion to introduce himself. Besides, it wasn't fair to disturb him on his weekend off.

But by the end of November he began to notice a marked change. The borders looked groomed, the soil was a rich brown and free of weeds, the dead clematis that had scaled the front of the house was pulled down and carted away. Great heaps of rotten foliage were piled high in the vegetable garden ready to be burned. The stones along the thyme walk had been weeded, the balls of topiary trimmed into perfect spheres. The gardens were a pleasure to behold, even in winter. He didn't usually bother to walk around his estate, from a combination of inertia and lack of interest, but now he was drawn away from golf to enjoy the marvels of his property.

The more David saw, the more his admiration grew. Miranda showed him around enthusiastically, pointing to the things Jean-Paul had done, deriving pleasure from these rare moments together. She watched her husband's astonishment with a real sense of achievement, feeling her spirits soar to the bright blue skies where a buzzard now wheeled in search of prey. She wanted to take his hand like they had done in the early days of their marriage, when they used to spend Sunday mornings wandering around the Serpentine before nipping into Jakobs for lunch, but something stopped her.

"The children help. They rush home from school to dig up all the weeds and fill the wheelbarrow. He showed them how to roast marshmallows on the bonfire. Even Mr. Underwood was dancing around it like a Red Indian. It was so funny." She recalled that she hadn't laughed like that with David in a very long time. Perhaps she never had.

David started to feel uneasy. "I'd better meet this Jean-Paul. He sounds like Mary Poppins," he said grudgingly.

"That's exactly what he is! The children can't get enough of him. Storm has made friends with Jeremy's cows and Gus has taken an interest in planting bulbs. He likes playing with the worms he digs up."

"Well, let's go down to the cottage and see if he's there."

"I don't think we should disturb him on a Saturday."

"I'm the boss. I can disturb him whenever I like." He sounded more severe than he meant to. Miranda followed him across the field. The children waved from their tree then disappeared inside.

"That tree is a godsend. It keeps them busy for hours. They never tire of it."

"I suppose it's better than television," he grunted. Miranda frowned. A moment ago he had been so happy. She mentally replayed their conversation, wondering if it was something she had said.

At the cottage, smoke billowed from the chimney, suggesting that Jean-Paul was at home. David knocked on the door and shoved his hands into his pockets. It was bitter out of the sun. Jean-Paul had been painting in the spare room. When he heard the knock on the door, he put down his brush and went downstairs to open it. David extended his hand and introduced himself formally. He did not smile. Jean-Paul was not what he expected, though he was relieved to see how old he was.

"Please come in," said Jean-Paul, standing back to allow them into the hall. "It's cold outside."

"But beautiful," Miranda added, shrugging off her sheepskin coat. "The children are in your tree. We can't get them out!" David noticed the excitement in her voice and felt his irritation mount.

"I see you've been busy in the garden," he said, wandering into the sitting room. The fire glowed, Crystal Gayle sung out of the CD player. "Do you really like this music?" he asked.

"Of course," Jean-Paul replied with an affable shrug.

"I suppose you are a different generation," David went on. Miranda began to feel uncomfortable. She so wanted her husband to like him.

"Please, sit down. Can I make you coffee or tea?"

"No thanks, we're not staying. I just wanted to meet you. I trust my wife's judgment, but I like to know those I employ."

"Naturally." Jean-Paul looked like a father might look at his son. He understood the younger man's disquiet. David was as transparent as the river Hart. "I hope you are satisfied with my work so far. You have a beautiful home. You could not have chosen a more charming house anywhere else in England."

David straightened up, flattered by the Frenchman's words. "I'm impressed with the tree house," he said, returning the compliment. He found the ease with which Jean-Paul had mollified him almost as irritating as his jealousy. "It's good to see them enjoying themselves."

"You were right to leave the city. Children need to be in the countryside where they have space to run around. They are full of energy. You must be very proud."

"I am," he replied. "We both are." He turned to Miranda and took her hand. The sensation of his skin against hers made her flinch. "You're doing a wonderful job."

"Thank you." Jean-Paul smiled. Miranda's heart flipped and even David felt moved to smile in return. "If there's anything you need, let me know. Before you arrived I hadn't turned my thoughts to the garden so we're probably in need of tools and things."

"You have everything. The previous owners left everything behind." Jean-Paul's face grew suddenly serious.

"Good. Well, we'll leave you in peace. Maybe take the children for a walk." Miranda looked at him in astonishment. He had never taken the children for a walk, nor, as far as she could remember, ever taken *himself* for a walk.

Once outside, he dropped her hand. "He's perfectly nice," he said, striding towards the bridge. "I see he's taken a shine to the children."

"They've taken a shine to him, too," she replied.

"He's not what I expected."

"Really? What did you expect?"

"Another Mr. Underwood."

"Oh no," Miranda laughed. "He's well educated."

"What's he doing gardening then, if he's so well educated?"

"Perhaps he loves it."

"Doesn't make much money."

"I don't think he cares about money."

"Has he left a wife back in France?"

"Not that I'm aware of."

He chuckled cynically. "He'll soon make his way through all the women in Hartington. I wouldn't trust him as far as I could throw him. He's much too good-looking."

"Oh, really, darling! He's not like that at all."

"Just because he doesn't flirt with you." She dropped her eyes to the ground and shoved her hands into her pockets. There was a sharp edge to his words which caused her pain.

"No, he doesn't."

"I should hope not. He knows his place."

When they reached the hollow tree David announced that they were all going for a walk. "I want you to show me your cows, Storm," he said, watching her crawl excitedly out through the hole in the bark. Her hair was strewn with twigs and pieces of moss and her cheeks glowed. Gus jumped down from halfway up the ladder, wishing he had something to show his father.

With Storm leading the way, they retreated over the bridge and along the riverbank towards the field of cows. Jean-Paul heard their voices and went to watch them at the window. He stood awhile, enjoying the sight of the little girl skipping through the long grasses. Poppy used to walk with a dance in her step, her dark hair flying about her shoulders in the wind, pretending to be a butterfly or a reindeer. Storm was beginning to learn the magic of the garden that Poppy had known instinctively. It was an enchanted world, ready for her to explore. He looked forward to showing her spring, when the ground would come to life and all the work they had put in would reward them with flowers. Then the magic would really begin.

Gus walked behind his father, whacking the grass with a stick, as if he carried the weight of the

world on his small shoulders. There was something angry about him, simmering at his core like
lava. His eyes were cold as if to protect himself
from disappointment and he always looked up
from under his fringe with a mixture of expectation
and mistrust. Now that Jean-Paul had met both
parents, it was easy to understand the boy's frustration. He knew that children needed to be listened
to, needed love and time. He didn't doubt Miranda
and David loved their children, but they had little
time to give. He recalled the little gestures that
daily demonstrated Ava's love for her children.
That sort of foundation was a priceless gift for a
child; a solid base camp from which to embark
upon life.

He returned to his painting. With each brush-
stroke on the canvas he felt connected to her again.

Storm talked to the cows as if they were her
friends, stroking the short hair between their eyes.
"You see, they know me," she said proudly. "Jean-
Paul says they have five stomachs."

"Lucky them," said David. "I wish I had five
stomachs. Then I could eat five times as much of
Mrs. Underwood's crumble and custard." Storm
giggled. Miranda watched her happily. It had been
a long time since they had all done something
together. Gus sat on the riverbank and picked the
grass absentmindedly. Miranda went to join him.

"Can you see any fish?" she asked.

"No."

"I need to buy you a rod. I'm sure Jean-Paul knows how to fish."

"He's going to get me a net so I can catch them." The boy's eyes lit up. "We're going to build a camp in the woods so we can watch deer. He says we'll see little ones in the spring. We might even see a badger. I'm going to make a spear so I can kill them."

"I'm sure that's not Jean-Paul's idea!"

"Can I have a penknife for Christmas?"

"I'll have to ask your father."

"Please!"

"We'll see." The thought of Gus with a penknife was rather alarming.

After lunch David didn't retreat as normal but suggested they light the bonfire in the vegetable garden. Gus informed him that it was Jean-Paul's pile of rubbish to be burned the following week. "We're going to be Red Indians again," he said, demonstrating by making a whooping noise with his hand over his mouth.

"It's my house and therefore my pile of rubbish," said David, striding off to put on his boots. Miranda realized he was jealous of Jean-Paul. That was why he had taken her hand and why he had gone for a walk with the children. Jean-Paul was a better father to the children than he was. Instead of reveling in David's jealousy, she felt ashamed of it;

ashamed that her husband had to compete with the gardener to prove himself a worthy father.

That night they made love. After weeks of no contact Miranda knew she should have felt grateful, but she felt only resentment. She knew his actions were motivated by the presence of Jean-Paul. He was marking his territory like a dog pissing on a tree. She closed her eyes and tried to put Jean-Paul out of her mind. But suddenly it was Jean-Paul's mouth kissing her and his hands caressing her and, in that delicious moment, she realized that the Frenchman excited her. With unexpected ferocity she held her husband close, wrapped her arms and legs around him and tried to focus on the familiar feel of his skin, as if afraid those disloyal thoughts would drive him further away.

The following morning they went to church. As it was their first visit, they were viewed with the same excited curiosity as new animals at the zoo. The Reverend Freda Beeley clasped David's hand enthusiastically between her own doughy ones. "It is such a pleasure to see you. I knew you would come eventually." Her voice was thick and fruity. Storm and Gus giggled at the sight of her fearsome bosom that wobbled beneath her robes as she spoke, giving her the shape of a blancmange.

As they walked down the aisle, Miranda caught the eyes of Troy and Henrietta and smiled in surprise. She had thought only old people went to church. Troy's eyes widened at the sight of her belted Dolce & Gabbana coat, leather boots and fur collar, and Henrietta waved discreetly, envying her effortless glamour and slender silhouette. David made for the front pew, fully expecting it to be on permanent hold for them, the first family of Hartington, but it was occupied by old Colonel Pike, scowling at all that was bad about the modern world, like female vicars, and Joan Halesham and her octogenarian beau, studying the prayer book through thick spectacles. Grudgingly he sat in the pew behind.

Storm and Gus would have been bored by the service had it not been for organist Dorothy Dipwood, speeding up and slowing down during the hymns without any regard for the congregation. Only the last line was sung in time with the organ. The Reverend Beeley bounced about the nave, gesticulating wildly and speaking with emphasis as if she were talking to children. David thought it amusing while Miranda, who had never liked church since being made to go so often as a child, was more entertained watching her children. Her eyes wandered about the pretty church, at the ancient stone walls and vaulted ceilings and wondered how on earth they had managed to build it all those centuries ago without the help of modern technology—anything to keep her mind off Jean-Paul. The vicar's sermon was about taking the time to enjoy the small things in an increasingly frenetic world, but neither Miranda nor David was paying attention.

On the green outside, Colonel Pike invited David to his home to show off the medals he had won in the war. Miranda found Troy and Henrietta, while the children discovered the gravestones, which they jumped on and off as if they were large stepping-stones in a river. The sun shone brightly down as the congregation lingered to chat. Miranda felt warmth on her face and the unfamiliar sense of being a part of the community. She found herself enjoying standing there with her children and husband, talking to the locals, knowing that Mrs. Underwood was cooking roast beef and Yorkshire pudding in the kitchen at home. Things were beginning to feel right.

"Why don't you come and have a trim, darling?" suggested Troy. "Your hair's lovely and shiny, but a few layers would give it more body."

"Oh, I don't know. I've never had layers," she replied, doubtful that anyone other than Robert at Richard Ward could do a proper job.

"Well, come and have a cup of tea in the salon then. Just the three of us."

"I'd love to. Tomorrow morning?"

"Come as soon as the kids are at school, I haven't got an appointment until ten."

"And I don't open until ten," Henrietta added.

"I'll bring some hot croissants from Cate's, but

we'll have to hide in the back. If she sees us she'll go mad."

"Wouldn't it be simpler to meet in her shop?" said Miranda.

"No!" they replied in unison.

"No," repeated Troy sourly. "I've had a little too much of Cate recently."

"Why do you carry on seeing her if you don't like her?" Miranda asked.

"Habit," Troy replied nonchalantly. "Like drinking too much alcohol—you know it's not good for you and that you're going to feel terrible afterward, but it's part of life."

David was in high spirits after their sociable morning, promising the children he'd take them to Jeremy's farm after lunch to play on the tractors. Storm had found a few friends from school and Gus had managed to join in without frightening them. Miranda had had to drag them away promising play dates after school. She was uplifted. With the clear skies and the banquet Mrs. Underwood had cooked she was sure an idyllic afternoon was to follow. Then David appeared in the hall with his bag, announcing that he was going to catch the early afternoon train to London. Miranda was disappointed. Everything had been going so well. Didn't he want to spend more time with them? What was the hurry? Weren't the important things in his life here in Hartington? She kissed him good-bye, but his kiss was hasty and he didn't hold her. These weeks apart were turning them into strangers. She knew she should trust him. She had no reason not to. But a nugget of doubt had started to worry her, like a stone in her shoe. Could he be seeing someone else?

Gus watched his father disappear up the drive in a taxi and felt a sharp stab of disappointment. He had been looking forward to playing on Mr. Fitzherbert's tractors. Once the car had gone, Storm disappeared inside with their mother. Gus picked up a stone and threw it at an unsuspecting blackbird, then headed for the woods. When he came to the dovecote he stopped. There, nestling in the long grasses was a hedgehog. He crouched down to get a better look. The hedgehog eyed him fearfully. With a finger Gus prodded its face. The hedgehog rolled into a ball. Gus grinned. It would make a good football.

"What have you found there?" came Jean-Paul's voice behind him. Gus stood up guiltily, the blood rushing to his cheeks. "A hedgehog?" Jean-Paul knelt down. "Do you know why he has rolled into a ball?"

"Because he's frightened."

"That's right. Come, let's take a closer look. I think he's hurt," said Jean-Paul, sensing an opportunity to teach the child a valuable lesson. "Can you see he's trembling?" Gus nodded. "You know, the funny thing about animals is that they have a very heightened sixth sense. They know who to trust and who to be afraid of."

"They do?" said Gus, thankful that the hedgehog didn't have a voice to tell tales with.

"Watch." Jean-Paul placed his hands under the hedgehog and scooped him up. He held him gently, close to his shirt. It wasn't long before the animal uncurled and began sniffing Jean-Paul's skin with his wet nose. "Let's take him back to the cottage and make him a bed. I think he's unwell, don't you?"

They went back down the thyme walk. Jean-Paul began to tell Gus about animals and how to respect and care for them. He was inspired by Ava's voice echoing across the years, teaching her children the same lessons. Once they reached the cottage Jean-Paul wrapped the hedgehog in a cloth and gave him to Gus. At first Gus was alarmed, afraid that the hedgehog would bite him for having prodded his face. But Jean-Paul reassured him. "The hedgehog can read your mind. If you think loving thoughts, he will pick up on them and cease to be afraid." Sure enough the hedgehog stopped trembling and began to sniff the palms of his hands.

Gus giggled. "He wants to eat me."

"No he doesn't, he's just exploring. However, I do think he's hungry. We'll put him in this box and give him some milk."

"Will he be all right?"

"Oh yes. We'll feed him up, keep him warm,

then put him back in the wild tomorrow. He's probably eaten something that's disagreed with him."

"He's got a sweet nose," said Gus, laughing again as it tickled him.

"You know that hedgehog probably has a mummy and a daddy who are missing him. He might have brothers and sisters, too. When we put him back we'll see if we can find them."

"That's a good idea."

"If someone hurt you your parents would be very upset, wouldn't they?" Gus nodded. "If you hurt this hedgehog, his parents would be upset as well, don't you think?" Gus shrugged, feeling bad. "He's not very different from you. He has just as much right as you do to be on the earth. We all live here together and we will all die here one day. You must respect God's creatures, even the smallest ants. You will do that for me, won't you?"

"Yes," said Gus, stroking the hedgehog's face with his finger. The animal seemed to be enjoying it.

Jean-Paul poured some milk into a bowl. "What's your sister up to this afternoon?"

"With Mummy. Daddy went up to London." The boy's face clouded.

"Are you disappointed?"

"He said he was going to take us to Mr. Fitzherbert's farm to play on the tractors."

"He's very busy, isn't he?"

254

"He's always busy. He never has time to play with us." Quite unexpectedly, Gus opened his heart to Jean-Paul. Feelings he had never put into words poured out in a jumble. "They want to send me away to boarding school—but it's not my fault—I never started it—I only bit him because he called me names—Daddy always promises to play with me—but he never does—he's always too busy—other daddies play with their children— why can't he play with me?" The little boy began to sob. Jean-Paul put his arm around him, listening to the barely comprehensible soliloquy of injustices. Finally, Gus grew quiet, his body jerking with the odd sharp intake of breath he was unable to control.

"Grown-ups are very hard to understand sometimes. It's not fair that your father promises to play with you then lets you down. But the intention is there. He wanted to play with you and meant to do so. Perhaps he was called away urgently and he's as disappointed as you are." Gus sniffed, incredulous. "You must tell them you don't want to go to boarding school."

"They won't listen. They never listen."

"Then you must ask them to listen and be strong about it. But be calm and steady and don't get cross. You have to set them a good example. They will do as you do." Gus looked unconvinced. "Do you still want to play on the tractors?" The boy's eyes lit up. "Come on then, we have time before tea."

Miranda wasn't the sort of person to snoop. There were no secrets between herself and her husband. But after the children had gone to bed, exhausted from playing on the farm, she began to go through his desk. He kept everything immaculately tidy. There were files for letters, household maintenance, invoices and insurance, but anything incriminating would surely be kept in London. If he had anything to hide, he'd hardly keep it at home. She ran a hot bath and soaked in lavender oil, closing her eyes and inhaling the steam. She cursed herself for having a suspicious mind. They just needed to spend more time together. She resolved to discuss it with him the following weekend.

That night she lit a scented candle, curled up in bed and opened the scrapbook. There was a strange magic to it, like opening the door into a world infinitely more beautiful than the one she lived in. It absorbed her, the memories wrapping their silver threads about her heart and pulling her in. She could feel the love like the heat of the sun and the pain as if it were her own suffering. While she read, she escaped from the increasing coldness of her marriage into the warmth of someone else's secret.

Ours was a love doomed from the very beginning. It was as transient as sunset. You once said that the setting of the sun was a tragedy, filling you with melancholy as you tried unsuccessfully to hold on to it. Perhaps its transience is its beauty. Perhaps our love is made sweeter by its hopelessness. If one could halt the sunset and live in a perpetual dusk, would it retain such magic? Would our love be as tender without the expectation of loss? We will never know, because all we have is loss and the memory of the crimson and gold.

XVIII

Pink cotton candy clouds at sunset. Spiders' webs sewn into the bushes like lace.

Jean-Paul stood on the stone bridge. It was dark and cold, the sky a deep navy studded with stars. The moon was high, not quite full, surrounded by an aureole of mist. He put his hands on the stone balustrade and leaned over to look at the water. The light bounced off the ripples as it flowed gently down to the sea. He stared for so long that his eyes stung, but before he blinked he was sure he could see her face, reflected with the moon, gazing back at him with the same yearning.

He couldn't sleep. It was hard to find peace in the cottage that used to be theirs. Every room echoed with her presence, every sound triggered a memory, the smell of orange blossom tormented him with longing. Yet he was drawn to it, like a loose tooth that he kept probing with his tongue, taking a strange pleasure from the pain. He could leave tonight, but the thought of the empty château caused him more discomfort than the cottage. If he couldn't spend his future with her, then he'd have to be satisfied in the past still warm with her memory.

The following morning Miranda took great care choosing her clothes. She put on a pair of faded gray Ralph Lauren jeans, brown leather boots and a gray cashmere Ralph Lauren polo neck. Just because she lived in the middle of fields didn't mean her standards had to slip. She applied makeup and sprayed herself with perfume, filling the bathroom with the scent of lime, basil and mandarin. With a bounce in her step she went to give the children breakfast.

As she was due at Troy's at nine, she decided to take the children to school by car, leaving their bikes at the end of the drive for them to cycle home on their return. She was on the point of setting off when the telephone rang. She half expected it to be Troy canceling their coffee morning. Cancellations were as frequent in London as unforecast rain.

To her surprise, the caller was a shop assistant from Theo Fennell, the jeweler in London where Miranda had been a good customer for many years. "I'm sorry to call you so early in the morning, Mrs. Claybourne," said the girl, her voice breathy and upper class. "But I've mislaid your husband's office number and he's keen to get an engraving done before Christmas. I wrote it on my pad, but my pad has gone missing. I'm new and I'm really embarrassed to have been so silly. Theo would kill me!" Miranda's curiosity was aroused. Perhaps David was buying her something expensive for Christmas. He knew Theo's was one of her favorite shops.

"What's he doing shopping in there?" she laughed, angling for more information.

"I don't think I should say," replied the girl nervously.

"No, perhaps you shouldn't. I'll give you the number, but don't tell him you spoke to me. If it's a surprise I don't want to ruin it. He'll be terribly hurt."

"Thank you, Mrs. Claybourne." The girl sounded relieved. Miranda dictated the number and hung up. A beautiful piece of jewelry from Theo Fennell would certainly go towards making up for his long absences. How could she have doubted him?

When Miranda arrived at Troy's, Henrietta was already there, biting into a hot croissant. The salon smelled sweet, of shampoo and hair spray, and the heating was on high. She took off her navy cashmere Celine coat—it had looked so forlorn in her closet she felt it was only fair to take it out, although it was much too glamorous for Hartington—and put her sunglasses in their case. Troy hissed at her to hurry to the back before Cate looked out her window. The three of them sat huddled in the little room, amongst boxes of products and a desk piled high with paperwork. The air was charged with excitement. It wasn't often that they defied Cate. "If she finds out, we're in shit," said Troy, handing Miranda a mug of tea.

"Then she'll never tell us when that gorgeous Frenchman comes in again," added Henrietta.

"We're all in love." Troy sighed dramatically.

"Who with?" Miranda asked.

"He's a mystery Frenchman," said Henrietta breathlessly. "He first came in October. We thought he was a tourist. Now he's back. We've spotted him across the road. He has black coffee and a croissant for breakfast. But as much as Cate asks him about himself, and you know her, she can be quite persuasive, he won't reveal anything!"

"You're not talking about *my* Frenchman, are you?" They both stared.

"I didn't know you had one, darling," said Troy.

"I don't *have* him. He works for me. In his fifties, very good-looking, deep-set brown eyes, longish graying hair, devastating smile."

"Oh my GOD!" Troy gasped. "He *is* your Frenchman! What does he do for you?"

"He gardens."

"Gardens?" they repeated in unison.

"Yes, he's a gardener."

"Don't be silly," said Henrietta. "He's a film producer or a writer. He can't be a gardener!"

"Well, he is," Miranda replied simply.

"How on earth did you find him?" asked Troy.

"He found me, actually. It's a long story."

"We have all morning."

Miranda recounted the tale during which time neither Troy nor Henrietta said a single word. "So," she concluded, "he brought Storm home and we got talking. I asked him what he did and he said he gardened. I asked him if he'd do ours and he accepted without hesitation. It was very bizarre."

"Is he married?" Henrietta asked.

"No," Miranda replied.

"Oh, good!" she exclaimed, determined to start a new diet as soon as she'd finished her croissant.

"Is he gay?" asked Troy.

"That I don't know," said Miranda. She flushed as she recalled her improper thoughts. "But I doubt it. Just a hunch."

"How do you control yourself during the week when your husband's in London?" Troy asked.

"I don't fancy him," she lied, giving a little shrug.

"That just goes to show what a happy marriage you have," said Henrietta, sighing with envy.

"Your husband must be mad with jealousy," said Troy.

"Miranda's husband is very attractive, Troy."

"But not as attractive as the Frenchman. What's his name?"

"Jean-Paul," said Miranda.

"Oh God! How sexy! Jean-Paul. Isn't it irritating that Cate was right all along?"

"What do you mean?" asked Miranda, sipping her tea.

"She insisted you found your gardener thanks to her notice board."

"Well, she's wrong then, isn't she," Miranda retorted.

"No," said Henrietta slowly. "We saw him in Cate's in October. He asked her about the house, who lived there. That's why we assumed he was a tourist."

Miranda put down her mug and frowned. "Did he see my notice?"

"He couldn't miss it, darling," said Troy. "Everyone in Hartington saw your notice."

Miranda suddenly felt uncomfortable. "He never said anything about it when I spoke to him."

"You probably jumped in there before he had a chance," suggested Henrietta.

"Yes, you're right. I think I did. I barely gave him a moment. I get like that when I'm nervous. A little too loquacious."

Troy grinned. "So you did fancy him?"

Miranda grinned back. "A little, but not any-more," she added hastily.

"What a relief!" he exclaimed. "She's human after all!"

Miranda drove home, dispelling her doubts about Jean-Paul. There was no reason for him to mention her advert. Perhaps he hadn't considered the job until she spoke to him about it. After all, it was Storm who brought him to the house. He might not have come otherwise.

When she got home Fatima was in the kitchen clearing up breakfast. "Good morning, Mrs. Claybourne," she exclaimed when she saw Miranda. "Leave it all to me," she added in her singsong voice, bustling about the room with the energy of a woman half her age. "You go and work, I will make your house shine shine shine!"

Miranda sat in her office trying to write an article for the *Telegraph* magazine, reining in her mind every time it wandered off. She thought of Jean-Paul in the garden, the children, who really needed some new winter clothes, and her growing desire to quit these soulless articles and write a proper novel. It would soon be Christmas and she hadn't begun to buy presents. They had decided to spend Christmas in their new home as a family, inviting Miranda's parents and her spinster aunt. Her sister had married and gone to live in Australia, which wasn't a great surprise to Miranda, who rather envied her for having put such a great distance between herself and their mother. She was dreading the whole event.

Just as she was typing the end of the first paragraph, Mr. Underwood entered with an armful of logs, which he dropped into the basket beside the fireplace. Miranda looked up and smiled, then made the mistake of asking how he was. "Well, Mrs. C., ma'am, seeing as you ask, I've had a tickle in my throat for some time now, just a tickle, as if there's a little ant in there. I know there isn't, but it feels like an ant. Or a spider with lots of wiggling little legs. Trouble is, it makes me cough. I went to the doctor and he couldn't find anything wrong with it. Still bothers me." He coughed to make his point.

"I'm sorry to hear that," said Miranda, sorrier to have asked him in the first place.

"Mrs. Underwood says I should have spoonfuls of honey. Trouble is, I don't much care for honey. It's too sweet and I'm a savory man. I like salty things, like bacon." He stood a moment watching her, as if he expected her to continue the conversation.

"Well, I'd better get back to work," she said, hoping he'd take the hint.

"Oh, yes, don't let me bother you. Don't want to stop the creative flow. I spoke to J-P early this morning, he's up with the lark, been up an hour already before I arrived at eight. We're going to rip out the cottage garden. Rip it out, all of it, and start again."

Miranda was horrified. She immediately thought of Ava and the garden she had created with M.F. She couldn't allow Jean-Paul to rip it out. "What, all of it?" she asked, incredulous.

"Aye, Mrs. C., ma'am. Rip it out, all out, every bit of it." His eyes blazed at the prospect. "Then we'll burn all the weeds. Build a big fire and burn the lot."

"I must go and talk to him. There must be something we can save."

"Oh, no. It's all dead or rotting."

"I'll be the judge of that," she replied, though, with her inexperience she wasn't qualified to judge anything. As she reached the door she heard her computer ping with another e-mail. Damn it, she thought, then, with a triumphant smile, she ignored it and walked into the hall.

She found Jean-Paul sitting on the blue bench that circled the mountain ash in the middle of the cottage garden. He was leaning forward, his elbows on his knees, rubbing his chin, deep in thought. Her heart stumbled when she saw him looking so sad. "Good morning," she said, not wanting to startle him. He turned and looked at her, his brown eyes so intense she blushed.

"I was miles away," he said, sitting up with a heavy sigh.

"Anywhere nice?" she asked brightly.

"Oh yes," he replied. "The past is sweet." He said it with such longing that her curiosity was aroused and yet, there was something about him that made it impossible for her to inquire further. She sat beside him on the bench.

"Mr. Underwood tells me that you want to rip out this garden."

"No. Not everything. Some things we can save, some things need to be replanted. We are late, it is already December. But the weather is unusually mild, and with a little magic . . ."

Miranda bit her lip. "I know you asked me to leave you to it. That I could trust you," she began carefully. "I'm sure I can. The thing is, Mrs. Lightly really loved this garden. In fact, it was very special to her. I don't think it would be right to change it."

Jean-Paul looked at her suspiciously. "How do you know about Mrs. Lightly?"

"Oh, I've been told. She was very popular here. Everyone knows about her gardens. Apparently, this garden was very dear to her." She longed to share the scrapbook with someone, but she was too deeply involved now to betray the woman who had made it.

"Listen, Miranda. I understand that you do not want to ruin what your predecessor created. I don't want to ruin it either. In spite of the weeds I can see what was there. I will endeavor to recreate it exactly as it once was."

Miranda was relieved. "You will?" He nodded. "Oh, thank you so much. I couldn't bear her to come back one day and see that we had spoiled it."

"You think she will come back?"

"You never know, do you?"

"No." He shook his head wistfully. "You never do."

So Jean-Paul and Mr. Underwood began the task of recreating the cottage garden. How different it was from the week Jean-Paul had originally planted it with Ava, Hector and her children. They had chattered and laughed together in the sunshine, the dogs frolicking about on the lawn, the pigeons cooing from the rooftops. It was during those days that she had slowly stolen his heart, little by little, so that he barely noticed until it was too late.

Miranda gave up on her article. She didn't feel in the least bit inspired. She found it hard to concentrate, her eyes wandering outside to the gardens, her mind drifting to the children and to Jean-Paul. She felt restless at her desk, irritated by the e-mails offering her more work and dissatisfied with her own writing that no longer came easily. Instead of battling with her piece, she lay on her bed and opened the scrapbook. She picked up the painting of the cottage garden and leaned back against the pillows to study it carefully. It was painted with confident strokes and vibrant colors. She would have loved to show it to Jean-

267

Paul so that he could copy it, but there was no point wishing. She would never show it to him or anybody. One day, if she were to meet Mrs. Lightly, she would return it to her.

XIX

Those mischievous squirrels on the cottage windowsill.
They feel the love inside like sunshine and want to bask in it as we do.

The children broke up from school. Miranda had taken to driving them to school in the mornings, meeting Troy and Henrietta either in the salon or at Cate's Cake Shop after the drop-off. Slowly she began to be integrated into the community. She hadn't intended to, resisting like a barnacle clinging to a rock. It happened without her noticing. Slowly and insidiously, like enveloping fog. They began to linger after church on Sundays, chatting to the locals. David visited Colonel Pike who proudly displayed his collection of medals and invited him to breakfast in Cate's Cake Shop on Saturday mornings. Miranda struck up the odd conversation with other mothers outside the school gates and attended the parent teacher meeting alone, as David was busy in London. She had arrived with a knot of anxiety in her stomach. But Mr. Marlow had greeted her with a friendly smile, delighted to tell her that Gus was finally settling down. He hadn't bitten anyone since October, but had yet to make friends. "He's a loner," she explained in his defense. Mr. Marlow had pulled a face. "Not a loner, Mrs. Claybourne, alone. There's a big difference. Your son would benefit enormously from having friends."

She was pleased when the term ended and Gus came home where there was no one to judge him. As far as she could see, her son was now playing contentedly with his sister in the tree house that Jean-Paul had built them. The fact was he didn't enjoy going to school and she didn't blame him. She hadn't much liked school either. Gus was happiest at home, she concluded. She watched him trail after Jean-Paul and realized that, above all, he was happiest with the gardener.

In order for Miranda to go to London to do her Christmas shopping, Henrietta agreed to look after Gus and Storm. Clare was perfectly capable of manning the shop in her absence, and Henrietta secretly longed to meet the elusive Jean-Paul, who drank his black coffee in silence every morning, reading the papers in Cate's Cake Shop.

Miranda departed on the early train, leaving Henrietta at the breakfast table with the children.

Troy had layered Henrietta's hair and given her spirits a lift. No one had noticed except Cate who had told her it made her face look rounder. "I mean that nicely," she had added. "It looks sweet."

Knowing that she was more than likely to bump into Jean-Paul, she had applied mascara. She didn't feel at ease wearing makeup, but today she had felt her confidence needed a little boosting. However, she didn't feel brave enough to show her fulsome figure, hiding it beneath a large woolly sweater.

Henrietta adored children. Gus and Storm sensed it immediately and began to show off. Not since Jean-Paul had they had such an attentive audience. She listened to them, laughed at their jokes and let them show her their bedrooms and toys. She admired Storm's pink playhouse, cuddled her cushions and gushed about the fairy dresses hanging in her closet. Gus showed her the tree house, scaling the ladder like a squirrel. "Jean-Paul made it for us," he told her. "I can see for miles. J-P!" he shouted.

"J-P?" repeated Henrietta with a laugh.

"That's his nickname. He's J-P, I'm Gus-the-Strong and Storm is Bright-Sky."

"I like it," she enthused.

He shouted again. "He's probably in the cottage garden. He's always in there." Henrietta longed for Jean-Paul to appear, but he didn't. Gus scampered down the ladder and disappeared inside the hollow tree.

At eleven she took them hot chocolate and digestive biscuits in their tree house. She went down on all fours, not caring that her knees were in the mud, chasing them around the tree, pretending to be Captain Hook. Then she thrust her head into the aperture and shouted, "Ooh-aah, me hearties!", her large behind sticking out like a mushroom. That is how Jeremy Fitzherbert's dogs found her. They sniffed her bottom with excitement as she struggled to extract herself. When she emerged, her hair was a mess, her face flushed and her blue eyes were glittering like dewy cornflowers. "I hope I'm not interrupting anything," said Jeremy, grinning at the sight of her.

"Oh God, I'm so sorry," she gushed, pushing herself up. "I'm a pirate."

"You make a very good pirate," he replied, looking her up and down. She tried to smoothe her hair.

"More like Pooh-Bear stuck in Rabbit's front door, I think. You got the wrong end, I'm afraid."

"Nothing wrong with that end. It looked perfect to me."

"Have we met?" she asked, puzzled.

"Indeed. You're Henrietta Moon, aren't you?"

"Yes." She frowned.

"I'm Jeremy Fitzherbert. I own the neighboring farm."

"Of course we've met," she replied, as everything clicked into place.

"I've been into your shop. You sell those large jars of candy sticks. They're my favorites."

"Mine, too," she exclaimed, feeling bad at not

having remembered him. "The butterscotch ones especially."

"Exactly. Once I start I can't stop."

"Unfortunately that's my problem, too."

"You look very well on it."

She stared at him, not knowing what to say. She wasn't used to compliments. She didn't imagine for a minute that he meant it. There passed a moment of awkwardness while Henrietta struggled to move her tongue and Jeremy found himself swallowed into her aquamarine eyes. He wanted to tell her how beautiful they were, but immediately felt embarrassed. She had probably heard it a hundred times before.

"*Bonjour*, Jeremy," came a voice. They both turned to see Jean-Paul striding up the path towards them, his jovial greeting breaking the silence. Henrietta caught her breath at the sight of his smile and felt her stomach lurch like it used to do as a child on fairground rides. "*Bonjour, madame*," he said to her. He took her hand and raised it to his lips, bowing formally. Henrietta didn't know where to look. She felt the prickly heat of embarrassment rise up her neck to her throat, spreading across her skin in a mottled rash. No one had ever kissed her hand before. It must be a French thing, she thought, struggling to recover.

"I've brought you the small tractor and trailer you wanted," said Jeremy. It appeared that neither had noticed her sudden wilting. Storm and Gus wriggled out of the hole in the tree to run about with the dogs.

"Thank you," said Jean-Paul. "That will be a big help." They talked about the gardens, the farm and the weather, unusually warm for that time of year, while Henrietta listened, too shy to utter a single word. Finally, Jean-Paul turned to her. "I gather you are looking after Gus-the-Strong and Bright-Sky today," he said, his eyes deep and twinkling.

"Yes," she croaked.

"How do you like my house?"

"It's terrific, it really is."

"I see you completed the ladder," said Jeremy, patting the wood. "Good solid oak, that." Henrietta envied the ease with which he spoke to Jean-Paul. "Have you been up?" he asked her.

"No," she replied. "As you saw, I had difficulty getting out. I'm sure I'd suffer worse coming down!"

"Not at all. Come on!" Jeremy stood on the first rung of the ladder. "Feels solid," he said.

"It should be. I made it to take the weight of an elephant," said Jean-Paul.

"Then it should hold me," Henrietta laughed nervously, praying that it wouldn't collapse beneath her weight. She regretted every croissant she had ever eaten. Jeremy climbed up first, then he encouraged Henrietta to follow. She placed her feet tentatively on the first rung, then the second, waiting for the crack as the wood snapped in two.

"Don't be afraid," said Jean-Paul behind her. "The ladder is solid, I promise. Are you frightened of heights?" She couldn't tell him she was frightened of her own size.

"A little," she lied. She looked up to see Jeremy holding his hand out for her. When she reached the top she took it gratefully and stepped onto the platform on which the house was built. She took a deep breath and looked around. Gus was right, the view was stunning.

"How beautiful the church spire looks rising above the trees," she said.

"If it weren't for the trees we'd see my farm," said Jeremy.

"I'd like to see your farm," Henrietta replied, remembering picnics as a child watching the combines.

"You can come over any time," he said softly, wondering why he had never noticed her before. She was delicious, like a toffee apple. He glanced down at her left hand and saw she didn't wear a ring.

Henrietta noticed Jean-Paul didn't join them. He stood on the grass below, talking to the children who were roaring with laughter. They clearly adored him. Jeremy watched her watching Jean-Paul and felt a jolt of disappointment. Not that it surprised him; how could a man like him compete with Jean-Paul?

He left them at the tree and returned to his farm.

There was a leak in the corridor outside his bathroom that needed mending. He changed into his blue coveralls, placed his tweed cap firmly on his head and went to collect the ladders from the vegetable garden where they lay against the side of the greenhouse. Mr. Ben and Wolfgang trotted along beside him. Life with Jeremy was always an adventure. The house dated back to the sixteenth century and was in constant need of repair, which Jeremy took upon himself to carry out. He was practical and innovative, though most would say eccentric. Replacing cracked roof tiles was a dangerous procedure requiring two ladders and a great deal of daring. The job took his mind off Henrietta Moon and the way she had blushed when Jean-Paul had kissed her hand. The Frenchman had charm, there was no doubt about that. If *he* started kissing hands everyone would fall about laughing. But Jean-Paul with his thick accent and deep-set brown eyes could carry off any outdated ritual of chivalry and everyone would think him the most romantic man to set foot in Hartington. Jeremy didn't stand a chance. He unhooked the cracked tile and tried to think of something else.

Henrietta managed to overcome her shyness in the company of Jean-Paul. The children took her off to the cottage garden to help with the planting. Mr. Underwood was there with his shirtsleeves rolled to his elbows, cap on his head, eyes bright with enthusiasm. He enjoyed having the children around. They reminded him of his own boys who used to sit on the tractor as he ploughed old Fitzherbert's fields. Now they were grown up, driving tractors with their own sons. If there was one thing he knew about children, it was that they liked to be included. Storm and Gus dug the holes and, together with Jean-Paul, placed the bulbs inside with great care as if they were hibernating animals. The weather was uncharacteristically mild so the earth was still soft and warm. Henrietta got into the spirit of it, too. She listened to Jean-Paul teaching the children about plants, patiently answering their questions. Then, every now and then he'd let out a roar of laughter at something one of them said and they'd all laugh together in blissful abandonment. It occurred to Henrietta that perhaps Jean-Paul was more comfortable with children than with adults and she wanted to ask him why he had never had any of his own.

Miranda had arrived in London early, hitting Peter Jones as it opened at 9:30. She inhaled the smell of carbon monoxide and felt a shiver of happiness. She was back where she belonged. The traffic rumbled, horns hooted, sirens screamed, people shouted, the pavements were crowded with jostling bodies. No one looked anyone in the eye, everyone went about their own business anonymously. She noticed no one smiled. But she did, from ear to ear.

She spent all morning buying presents. She went to Daisy & Tom for the children, where laughing toddlers rode the carousel and upstairs sat enthralled by the Peter and the Wolf puppet show. She bought David a couple of sweaters from Yves Saint Laurent on Sloane Street and a pair of shoes from Tod's. Finally, inside the temple that was Harvey Nichols, she wandered about slowly, relishing the familiar smell of perfume, gazing at the counters laden with boxed gifts and glittering pots of creams promising eternal youth. It was her wonderland. She bought some Trish McEvoy makeup in celebration of her return.

By lunchtime she had ticked almost everything off her list, except for the children's stocking fillers, the majority of which she'd buy in Hartington. She made her way to the fifth floor to meet Blythe and Anoushka for lunch. Catching herself in the mirror as she stood on the escalator, she was satisfied that although she lived in the countryside, she still retained her urban glamour. In jeans tucked into leather boots, a gold, fur-trimmed Prada ski jacket and Anya Hindmarch handbag, she felt confident that her girlfriends would be impressed.

She found them already sitting at the table, heads close together, gossiping. "Hello, girls," she said, standing before them. They sprang apart, clocking the jacket and bag almost before they greeted her.

"Darling, you look gorgeous," said Blythe, her

green cat's eyes sliding silkily up and down Miranda's body in appreciation. "No one can say the country isn't doing you good!"

"Thank you," she replied, sitting down. She kissed them both, almost tasting their perfume on her lips.

"Oh, it's so good to see you," said Anoushka in her Anglo-American drawl. "Where are the boots from?" She tossed her wavy blond hair, aware of the man at the next-door table appraising her.

"Tod's," she replied.

"This season?" Anoushka's voice had an edge to it.

"Yes."

"They look great. I wonder if they've got any left. You don't mind if I just call them quickly, do you?" She pulled out her mobile telephone and pressed the numbers with blood-red fingernails.

"So," said Blythe. "How's it all going down there?"

"It's taken a while, but I'm beginning to settle in now. You'll have to come and stay after Christmas."

"I'd love to, when I'm back. We're off to Mauritius for ten days. I've rented the private villa at the Saint Géran. The bastard has made me so miserable I have no qualms about spending his money. You know he's dragging the whole thing on and on and on. I bet he won't give me a divorce for the full two years. Even if it costs him more in the long run, he just wants to drag it out to torment me."

"I'm sorry. It's such a mess. I wish he'd give you a divorce and bugger off, then you can both get on with your lives. David tells me he's been giving you advice."

"David," she repeated, smiling tenderly. "Your husband has been a real support. I don't know what I'd have done without him. With you tucked away in the country I had no one to turn to. Then in he rides like a knight in shining armor. He's so patient and thoughtful."

"Oh good," Miranda replied, wishing he was as patient and thoughtful with her.

"He's given me invaluable advice. Thanks to him I'm going to fleece the bastard. He's going to wish he had treated me better. David is my secret weapon."

"Isn't he begging you to come home?"

"Only because he doesn't want to part with fifteen million."

"I can't say I blame him. That's not exactly pocket money."

"I deserve it for having put up with his infidelities for the last ten years. I might embark on some infidelity myself."

"Have you found someone?"

"Maybe." She looked coy.

"You have!" Miranda exclaimed. "Do I know him?"

"No," said Blythe quickly. "No one knows him. It's not big love, but it is big sex. He's delicious in the sack. Makes me hit the ceiling every time."

"Is he married?"

Blythe pulled a face.

"Oh, Blythe!" Miranda exclaimed. "Be careful. Remember how it feels. Don't put some poor wife through the hell you went through."

"It won't last," she said dismissively. "It's only a bit of fun. I promise you, no one will get hurt. It's not like I'm his mistress."

"Then what are you?"

"A friend who fucks," she replied with a self-satisfied smile. "Let's order some champagne. We're celebrating your return to the big smoke." She called over the waiter with a brisk click of her fingers. Anoushka came off the phone having succeeded in reserving a pair of boots in a size seven.

"Such a relief," she exclaimed. "I'd have died had they not had them. Now, let's fill you in on the gossip," she said. "There's so much, I barely know where to start."

Miranda listened while they recounted the scandals and misadventures that had kept London gossips busy in her absence. They drank champagne, picked at grilled fish with salad and hadn't a nice word to say about anyone. Miranda felt oddly remote, as if a pane of glass separated her from the two of them. Once she had had news to contribute; now she had nothing to add. She would have liked to share Ava Lightly's scrapbook and Jean-Paul, but Hartington was a world away from Knightsbridge. Small town news wouldn't interest these big town girls.

There were plenty of affairs and divorces going on in London to keep those two vultures happy, pecking with relish at the exposed flesh of the hurt and vulnerable. Miranda sat back and listened with a mixture of intrigue and disgust. Having been away for a few months she was able to observe them with an objectivity she hadn't had before. As the lunch progressed, her two friends became somewhat grotesque. Their collagen-enhanced lips grew swollen with champagne, their Botoxed foreheads took on an alien quality, robbing them of humanity. The more they rummaged about the lives of London's broken, the less compassionate they became. Miranda left to resume her Christmas shopping with a sour taste in her mouth. Suddenly London didn't hold so great an appeal. The traffic was too loud, the pavements too crowded, the people unfriendly, even the smell of perfume on the ground floor of Harvey Nichols had become unbearable. She longed to return to the peace of Hartington.

When she reached home, Miranda was a little surprised to see that Henrietta had put the children to bed and was sitting in the kitchen having supper with Jean-Paul. "I hope you don't mind," said

Henrietta. "We've been in the garden all day planting things. The children are done in; they fell asleep the moment Jean-Paul finished telling them the story of the velveteen rabbit. We thought we'd celebrate the end of a hard day's work."

"I'm delighted," Miranda replied, drawing up a chair. "I can't thank you enough for looking after them for me."

"You look exhausted," said Jean-Paul. "Let me pour you a glass of wine. There was a time when I thought the city was the only place to live. Then I discovered how shallow and empty it was. Like icing on a rotten cake. Underneath it was all bad."

"God, that's just how I feel. I was so excited to get up there, walking those pavements again, but by the end of the day all I wanted was to come home."

"I've never liked the city," said Henrietta. "Much too unfriendly. Here in Hartington there's a sense of community. I like belonging."

"So, have you finished my little garden?" Miranda asked, already feeling better for their company.

Jean-Paul's smile poured warm honey over the sour taste that had been with her since lunch. "We have completed the planting. With a little magic, it will flower in spring."

"Why do you always say magic, Jean-Paul?" Miranda asked. "Do you mean nature?"

"Magic is love, Miranda. If you love someone

they grow in beauty and confidence. They flower before your eyes. A woman who isn't beautiful becomes beautiful in the warmth of love. The garden is the same. With love it will grow better and brighter and more abundant. There is no secret to love or magic, just the limitations of our own courage and self-belief."

"I don't understand."

"Love requires effort, exertion and will. True love begins with loving ourselves. Love is not purely a feeling but an act of will. The man in a bar who neglects his family will tell you with tears in his eyes that he loves his wife and children. Love is as love does. A very exceptional woman taught me that a long time ago."

Henrietta and Miranda sat in silence. The more he spoke, the less they knew him and the deeper the pool of his experience and wisdom seemed. Both recognized the terrible sadness in his eyes but neither had the courage to ask him its cause. Henrietta dreamed of being loved by him; Miranda knew loving him was only a dream. Both hearts reached out to the man who would only ever love one woman. The woman he was slowly bringing to life in the tender planting of their garden.

XX

The wistful light of dusk turning the dovecote pink, but only for an instant like the soft outward breath of heaven

Jean-Paul returned to the Château les Lucioles for Christmas. He drove through the large iron gates, up the drive that swept in a magnificent curve around an ancient cedar tree and parked the car on the gravel in front of the impressive façade. The pale blue shutters were open, the windowsills covered with a thin sprinkling of frost. He gazed up at the tall roof where small dormer windows peeped out sleepily and towering chimneys stretched into the crisp blue sky. Françoise unlocked the door with much rattling of keys, complaining bitterly of the cold even before she saw him. "*Monsieur*, come inside quickly before you catch your death. Gerard has lit fires in the hall and drawing room. Are you hungry? Armandine has left a daube in the oven and there is a fresh loaf of bread. She was not sure whether or not you would have eaten. She will come back tonight to cook your dinner. Don't waste time outside. Come come, it is cold." The housekeeper beckoned him inside, closing the door behind him with a loud clank. "These big houses are hard to keep warm," she muttered, shuffling into the hall.

"Is Hubert here?" he asked, thinking only of the garden.

"Yes. Why don't you eat first, see him later? He is outside."

"Has there been much frost?"

"Only in the last week. It has suddenly got very cold after a mild autumn."

He glanced about the hall, at the blazing fire in the grate, the shiny flagstone floor and faded Persian rugs, and sighed with pleasure. It was good to be home. He took off his coat, handing it to Françoise. "I will see him now in the drawing room," he said. "You can bring the daube in on a tray. I'll eat in there."

"Shall I let the dogs in?" she asked. "They have been restless all morning. They knew you were coming home."

"Yes. I've missed them."

"Are you here to stay?"

"No. I'll leave in ten days."

She pushed out her bottom lip. "Such a short visit?"

"Yes."

"If your mother were alive . . ."

"But she is not," he retorted briskly.

"Why do you stay away? The animals miss you." She lowered her eyes. "So do we."

He looked at her tenderly. "Ah, Françoise, you are a sentimental woman underneath that efficient exterior."

"And what of you, *monsieur*? Why don't you find a nice young woman and settle down and have a family? This is a large château. It is not right that it is empty all year. It echoes with the voices of ghosts because it is not inhabited."

He shook his head. "Things don't always end up the way they were planned."

"What plans did you have?" He caught her looking at him with a mother's concern.

"Those I cannot speak of to anyone," he replied grimly. "Now bring me my food, I'm ravenous. And tell Hubert I want to see him."

Two Great Danes bounded into the drawing room, rushing up to him excitedly. He fell to his knees and embraced them both, allowing them to lick his face. "I've missed you, too!" he told them, gently pulling their ears and patting their backs. There had always been Great Danes at Les Lucioles. A house of that size needed big animals to fill it. He sat on the club fender, the fire warming his back, looking out through the French doors that led into the garden, now hidden beneath frost. He had hoped to return with Ava. To show her the gardens he had created for her. To live out the rest of their lives together. She had promised. He had promised, too. Promises sealed with love. He had kept his side of the bargain, but what of hers?

Françoise entered with his lunch on a tray. "Are you going to spend Christmas on your own?" she asked.

"I have no choice."

"What a shame. A handsome young man like you."

"Don't pity me, woman," he growled.

"If your mother were alive . . ."

"But she is not," he repeated. "If she were alive she would spend it with me. As it is, I am alone."

"Of all the men worthy of love it is you, *monsieur*. I have known you since you were a little boy. It causes me pain to see you live alone. Yes, it is all very well taking lovers, but I want more than that for you. I want a good, honest girl and a brood of healthy children."

"I'm past that now."

"Not if you marry a fertile young woman."

"Françoise, you are dreaming." He chuckled cynically. Hubert entered, cap in hand.

"*Bonjour, monsieur*. I am glad you have returned safely." He bowed formally.

"I am being cross-examined, Hubert. Françoise, bring Hubert a glass of brandy. Now tell me. How are the gardens?"

Françoise retreated into the hall. She was stiff in the joints and her back ached constantly. She should have retired years ago but she remained out of loyalty to Jean-Paul's late mother and to Jean-Paul, whom she loved as a son. She had seen him return from England twenty-six years before, a broken young man, determined to remain true to the woman he loved but could not have. Françoise had briefly known love and lost it so she had understood his pain. That kind of sorrow is healed over time; hers was now nothing more than a thin scar across her heart. But Jean-Paul had never healed. His heart was still open, raw and bleeding. Like a dog beside the dead body of his master, Jean-Paul let his love starve him slowly to death. His mother never experienced the joy of grandchildren. His father's dreams for him were never realized. Neither knew why. But Françoise knew all the secrets, for like a shadow, she lingered in every corner of the château, invisible but omnipresent. Only she had seen the paintings stacked against the wall, the letters written and never sent, and the flowers planted in the hope that one day he would bring her back and show her how he had dedicated his life to her with as much attentiveness as if she were beside him.

She clicked her tongue and lumbered across the stone slabs towards the kitchen wing and her cozy sitting room. Some things were better forgotten. Life was short. What was the point of pining for the unattainable? Hadn't she closed the chapter, put away the book and begun again? It wasn't easy but it was possible. She lowered herself carefully into an armchair and picked up her needlepoint. At least he was home, for that she was grateful.

Back at Hartington House Miranda missed Jean-Paul's presence. Her parents, with her father's sister, Constance, arrived in a silver Land Rover packed with presents and luggage. This was their first visit. Diana Stanley-Kline had much to comment on, wafting about from room to room in ivory slacks, matching cashmere sweater, suede shoes, and pearls the size of grapes. "Oh dear," she sniffed at her daughter's kitchen stools. "The distressed look might be very fashionable, but you wouldn't want to sit on one of these in your best tights." She raised her eyebrows at the large ornamental glass vases in the hall. "What odd things to have in a house with small children!" And when Miranda told her about the gardens, how they had once been the most beautiful in Dorset, she scrunched her nose and remarked: "Well, everything's relative." As usual nothing could please her mother. Miranda longed for it all to be over and for everyone to go home.

Constance had the annoying habit of interrupting. She'd ask a question but not listen to the answer, preferring to give her opinion instead, cutting one off midsentence. After a while Miranda gave up trying and sat back and listened with half an ear, making the right noises in the right places to suggest that she was paying attention. David liked her father, Robert. They sat smoking cigars, discussing politics. They shared the same opinions, both right wing and equally pompous.

The children played outside in their boots and coats, their laughter rising into the damp air. But

Gus seemed lost without Jean-Paul. He tried to get his father to play with them, but David was busy with their grandfather. The child lingered on the stone bridge, gazing forlornly at the cottage that was empty and cold. Storm returned inside to play Hama beads on the kitchen table while Mrs. Underwood cooked lunch. Gus was left alone to wander about in search of entertainment. Without Jean-Paul to keep him busy he reverted to what he knew best: tormenting small, defenseless creatures.

He found his target along the thyme walk. It was a large spider with black hairy legs and a round, juicy body. Having been prodded with a stick it was cowering under a leaf, but Gus could see it clearly. It waited, frozen with fear. But in spite of its experience of birds and snakes, the spider couldn't have imagined the nature of this predator.

Gus rolled onto his stomach where the paving stones were still damp from drizzle fallen in the night. It was no longer raining but the sky was darkened by clouds and the wind was edged with ice. Slowly, so as not to frighten the spider away, Gus moved his hand. The spider remained motionless, hoping perhaps that the predator might not see it if it didn't move. But Gus was an expert when it came to spiders. He wasn't afraid of them, like his sister and her friends. With a swiftness that came from years of practice, Gus thrust his fingers forward and grabbed the creature by one long, fragile leg. "Gotcha!" he whispered triumphantly. The spider tried in vain to escape. Gus pulled it out into the light and very slowly, while still holding one leg, plucked another off the body. He couldn't hear the spider wail or see the look of pain in its eyes. Perhaps it felt no pain at all. It didn't matter. One by one he pulled the legs off until all that remained was the soft round body which he left on the stone for a bird to eat. The legs lay like tiny twigs discarded by the wind.

His sense of satisfaction was short-lived. He thought of Jean-Paul and how he loved all God's creatures, and was suddenly gripped with shame. Hastily, he squashed the little body under his foot, hoping to wipe away the deed, pretend it had never happened. He ran off into the vegetable garden, closing the door behind him, and found a warm place in one of the greenhouses. To his surprise it was full of pots. Each pot was packed tightly with earth, lined up in neat rows. There were about fifty in all and Gus swept his eyes over them in awe. He knew instinctively that Jean-Paul had planted something special in each that would grow in the spring. He sensed them hibernating beneath the soil. *So this is garden magic*, he thought excitedly, wishing that Jean-Paul were there to explain it to him. He spotted a beetle lying on its back on the concrete floor, legs wiggling frantically as it tried to right itself. Gently, so as not to hurt it, Gus flipped it over with a leaf and watched it scurry beneath a terra-cotta pot. His spirits rose on account of his good deed.

Miranda showed her mother and Constance around the garden. She found it easier to handle her mother's barbed comments out there where Jean-Paul had sown his magic. She felt close to him, as if his presence warmed the air around her and filled her spirit with serenity. Constance rattled on enthusiastically, while Diana sniffed her contempt. "Goodness, do you really need such a large property? Terribly hard to maintain."

"We have two gardeners," Miranda replied grandly, smiling to herself as she thought of Jean-Paul.

"At your age I did everything myself. It's terribly extravagant to employ so many people . . ."

"What nonsense, Diana," interjected Constance. "You said so yourself, it's a hard property to maintain. I would imagine you'd need more than two. I hope they're good!"

"As you can see . . ."

"I certainly can, Miranda," Constance interrupted again. "There's not a weed to be seen anywhere. I do hope to see it in spring. It'll burst into glorious flower."

"Oh, spring will be lovely," Diana agreed. "But by summer, everything will grow out of control and then you'll realize you've taken on more than you can chew." Miranda was relieved when Mrs.

Underwood announced that lunch was ready and they returned inside.

"I must say, Miranda. You've done a splendid job, you really have," said Constance when Diana was out of earshot. "You really have to be a terrible old sourpuss to find fault with it. Think nothing of it, my dear. The problem does not lie with you, but with your mother and the very ugly green monster that's got under her skin." The older woman winked. Miranda smiled and followed her into the cloakroom to hang up her coat.

Diana took her place at the dining room table. "Funny to have used such pale colors on the walls," she said to her daughter. "It's very London. I think warm colors are better suited to the countryside."

"I don't think . . ." Miranda began, but Constance dived in there before she could finish.

"It's very pretty, Miranda. You've done the house beautifully, hasn't she, Robert?"

"Yes, indeed," her brother replied, having not considered the decoration for a moment. "Very tastefully done."

"Gus and Storm, come and sit next to your grandmother. I see you so rarely. Miranda never brings you to stay with me. She should share you both a little more. Poor Grandma!" Miranda rolled her eyes and watched the children do as they were told, though without enthusiasm. "So pleased you've got a cook, Miranda. It wouldn't be worth

293

us coming all this way if we had to stomach your efforts." She gave a little laugh as if it was meant in jest, but Miranda turned away, bruised. No wonder her sister had gone to live on the other side of the world.

Mrs. Underwood entered with a roast leg of lamb. The room was at once infused with the scent of rosemary and olive oil. Diana inhaled deeply but said nothing. Miranda wondered whether she'd have the nerve to criticize Mrs. Underwood. Now, *that* would be a skirmish she'd pay good money to see. She waited as her mother took her first bite while Mrs. Underwood went around the table with the dish of roast potatoes. Diana chewed in silence, her cheeks flushing with pleasure. Finally, she spoke.

"Very good," she said briskly, piling another load onto her fork.

"Of course it is," replied Mrs. Underwood, watching David help himself to four large potatoes. "It's organic Dorset lamb. You won't get better than this." Diana knew better than to argue.

On Christmas Eve Gus and Storm put their stockings out for Father Christmas and went to bed without any fuss. Gus declared that he was going to lie in wait for him, while Storm argued that if he did Father Christmas wouldn't come at all and neither of them would get any presents. Miranda tucked them up and returned to the drawing room to add a log or two to the fire and turn on the Christmas tree lights. She closed the curtains, put on a CD and sat a moment on the fender. She missed Jean-Paul. She missed his reassuring presence around the place. She wondered how he would advise she deal with her mother. He had answers for everything, like Old Father Time. Suddenly she had a longing to return to the scrapbook and for her parents and Constance to go home so that she could lie in peace on her bed and disappear into the secret life of Ava Lightly.

At that moment, David entered in a burgundy smoking jacket and matching velvet slippers. He saw his wife on the fender and smiled at her. "How are you, darling?"

"Surviving," she replied.

"Are the stockings ready for me? I'm rather looking forward to playing Santa!"

"I hope Gus doesn't stay awake for you. I'm afraid you'd be a big disappointment to him."

"He's been out all day. He's exhausted. I don't imagine he'll manage to keep his eyes open for more than five minutes."

"Mummy's being very awkward," she said, changing the subject.

"Only because you let her." He popped open a bottle of champagne.

"It's been like that all my life and I still don't know how to handle her."

"You're a grown woman. Just tell her to shut up."

"Easier said than done."

"Since when have you been such a wilting wall-flower?"

"David!"

"Well, darling. People treat you according to how you let them. All you have to do is say 'no.'"

She frowned at him. "I can see why Blythe raves about you."

"Does she?"

"Yes, she says you give good advice. Now I know she's right." He poured her a glass of champagne.

"Here's to you, darling," he said, kissing her cheek.

"What's that for?" she asked.

"Just to tell you how much I appreciate you. I've bought you a splendid present." Miranda smiled, thinking of Theo Fennell.

"Have you?" she asked coyly. "When are you going to give it to me?"

"I could give it to you now," he said, kissing her again. "You smell delicious. Why don't we sneak upstairs for ten minutes? I heard your mother running a bath, they're going to be a while."

"I haven't had a bath either."

"Good, I like you better before you go and cover yourself in oil. Come on!"

He took her hand and led her upstairs, both giggling like a couple of children afraid of being caught. Once in the bedroom he pushed her playfully onto the bed and settled himself beside her. He kissed her again. She forgot about the present as he pulled her shirt out of her jeans and ran his hand over her stomach. He undid her bra and cupped her breast, rubbing the nipple with his thumb. Then he buried his face in her neck, kissing the tender skin until she wriggled with pleasure. Aware that they could be disturbed at any moment they made love quickly. Miranda didn't think about Jean-Paul. It had been so long since David had looked at her in that way, his eyes sleepy with lust, his mouth curled with admiration, that she remained in the moment with him.

When it was over they lay together, bound by the intimacy of their lovemaking. "You were a feast, darling!" he exclaimed. "Now I'll give you your reward." He got up and wandered naked into his dressing room. Miranda covered herself with the sheet and prepared herself for her gift.

"I hope you haven't gone mad!" she said. It was impossible not to go mad in Theo Fennell.

"Don't you think you deserve it, darling? I leave you down here all week. This is to tell you how much I appreciate and love you." He returned holding a red box. Miranda knew immediately that it couldn't be from Theo Fennell, whose boxes were pink and black. She felt a wave of disappointment but made an effort to dissemble. "Happy Christmas, darling."

"Thank you." She hesitated a moment before opening it. "What have you gone and bought me?"

"Go on," he encouraged, smiling in anticipation. Inside the box was a diamond heart pendant. If she hadn't had the call from Theo Fennell she would have been thrilled with it. What woman could be unhappy with diamonds? But all she could think of was the piece of jewelry David had had engraved. If it wasn't for her, who was it for?

Spring

XXI

The happy sight of pussy willow.
The first glimpse of a daffodil
shooting through the soil.

Hartington House, 1980

The change of season brought on a change in me, a blossoming, like an unexpected flower bursting through snow. Outwardly, I continued as if nothing had been said, but inwardly I could not forget M.F.'s declaration of love. Suddenly, something I had never considered lingered at the forefront of my mind, like a carrot before a donkey who had always been content with grass. I should have sent him home and avoided the terrible anguish and pain that was to strike us both in the heart. But how could I have predicted what was to come when at the time I truly felt nothing but affection? As winter thawed I found myself thinking more and more about him. Moments when my mind was normally empty were filled with his laughter and that wide, infectious smile, so handsome my stomach flipped at the merest thought of it. The nights grew increasingly tormented, the days charged with electricity that continued to build between us like humidity in

301

summer before a storm. Perhaps if Phillip had been at home more, it might not have happened. But he was away so much. I was lonely. His absences allowed me and M.F. to grow close. And I, starved of company, allowed it to happen. I fought with the guilt.

My moods swung from joy to despair, when I would sit alone on the bench in our cottage garden and ponder the hopelessness of this forbidden love. Every time I indulged those impossible dreams the faces of my children rose up before me, cutting them down before they could take root. I loved M.F., but I loved my children more.

Phillip continued in his merry way, disappearing to France and Spain for weeks on end, even traveling as far as Argentina and Chile in search of new wine. He was oblivious of the growing kernel in my heart. At first I pretended I had not seen it, then I concealed it, but as it grew I was unable to ignore it, that feisty seed of love that M.F. had planted that day in the woods.

Ava was plagued with confusion. How could she love two men at the same time? Her love for Phillip had not diminished, not even an inch, and yet, she found herself growing more and more attached to Jean-Paul. She had presumed affairs happened when there was already discord in the marriage. Yet, there was no discord in her marriage. Not even boredom. There was no reason why she should be attracted to Jean-Paul when everything in her life was as it should be.

At first she tried to distance herself from him. She sent him to the far corners of the garden, but even though he wasn't physically present he was constantly on her mind. Then she dismissed her feelings as sisterly fondness. After all, they had worked closely together in the garden now for six months—it was natural that she should feel like his big sister. But as winter thawed and the snowdrops and daffodils began to raise their heads, she could deny it no longer. Her feelings were sexual and they weren't going away.

She had witnessed a transformation in Jean-Paul. He had arrived in autumn an arrogant, insouciant young man. Little by little the garden had changed him. She would not have imagined the part she had played in that change. That he had watched her with her plants and animals, with her children and her husband, and when she was alone with him. Ava had no knowledge of her own intrinsic magic. Whether it was Ava or the garden, Jean-Paul had undergone a definite change for the better. He had become more sensitive, more understanding. The root of that change, of course, was love. The more love he felt in his heart, the better a human being he became.

One day in March Jean-Paul suggested they

drive to the beach for the morning. "We can have lunch in a pub. I'd like to see a little more of Dorset." He put his hands out and shrugged. "It's drizzling. There is little we can do in drizzle." His grin of entreaty made it impossible for her to refuse.

"That's a good idea," she replied, trying to mask her anxiety. It was all very well being alone with him in her garden, but somehow the idea of spending the day together on the beach felt improper. "I'll tell Phillip. Perhaps he'd like to come." Jean-Paul's face fell at the suggestion. "He's probably too busy, but I know he'd appreciate being asked," she added hastily, making off towards the house.

Phillip sat in his study in a worn leather armchair, the dogs lying on the rug beside the fire, classical music resounding from the tape recorder in the cupboard. He was so deeply engrossed in a book that he did not hear his wife enter. "Darling," she said, drawing near. He raised his eyes, startled a moment, then smiled at the sight of her. "Sorry to interrupt."

"You never interrupt, Shrub," he replied, putting the book on his knee.

"Jean-Paul has suggested we go for a walk on the beach. It's a miserable day. We'd have lunch in the pub. He wants to see more of the countryside. Why don't you join us? It'll be fun."

"As much as the thought of strolling in drizzle

with my wife appeals to me, I will decline," he replied and Ava was horrified that she felt such relief. In an effort to assuage her guilt she managed to look suitably disappointed, planting a lingering kiss on his cheek. "You're very transparent, Shrub," he said with a chuckle.

"Transparent?" she repeated, blushing.

"Yes." He scrutinized her face. "You think you'll be bored with Jean-Paul on your own, don't you?"

"No."

"I know you, Shrub. I can read you like a book. You're my number one bestseller." He laughed. "I'm afraid you'll have to go alone. I'm sure you'll survive."

"You're a beast!" she exclaimed. "You leave him to me all the time. You owe me for this. You know that, don't you?"

"Whatever you want is yours," he replied.

"I'll hold you to that."

He pulled her down and kissed her on her forehead. "I hope you do," he said. With a bounce in her step she left the room, closing the door softly behind her.

Jean-Paul and Ava drove down the narrow winding lanes towards the coast. Ava felt unusually nervous, like a teenager on her first date. Jean-Paul looked relaxed, clearly enjoying her company and the sight of the newly budding countryside. The windscreen wipers swept the rain off the glass with the regularity of a ticking clock. Ava sensed more keenly than ever the swift passing of time. At the end of the summer he would return to France, having picked her up and dropped her like a tornado. They would both recover from their infatuation. She would reflect on what might have been, certain that as a married woman she had had no choice but to refuse him.

She parked the car in a lay-by and led him down a snake path to a secluded beach. "No one comes here," she told him. "It's stony. But I love the roughness of it and the sound of pebbles under my feet." It was drizzling steadily, but she was dry under the cowboy hat Toddy had bought her in Texas some years before, a poncho she had acquired in Chile as a teenager, jeans and gumboots. Her hair was stuffed into the hat, escaping in a few curly tendrils down her neck. She had never considered herself good-looking, but the way Jean-Paul looked at her told her she was the most beautiful woman in the world.

On the beach, Jean-Paul walked beside her. He wasn't towering like Phillip, but next to Ava, who was a little over five feet six, he walked tall. The sea was benign, sliding smoothly up the stones, polishing them with surf before withdrawing in a flirtatious dance. The wind tasted of salt, blustering one moment, dropping the next, reflecting the awkward exchange between Ava and Jean-Paul. He wanted so much to hold her in his arms, to release the words locked inside his heart and tell her how deeply he loved her. He thrust his hands into his pockets and walked, commenting inanely on the flight of a seagull or the remains of a crab washed up on the beach, anything that came to mind to prevent him from spilling his soul. She in turn burned with the desire to be held by him, if only for a moment, a forbidden second on which she could feed during those interminable nights when she longed for him. She was reminded of the tragedy of sunset and without warning, she began to cry.

Jean-Paul stopped and held her shoulders, anxiously searching her face. "I'm sorry," she whispered.

"For what?" he asked and his voice was so soft that it made her cry all the more.

She shook her head. "It's no use, Jean-Paul."

"I don't understand."

"It's like a sunset. Something so beautiful I want to hold on to it. But then it's gone."

"Ava . . ."

"Or a rainbow," she sobbed. "Loved from a distance, but impossible . . ."

He didn't wait for her to finish, but pulled her into his arms and kissed her ardently. She didn't have the strength to resist. She let him hold her and closed her eyes, relinquishing control. His kiss was urgent yet gentle and she wound her arms around his neck, letting him take her, willing the moment to last. But like all beautiful things the end was but a breath away and the anticipation of it made the kiss even sweeter. The high was followed by a terrible low, like falling off the arc of a magnificent rainbow into gray clouds. She thought of her children and Phillip and was flooded with guilt. She pulled away.

"I can't," she gasped, touching her lips still warm from his kiss. He stared at her in mortification, as if she had just pulled the earth away from under his feet. "Don't look at me like that. I can't bear it." She placed her fingers on his cheek, cold from the wind and wet from the drizzle. "We shouldn't have come. In the garden everything is as it should be. We each have our place. Out here, there are no boundaries to keep us apart."

"But we can't go back now," he said. "We have come too far for that."

"Then what can we do?"

"I don't know, Ava. All I know is what is in my heart. The more time I spend with you the more of my heart you take." She rested her head against his chest and gazed out over the sea. It was misty on the horizon. She listened to the sound of the waves and the plaintive cry of a gull and felt her spirit flood with sadness.

"It is not meant to be, Jean-Paul," she said at last. "I can't betray Phillip. I love him, too. And the children . . ." Her voice cracked for he suddenly grew tense with anguish. "There is nothing in the world that would make me leave them."

"Then I will go back to France."

"No!" she exclaimed fiercely, pulling away.

"I have no choice, Ava."

"But I want to share spring with you, and summer. I want to enjoy the gardens with you. No one understands them like you do." She swallowed hard and gazed at him, debilitated by his stricken face. "No one understands me like you do."

"No one loves you like I do," he retorted, holding her arms so tightly she winced. "But you are right," he said, letting go. "I cannot live without you, so I have only one choice—and hope."

"Hope?"

"Hope that the rain will last and the sun will break through and there will shine the most exquisite rainbow."

They tried to continue as if the kiss had never happened, but although they spoke of other things, the memory of it remained. Jean-Paul had been given a taste of paradise and was left wanting more, while Ava had been singed by her rashness and was relieved she had put a stop to it before it went too far.

Neither felt like eating. They drove home in silence. The mist had drifted inland. Ava turned on the fog lights, but it was hard to tell where she was. She drove slowly, anxious to return to Phillip and normality. Jean-Paul put on the radio. Mama Cass's voice sang out rich and low. At last they turned into the drive. It seemed as if they were waking from a dream; neither said a word. *We can't have everything we want in life*, Ava thought to herself. *I must appreciate what I do have and not jeopardize it for my children's sake. For Phillip's sake.* Jean-Paul had nothing to lose. He had arrived with nothing, he would leave with nothing, but his heart would be forever altered.

Jean-Paul returned to his cottage, where he lit a fire and began to express his sorrow with violent strokes of paint on canvas. Ava returned to her husband. She crept up to where he was standing in front of his bookcase, running his long fingers over the spines, and wrapped her arms around his waist.

"So you're back," he said jovially.

"Have you eaten?" she asked.

"I found some crumbs in the fridge," he replied.

"I bet they were delicious crumbs."

"They were made by an expert." He turned around. "You've caught the wind," he remarked, noticing her red eyes and cheeks.

"It was blowing a gale down there."

"So I see." She sank into his arms. "Are you all right, Shrub?"

"I'm fine. Just a bit of a headache."

"Do you want me to pick up the children?"

"Would you?"

"Of course. Why don't you have a lie-down?"

"I will."

"Did you have fun?"

"It was okay. He's sweet," she replied, burying her face in his sweater. She shut her eyes. How close she had come to putting in danger the things she cherished the most. Phillip held her close. "That feels good," she murmured. But Phillip couldn't know just how good it felt.

XXII

Snowdrops peeping through frost.
The first signs of spring.

Ava awoke early. She hadn't slept well since that kiss on the beach. Her heart beat wildly, a confusing mixture of excitement and fear that sent the blood pumping through her veins. She lay listening to the cheerful clamor of birds in the trees and thought of the garden stirring to life with the warmer weather and longer days. The dawn light spilled into the room, flooding a slice of carpet with enthusiasm and yet, for Ava, it filled her with dread. The light signaled another day's struggle with Jean-Paul and her own, uncontrollable desires. They worked in each other's company like a couple of magnets fighting the force that pulled them together. They talked about anything but their true feelings; both suffered the same frustration inside, and the same struggle to dissemble.

Phillip lay on his back, his hand by his ear in

carefree abandon. Ava turned on her side and watched the rise and fall of his chest as he breathed with the slow regularity of a man contented with his lot. He had done nothing to deserve her betrayal. They enjoyed a solid marriage in spite of his long and frequent trips abroad. He left her in no doubt that he loved her greatly. She, in turn, held him in the highest esteem; she respected his opinion about everything and admired his intellectual brilliance. She relished his lack of arrogance, his reliability, his strong moral code, his deep wisdom. So, why did she risk it all by loving a man she couldn't have? Was it worth losing everything for a moment's ride on a rainbow?

She thought of her children. Those three trusting people whose lives depended on the solidity of the foundations she built for them with Phillip. If she were to shake those foundations, what future did they have? But even while she held their futures in her hands like fragile feathers she was still distracted by the irresistible draw of Jean-Paul. There was only one thing to do.

She didn't wait for Phillip to wake up but maneuvered herself on top of him, nuzzling her face in his neck. He stirred as he felt her warm body on his and wrapped his arms around her dreamily. "I want another baby," she whispered into his ear. Phillip awoke with a jolt.

"What?" he mumbled, struggling to consciousness.

"I want another baby," she repeated.

"Shrub, darling. Another baby? Right now?"

She held him tightly, frightened of losing him. "Yes."

"I think we should think this through sensibly."

"I've thought it through. I can think of nothing else." *Nothing else to tie me to home so I don't run away . . . I can't trust myself anymore.*

"I don't think I could give you a baby right now even if I wanted to," he said, pushing her gently off him. "That's not the sexiest way to wake a man."

"I'm sorry," she said, rolling onto her back and throwing an arm over her face. "You know how I am. If I have an idea I have to act upon it immediately."

"Usually one of your most endearing qualities," he said drily, stumbling into the bathroom.

"I'm getting on for forty. If I don't have another now I'll miss my chance."

"Aren't three enough?" Her reply was drowned by the sound of water gushing out of the tap as Phillip brushed his teeth and splashed his face with cold water.

"Then let's go away for a few days," she suggested when he emerged. "Just the two of us."

He looked at her and frowned. "Are you all right, Shrub?"

"Yes, of course."

"I didn't think wild horses could drag you from your children and gardens."

"It's been so long. I never see you. You're in your study working, or abroad. I need to see more of you." There was an edge to her voice he hadn't heard before. He sat on the bed beside her.

"If that's what you want. I'm sorry, darling. I had no idea."

"I want to spend some time with you without the children. I want you to look on me as a woman and not just a mother."

"You're all woman to me, Shrub." He tried to smile, but her sudden, uncharacteristic outburst worried him.

"Marriage has to be worked at. If there are chinks, things can get in. There can't be any chinks. Do you see?"

"I'm trying very hard to see. It's a little early in the morning to see much."

"Let's go abroad. Somewhere warm. We can lie in the sun and read. Walk hand in hand on a beach somewhere. Do you remember before Archie was born?"

"Tuscany. Of course I remember. We were young and in love." He laughed.

"We made love all afternoon after big glasses of rosé and big plates of pasta. It was warm and balmy. I remember the smell of eucalyptus that scented the air. At night we wandered the streets of Siena and Florence without a care in the world. Let's do it again." Her eyes blazed with enthusiasm and Phillip's anxiety ebbed away.

"I remember you in that black and white polka-dot sundress. You were the most lovely creature I had ever seen." He kissed her forehead. "You still are, you know."

"We can make a baby in Tuscany. A celebration of our marriage and our love. Oh Phillip, it'll be so romantic."

"I'm not sure sleepless nights and nappies are very romantic. Think about it, Shrub. You're talking about another human being. Another member of our family. A child too small to play with his siblings. I'm old, don't forget. And I'm not going to get any younger. If you really yearn for another child I won't deny you. But I want you to think about it very carefully and to consider the sacrifices. Are you ready for them?"

With those thoughts she prepared to face Jean-Paul. Having suffered guilt that morning in the arms of her husband, she now suffered it all over again as she stepped into the garden in search of Jean-Paul. She was considering bringing another child into the world solely to prevent herself from yielding to him. Suddenly that felt like a betrayal, too. *I should send you away*, she thought unhappily, *but I couldn't bear never to see you again.*

She wandered into the wildflower garden and stood in the sea of daffodils. The sky was clear and fresh, the air sweet with the earthy scent of fertility. All around her the gardens were stirring with life, the trees vibrating with hundreds of

315

nesting birds jostling each other for position. Instead of uplifting her, they made her sad. A vital part of her would never flower but remain stunted, like a bud killed off by frost. She would always wonder what life would have been like beside Jean-Paul. In her heart she knew she would die not knowing, for the sake of Phillip and their children. *My life does not belong only to me,* she concluded. *I'm bound to my family by love and nothing will ever change that. I have chosen my life and the lives of four others depend on me. I must be content with his friendship. Friendship is better than nothing.*

She lifted her eyes to see Jean-Paul striding purposefully up the meadow towards her just as Phillip's car disappeared down the drive. The sleeves of his blue shirt were rolled up, his forearms brown and strong, his shoulders wide, even his gait had changed in the months he had been at Hartington. He was no longer a precious city boy used to long lunches on the rue Saint Germain but a man of the land, who loved it as she did. Her spirits rose and her resolve weakened. As he approached he seemed to transform the gardens around him into something magical. The sight of those daffodils and the almost phosphorescent green of the newly emerging leaves on the trees caused her intense happiness.

His face was drawn. Before she could speak he took her hand and pulled her behind the hollow tree, wound his fingers through her hair and kissed her on the mouth. Finally, he pulled away.

"I can't go on like this," he said at last. "Every day I love you more. Don't you see how you torment me? What began as a pleasure simply to be with you is now a curse. I am permitted to look but not touch and that, my beautiful Ava, is slowly killing me. So, I have decided to go back to France."

His words winded her as violently as if he had struck her. "You're leaving?" she gasped.

"Don't look so sad. You'll make it harder for me."

"I don't want you to leave."

"Then be with me!" he argued roughly, taking her by the shoulders. "Be with me!"

"I can't," she replied hoarsely. "I want to, but I can't."

"Then what is there for me here?"

"I don't know. At least we're together."

"But at what price?"

"I can't live without you, Jean-Paul. Please don't make me live without you."

"I can't live with you if I'm not able to hold you," he replied gruffly. "I'm a man, Ava. *Un homme qui t'aime.*"

"Et je suis une femme qui t'aime."

He stared at her in astonishment. "You speak French? My God, I thought I knew everything about you." He traced a finger down her cheek and across her chin as if willing himself to remember every contour.

"Will I never see you again?"

He wiped the tears with his thumbs. "I don't know."

"Jean-Paul, you can't leave me like this. Just when the garden is bursting into flower. All that we've created together . . ."

"Will remind you of me." He laughed cynically. "Maybe it will convince you to come and join me." He drew her close. She heard the frantic beating of his heart and inhaled the spicy scent of him she hoped she'd never forget. She closed her eyes but the tears escaped, soaking his shirt.

"What will I say to Phillip?" she asked.

"Tell him I have had enough."

"I don't want him to think badly of you."

"Then tell him I had to leave on account of a woman. It is always easier to add a little truth to a lie."

"Oh, Jean-Paul, please stay, I beg you." But she knew it was useless. "What will your father say?"

"I don't care."

"But your inheritance?"

"I'll transform his gardens at the château and show him what I am capable of."

"But we've only just begun. There is so much more to learn."

"Then I will have to teach myself."

"You won't see your cottage garden in full bloom."

"I don't care about the cottage garden. I care

only about you. I will never see you in full bloom and for that I am heartbroken." He lowered his head and kissed her again.

This time she shut her eyes and parted her lips and let him kiss her deeply. She didn't think about her children or Phillip. Jean-Paul was walking out of her life forever and while he kissed her, nothing in the world could distract her from him.

Ava ran to the house and threw herself on her bed where she cried like a child. She focused on that final kiss under the tree and tried to hold him there where she could still feel him. It seemed unreal that she would never see him again. He had become so much a part of Hartington that the place would feel empty without him. She thought of the cottage garden exploding into flower and cried all the more. It was *his* dream. His creation for her. It was wrong that she should enjoy it alone.

What would she tell the children? They loved Jean-Paul, too. He was part of the family. She was more determined than ever to have a baby, to hold her here and concentrate her mind. A child to stand between her and the door to remind her where her place was. Archie, Angus and Poppy were at school all day. How was she to fill the hours except in the gardens they had tended together? Every plant would remind her of him. What if her longing grew too much? What if it corroded her reasoning and her judgment? What if it drove her crazy like Daisy Hopeton and she was unable to stop herself? A new baby would stop her more surely than anything.

She didn't know how she was going to tell her family that Jean-Paul had gone. She decided to tell them that he had gone home to see his mother. That way, if he changed his mind, he could always come back. How she hoped that he would change his mind. She told the children at teatime, hiding her face in the tomato and basil sauce she was cooking for their spaghetti. They gave it a moment of their attention before returning to more important things like building a camp under the refectory table in the hall. Ava stared into the saucepan, holding back her tears. They would never know the sacrifice she had made for them.

Ava had made a cheese soufflé and roasted a pheasant in order to take her mind off Jean-Paul's departure. The children had played in the hall with the dogs, diving in and out of their camp, pulling the books off the table in their exuberance. Ava cooked to the sound of the radio, but the country songs she liked just made her cry, so she tuned into Radio Four and listened to a short story instead. When Phillip returned for dinner, the children were in bed. Ava handed him a glass of red wine warmed by the Aga and kissed him. Seeing his smiling face in the doorway confirmed that her sacrifice had been worth it. What sort of woman would she be if she left him and the children and ran off to France?

However, the fact that she had made the right decision didn't make it any easier to bear. She tried to pick the right moment to tell her husband: it was vital that she showed no emotion. Tears, blushing, wobbling lower lip and chin would only give her away. She had never been very good at acting. In her school days she had always been given the least responsible parts, like janitor, cook or "member of crowd scene." Now she was required to give an award-winning performance, but she was insufficiently talented to pull it off. So instead of telling him at the table she decided to toss the news to him while she was bent over the dishwasher, stacking the soufflé plates.

"Darling, Jean-Paul has gone home for a break, to see his mother." She closed her eyes at the mention of his name and squeezed back tears. Her throat constricted and her face reddened. She stood up and faced the window where her miserable reflection stared back at her from the glass.

"Good" was his reply. "You know, I've been thinking about your holiday idea."

"Oh?"

"Yes, I think we both deserve a break. Do you think your mother could come and look after the children?"

"Well, I was thinking perhaps Toddy would take them."

"No, she's got too much on her own plate to take on our three." Finally, it was safe to turn around.

She took the pheasant out of the oven and lifted the lids off the vegetables.

"I'm sure Mummy would love it, and the children adore Heinz," she replied, relieved as she felt the shame drain from her face. "We could ask Mrs. Marley to cook, that way she won't have to worry about food. I'll get Toddy to keep an eye. Maybe she could take the boys off Mummy's hands a little and have them for a couple of afternoons."

"Splendid."

"When were you thinking of going?" They served themselves and sat down.

"The end of May. The children will be at school all day so Verity won't have to do much more than get them up in the mornings and pick them up after school and put them to bed. I think a week would do."

Ava pulled a face. She didn't like to leave the children. "You don't think that's too long?"

"Seven days? No, you need a proper rest."

"Make it five, darling. I'll get twitchy after that and they'll miss us. Why not leave on a Monday and return on a Friday, that way we're back for the weekend."

"It's up to you."

"Yes, that's better. Five days. Where shall we go?"

"Leave it to me. Tuscany perhaps, or somewhere in Spain. I'll think about it."

"Thank you," she said, sighing heavily.

"Are you all right, Shrub? You don't look happy." He took her hand across the table and studied her face. "You don't look happy at all."

"Oh, I'm fine," she said brightly.

"You're still thinking about having another baby, aren't you?"

"It's on my mind, yes."

"It's worrying you."

"It's a big decision."

"Very big. You've got plenty of time to decide. Don't let it make you miserable. If you really want another child, Shrub, I'll do my best to comply. You know I can't deny you anything. It should give you joy, not make you sad."

"I know. I'm just not sure I'm doing it for the right reasons."

"We have three beautiful children who give us tremendous pleasure."

"I know."

"Think about it on holiday. The sunshine and rest will do you the power of good and put life into perspective. Now, give me a smile, darling. You've made a feast. I raise my glass to you. You're a wonderful woman, Ava." He brought her hand to his lips and kissed it. "And you're *my* Shrub." Ava was stunned. That was a gesture unique to Jean-Paul. Phillip had never kissed her hand before. She felt her cheeks burn and the overwhelming desire to cry. "Darling, you look like you're about to burst into tears."

"You're so good to me," she said, unable to hold back anymore. Phillip chuckled, assuming her tears were inspired by his loving reassurance.

"You deserve nothing less." She wiped her eyes with the back of her hand. "When I married you, you were a girl. You've grown into a woman I am so proud of. You're beautiful, intelligent, interested in everything, but, above all, unique. There's not a person in the world who resembles you in any way. I'm the luckiest man in the world to have found you."

"You're making me cry," she said, grateful for the excuse.

"Cry all you like, Shrub, darling," he said gently and kissed her hand again.

XXIII

First bees and insects on the flowers of the ivy on top of the wall. Lavender crocuses appearing in the grass.

Ava expected Jean-Paul to come back. The place was so empty without him it seemed inconceivable that he would not return to fill it. He belonged there now as much as the dovecote and the hollow tree, and his absence upset the harmony of the garden. Like a homing pigeon she made her way to the cottage, hoping that she would see the lights on and smell the smoke wafting out of the chimney; but it was cold and empty and unwelcoming. She stood on the stone bridge and leaned over, gazing at the hypnotic flow of water below. The breeze was warm and sugar scented, caressing her skin like soft fingers. The bushes and trees rang out with the song of birds. Above them all sang the skylark, its voice brave and clear and unwavering. Little violets opened their purple faces in the sun and white periwinkle trailed its wreaths along the riverbank.

She wandered through the gardens in a daze, allowing her melancholy to possess her like a malady. She lingered amidst the sweet smells of daphne odora and viburnum, drawing them in through her nostrils, anticipating the ecstatic soaring of her spirits, but nothing came. Her sorrow was heavy like stone.

Finally, she climbed into the car and drove to Toddy's, a rambling old farmhouse nestled in the valley five miles up the road. She turned into the drive, not noticing the pink cherry blossom fluttering in the sunshine like clusters of little butterflies. She parked her car outside the house and walked around to the back where Toddy was busy in the stables with her horses. When she saw Ava she waved heartily. Ava returned her wave with a forced smile.

"What a pleasant surprise first thing in the morning!" Toddy exclaimed, emerging from one of the stables in riding boots and jodhpurs that clung to her legs like a second skin. "Are you all right? You look frightfully pale."

"I'm fine, just a bit down," Ava conceded. There was no point pretending.

"Anything specific?"

Ava shrugged and took a deep breath. "I'm just tired," she replied, thrusting her hands into the pockets of the long stripy coat she wore over jeans. "Phillip's gone off to London. I barely see him these days. He's so engrossed in his book."

"Men! At least he's got an interesting job, unlike Ben who can't even mention his business without my eyelids drooping. Of all the men in the world, I have to marry an accountant!"

"Keeps you on the straight and narrow!"

"I've learned to be devious over the years, trust me. Come inside. I could do with another cup of coffee. You look like you could do with something stronger."

Lying on a beanbag in the middle of the kitchen table was Mr. Frisby. "He's been unwell," Toddy informed her, running a hand over the sleeping animal's back. "Nothing serious, just a cold. Must have caught it from the twins. Earl Grey or bog-standard builders' tea?"

"Earl Grey," Ava replied, sinking into the arm-chair. The kitchen smelled of coffee and toasted currant buns. Toddy clattered about taking cups from the cupboard and fishing two spoons out of the dishwasher she hadn't bothered to unload.

"How's the devilishly handsome Jean-Paul?" she asked, reaching to the back of the cupboard for the box of Earl Grey. Ava hadn't anticipated the mention of his name and blanched.

"Gone to visit his mother," she replied.

"Shame," said Toddy with a chuckle. "The girls will be disappointed."

"The girls?"

"Samantha and Lizzie. Sadly, no great romance to report there. I don't think they're his type. He probably finds English girls very unsexy."

"Probably."

"Still, he's hung in, hasn't he? I thought he'd be bored stiff here in Hartington. Do tell him to come out riding again when he comes back. I think he really enjoyed himself."

"Oh, he did," said Ava hoarsely, barely daring to speak in case the tremor in her voice gave her away.

"To think you thought he'd last a week." Toddy poured boiling water into one of the cups. "Do you remember Daisy Hopeton?"

"Of course. Mother never stops talking about her." Ava was relieved to change the subject.

"Well, she's back."

"Back?"

"Yes. Staying with her mother. You should give her a call. Wasn't she once a good friend of yours?"

"Yes, she was."

"Well, she's come for her children. She wants to take them out to South Africa. It's all rather messy."

"How terrible. Poor Michael."

"To lose your wife and then your children. He might be a dullard but he's a good father." She handed Ava the cup of tea. "Sure you don't want me to add a little brandy?" Ava shook her head. Brandy couldn't cure the pain in her heart.

"I'm rather relieved, actually," said Ava, thinking of herself. "I don't think I could understand a woman who leaves her four children. However in love she is, surely the greater part of her heart resides with them."

"Love can be a terrible thing. It clouds one's judgment. In the throes of passion it's probably quite easy to forget one's children." *No it isn't*, Ava thought to herself. Even Jean-Paul's kisses couldn't distract her from her love for Archie, Angus and Poppy. But she kept her thoughts to herself. "I don't blame her running off with a dashing South African though. Michael's a real old fart. Nice but very boring. You can tell just from his face that he's never had a really good laugh."

"She chose him," said Ava.

"She made a mistake."

"But it was her choice. She should live with it."

Toddy looked at her friend in bewilderment. "You don't really believe that, do you?"

"I do," she said emphatically. "She shouldn't

break up a family and five people's lives for her own happiness. It's selfish. Compromises have to be made. For the sake of her children she should have stayed."

"You sound like your mother."

"Do I?"

"Yes. It's not like you to be so judgmental. Surely, if the poor girl's miserable it's better for all of them if she leaves."

"She should make the best of it. Those children depend on her."

"They'll get over it."

"That's where you're wrong. They'll never get over it. It's no coincidence that the first question every therapist asks is 'tell me about your child-hood?' The foundation blocks are deeply impor-tant. Crack those and you jeopardize their entire future."

"You've been spending too much time with Verity."

"I don't always agree with my mother, but in this case, I think I do." She looked up at Toddy and nar-rowed her eyes. "Could you leave your children for a man?"

"He'd have to be one hell of a man."

"I'm serious."

"I don't know. I don't think one can speculate. If I find myself in danger of doing a Daisy, I'll call you and we can discuss it. Perhaps you'll be a little kinder to me."

"I wouldn't. I'd be thinking of the twins. Personally, I couldn't. I can tell you that now. I really couldn't, not even for one hell of a man." She lowered her eyes and stared into her tea. "I couldn't bear to hurt Phillip either. He's so good to me."

"You're really not yourself today, Ava," said Toddy, drawing her chair closer. "Is there something you want to tell me?"

"No," she replied hastily, shaking her head. "I'm feeling weepy for no reason. It's the prettiest time of year and I feel low. Silly really. Not like me at all."

"Hormonal," said Toddy knowingly.

"Yes, that must be it."

"The monthly blues."

"Poor Daisy Hopeton and those dear children. It breaks my heart. She will never be happy. How can she be, out of the mess she has made? I wouldn't want that on my conscience."

"Let's go for a ride," said Toddy, draining her coffee cup. "It'll do us both good. The wind in your hair, the smell of spring in the air, galloping over the hills. Come on!"

Ava borrowed a pair of boots and a hat and took to the hills with Toddy. Her friend was right, up there she could see for miles and the leaden feeling in her heart slowly grew lighter. As much as she pitied Daisy Hopeton and disapproved of her actions, she couldn't help but feel jealous that she had done what Ava herself would never have the courage to do. Daisy would return to her lover in South Africa and no doubt she'd bring the children with her. Daisy would have her cake and eat it in great big mouthfuls. Ava would never know how such a cake tasted.

The following weekend it snowed. The cold almost silenced the birds. Ava threw bread onto the lawn and broke the ice on the birdbath. The starlings and cock chaffinches looked so pretty in their new spring coats, flying down to eat the crumbs. By midmorning the sun had melted most of the snow away, except under the bushes and in the shadows of the trees where it still remained cold. The dogs rolled about in it and the children tried to make a snowman, but by lunchtime he was a sorry heap of sticks and slush. As the days progressed the weather grew warmer again. The garden burst into blossom, the bees awoke from their winter sleep, and Ava called Daisy Hopeton.

To Ava's surprise, Daisy sounded thrilled to hear from her and promptly asked her over for coffee. She seemed upbeat, not at all chastened by her appalling behavior. Ava wondered how she managed to look herself in the mirror after having hurt so many people. A hair shirt would be more appropriate. It wasn't fair that she was happy after having made her husband and children so *un*happy—holding the prize of a future with her lover that Ava denied herself.

Daisy's mother, Romie, lived the other side of Blandford, about half an hour away, in a pretty white house adorned with pink montana.

Ava followed Romie into the tiled hall. The ceilings were low and beamed, the walls white, the rooms small and cozy. Ava remembered the times she had stayed there as a teenager for dances and dinner parties. Before she could dwell on the memory of a certain pink satin dress, Daisy was striding out of the kitchen to greet her. "I can't tell you how nice it is to see you, Ava! Most of my friends have disowned me." The two women kissed. Daisy smelled of Yves Saint Laurent's Paris. "Come and have some coffee. I've opened a packet of biscuits."

"You're just in time," added Romie from the butcher's table. "She's off to South Africa on Friday."

"For good?" Ava asked.

"Forever," said Daisy, pouring coffee into the cups.

"Oh, Daisy. You must have gone through hell."

"It's been terribly hard. But I've done enough weeping and wailing. One has to look on the bright side or one would go mad."

"How did it happen?"

Daisy smiled resignedly and shook her head. "I'm amazed you came to see me, Ava. I know your mother disapproves very strongly."

"Duty and all that," said Ava, embarrassed that word had got back. "She's a different generation."

"Listen, she's not a lone voice, I assure you. What I did was unforgivable. I fell in love with another man. But I was so unhappy, Ava. I was a shadow of myself. Wasting my life with a man I no longer loved, loving a man I couldn't have. My love consumed me. I was a terrible mother and a terrible wife, no good to anyone." She swept her curly brown hair off her face and Ava glimpsed a hint of weariness in her eyes. "Michael and I weren't like you and Phillip. If we had enjoyed a contented marriage it would never have happened. Unhappiness is the perfect breeding ground for infidelity." *Loneliness is, too*, Ava wanted to add, but kept her thoughts to herself.

"How did you meet him?"

"We were in Cape Town for a wedding. It was love at first sight. I thought long and hard, Ava, but in the end I felt it would be better for the children to grow up in a house of joy rather than a house of sorrow." She nibbled a biscuit reflectively. "You see, Ava, we never had the beautiful estate that you have. My children are going from an ordinary little suburban house to a stunning country house in the middle of mountains. It's an idyll. They'll love it. South Africa is beautiful."

"But what about Michael?"

She lowered her eyes. "Don't," she groaned. "He'll see them in the holidays. They'll get the best of both worlds." But she clearly knew that wasn't true. Nothing could replace their father. She suddenly looked old and deflated. It was the first time that Ava had seen the true face she hid behind her smile.

"You're doing your best," said Ava gently. "You can't replace the eggs once the shells are broken. But you're making the best omelette you can."

Daisy laughed. "Trust you to come up with something like that. I *am* doing my best. God, I've had every accusation thrown at me. From callously leaving my children to suing Michael for hundreds of thousands. First, I never left my children. I was always going to come back for them. Michael knew that. Second, poor old Michael doesn't have any money, so I can hardly fleece him of what he doesn't have."

"So, what's this South African like?"

Ava and Daisy took their coffee cups and strolled around the garden. It was a beautiful morning, clear and bright, the freshly emerging leaves still glittering with dew. "How has your mother taken it all?"

"She puts on a good show, but she's ashamed, of course. But what can she do? She's my mother, she has to support me. I'm running off to South Africa, she has to stick around and answer to all her friends. You wouldn't believe the people who have turned their backs on us. The least expected." She shrugged. "At least I now know who my friends are." She turned to Ava. "I can count on you, can't I?"

Ava smiled. "You can," she said firmly. "I understand. Love is never simple. It can turn the sanest mind mad with longing. It distorts everything. Once the dust settles, you'll be happy out there with your Rupert. You've got courage. I don't think I'd ever be as brave as you. I suppose one has to weigh it all up—do I live for me, or for others?"

"And you never know how you're going to act until it happens to you."

Ava drove away envying Daisy. She had got what she wanted, but at what cost to Michael? Ava loved Phillip too much ever to hurt him like that.

Just when Ava was beginning to tolerate life without Jean-Paul, Phillip announced he'd had a telephone call from Jean-Paul's father, Henri. Ava was in the vegetable garden planting seeds with Hector. When she heard the news she stood up, trowel in hand, her face and hands grubby with mud. "You've heard from Henri?" she repeated, anxious to hear more. "What did he say?" *Is Jean-Paul coming back?*

A smile played around Phillip's mouth, for he knew the news would please his wife. "He's asked us to stay at the beginning of May."

"To stay?" she repeated, incredulous.

"Yes. I thought you'd be pleased. We could take our holiday there. You'll love Henri, he's a real character and Antoinette, his wife, is a keen gardener like you."

"What about Jean-Paul?"

"What about him?"

"When is he coming back?"

"I don't know. Didn't he tell you how long he was going to be away?"

"No," she replied quickly, wiping her forehead with the back of her hand. "So he'll be there?"

"I'm sure he will. I told him we're very pleased with Jean-Paul's work. That he's learning a great deal. I told him he's indispensable to us now— thought a little exaggeration wouldn't hurt."

"Didn't he think it odd that he had gone home?"

"Clearly not. Why is it odd?"

"He's been away three weeks."

"You're not missing him, are you, Shrub—the woman who said she wouldn't last more than a week with him?"

She turned away, pretending to be keeping an eye on Hector. "Well, we could do with his help. There's an awful lot to do around here."

"So, what should I tell Henri?"

Ava lost her focus among the greenhouses, aware that she was standing at a crossroads and that her fate and perhaps the fate of her whole family depended on the choice she made now. She thought of Daisy Hopeton. How she had disapproved. But was *she* any better? Then something pulled at her. An invisible cord attached to her heart, pulling her across an unseen threshold. "Tell him yes," she said slowly, knowing that she should have taken the other path. "Tell him we'd love to."

"Good. I knew you'd be pleased. Don't I always come up with the goods?" He chuckled and wandered through the gate in the wall back to the house. Ava felt the familiar tingle of excitement and the rising of her spirits out of the smog that had been her unhappiness. Suddenly she was able to see the sunshine and feel its warm rays on her face. She looked around at the budding trees and bushes and breathed in the fertile scents of flowering shrubs and new grass, allowing spring to uplift her as it always did.

She knelt down and continued to plant the marrow seeds for Poppy. Inside, her stomach was filled with bubbles. Then she felt the guilt, pricking each bubble one by one, spoiling her joy. She told herself that her desire to see Jean-Paul again was innocent. That all she wanted to do was to be in his company and convince him to return with them to Hartington. They would be dear friends. That was all.

That night Phillip made love to her. She was so overwhelmed with happiness that she received him enthusiastically, pulling him into her arms, kissing him passionately, savoring his attention, telling him how much she loved him. Masking the secret feelings she had for Jean-Paul.

"You're back, Shrub," he said afterward, scrunching her tousled hair in his hand. "You haven't been yourself."

"I'm sorry."

"Don't apologize, darling. I don't like to see you unhappy, that's all."

"You're very sweet to put up with the potato face."

"It wasn't a potato face, Shrub. More like a weeping willow. I want you to be a sunflower all year round."

"So do I."

He paused a moment. She began to plan what she would pack. "You're not unhappy with Jean-Paul, are you?"

"What do you mean?"

"I know you and he haven't exactly gelled. Is it going to ruin your holiday if he's there?"

"No. Not at all."

"He might have returned by then anyway."

"Exactly. But I don't mind. I like him. I really do. He's pleasant to have around and he's changed a lot since he arrived. It would be nice if he were there. He can show us around the château gardens himself."

"Good. I want you to have a good rest, Shrub. We don't have to hang around with them all day. We can venture off on our own and explore. I know you want us to spend time together."

"That's okay. I'm sure they're charming."

"Yes, but I promised you we'd have time alone. You know I always keep my promises."

This time she wouldn't mind if he didn't.

XXIV

Raindrops on bluebells.
The eccentric sound of a cuckoo.
The uplifting sight of flirtatious
mallards in flight.

They were met at Bordeaux airport by Henri's driver. He held up a sign saying PHILLIP LIGHTLY, WELCOME! He spoke no English and Ava was thrilled to speak French to him. Phillip listened with pride as she chatted easily. He had never seen her look more beautiful. Her hair was loose and falling down her back in shiny curls. Her cheeks were pink which accentuated the sparkling green of her eyes, and her face had tanned the color of warm honey. She wore glittery pink velvet slippers on her feet and a rather old-fashioned black dress printed with small pink flowers, and a short olive green cardigan. He noticed that she walked with a bounce in her step and was pleased that he had gone ahead and organized this break away from home. It was just what she needed.

Ava was as taut as a tightly strung violin. Outwardly she put on a good show of simply being excited by the holiday, but inside she was quivering with nerves. What would Jean-Paul think of her appearing at his home? What if he had chosen to spend the week in Paris in order to avoid her? Or worse, what if he interpreted this trip as an indication of her readiness to give herself to him body and soul? She stared out of the window and pondered the wisdom of her decision.

France was in the full throes of spring. The trees were all in leaf, tall white candles adorned the horse chestnuts, and undulating fields of vines shimmered with their first leaves. Roses grew in abundance. The driver told Ava that they were planted at the ends of the rows to stop the ploughing oxen from nibbling the vines as they turned around to start the next row. To her delight she spotted a pair of swallows on the wing and a pretty brown thrush.

Finally, the car swept up a long curved drive, beneath an ancient avenue of towering trees that plunged them into shadow. At the end, the house stood bathed in sunshine. It was a majestic, neoclassical building on a grand scale. Built in pale, sand-colored stone, symmetrical, with tall windows framed by blue shutters and ornate black balconies, its beauty distracted Ava from her fears and filled her with wonder. Virginia creeper scaled the walls with honeysuckle and wisteria. As they approached, she could see the steep roof of slate tiles and charming dormer windows, each one capped by a curving pediment like a graceful eyebrow. Narrow stone chimneys reached into the sky with fanciful, cone-topped towers, decorated by a sudden spray of small birds.

The car drew up on the gravel outside the house. A pair of Great Danes charged out of the open door, their deep barks biting into the still air and echoing off the walls of the château. Ava climbed out of the car, her heart beating with anticipation. She raised her eyes to see an elegant, olive-skinned woman standing at the door. With her black hair pulled into a chignon that showed off her beautiful bone structure and deep-set brown eyes, she was obviously Antoinette, Jean-Paul's mother.

Antoinette smiled serenely. "Welcome," she said, stepping onto the gravel. "I hope you had a pleasant journey."

"Splendid," said Phillip, striding over to her. She gave him her hand and he leaned forward to kiss her. She was tall and willowy in flowing white trousers held at the waist with a brown crocodile belt. She wore a man's striped shirt beneath a cream waistcoat lined with black-striped ticking. Ava thought she was the chicest woman she had ever laid eyes on. "This is my wife, Ava," Phillip added, introducing her.

"I have heard so much about you," she said warmly. "Jean-Paul is so fond of you." Ava shook her hand, thin and surprisingly cold to touch, and wondered how much he had told her.

"Please come inside. I hope you don't mind the dogs, they are rather large but very friendly."

"We adore dogs," said Ava, trying to hide her

nervousness behind a veneer of enthusiasm. "We have two of our own."

"Of course you do. Well, you will feel quite at home then."

They walked across the hall dominated by a sweeping stone staircase and a giant fireplace full of neatly cut logs piled one on top of the other. On the mantelpiece were ancient bottles of wine lined up on display. The floor was of big square flagstones that shone, except along the middle where they were worn away by centuries of treading feet. Antoinette took them through to the drawing room, a grand red salon with high ceilings and long crimson curtains framing French doors that opened onto a wide terrace, surrounded by a stone balustrade. Faded tapestries of hunting scenes hung on the walls, flanked by gilded portraits of the family ancestors. Ava ran her eyes over them, seeking out any similarities with Jean-Paul. A maid entered the room and Antoinette asked her to bring a tray of drinks to the terrace. "And where is my son, Françoise?" she added. Ava's stomach flipped and she grew anxious that she wouldn't be able to hide her feelings.

"He is out," she replied.

Antoinette sighed. "And Henri?" Françoise shrugged. "Well, go and find him and tell him our guests have arrived. I said they would be here by noon."

"Yes, *madame*," said Françoise obediently and left the room.

"Come, let us sit on the terrace. It is warm there in the sun. Françoise will bring us some wine." She opened the French doors wide and stepped outside. The dogs followed her, trotting off to sniff the borders and cock their legs against the balustrade. Below, the gardens stretched out to an old wall covered in climbing roses and pink bougainvillea, where ancient trees watched over the grounds and, beyond, the domed roof of a dovecote silhouetted against the sky. Ava could see at once why the château was so special to Jean-Paul and why he did what his father asked of him in order not to lose it.

"Ah, my friends, you have arrived!" exclaimed Henri, approaching the terrace from around the side of the house. His voice was loud and booming, like a trombone. "You should have sent Françoise to find me," he added to his wife.

"I did," she replied coolly. He embraced Phillip with the warmth of an old friend and kissed Ava's hand as his son had done. He smiled broadly, dark eyes appraising her beneath a thick head of rich brown curls. Ava remembered Jean-Paul telling her that he had a mistress in Paris. It didn't surprise her. He was devilishly handsome, like his son. "Where's the wine? Françoise!" he bellowed. Françoise appeared almost at once, struggling beneath the weight of a large tray heavy with bottles and glasses as well as a jug of iced water.

Henri made no move to help her. "Good! We were in danger of dying of thirst," he said in English so that the maid couldn't understand. He sat down and pulled out a cigar. "So, Phillip, my friend, how is the book?"

Antoinette turned to Ava. "Would you like to see the dovecote? Jean-Paul tells me you have one in your garden."

"I would love to. Is that its dome over there?"

"Yes."

"It's far more magnificent than ours."

"Jean-Paul says you have the most beautiful estate."

"I wish he were there now. Everything is bursting into flower—and the smells, it's never smelled more delicious."

"Come, I need to talk with you."

Ava followed her down the wide steps to the garden, leaving the men talking and drinking on the terrace. Once again she felt the blood rushing through her veins with panic. Had Jean-Paul told his mother that he was in love with her? Was she going to warn her off? Say he needed to marry a young woman from his own country and have a son to inherit as he would do? She began to feel nauseous and rubbed her forehead in agitation. The sun was very hot, in spite of the cool breeze, and the twittering birds were drowned by her own pulse thumping in her ears.

"May I speak with you plainly?" Antoinette

asked as they walked across the lawn towards an iron gate built into the wall.

"Of course," Ava replied.

"It's about Jean-Paul." Antoinette glanced across at her. "He is my only child, you know, and I love him deeply."

"I know, he's told me a lot about you."

"I'm sure. The trouble is that he has a terrible relationship with his father. Henri is insensitive to his needs. Jean-Paul is a talented artist but Henri does not like him to paint. He writes beautiful poetry but Henri thinks nothing of poetry. Henri had an uncle who wasted his life painting unremarkable paintings. He does not want Jean-Paul to waste his life like him. It's not just the painting. Jean-Paul spent months in Paris doing nothing but dating inappropriate girls, which was a good thing on one hand—Henri was afraid he was homosexual—but on the other hand it is no life for a young man who will one day inherit an estate such as this. Henri wants him to help run the vineyard here, but he was never interested, until now."

"Now?" Ava wondered where the conversation was leading.

"He wants to stay here and learn about the vineyard, but Ava, he needs to go back with you." Ava was unable to reply, her throat was so tight with emotion. "I think he wants to stay for me. You see, I'm alone here most of the time. Henri lives in Paris. I'm sure he told you. He speaks about you

345

with such affection, Ava. It makes me so happy to know that he is understood. He told me he painted a garden for you."

"It is the most beautiful painting, Antoinette. We have planted it just as he painted it. He has such imagination and flair."

"I know." She smiled again and shrugged. "I understand him, of course." She opened the iron gate, which whined on its hinges like an old dog, and led her into a wild meadow in the midst of which stood the round stone dovecote. "He is not ready to come home, Ava. I can tell he is unhappy. If he comes home now he will not be free of his father. Not for a moment. With you he is able to enjoy freedom to be himself. I couldn't bear it if he sacrificed that for me. This is an opportunity of a lifetime and I want him to enjoy it. I will still be here in the autumn. Tell him, for me, that he has to return. I know you can persuade him. His father thinks he has come home for a break. He will never forgive Jean-Paul if he thinks he has let you down, after all your kindness. You see, he has to return with you. There is no other way. Do it, please, for me."

"I'll try," Ava replied huskily.

Suddenly, from around the back of the dovecote Jean-Paul appeared. He stood with his hands in his pockets, looking up at them from behind his fringe. He watched them warily. "Jean-Paul, show Ava the dovecote. I must check on lunch." She looked at her watch. "Goodness, it is nearly time. Don't be long." She turned and slipped through the gate, leaving them alone.

"Why have you come?" he demanded, his tone aggressive. He stared at her impassively, awaiting her response, expecting rejection. Ava ran a hand through her hair, feeling awkward. It had been a terrible mistake. Then he shifted his gaze, suddenly looking as vulnerable as a boy. Her heart buckled. He looked so sad.

"I'm sorry," she whispered, slowly approaching him. "I'm miserable, too."

His face softened. "You look radiant," he replied, a small smile curling the corners of his lips.

"That is because I knew I was going to see you."

"Then you have missed me, too?"

"Yes."

He slipped his hand around the back of her neck, beneath her hair, and pulled her to him, pressing his lips to hers. She didn't push him away. She didn't think of her children or Phillip. She existed in the moment, riding the arc of the rainbow, although, in her heart, she knew it would never last. His mouth was soft, his kiss ardent. She parted her lips and let him in, winding her arms around his waist, feeling the muscles tense beneath his shirt as she touched him. His breathing grew heavy, his body hot and taut. He pulled her around the building so they could not be seen from the gate. Ava felt reckless. She was so far from home. She felt like a different person. Intoxicated by the feel of his body in her arms, combined with the scents of France, she forgot that her husband sat on the terrace with Henri and that lunch was a few minutes away in the dining room of the château. She dwelt in a fantasy world where only she and Jean-Paul resided. A limbo where anything was possible.

He took her hand and led her to the door of the dovecote. Inside it was warm and sweet smelling. He closed it behind him and lay down with her on the straw. She caught her breath as he moved on top of her, parting her legs with his knees. He buried his face in her neck, breathing in her familiar, forbidden scent. Her stomach swam with pleasure as he ran his tongue over her skin. Then he was kissing her chest and unfastening the buttons on the front of her dress. He slipped his hand inside and felt the warm softness of her breast, caressing it with his thumb. Her head fell back as he took it in his mouth. She could feel his bristles against the tender flesh and the wet sensation of his tongue as he toyed with her nipple, and her body shivered with the guilty pleasure of enjoying what she had dreamed of for so long in the secret recesses of her imagination.

She let out a deep moan as he lifted her dress over her stomach and helped her wiggle out of her panties. She felt hot and wanton like a teenager, and smiled at her brazenness. When she opened her eyes she saw that he was looking at her as if she were the most beautiful girl in the world. He smiled at her appreciatively and she smiled back, parting her thighs to let him inside her. As they made love he took her hand and entwined his fingers through hers. She didn't regret her adultery, not for a moment. If she had taken a second to reflect on Daisy Hopeton she would have realized that there wasn't such a great difference between them, after all.

"Will you come back to Hartington?" she asked when they lay together, bathed in a pool of light dropped from a little window above them.

"Yes," he said. "You know I would move mountains for you."

"You don't have to, my darling," she replied, lovingly caressing his face. "I'm here now."

Hastily, they tidied themselves in preparation for lunch. Ava fastened the front of her dress and smoothed it down, brushing off any telltale wisps of straw. Jean-Paul made for the door, then turned and kissed her again. She laughed and kissed him back. "You look beautiful," he said, stroking her face with his eyes. "I don't think I've ever seen you in a dress."

"I wore it for you."

"It suits you. And your hair is down. I like it down. What happened to the pencil?"

She laughed at his teasing. "Seriously now, how do I look?" She wiped her mouth with the back of her hand.

"Flushed." He took her hand. "Come, we'll walk the long way around, that way any evidence will be blown away by the wind."

When they reached the terrace, Antoinette, Henri and Phillip were just getting up to go in for lunch.

"Perhaps you'd like to freshen up in your room," said Antoinette to Ava. "I'm sorry, I should have offered when you arrived. Françoise will show you."

Ava followed the older woman up the stone staircase and along a corridor until they reached a door at the end. Françoise opened it to reveal a large bedroom with a four-poster iron bed draped in white linen. A window was wide open, giving on to the dovecote and the fields of vines beyond, and a pair of white curtains billowed on the breeze that blew in from the garden. Françoise was surprised that she spoke French. "Is there anything I can do for you?" she asked, grateful to be understood.

"No, thank you. I'll be down in a minute." She noticed that her suitcase was on a stand, open and ready to be unpacked. She delved inside for her sponge bag and hurried into the bathroom to wash away the evidence of adultery. Catching herself in the mirror she paused to see if there was anything in her appearance that might give her away. Her cheeks were rosy, her eyes shining, her hair tousled and tumbling over her shoulders. She pulled out a piece of straw that had gone unnoticed. Instead of throwing it in the bin she put it in the pocket of her sponge bag. Something to treasure. It would always remind her of the first time they made love.

She leaned out the window and surveyed the gardens. The sky was clear blue, the scent of newly cut grass and sweet-smelling shrubs rose up on the air and, beyond it all, stood the dovecote, their secret place, half hidden behind the wall. She smiled to herself and thought of Jean-Paul, recalling his kiss and his touch. She closed her eyes and wished the week would last forever.

XXV

The sweet scent of unfurling leaves.
The tremor of my childlike
excitement at the sight of spring.

Ava sat through lunch exuding a radiance that affected them all. Phillip delighted in his wife's happiness and silently congratulated himself on arranging this break away from home. It was obviously what she needed; she was back on sparkling form, looking lovelier than ever. Henri smelt Ava's sexuality like a dog sensing a bitch on heat and flirted with her in his coarse, bombastic manner. Jean-Paul watched her with dreamy eyes, holding her gaze a little longer than was prudent, throwing his head back and laughing in a way he hadn't laughed for weeks, certainly in a way he never behaved in the presence of his father.

Antoinette reveled in his joy and knew that Ava had done as she had asked and persuaded him to return to England. Ava slipped back to her normal, ebullient self, holding the table with her stories and making them all laugh with her impeccable timing and witty repartee. She felt electrified by Jean-Paul's presence in the room, as if he were spring incarnate, coaxing her winter branches into blossom.

After lunch, Henri insisted on showing them around the vineyard. Antoinette declined gracefully, floating off for a siesta. She kissed her son, leaving him with an affectionate look, then smiled conspiratorially at Ava. Ava panicked. A mother's instinct perhaps? Then she shook off any feeling of unease. She couldn't possibly know. Her complicit look must refer to the fact that Ava had succeeded in getting her son to change his mind and return with them to England.

Ava walked behind Phillip and Henri with a bounce in her step, her shoulder almost touching Jean-Paul's arm. She was unable to hide her exhilaration, taking pleasure from every stolen moment. Henri led them down the garden to the dovecote. "Thank goodness doves can't talk," Jean-Paul commented under his breath as they slipped through the gate.

"Les Lucioles has been in my family for five hundred years," said Henri, puffing his chest out with pride. "This dovecote was built in the time of

Louis the Thirteenth." He patted Jean-Paul on the back, feigning fatherly affection. "One day my son will take over from me. Once he has found a wife and produced an heir. Am I right?" He pulled a face and gave a few exaggerated nods, appraising his son like an old king. "Yes, one day you will inherit all that is mine. It has lasted five hundred years; there is no reason why it won't last another five hundred. Eh?"

Ava winced as he flung open the door so that it crashed against the wall, sending the doves shooting into the air like bullets. "It's beautiful," she commented, stepping inside.

"It is very special to me," said Jean-Paul without looking at her. Then he put his hand on his heart. "Very special."

Phillip glanced at his wife. "Slightly more charming than ours, don't you think, Shrub?"

"Oh, I think ours has a lot to recommend it."

"No doves," he added.

"We should buy some. We can't have a dovecote without doves."

"And give it a lick of paint," Phillip continued.

"No, no. Don't paint it. You will ruin it if you paint it," said Jean-Paul. "I like it just the way it is. It has a secret magic." Ava pretended to be distracted by something in order not to have to look at him.

"So, when are you planning on returning to Hartington?" Phillip said to Jean-Paul.

"Next week," he replied coolly. "I needed to spend some time with my mother."

"Can't you find him a suitable English girl?" Henri interrupted. "Don't they make them like you anymore?" he added to Ava with a wink.

Ava smiled sweetly to hide her embarrassment. "You flatter me," she replied, shrugging off his comment with a laugh.

"Come, let me show you Antoinette's garden." He put his hand in the small of her back and escorted her out of the dovecote. Jean-Paul walked behind with Phillip, but she felt his eyes upon her and the frisson of excitement they caused. "We need to find him a girl," he said, lowering his voice.

"He's young," Ava replied in his defense.

"It is time he settled down. Between you and me, I had to get him out of Paris. He was living the life of a playboy, dating the most unsuitable girls. I will not hand over the estate to a woman of that sort, who will piss it all away on frivolity."

"Don't you find him changed?" she asked, suddenly realizing that she was in a position to help him. "When he arrived in England, I'll be honest, I didn't think he'd last a week. He had never done a day's work in his life and it showed. He was completely ill equipped to work in a garden and arrogant with it. But he's changed. Can't you see it?"

"He looked as miserable as a dog!" said Henri

unsympathetically. "I said to Antoinette, 'That boy's in love.'"

"With the garden," replied Ava deliberately. "He's in love with my garden. You wouldn't believe it unless you saw it with your own eyes, but he's put his heart and soul into it. He's worked so hard to create something really beautiful and he's never too proud to learn. When he comes back he'll enjoy the fruits of his labor."

"I am pleased." Henri shrugged. "I wouldn't believe it had anyone else told me but you."

"I think he worries about Antoinette," she added carefully.

"She's stronger than she looks."

"I'm sure. He's a dutiful son."

"He's her only son. That makes her very anxious. You understand, you're a mother. She's overprotective and over-indulgent. If he came back from Paris with one of his strays she'd accept her. Anything to make him happy."

"And you're tougher, to compensate?"

"Perhaps." He looked at her with narrowed eyes. "You're very perceptive, Ava Lightly."

"It's easier to see if one's not involved."

"I can see the bigger picture. Life is not a fairy tale. I need a son who is a man. I entertain on a grand scale. Some of the most important men in the land walk through my gates. I cannot hand the business over to a man who does not accept his responsibility with a grubby tart for a wife."

"You want your son to be like you," she said, feeling sorry for Jean-Paul, his destiny all mapped out for him like that. Even though it was a magnificent destiny, there was still so much pressure to conform. While his father was alive, there was no hope of freedom, except in England with her.

"I need my son to be as solid as me," Henri replied. "With a good head for business. He must find a decent girl and start a family. A girl who knows her place, not a flighty girl with ambitions of her own."

"Like Antoinette."

"Jean-Paul needs to return to England in order to stay away from his mother. Sometimes love can be suffocating. There is nothing wrong with love, but we all need a little space. Relationships work better when the air is able to circulate between two people. Antoinette would have liked more children. It would have been easier for Jean-Paul if she had. *Tant pis*!"

"He will make a wonderful vigneron," she said diplomatically.

"He has watched the machinations of the business since he was a little boy and then, bam, all of a sudden he lost interest and I lost him."

"Don't all children go through that stage? They rebel against their parents when they try to work life out for themselves and gain a little independence. He'll come back to you."

"I don't know. I had such high expectations of him."

"Don't be too hard, Henri. On yourself or on him. If you give a horse a long rein he won't run away; if you pull it in tight, he'll bolt."

"You are wise for someone so young."

"It's all the spinach I eat. Good for the brain," she quipped.

"Then I should eat more than I do."

Antoinette's garden was bursting into flower. Pink roses were budding against a wall where great stone urns of white tulips sprang up with yellow senecio and violas. Box hedges were frothy and pale green, and wild yellow narcissus grew in abundance among rampaging honeysuckle and daisies. The air was sweet with the scent of spring, stirred by the merry twittering of birds as they flirted in the cedar and sycamore trees. In the middle of her carefully designed garden was an ornamental pond, the statue of a little boy, his hand outstretched, touching the wing of a bird in flight. Ava was drawn to it. She stood beneath the sculpture, admiring the way the boy's fingers barely touched the bird so that it appeared to be totally unsupported. Jean-Paul came up behind her.

"Isn't it incredible?" he said.

She turned and smiled at him. "It reminds me of the little boy and dolphin that stand on the Embankment in London."

"This was commissioned for me, by my mother."

"Really?"

"Yes. I am the little boy, the bird symbolizes freedom. As you can see, I can almost touch it."

"You can be free at Hartington."

"I know," he replied, so softly she could barely hear him. She felt the breeze ruffle her hair. "I want to kiss your neck," he added.

"Be careful."

"I'm French, I say what I feel."

"I ask you to take care, Mr. Frenchman. We are being watched."

"They are not interested, *ma pêche*. Look, they are busy discussing the history of the *cave* and the great freeze of ninety-one. Papa will not cease to worry about frost until *la lune rousse*." He sighed heavily. "But I couldn't care less about frost. I want to lie with you and make love to you in the warmth of my cottage, up there under the eaves. I want to kiss you all over, slowly, carefully, savoring the taste of you inch by inch."

"Stop," she pleaded. "Phillip . . ."

"Your Phillip is enraptured by my father. Listen, they are discussing the quality of the grape."

"There's nothing that interests him more than that."

"Then leave them to it. He is happy. Come."

"We can't," she protested.

"I want to show you the greenhouses. They are spectacular."

"It's too obvious!"

"Only to you. They suspect nothing. Isn't it natural that I should want to show you my home?" He began to walk towards the yew hedge.

Ava turned. Phillip raised his eyes, she waved, he waved back, then she was gone through the hedge and Jean-Paul had taken her hand and was leading her down a gravel path.

Once inside, he closed the door and kissed her. It was hot and humid, smelling of damp earth and freesias. She felt his excitement as he pulled her hips towards him. "We can't . . ." But it was useless to protest. His mouth silenced her and his arms wound around her in a passionate embrace.

"I wish we were alone. You drive me crazy," he gasped. "I want to take your dress off and feel your flesh. I want to lie naked with you so nothing separates us but skin and bone."

"Darling Jean-Paul, it's not possible here. Phillip and your father could come in at any time."

"Curse them both!" He scowled. "I will engineer it so that we can be alone."

"How?"

"You will see. I have a plan. Trust me."

Ava pulled away to inspect the greenhouse. There were pots of highly scented tuberose, rows of orchids in myriad colors, and pretty nerine lilies, just opening. Jean-Paul followed her, holding her hand, turning her around every few minutes to steal another kiss. It was fortunate that when Henri entered with Phillip they were on either side of a table of rare purple orchids. "Phillip, do come and look at these," she called to her husband. "They're almost checked."

Phillip strode over, admiring the plants as he passed them.

"This is quite something," he agreed.

"Oh yes, Antoinette is a keen amateur," said Henri.

Jean-Paul remained apart, watching Ava's every move. "I think you should take them around the vineyard in the truck," Jean-Paul suggested to his father. Henri enjoyed nothing more than showing off to his guests.

"We have just started spraying the crop," he said. "Would you like to see?"

"That would be splendid," said Phillip.

Jean-Paul waited for Ava to back out so that they could be together at last.

"I think I'll leave you boys to it," she said on cue. Jean-Paul threw her a secret smile.

Phillip frowned uneasily. "Why don't we go for a walk?" he asked his wife. Jean-Paul looked at him in alarm.

"A walk?" Ava repeated.

"How far is it into town?" he asked Henri.

"A fifteen-minute walk. It's a nice walk. There are some pretty shops you might like, Ava. Women's shops, soaps and things."

"I'd love to," she replied. She wanted to explain

her actions to Jean-Paul. They had to behave with caution. The last thing she wanted to do was hurt Phillip. Her desire to be alone with her lover would have to wait.

"I can show you the vines tomorrow," said Henri. "Now, let me show you how to get to town."

Ava was sure that Jean-Paul would sulk. She braced herself for a sullen face, but to her surprise he simply shrugged. She smiled at him gratefully and he seemed to say "It's okay, we'll have plenty of time." Reluctantly, she left him in the garden by the fountain and accompanied her husband to the front of the house. "Isn't it a beautiful place?" she said as they walked down the drive beneath the shimmering plane trees.

"Beautiful," he agreed. "Now you can see why it matters so much to Henri that his son gain experience of running an estate."

"Completely. But I think he's matured so much since he came to stay with us."

"He's a different man."

"That's what I said to Henri. I want him to know that he has a very talented son. I think he's hard on him." Phillip nodded. "His mother overcompensates."

"It's good for Jean-Paul to get away from both of them."

"Do you think someone will be saying that someday about Archie and Angus?"

"Of course not, Shrub," he reassured her. "You and I are pretty solid parents."

"I hope so. I'd hate to think of them escaping to another country to avoid us."

"Children go through stages. They have to spread their wings and fly. We have to let them. Jean-Paul will come back in the end and run this place as his father did. You can see how much he loves it and why."

"I never imagined it to be so spectacular," she agreed.

He took her hand. "So, you're not missing the children?"

"Not yet."

"You're happy I brought you here?"

"Very happy."

"And your thoughts on motherhood?"

"I've moved on," she said simply.

"Good."

"I've decided I don't need another child. I don't want to be chained to the nursery again."

"Quite."

"I'm just beginning to enjoy my freedom."

They wandered around the town, a pretty cluster of reddish-brown buildings built around a square dominated by an ancient church and a town hall. In the middle was a fountain shaded by neatly clipped trees. A couple of old men in caps sat smoking pipes on a bench, and a grandmother and child threw crumbs to a flock of pigeons. There was a small market where wizened country folk sold fruit and vegetables and tall bottles of olive oil. A skinny dog played with an empty Coke can. They drank coffee in a little café that spilled onto the pavement, served by waiters in black and white. A group of men in waistcoats played draughts in the corner and a couple of salesgirls smoked and gossiped. The streets were cobbled and narrow so that people were forced to park their cars and walk. A few tourist shops sold patterned tablecloths and soaps. Ava bought some lavender bath oil for her mother and sprayed herself with orange blossom perfume. Then she bought the scent. A small indulgence, but Ava was not extravagant and she couldn't remember the last time she had bought something for herself beside plants. "This will always remind me of France," she said, sniffing her wrist, then she walked lightly out into the street, where Phillip was looking into the window of an antiquarian bookshop.

"Shame they're all in French," he said.

"Come on, don't you have enough books?"

"Oh no, there's always room for more."

They returned exhilarated from the walk. Antoinette appeared in the hall from the drawing room. "You must need some refreshment," she said. "Tea or lemonade?"

"Tea would be lovely," Ava replied.

"Same for me," said Phillip, following

Antoinette into the drawing room where the two Great Danes lay in front of the fireplace.

"I'm going to go upstairs and put my shopping away," she called after him.

"All right, darling," he replied. She clutched her parcel, excited by her purchases, and ascended the stairs. As she was walking along the corridor towards her room, a door opened and a hand grabbed her, pulling her inside where it was dark and cool.

"Don't say a word," Jean-Paul hissed. Ava was stunned. He had closed the shutters; thin beams of light filtered through the cracks.

"You're crazy!" she hissed back.

"Crazy for you!" he replied, pulling her onto the bed.

"What if someone . . ."

"They won't. Relax, *ma pêche*. I said I would arrange something and I have."

"How long have you been waiting?"

He laughed, then looked at her with an expression so serious and so tender that her stomach lurched. "For you, I would wait forever."

XXVI

The delight of fresh herbs and vegetables grown in our own garden, sown with our own secret magic.

Hartington House, 2006

Miranda sat at her desk. The usual place, the usual music, but while her fingers hovered expectantly over the keys of her laptop, inspiration didn't come. She had been asked by the *Daily Mail* Femail section to write about her experiences of moving out of London to the countryside. How the reality had turned out to be less blissful than the vision. She could have written it on autopilot a couple of months ago, but now she felt different. She could hear the children's voices behind the wall of the vegetable garden and yearned to be with them. Country life was an adventure with Jean-Paul when they were home. He took them camping at night to watch badgers, to the river to catch fish, up to the woods to build camps and light fires, to watch the pheasants feeding and the rabbits playing. Her children, who at first had found nothing to do in the countryside except miss the city, were as much part of nature now as the animals they watched.

As for her, she had grown accustomed to leaving

her hair unbrushed and wearing little makeup. There was no pressure in Hartington to look glamorous all the time. It was a relief. She didn't mind wearing gumboots and, although she still retained a muted longing to wear the beautiful clothes that languished in her wardrobe, she had no desire to return to the frenetic social life that had driven her to exhaustion in London.

She wrote a swift e-mail to the editor suggesting the article be a positive one. The editor replied it had to be negative; they already had another journalist writing the positive now. To hell with it! They'd have to find someone else. "Right," she sighed, standing up. "That's the last time she'll ask me to write for her. Another door closes!" But as she wriggled her foot into a Wellington boot she realized that she didn't care. *I should be writing a novel, not picking away at meaningless articles.*

Miranda went out to the vegetable garden where Jean-Paul was planting seeds with Storm and Gus. The children were on their knees, their small hands delving into the earth. Mr. Underwood leaned on his pitchfork, having done very little all morning except stand about making obvious comments like: "I'll be damned, there's a caterpillar, Storm." Or: "Well, that'll be a worm." Miranda didn't mind. She was in good spirits. Jean-Paul was more uplifting than sunshine. In fact, just being near him was a bolt of excitement. He made her feel good about herself. Not that he asked her much about her life—they talked mainly about the garden—but he took an interest in what she said. He encouraged her to learn about plants, to take pleasure from the bulbs emerging from the soil and the small creatures who lived among them. He enjoyed simple things and his fascination was infectious. Miranda soon found herself on her hands and knees planting potatoes and flicking through cookbooks to find interesting things to make with them when they were ready to harvest. She took pride in herself and her home, but most of all she began to enjoy being with her children to the exclusion of everything else. They all shared their enjoyment of the garden and that was thanks to Jean-Paul.

The garden looked magnificent. The blossom was out, the lime green leaves on the trees were turning frothy, birdsong filled the honey-scented air. Fat bees buzzed about the borders where bulbs were now flowering. The wild garden was peppered with buttercups, purple camassias, cowslips and feathery dandelions. In the cottage garden a luxuriant bed of green shrubs grew up with tulips, narcissi and primulas. In the middle of it stood the mountain ash like a sailing ship in a winding river that was the grassy path. Beneath her canopy of white flowers was the circular bench where Jean-Paul sat from time to time, his brow furrowed in thought. Miranda had often seen him there, though what troubled him she was still too polite to ask.

"Mummy, look at this one!" Gus beckoned his mother to observe the worm he was waving in the air. "It's enormous."

"I want to keep one as a friend," said Storm. "Can I, J-P?"

"Of course. We can put it in a jar and give it a name."

"Why not call him Worzel the Worm," suggested Miranda. Then, inspired by the idea, she announced that she would go get a jar.

"Clever Mummy," said Storm, spotting another worm hiding in the soil and bending down to pull it out.

"That's a fat one," said Mr. Underwood, chuckling happily. "You've got quite a few there."

"Bring something to drink," Jean-Paul shouted after her. "This is thirsty work, eh!"

"*Je suis faim*," said Storm.

"*J'ai faim*," Jean-Paul corrected. "*J'ai aussi soif*," he added.

"That means thirsty," said Gus.

"Gus-the-Strong and Bright-Sky, you are learning fast!"

"That'll be French," said Mr. Underwood, nodding admiringly.

"Correct," said Jean-Paul, grinning at him. "You, Mr. Underwood, are as clever as an old fox!"

While Miranda was in the kitchen, the telephone rang. It was Blythe. "Hi there, stranger." Miranda was pleasantly surprised. She hadn't heard from her friend since their lunch before Christmas.

"How are you?" Miranda asked.

"Fine. I have to go to court next Monday for the settlement."

"Don't let him get off lightly. Remember what David advised."

"How is he? I haven't seen him for a while." She sounded down.

"Truth is, Blythe, I don't see much of him either. He's working really hard. Comes down late on Friday night and leaves early Sunday afternoon."

"You should take a lover," said Blythe brightly. "That's what I'd do if I were stuck in the middle of the countryside. Happens all the time, I should imagine."

"Don't tempt me," she replied, thinking of Jean-Paul.

"I just want the whole thing over and done with, then I can move on with my life."

"Why don't you come down for the weekend?" Miranda suggested. "David would love to see you. The gardens look beautiful and I'd like to show off the house."

"You're settling in then?"

"Yes. Right now, there's no place I'd rather be. I wake up every morning to the sound of a hundred birds in the trees and the scent of flowers wafting in through my window. It's heaven. Do come, I'd love to see you."

"I thought you were a city girl."

"I was, I've just got out of step with the rhythm of London. I prefer the slower pace down here."

"I haven't seen many of your articles. Have you stopped working as well?"

"Just a little pickier!"

"Has the countryside quelled your ambition?"

"There's just so much to do down here, I don't seem to find time to get to my computer."

"It sounds blissful. When do you want me?"

"Whenever you like. Things are very relaxed in the country. I have no plans."

"This weekend I'm tied up but the one after I'm free."

"Great. I'll tell David, he'll be thrilled. If you're not careful he'll give you some more of his advice. Great big pearls of wisdom." She laughed.

"I could do with that, believe it or not. You know, most of our friends have taken the bastard's side. I'm known as a scarlet woman."

"Ignore them. He's just got a bigger mouth than you."

"Oh, I do miss you, Miranda. You're such a good listener." She sighed. "You've made me feel so much better."

"Come down here, my garden will make you feel wonderful. I feel utterly transformed."

"You *sound* utterly transformed. Though I wonder how long it will take before you scamper back up to the city?" asked Blythe cynically. "All those designer collections. You can't have changed that much."

"We'll see," Miranda replied nonchalantly, feeling not an ounce of envy for her friend. She put down the receiver and passed her eyes over the jug of cow parsley that sat on the kitchen table and the three baskets of lilac hyacinths Jean-Paul had put on the windowsill. The air was infused with spring.

She made up a jug of elderflower cordial and found an empty jar in the storeroom. As she walked back into the hall she glanced into her study, where her laptop sat in shadow. She didn't feel guilty or frustrated. She almost skipped through the French doors onto the terrace. The sun was out, the air was warm, Jean-Paul was in the garden, transforming the place with his own unique brand of magic. Magic she was beginning to understand.

The children had gathered a merry collection of worms and beetles, which they poured into the jar along with a few leaves and blades of grass. "Will they die?" Storm asked Jean-Paul.

"Not if you only keep them for a short while. Put them back at the end of the day. They belong in the garden." The children set off in search of more. Mr. Underwood finished his cup of juice and returned reluctantly to the dovecote. A few trees had come down in February. He took up from where he had left off before the children's laughter had lured him into the vegetable garden.

Miranda sat on the grass with her own cup of juice as Jean-Paul set about putting up the sweet pea frame with pig wire. She watched him work, his fingers rough, his nails short, the hands of a man who had worked in gardens all his life. There was something rather moving about those hands and the way his face looked sad in repose. "Have you always been a gardener?" she asked.

"For as long as I can remember." His hands paused a moment. "My life before meant nothing. I tossed it away on frivolities."

"What inspired you?"

"My mother. I grew up on a vineyard in Bordeaux. She was a passionate gardener."

"Is she still alive?"

"No. She died last summer."

"I'm sorry. You were close?" She slowly prised him open like a rare and mysterious shell. She knew there was something beautiful inside if only she could get in.

"I was her only son. We were very close."

"What was she like?"

He looked at her steadily, as if weighing up how much he should tell her. His eyes took on a softer shade of brown. "She was dignified and quietly spoken. She had an air of serenity. She was very strong."

"Was she beautiful?" she asked, knowing the answer.

"She had black hair that she tied into a chignon. I

rarely saw it down, except at night before she went to bed. She would kiss me good night when I was a boy and I would see her like that, with her hair down, and I thought she must be an angel, she was so beautiful. It would fall down her back shining like silk. As she got older it went gray. Then I never saw it loose. She never lost her dignity or her serenity, right up until the day she died."

"If you don't mind me asking, how did she die? She can't have been old."

"She was seventy-three. She died in her sleep, peacefully. There was nothing wrong with her. She simply didn't wake up." He shrugged and shook his head. "Like a clock, her heart ceased to tick."

"Is your father alive?"

"Yes. He lives in Paris. They were not close."

Boldly she asked the question she had been longing to ask since she first met him. "Jean-Paul, have you ever been in love?" For a moment she feared she had gone too far. His face closed into that of a stranger, pulled down and gray with sorrow. Startled, she was about to change the subject, ask him about the vineyard, coax some more memories from him, but he answered before she had time to speak.

"Once," he replied evenly. "And once only. I will never love again."

Miranda felt a wave of disappointment, as if his answer had crushed her heart. She stared into her empty cup. "Would you like some more juice?"

she asked, endeavoring to break the silence and return to the way they were. But the shell had snapped shut.

"So you pour all your love into the gardens," she said hoarsely. He didn't reply, but his face softened and his lips curled at the corners. "You have a gift, Jean-Paul," she continued, emboldened. "Your love not only makes the garden grow but my children, too. They've blossomed like those cherry trees. Thanks to you they don't fight all the time. They've stopped watching television. You've taught them the wonders of nature and the fun there is to be had among the trees and flowers. I'm so grateful."

"It's not all me," he said, taking a pot of sweet peas to plant beneath the frame. "Your children want to be with you and David."

"I didn't know what to do with them before," she admitted. "In London they had a nanny. I realize now that I never really saw them. They'd leave in the morning for school and Jayne would pick them up in the afternoon and whisk them off until six. All I had was bath time and bedtime. I was afraid of upsetting them so I let them watch videos when I should have read them stories and listened to them. Gus was such a problem, fighting with the other children at school, disrupting the classes. Moving out here has been the best thing we ever did for him. He's really settled down. It's thanks to you, Jean-Paul. You and the garden."

"Gus just wants to feel important and valued, Miranda. Have you noticed how he looks at you?"

"*Me?*"

"Yes. He wants your approval and your admiration. Children are very easy to please; they just want your attention and your love."

"I *do* love them."

"It is not enough to tell them you love them. You have to show them. Words mean nothing if they are not backed up with action."

"How come you're so wise when you don't have children of your own?"

"Because I learned from a very special woman many years ago. She put her children above everything, even above her heart's desire. They came first."

"Is it wrong to be a working mother?"

"Not at all. You have to satisfy yourself as well. If you are unhappy they sense it. Children need their mothers and fathers. Gus needs his father."

"I know." *But he has you. You're better than any father. You include him, inspire him, play with him, build him up, make him feel special and important. You're the one he looks up to. You're the one he loves. David only thinks of himself.* Suddenly, a dark cloud of resentment cast her in shadow. "I need a husband, too," she confessed huskily.

"Tell him," he said simply.

She stood up, collected the empty cups and jug

and sighed. "Life is so complicated. Love is complicated."

"But life is unbearable without it."

"Then how do you bear it?" she asked before she could stop herself. She realized that David had shifted away from the center of her world. Jean-Paul had taken his place in her affections. She loved him. She couldn't help herself.

"Because I have no choice," he replied. She walked away, turning as she reached the gate, hoping that he might still be watching her. But his head was bent over the sweet peas, lost in thought.

It occurred to Miranda that her life was beginning to mirror Ava's. The parallels were startling. Both women had fallen in love with their gardeners. David appeared in her mind like a small boat drifting away on the current. If she shouted would he hear her? Would he care? Would he take the trouble to row back?

Suddenly she was inspired to write. With a pounding heart she realized she had found her story. A great love story in the grand style of *Anna Karenina* and *Gone with the Wind*. It was right here beneath her nose. She was living it. If she couldn't have Jean-Paul she would satisfy her desire in a work of fiction.

While the children played in the gardens, she opened the windows in her study, filling the room with the honey-scented blossom from the orchard.

She chose a CD of light classical music and sat at her desk, in front of her computer screen. The music carried her deep into her imagination where her longings lay like dormant seeds in a bed of rich and fertile soil. Her fingers tapped over the keys, faster and faster as she watered those seeds with expression and felt them grow. She inhaled, sure that she could smell the tangy scent of orange blossom.

That night, as she read the children a bedtime story, Gus snuggled up against her, resting his head on her shoulder. She was moved by the transformation in her little boy; he was no longer the troubled child he had been in London. But she could tell by his frown that something was troubling him now.

"Mummy, why doesn't Daddy ever play with us?"

"Because he's very busy, darling."

"But you play with us."

"That's because I'm here all week and he has to work in London."

"But on weekends?"

"He's tired."

"I wish J-P was my daddy." Miranda felt a cold fist squeeze her heart.

"You don't mean that, Gus," she replied.

He wriggled uncomfortably. "J-P loves us like Daddy should."

"Daddy loves you very much." Gus looked

unconvinced. "He would love to spend all day with you like Jean-Paul does. But he has to work in the City to earn money so we can live in this beautiful house and so you and Storm can go to school . . ."

"But he's going to send me away to boarding school."

Miranda took a deep breath. She couldn't deny that boarding school was on the cards for both children. "You'll love boarding school, Gus. You'll play sports all day and make loads of friends." He looked away. "And you'll come home on weekends. Only big boys go to boarding school."

"I don't want to be a big boy," he whispered.

XXVII

Planting sweet peas, watched over by those softly cooing doves on the wall. The bliss of being alone in the early evening light.

When David came home that weekend he was tired and irritable. Miranda was in high spirits. Having acknowledged her love for Jean-Paul she had put the children to bed after reading them *The Three Little Wolves* in a very theatrical voice, and returned to her computer to write until four in the morning, stopping only to make herself a cup of coffee. The words had spilled out from deep inside her. Inspired by love, and Ava's secret scrapbook, she had written prose so lyrical it was as if someone else were writing through her.

David strode into the hall enveloped in a cloud of fury. For the first time Miranda was impervious to his mood. She kissed him cheerfully, smelling of lime, basil and mandarin and announced that she had tried a new recipe for dinner. "Salmon pancakes. Why don't you have a glass of wine, darling. You look exhausted." David was startled by the change in his wife. She seemed in her own happy world, unaffected by him. He sensed the shift but couldn't guess how or from where it came. He followed her into the kitchen. She looked good, too. Her eyes sparkled, her skin glowed and she walked with a spring in her step. Her exuberance made him feel all the more bad tempered.

"How are the children?" he asked, taking the glass of wine she handed him.

"They're on very good form. Gus has asked to bring some school friends home. They're coming for tea tomorrow. It's a big step for him. He's never had friends before. Storm has invited Madeleine. They're all going fishing with Jean-Paul. He's made them all nets. I'm sure they won't catch any-thing, but I'm going to make them a picnic. You can join us if you like."

"I might," he replied noncommittally.

"Good wine, isn't it?" she said, taking a sip. "Fatima's son, who owns the convenience store, recommended it to me. He says it's as good as Château Latour."

"I hope it's not as expensive as Château Latour."

"Twelve pounds a bottle."

He took a sip and raised his eyebrows. "Not bad."

"Dinner will be at eight-thirty. I've got one or two things to do in my study. Why don't you have a nice bath? Oh, by the way, I've asked Blythe down next weekend."

He looked even more furious. "Why?"

"Because I haven't seen her since Christmas and I've been meaning to ask her for ages. I want her to see the house. Why? Do you have a problem with it?"

"No," he replied hastily.

"Good." She disappeared up the corridor. David was left in the kitchen wondering why everything felt wrong.

Miranda printed out the novel so far. It began the day Jean-Paul had turned up with Storm, although she had changed the names of all the characters and added a little invention to detach it as best she could from her own life. She was particularly pleased with the central character, whom she called Angelica. She could see her clearly in her mind's eye: small, slight, with a long straight nose, tousled hair the color of sun-dried hay, twisted up on the top of her head and secured casually with a pencil. Her eyes were pale green, the color of early leaves, and her smile was wide and infectious. She made her eccentric, a great entertainer with a dark, solitary side to her nature. She came to life on the page as if she already existed and had suddenly found a channel through which to express herself.

While Miranda wrote, little else mattered. She was overcome by the need to put the story down on paper and her fingers seemed to move automatically, the story writing itself. She reread the first couple of chapters and was impressed. She never knew she had the ability to write like this.

That night, while David made love to her, her mind was in the gardens with Angelica and Jean-Paul, with Ava and the enigmatic young man who dominated her secret scrapbook. She closed her eyes and imagined David was Jean-Paul. Swept away on her imagination, more fertile now than ever before, she enjoyed his attentions. Afterward he seemed satisfied that she still belonged to him. That his world was still as it should be. He rolled over and went to sleep, but Miranda lay awake, staring at the ceiling through the darkness, her mind jumping about like a restless cricket.

In the morning she got up early, leaving him asleep in bed. Gus and Storm were in a state of high excitement anticipating the afternoon with their friends. Miranda slipped into a pair of jeans and a shirt, not bothering to apply makeup. She tied her hair into a ponytail and skipped about the kitchen humming to herself while she made breakfast for her children.

She had just poured herself a cup of coffee when Jean-Paul appeared at the window. The children waved excitedly. "Do you want to come in for a coffee?" she asked, holding up her cup in case he couldn't hear her through the glass. He grinned and nodded. Since their conversation in the vegetable garden Miranda felt as if the wall between them had lost a few bricks in the middle. She could see him through it and he seemed to welcome their newfound intimacy. A few minutes later he appeared in the kitchen in his socks, having left his boots at the front door.

"*Bonjour*," he said. The children replied in French, their small faces beaming.

"Fred and Joe are coming to play today," Gus reminded him.

"And Madeleine," added Storm.

"And we are going fishing, no?" said Jean-Paul. He took his coffee and perched on a stool. "Then we will make a fire and cook what we catch."

"Do you think you'll catch anything?" Miranda asked.

Jean-Paul shrugged. "If we don't, I have a fresh salmon in my fridge."

"Ah," she replied, grinning at him conspiratorially. Jean-Paul stared at her a moment. There was something unfamiliar about her. She was all fired up as if her heart were a burning coal. She no longer looked dry and stringy. He recognized it instantly as love. Ava had glowed like that, too, before the sun went in and the rainbow faded. Things must have improved between her and David. He was pleased.

After breakfast, Jean-Paul took the children off into the vegetable garden. Miranda telephoned Henrietta, her new friend, and asked her over. They had been seeing a lot of each other, their friendship blossoming with the apple trees. Cate had tried to inveigle herself into joining them for coffee, but Miranda didn't like the way she patronized Henrietta and lately they had met in Troy's or in Miranda's kitchen instead.

Henrietta arrived, looking flushed. Miranda poured her a cup of coffee and they sat at the table gossiping. "How's the diet?" she asked, observing that it had so far made absolutely no difference.

Henrietta's eyes glittered. "I can't do it," she replied, turning pink. "I'm fed up with it. Abstaining from all the good things in life just makes me miserable. Every time I go for a croissant I see Cate's thin face looking disapproving."

"Oh, Etta. What are we going to do with you? You don't know how lovely you are."

"I don't feel it. I love a man who'll never love me back." She stopped suddenly, aware that she had said too much.

"You're in love?" Miranda asked. "Who with?"

Henrietta bit her lower lip. "I can't say. I'm embarrassed. It's silly."

"Jean-Paul?" Miranda volunteered, pulling a sympathetic face. But Henrietta shook her head.

"I would never set my sights so high. I admit I fancy him, who doesn't? But it's like fancying Robert Redford. No, I love Troy."

Miranda stared at her for a moment. Of all the men to lose one's heart to, Troy was the very deadest of dead ends. "Troy," she repeated.

"I know. It's impossible. But I really love him."

"Does he love you back?"

"Yes. But he doesn't want to have sex with me. He wants to have sex with Tony the postman."

Miranda sighed at the scale of the obstacle. "I wish I could give you some advice, but there is none. He's gay. He's not going to give you children and snuggle up to you at night. He's probably repulsed by a woman's body. You've got no chance."

"I know." Her eyes began to well.

Miranda frowned. "We've got to do something about you. It's spring. The most beautiful time of the year. You should be feeling happy."

Henrietta pulled out a piece of paper. "This was posted on the board in Cate's Cake Shop." It was an advertisement for a new Pilates class which had been set up in a studio behind the church. "I thought, I don't know . . . I'm sure I'm not fit enough, but . . ."

"This is brilliant!" Miranda exclaimed. "I did a class like this in London. They use these incredible beds with straps you loop over your hands and feet. It's tough. Really hard work, but the results are quick and lasting. This is definitely for you, Etta."

Henrietta looked encouraged. "Really?"

"Really. I'll do it with you. We could do it a couple of mornings a week when the children are at school. We could start next week."

"Would you really do it with me? You're so slim, you don't need it."

"It's not about being fat or thin. It's about feeling good about yourself and keeping in shape. By the way," she said, narrowing her eyes. "You've got to do something about the way you dress. You can't hide under big shirts and sweaters anymore. You should celebrate your shape."

"Like Dawn French?"

"She's not a bad example, but you've got a way to go before you're her size. Have you ever watched Trinny and Susannah?"

"Of course, I wish they could give *me* a makeover."

"Their message is brilliant. It's not about killing yourself with diets, but dressing the best way for your shape. The results are instant and it really works. I'm going to buy you their book. Then we're going to hit London!"

"Oh, Miranda!" Henrietta couldn't believe

someone other than Troy was prepared to go to all this trouble for her.

"I'm going to give you a makeover. Consider it a present. It's not about finding a man but about feeling good in your skin."

"I've never had a friend like you," she sniffed.

"Well it's about time you did. Cate's a bad influence. By putting you down she pushes herself up. She's a bitter old cow! You've got a really pretty face, lovely soft skin, thick hair and a sweet, endearing smile. I'm not at all surprised that Troy loves you. But God made him gay. There's someone out there who isn't gay who will love you and give you marriage and children. I want you to look your best for him. I'm going to arrange for someone to look after the children while we're in London. We'll spend the morning in Richard Ward where Shaun will give you the best highlights you've ever had, and the afternoon in Selfridges. Leave it to me. We'll have fun over a glass of champagne and we'll spend an obscene amount of money."

"Oh, Miranda. I'm embarrassed."

"Don't be. It's not my money!" she replied with a wink.

Jeremy Fitzherbert sat alone at his kitchen table in front of a plate of bacon and eggs and a cup of tea. Mr. Ben lay on the floor watching him, hoping for another slice of bread and butter, while Wolfgang chased rabbits in his sleep. There was a lot to do in the garden, cutting back shrubs and trees and planting vegetables. However, he didn't feel inspired. Ever since he had met Henrietta Moon up at the house, he had been able to think of little else.

Jeremy had never been in love. He had enjoyed the odd relationship as a young man, but for most girls, after the initial excitement of dating a rich farmer with a beautiful big house, the reality of farm life had turned them sour. The odd one who had relished living on a farm had driven him mad with ideas beyond his means. The fact was, he was a simple farmer who loved the land. In Henrietta he saw a woman with simple tastes like his own, a voluptuous and juicy body like a delicious fruit, and a smile that revealed a gentle nature and tender disposition. She was perfect, but out of reach. That day up at the house he had given her his heart, even though she had clearly only had eyes for the hand-some Frenchman.

Jeremy had accepted defeat without complaint. How could a simple man compete with the daz-zling good looks and charm of a foreigner? Jean-Paul was exotic. His accent conjured images of vineyards and eucalyptus trees, foie gras and sun-shine. Jeremy had bowed to the greater power and made a dignified exit. However, he had found him-self going into town for no particular reason, pop-ping into Henrietta's gift shop under the pretense of buying a birthday card, or a bottle of bath oil for his mother. In fact, he had spent more money on trifles in the last few months than he had spent in an entire year. His bathroom was full of unopened boxes of soap and pretty glass bottles still in their wrapping. She always smiled at him, which caused his heart to sputter and spit like an old engine that hadn't turned in years. They chatted about the weather, and she always asked about his cows. He wanted to take her a bottle of warm milk straight from the dairy but every time he was on the point of filling one for her, he remembered Jean-Paul and his confidence stalled. He picked at his eggs and bacon and pondered his future. It looked as bleak as a January day. He wasn't getting any younger and was losing hair by the minute. Soon he'd be an old, bald farmer and no one would want him. He looked down at his dogs. "Thank God I've got you," he told them. Mr. Ben cocked his head and frowned. "You want another slice of bread?" Mr. Ben thumped his tail on the floor. Jeremy got up and buttered a piece of wholemeal. "There you go," he said, tossing half at Mr. Ben, half at Wolfgang who opened his eyes when he smelled it right in front of his nose and snaffled it up in one mouthful.

Jeremy was tired of holding back. Hadn't she said she'd like to come and see his farm? Feeling encouraged he finished his breakfast. He'd take that milk after all and extend an invitation. The worst she could do was decline.

David awoke and stretched, the space beside him empty and cold. He got up and showered. He felt disgruntled, remembering Miranda had asked Blythe down the following weekend. David was trying to distance himself from Blythe. It had been fun for a while, but she had grown needy, telephoning him throughout the day, insisting on seeing him. He had tried to let her down gently, but then she had turned up at his office in a fur coat, opening it a little so that he could see she was wearing nothing but a pair of lace stockings and a little shirt that barely reached her belly. Unable to resist, he had made love to her in the girls' lavatory, which he now regretted. It had given her the wrong message. Now Miranda had asked her down for a weekend. He resolved to organize a business trip and avoid it altogether.

The kitchen was empty, used cups in the sink and a pan of hot milk keeping warm on the Aga. He sighed resentfully. There was a time when Miranda had made him breakfast every morning, fussing over him like a geisha. Now she didn't even bother to stick around. He poured himself a cup of coffee, made a couple of pieces of toast and marmalade, and sat down at the head of the table to read the papers.

After breakfast he went into the garden. The sound of birds was loud and cheery, a background to the excited squeals of his children behind the wall of the vegetable garden. Curious to see what they were doing, he walked up the path and opened the gate to find Storm and Gus chasing each other up and down the gravel pathways that separated the vegetable patches, holding long worms between their fingers. Jean-Paul was on his hands and knees planting. More surprisingly, Miranda was on her knees, too, her face flushed, while her fat friend Henrietta looked on, hands on hips as wide as a small continent, laughing with them. David felt excluded. They looked like any happy family on a Saturday morning, enjoying the sunshine. He felt resentment claw at his stomach.

He had to admit it was beautiful, though. The white apple blossom, the neat borders of box that enclosed each vegetable patch, the arched frames that Jean-Paul had constructed for the sweet peas and beans. The old wall was covered in white wisteria tangling through blue ceanothus. Doves settled on the top of the wall, gently cooing, and a couple of squirrels played tag, jumping from tree to tree.

Miranda beckoned him over. "Come and join us!" He raised his cup and forced a smile. But he didn't feel like helping; he felt jealous, an outcast in his own home. The usurper was there with his knees in the mud, slipping into his place while he was in London. He was turning to leave, his heart heavy, when a high-pitched voice shouted after him. "Daddy!" Storm ran up to him. "Daddy, come and see what we've done in the garden." He looked down at her enthusiastic face and was left no option but to follow her. Gus stood watching warily from under his dark fringe. He looked at his son, suddenly so tall and handsome, and wondered how he had grown so much without him noticing.

"What have you been doing, Gus?" he asked.

Gus proudly held out the jar of creepy crawlies. "Say hello to our friends," he said, and Jean-Paul paused in his planting to watch.

Jeremy hesitated outside the entrance to Henrietta's gift shop. He shuffled his feet in the sunshine, carrying a bottle of warm cow's milk, straight from the dairy. He shook off his nerves, took a deep breath and opened the door. The little bell indicated his arrival but it wasn't Henrietta who emerged from the back room, but her sister, Clare. "Good morning," she said brightly. "How are you today, Mr. Fitzherbert?" Clare was slim and pretty with mousy brown hair and glasses. She wore a beaded necklace her six-year-old daughter had made at school and a bright red sweater emblazoned with the words *Naff Off*.

"Very well thank you," he replied nervously. The shop smelled of incense and soap. "Is Henrietta in?"

"No, she's at Miranda's," she replied. "Anything I can help you with?" She was used to seeing him in the shop. Today, he looked gaunt and pale. "Are you all right?" she asked sympathetically. "There's a horrid bug going around, two of my children have had it."

"Quite well, thank you," he replied. She settled her eyes on the bottle of milk he was carrying.

"What's that?"

"This? Milk."

"Milk?"

"Yes, I was going to . . . I was thirsty," he replied, changing his mind. He thought of Henrietta up at Miranda's with Jean-Paul and suddenly felt very foolish for having imagined he might have a chance.

Clare looked at him suspiciously. "Shall I tell her you came by?"

"No. I'll come back another time." He left the shop feeling like an inadequate teenager. *God*, he thought bleakly, *I'm forty-five years old. Too old for this sort of thing!* He returned home to his dogs and his farm and the prospect of another day trying not to think about Henrietta Moon.

XXVIII

Purple shadows on the grass cast by the clipped yews in the evening light

Blythe arrived with her son, Rafael, on Friday afternoon. She stepped out of the taxi and swept her eyes over David and Miranda's beautiful house with an uncomfortable mixture of admiration and envy. It was a warm afternoon, the sky a rich blue across which fluffy white clouds drifted like sheep. The birds twittered noisily in the trees and a pair of fat doves sat on the roof of the house lazily watching the hours pass. The sun turned the wild-flower meadow golden while a gentle breeze raked through the long grasses and flowers like fingers through hair. In the middle of it all stood an old oak tree where a group of giggling children played, their cries ringing out in joyful abandon. It was an idyllic scene, not at all what Blythe had envisaged. When she thought of the country she imagined rain, mud, gumboots, cold houses and boredom.

Gus shouted at Rafael excitedly from his tree house. Blythe held her son's hand. Gus was a menace. The last time they had played together Gus had hit him over the head with a heavy wooden train track and given him a swollen egg for a week. She had warned Rafael never to be left alone with him. "He's a horrid little boy," she had told him. "You don't want another egg, do you?" Rafael gazed longingly at the tree house.

Gus was Captain Hook in the eagles' nest of his ship, scanning the sea for enemies. Inside the hollow Joe and Madeleine were imprisoned Lost Boys, while outside, Tinkerbell, played by Storm, and Peter, played by Fred, were sneaking through the grass to rescue them. The game was halted while Storm and Gus shouted for Rafael to join them. Rafael hovered by his mother's side, nervous of Gus who looked so much bigger and more frightening at the top of that tree. Finally, his curiosity got the better of him. Pulling his mother by the hand, he dragged her over to the tree.

"Do you want to play?" Gus asked, jumping lithely down the ladder, a broad grin eating up the freckles on his face. Blythe was surprised. He didn't look like the surly child she knew. "He can be another Lost Boy if he likes." His politeness grated. She almost preferred him sullen and uncommunicative. It seemed as if Miranda had everything. Then she thought of David. *Almost* everything.

As Rafael was bundled into the hollow with Joe and Madeleine, Miranda stepped out the front door. She waved at Blythe. "I didn't hear your taxi," she said as she approached. Blythe studied her carefully. In a pair of jeans and shirt she looked radiant. *I never knew she had quite such long legs*, Blythe thought grudgingly, *even in trainers!*

"You look so good, Miranda, I'm feeling sick!" she gushed.

"Don't be silly!"

"You do. Your house is divine, by the way. Stunning. It's paradise down here. You're so lucky. I want it all and I want it now." She laughed huskily and delved in her handbag for a cigarette. "Do you want one?"

"I've given up."

"Hence the glow." Blythe sighed before popping a Marlboro Light into her mouth and flicking her lighter. "I'll give up once this bloody divorce is done with."

"How's it all going?"

"Dreadful. I feel like I've been through a mangle."

"You look well on it."

"That's because I have a lover," she whispered smugly. She couldn't resist. Miranda's perfect life was too much to bear.

"Same one?"

"Same one."

"Come inside and have a cup of tea," Miranda suggested. Blythe glanced at her son. "Rafael's fine here," Miranda added. "Gus will take care of him."

"It's Gus I'm afraid of," said Blythe drily. "He's Captain Hook!"

Miranda laughed. "Don't worry. His battle cry is worse than his hook."

"It's an amazing tree house. Did David make it?"

"No, Jean-Paul, the gardener."

"Wow. Some gardener! It's incredible."

"He's wonderful. I'll show you around. The garden is really beautiful. It used to belong to this fascinating old woman called Ava Lightly. When I arrived no one could talk of anything but her amazing garden. It didn't look like much when we bought the place. It had all been left to rot. The house was unoccupied for two years. Then Jean-Paul took over and agreed to bring it back to its former glory. He's done the most incredible job. I'd like to invite Ava Lightly over to see it. I think she'd be really pleased."

"Or appalled. Old people can be so ungrateful."

"I don't know. She sounds such a nice person."

"Do you have friends down here?"

"Yes. The people range from charming to eccentric. A mixed bag. You'd love Troy, he's gay and has a hair salon on the high street. Henrietta Moon, who owns the gift shop, has become a good friend. We've just started doing Pilates together, which is hilarious. Some of the other girls are really nice. We all have coffee together afterward. It's hard work, but great fun and the trainer is rather easy on the eye. If he were ugly I wouldn't do the extra ten!" As they walked into the hall Miranda added, "The vicar is putting on a drinks' party in the village hall tomorrow night in order to raise money. It's twenty-five pounds a ticket. If you'd like to check out the local flavor, we could go. Might be a laugh."

"Or hell!"

"David will go. He loves lording it over everyone. He's dragged me to church once or twice just so he can stride up the aisle and sit in the front pew, which I was amused to find was already taken by some oldies who weren't going to budge for him. You can imagine his disappointment. Once he heard that the Lightlys sat there every Sunday there was no stopping him. He chatted to everyone afterward, dispensing pearls of wisdom no doubt. The generous-spirited person that he is!"

"He's incorrigible," said Blythe, smiling as she thought of him. "What time does he come home?"

"In time for dinner."

Blythe gazed around the oval hall. At the end large French doors gave out onto a leafy terrace where she could see vast urns of tulips and a stone walkway that extended into the distance, lined by big fat topiary balls. In the middle of the hall stood a round table, neatly decorated with glossy books and a luxurious display of pink lilies. Their scent filled the room with the smell of spring. Miranda had painted the walls a warm ivory on which hung a collage of large black and white photographs in silver frames. The look was effective. "Did you get help from an interior decorator?" Blythe asked.

"No," Miranda replied. "I wanted to do it myself."

"You've done it beautifully. I want to repaint my house. What is that paint?" She pressed her nose up against the wall to take a closer look.

"Sanderson."

"Of course. Very subtle."

"I love light."

"There's plenty of that here. What happens outside?"

"Let's get a cup of tea, then I'll show you around."

"I think it's time for a glass of wine," said Blythe, needing fortification. Surely no one deserved to live in such a paradise.

Blythe took her glass of chardonnay around the entire house, taking her time to poke her nose into each room, commenting on the wallpaper and furniture as if she were a potential buyer. Once she'd seen inside, she asked Miranda for a tour of the garden. They wandered up the thyme walk, stepping across long shadows cast by the topiary balls, watching the setting sun bleed into the sky. The children's voices could be heard on the other side of the house, rising into the air like the loud chirping of birds.

Miranda showed her the vegetable garden, telling her proudly about sowing the vegetable seeds. "There was a time I couldn't live in anything but a pair of heels. Who'd have thought I'd learn to wear gumboots with style?"

"I thought you were miserable down here."

Blythe had preferred it when she had been unhappy.

"I was. Now I love it. I have Jean-Paul to thank for that." They walked up the meandering path of the cottage garden. Miranda pointed out the shrubs and plants beginning to flower. Blythe was surprised how she knew them all by name. Her friend had changed and she wasn't sure she liked it. The balance of power had shifted, leaving her at a disadvantage. Only her secret gave her consolation. They walked on until they came to the old dovecote, watched over by towering larches. "I want to buy some doves," said Miranda. "There's something very lonely about this place. It's like a neglected corner of the garden. Sad, somehow. Doves will put the life back, don't you think?"

At that moment, Jean-Paul strode out of the trees, pushing a wheelbarrow full of dead branches. Blythe caught her breath. "Hello, Miranda," he said, setting Blythe off balance with a wide smile.

"Wasn't Mr. Underwood supposed to clear away that tree?"

"Yes, but he's old." Jean-Paul shrugged and settled his eyes on her friend.

"This is Blythe," Miranda said. "She's come to stay for the weekend. I'm showing her around the garden."

"I've heard so much about you," said Blythe in French, gazing back at him coyly. "You've done wonderful things in this garden."

"Thank you," he replied, smiling again. "I commend your French."

"It's a little rusty."

"It sounds perfect to me."

"I'm so pleased. It's been a while since I've had a chance to practice it." She turned to Miranda. "You should speak to Jean-Paul in French."

"I don't speak French," Miranda replied.

"Oh, of course you don't. Silly me!" She settled her cat's eyes on Jean-Paul again and shrugged. "*Tant pis*!"

"I think I'll go and be a crocodile for a while," he said to Miranda.

"They'll love that," she replied, spotting the knowing twinkle in his eye as he departed. Blythe watched him walk away, her gaze lingering appreciatively on his slim hips and low-slung faded jeans.

"Christ, Miranda!" she exclaimed once he had gone. "No wonder you like it down here. He's delicious!"

"I know. Everyone fancies him." Miranda turned away so Blythe wouldn't see her blush.

"Are you fucking him?"

Miranda was appalled. "Of course not! I'm married."

"So? You said yourself, David's never here."

"What difference does that make? I love David. Why would I want to be unfaithful? There's more to life than sex."

"Is there? Life would be very dull without it!" They continued to walk towards the field where Charlie the donkey stood chewing grass. "You'd want him if you weren't married," she added with a smirk.

"That's irrelevant."

"I'm not married and I want him. How did you find him?"

"He just turned up here one day with Storm. He found her in a field and brought her back."

"What was he doing in the field?"

"I don't know. Looking for a job!" On reflection it was all very bizarre.

"In a field?"

"He was on his way here. He'd seen my advert in town. Anyway, what does it matter? He's a good gardener and that's what counts."

"He's obviously not married. Divorced?"

"I don't think so."

"You don't know? Haven't you asked him? Has he any children?"

"No."

"What were his references like? Who was he working for before he came here? A grand English family no doubt."

"I have no idea."

"You didn't check him out?"

"I didn't need to. I sensed he was right."

Blythe raised her eyebrows. "You hired him because he's handsome. He could be a criminal on the run, for all you know."

"I doubt it." Miranda grew irritated. "Look, Blythe, I don't care if he's a criminal on the run or has three wives across different continents. He does a wonderful job here and he's good company. I enjoy being around him. I don't ask him about himself out of respect. I don't want to pry."

"You mean you don't want to look too interested."

"I don't fancy him, Blythe!"

"Of course you don't." She gave a little snort. "But I do."

"You're unavailable."

"I don't know. My lover is about to dump me. Once he showered me with gifts, now he rarely has time for me. You know, I turned up at his office the other day in nothing but a fur coat and suspenders. He couldn't resist me then."

"You've got a nerve."

"It was fun. I like taking risks."

"Do you think he'll leave his wife for you?"

"I don't know." She surveyed the estate and fantasized living here. It was an appealing thought. "At the beginning we couldn't get enough of each other. Now, I'm not so sure. I don't think I'm wife material anymore."

"Have you met the wife?"

"Yes." Blythe cast a sidelong glance at Miranda, relishing her secret.

"What's she like?"

Blythe chewed the inside of her cheek as she

pondered the best way to answer without giving the game away. She knew she was taking a risk even discussing it with Miranda, but there was something about Miranda's perfect life—and perfect Frenchman—that made her want to burst one or two of her bubbles. "Nice," she replied carefully. "I'm a bitch!" She gave a throaty laugh, then pushed her wrist out of her sleeve. "Look, this is what he gave me for Christmas." Miranda looked at the Theo Fennell diamond watch and recalled the strange telephone call in December. Her stomach twisted with anxiety.

"It's from Theo's," she observed.

"Yes. Isn't it gorgeous? I'm loving the pink strap."

"Is it engraved?"

"Yes. It says Big Pussycat on the back. Private joke. But that was Christmas. He hasn't given me anything since," she pouted.

Miranda took a breath. *No, it can't be. It's just a coincidence*, she thought, suddenly feeling nauseous. *We're not Theo's only clients. Anyone could have bought her that watch.* But her mind began whirring with possibilities. Was David Blythe's lover? Is that why he spent so much time in London? Did Blythe, the friend she had known since school, have the malice to steal her husband? She glanced across at her, still watching the diamonds glitter in the sunshine, and concluded that it was impossible. If David were Blythe's lover, Blythe would have kept the affair secret.

Once, Miranda would have shared everything with Blythe. They had occupied the same bedroom at boarding school, exchanged stories about boyfriends and tales of family strife, fought and made up as good friends do. But they weren't schoolgirls anymore, and time had grown up between them, forming an invisible wall. The truth was that Miranda didn't know Blythe as she once had. Their lives were no longer joined by shared experience. Apart from their children, they had little in common. Instead of communicating her fears, Miranda kept them to herself. She no longer trusted her friend.

As they walked back to the house, Miranda tried to hide her anxiety by asking Blythe about herself and letting her rattle on, but she could not dispel the feeling that David was seeing someone else. She had become so involved in the garden and her children and her secret desire for Jean-Paul. But the more she thought about it, the more her suspicions were aroused.

They reached the hollow tree where Jean-Paul was playing with the children, pretending to be a crocodile. Gus was in his arms, wriggling about, trying to free himself, roaring with laughter. Miranda suddenly felt tearful. Jean-Paul was such a natural father. Her children adored him. He was full of inventiveness and enthusiasm. Why couldn't she be married to him?

When Rafael saw his mother he clambered down

from the tree house and ran up to her excitedly. "Mummy, J-P's a crocodile, quick, up the tree. You mustn't be eaten." Blythe thought how much she'd adore to be eaten, and lingered on the grass hoping the handsome Frenchman would play with her as well. She rather fancied being swept up into his arms. Jean-Paul put Gus down and laughed as he scampered back up the ladder, gloating happily that he had outwitted the crocodile.

Miranda went inside to make the children tea, leaving Blythe with Jean-Paul. She was relieved to be alone. If David was having an affair, what then? Was their marriage over? Was it worth saving? Did she still love him? She wasn't sure. Could Jean-Paul ever love her?

David had originally planned to be away on business for Blythe's weekend, but his desire to spend more time with Miranda and the children overrode his wish to distance himself from his mistress. When he arrived the children were watching a video in their pajamas. Madeleine, Joe and Fred had been taken home. The day had been a great success. Gus had played alongside his friends without picking a fight. He was proud of his home and wanted to show it off. Hartington House had given him a sense of security and belonging and a source of continual entertainment. Since Jean-Paul had arrived he had grown in confidence. Mr. Marlow had praised him for good behavior. He seemed to be enjoying school. Storm's friends were no longer afraid of coming home and she had little girls with whom to share her playhouse. Miranda read them bedtime stories and helped them with their homework. She delighted in these quiet moments together. Life at Hartington had become a joy. Yet, David wasn't part of it.

Miranda watched him greet Blythe with the scrutiny of a scientist observing an organism beneath a microscope. She didn't miss a thing.

XXIX

The battle to keep those naughty rabbits out of the garden. We lost to Mr. Badger, but oh, what a character he was!

David met Miranda warmly, sliding a hand around her waist and kissing her affectionately on her cheek. Miranda flushed with pleasure and surprise. Blythe's reaction to seeing him was not dissimilar to the way she had reacted to Jean-Paul. There was nothing in her body language to indicate she was intimate with him. Besides, she was a natural flirt. Despite having been irritated when Miranda had mentioned she had invited Blythe for the weekend, David seemed pleased enough to see her. He was tired from the week in the office and the train journey from London. He looked strained around the eyes. Miranda poured him a glass of wine and, after saying hello to the children in the playroom, he disappeared upstairs to have a bath.

Blythe sat with Miranda in the kitchen, watching her prepare the roast chicken for dinner. She sipped her wine and nibbled on a carrot. "David's looking very tired," she said. "Is he always this exhausted on a Friday night?"

"Every weekend it's the same. By the time he's recovered he's back on that train to start the whole process again. A banker's life isn't a life. It's just money. Frankly, I'd rather have a husband."

"I didn't know things weren't good between you." Blythe looked genuinely concerned. Her sympathy was reassuring and Miranda hastily dismissed her suspicions as irrational. After basting the chicken she picked up her wineglass and joined Blythe at the table.

"I just don't see much of him, that's all. It's hard to have a marriage when you spend so little time together."

"Perhaps this move out to the country wasn't such a good idea. I mean, for Gus and Storm it's been fantastic, anyone can see that. Gus especially. He's a changed boy. He was once so angry. Now he's charming."

Miranda's spirits rose at the compliment. "He has more of a relationship with Jean-Paul than he does with his own father," Miranda confided.

"Doesn't that sadden David?"

"I don't think he's noticed." Miranda laughed bitterly. "I have more of a marriage with Jean-Paul than I do with him. And no, I'm not sleeping with him. But I spend more time with him. We share more than David and I do."

"Can't he work at home, at least a day or two a week?"

"You know he can't."

"Does he know how you feel?"

"We never have time to talk. I've changed, too. You know something, Blythe, I don't think he knows me anymore."

"Darling, this is so sad. You and David are two of my dearest friends. I thought you had the best marriage in London." Blythe's reaction to her troubled marriage dispelled any fears of duplicity; she seemed genuinely saddened. If not, she was playing the role of her life.

"What should I do?" Miranda asked.

"Talk to him. Work it out. I would hate for you two to have to go through what I'm going through. It's hell. You'd lose this beautiful house for a start. You're so happy here, I'd hate for it to be washed down the drain in those shitty divorce courts."

Miranda and Blythe put the children to bed. Gus was sharing his room with Rafael, but they fell asleep immediately, exhausted by their games in the fresh country air. David came out of his bedroom, dressed in a pair of slacks and a clean, open-necked shirt. He saw the women hovering outside

Gus's room and went to join them. "Are they asleep?" he asked.

"Why don't you go and kiss them good night," said Miranda. "Even if they're half asleep, they'll like it." David nodded and disappeared into Gus's room. Blythe gave Miranda an empathetic look. Miranda turned away and began to walk downstairs.

Gus felt his father's prickly face as he kissed him on his cheek. He opened his eyes.

"I wasn't really asleep," he hissed.

"Just pretending?" said his father.

"Yes."

"Well, be a good boy and go to sleep."

"Rafael's asleep."

"What did you do today?"

"We played pirates. Jean-Paul was the crocodile," he said with a giggle.

"Was he?" David bristled with jealousy. "Didn't Captain Hook kill the crocodile?"

"No! I was Captain Hook and the crocodile ate me."

"You look in pretty good shape for someone who's been in the belly of a crocodile."

"I escaped."

"Clever you!"

"Will you play with us tomorrow?"

"What, be a crocodile?"

"You can be Smee."

David considered his proposal. "I'll think of a more exciting game," he said.

"Okay," Gus replied. But he knew his father would forget and find something better to do. Gus rolled over and closed his eyes. It didn't matter if his father didn't play with him: he had Jean-Paul.

Miranda was carving the chicken when David came in. He had a strange look on his face, as if someone had put a hand in his stomach and twisted his gut. "Are you all right?" Miranda asked.

"I'm fine. Just need a glass of wine. It's been a bad week." Miranda handed him his glass.

"Was Gus asleep?"

David grinned and took a swig. "No, the little monkey was just pretending. Clever boy."

"Like his father," said Blythe. "Clever, I mean."

David didn't react. "Here, let me help you with that," he said to Miranda. She handed over the knife and fork in surprise. "This looks delicious," he exclaimed.

"It's from the farmers' market. Should taste good."

"Let's have a try." He tore a piece off and popped it in his mouth. The color returned to his cheeks. "It'll do," he quipped, feeling better. "So, Blythe, how are things with you?"

"Rattling on. Same as usual. Should soon be a wrap, then I can move on. Find someone else, start again. God, I don't feel up to it."

"You won't feel up to it for a while," said Miranda. "Just take it a day at a time. Besides, Rafael needs you. He's been in the thick of it. The last thing he needs is a strange man coming on the scene. He's your man for the moment."

"I agree. Anyhow, I don't think marriage is for me."

"Don't rule it out. You're young and attractive. There's someone out there who'll convince you to change your mind," said Miranda.

"Perhaps," she said, giving a little sniff.

"Right, Blythe, come and help yourself," said David. He handed her a plate, then walked up to his wife, put his arm around her waist and planted a kiss on her temple. Miranda looked up at him. Perhaps their marriage wasn't on the rocks after all, she thought, noticing a warmth in his eyes she hadn't seen in a long time. The mystery engraving at Theo Fennell was probably a horrible misunderstanding. Must not have been David at all. They just needed to spend more time together. Get to know one another again. He worked hard to give them the life they enjoyed. She had been unfair to doubt him. "And how are you, darling?" he asked her.

"Well, the garden is looking stunning. I'd love to show it to you tomorrow. We've planted loads of vegetables. The children have invited friends home for tea. We wouldn't have imagined that happening six months ago, would we?" In her enthusiasm she was about to tell him she had started writing a novel. However, something made her hold back. Her novel was linked to Ava Lightly's scrapbook and her own, secret fantasies about Jean-Paul. She might try to publish it under a pseudonym. "Everything's good," she concluded.

David tucked into his chicken, drank half a bottle of wine and finally began to relax. It was extremely unsettling having Blythe in his house. Recently, he had begun to feel displaced in his own home. The sight of his wife and children in the vegetable garden with Jean-Paul had given him a painful jolt. They had looked like any ordinary happy family, laughing and playing in the sunshine. Miranda had treated him as if he were of little importance. She didn't smile at him the way she smiled at Jean-Paul. He had noticed the way her eyes lit up when he looked at her. The way they seemed to communicate silently like two people who shared secrets. He regretted his affair with Blythe. It had meant nothing. Just a bit of fun. But now he felt Gus and Storm drifting away from him like bright helium balloons in a big blue sky, too far away to reach. They had settled into Hartington with their mother. They all had a place there among the trees and flowers, but there didn't seem to be a place for him.

He chatted to Blythe as any friend would, hoping to give nothing away. It had been reckless of her to accept the invitation. He'd get through the weekend without raising suspicion, then he'd tell her it was over. He had tried to let her down gently, seeing less of her, not taking her calls. But she was strong and persistent and he had made the error of weakening at the sight of her in suspenders and fur coat. She had to be told straight. Their affair had to stop. He watched her in the candlelight, her features distorted by the shadows that fell across her face, and realized that he had made a massive error of judgment. She wasn't the type of woman to let go easily. In fact, if he didn't handle it right, she could create a lot of trouble.

After dinner they remained at the table discussing Blythe's divorce. There was nothing more gratifying for her than talking about herself, sweeping everyone into her drama. The more she drank, the less attractive she became. By contrast, Miranda looked serene, if a little detached.

Later, in bed, Miranda turned over onto her side, facing away from him. Her breathing was so quiet he could barely hear her. "Miranda," he whispered. "Are you still awake?"

"Yes," she whispered back.

"Come here."

"I'm tired," she replied without moving. She didn't feel like making love. He put an arm around her waist and edged close behind her.

"I want to spend time with the children tomorrow," he said.

"Good," she mumbled sleepily.

"What would they like to do?"

"Pirates."

"That's not my game," he retorted sharply.

"Then do something different. Take them up to the castle. I've never taken them there."

"Would they like that?"

"I'm sure they would if you make it fun." David thought about it a moment. He wanted to confess that he had forgotten how to make things fun.

"I'll do my best," he said with an awkward chuckle.

"You're making me hot," she said, not unkindly. He moved back to his side of the bed. The sheets were cold.

"What's happening to us?" he said suddenly. "We used to laugh all the time. We used to share everything. Now we exist in the same world but apart. Is it my fault?"

Miranda turned over to face him. She could see his distraught face through the darkness. "I don't feel very close to you anymore, David."

"You mean you're in love with someone else?"

"Of course not," she replied, then laughed. "I love the children and the gardens and this house. I want you to be a part of it. Gus and Storm want their father to play with them, but they never see you. I don't want to complain. You're up there all week working your backside off for us. It would be ungrateful to complain."

"I want to make it right between us. I want to go

back to the way we were." He reached out his hand and placed it on her hip. "I love you, Miranda. There's no one in the world like you. The trouble is I get so caught up in work, travelling up and down from London, that I forget to tell you I love you. I don't want to be cold or distant. I feel you drifting away. I don't want to lose you."

She ran her fingers down his face. "You're not going to lose me, darling. But we have to work at this."

"Then let's work at it. My family is more important to me than work. I'd quit my job in a heartbeat if I felt it was driving a wedge between us."

"You don't have to go that far. Just watch less golf on weekends. Gus and Storm are such fun. They just want you to spend time with them. They want to feel valued."

"You're so right. I wish Blythe wasn't here, then we could be alone together." He drew her into his arms and kissed her forehead. *I wish I had never fooled around with her*, he thought to himself. *I'll tell her it's over and put the whole stupid mess behind me.*

Blythe lay in bed unable to sleep. The room spun. She stuck her foot out and planted it firmly on the floor to steady herself. It wasn't much help. She seethed in fury. David hadn't paid her any attention. He had kissed his wife in front of her—what an insult!—and not even given her a secret smile or knowing look. He hadn't slipped her a note, arranging to meet in the pool house at four in the morning or in one of the spare rooms of the house. He had acted as if she were like any other guest. There was no fun in playing it so safe. So much for Miranda's floundering marriage. They looked as smugly content as any happily married couple could look.

As the room slowed down she resolved to get him on his own the following day. She'd drag him into a bush if she had to.

Henrietta sat in Troy's sitting room curled up on the sofa with a digestive biscuit and a mug of hot milk. "You know, Miranda's going to take me up to London for a makeover," she informed him. "We're going to the personal shopping place at Selfridges."

"Lucky you!" he breathed enviously. "You might even get Pandora."

"She mentioned her."

"Oh, she's famous! Gorgeous, blond, as bubbly as a magnum of Moët and Chandon."

"How on earth do you know that?"

"I make it my business to know important things." He laughed. "*Grazia* magazine or *InStyle*, I can't remember which one, but they gave her a whole feature. She takes care of the rich and famous. She'll turn Cinderetta into a real princess at the ball."

"You're silly!" She grinned at him fondly. "I'm rather excited. It's so generous of her."

"She's got a heart as big as her wallet and we love her for it!"

"She's given me Trinny and Susannah's book," she said, pulling it out of her bag.

"Great! Let's read it now."

"Now? But it's after midnight?"

"Well, you're not a pumpkin, are you?"

"No."

"You don't have anyone to get back to?"

"Sadly not."

"You can stay the night with me."

"But I haven't brought my toothbrush."

"I have enough of everything for both of us. I'll let you into my secret cupboard of cosmetics. It makes Selfridges look like the corner shop."

"Are you sure?"

"I've only got The Haggis coming in at nine and she always cancels." He snorted dismissively. "If you're going to meet the glorious Pandora, you must know what suits you. She needs to be briefed. Go on, open it!"

Five miles away, Jeremy Fitzherbert lay in his large wooden bed over which a week's worth of clothes lay draped. He never put anything away, leaving it all for his housekeeper who came once a week to wash and iron. He barely noticed the chaos until she had tidied it all away, at which

417

point he resolved to keep it neat, only to slip back into his old habits the day after she had gone. He slept with the curtains open, and a window ajar. He liked the smell of the countryside and the sound of birds in the early morning, and he relished the pale, liquid light of dawn. He listened to the wind sweeping through the leaves causing them to rustle gently. It was a clear night. Small twinkling stars shone through the darkness and a crescent moon hung low in the sky. He sighed, thinking of Henrietta and his abortive trip to her shop. He replayed the moment they had met and smiled at the recollection of her extricating herself from the hollow tree. Her face had flushed with embarrassment, but her pretty eyes had sparkled and her smile was so endearing he had wanted to kiss her right there. He liked full-bodied women. To Jeremy a full-bodied woman was a woman who ate enthusiastically from the tree of life.

He hadn't intended to go to the town hall party the following night. The older he got the more solitary he became. But there was a chance Henrietta might be there. He didn't want to miss her. As he drifted to sleep he considered his life. It was time he shared it with someone. There was only so much solace one could get from Mr. Ben and Wolfgang.

XXX

Pretty white candles on the horse chestnut trees, scattering their petals over the cottage roof like snow

David was up with Miranda and the children at 7:30 a.m. He heard the sound of footsteps on the gravel and bristled at the thought of Jean-Paul striding into the core of his family and taking it over. He peered through the window. Outside, the garden was bathed in the fresh, sparkling light of morning. Beyond, he could just see the spire of the church, nestled behind the trees. The sight assuaged his irritation. The place looked this beautiful because of Jean-Paul. David was wise enough to know that if his children preferred to spend time with the gardener it was his own fault.

"We're going to have a picnic at the castle," he announced over breakfast. Storm and Rafael wriggled on the bench excitedly. Gus looked at his father mistrustfully.

"What's there to do at the castle?" he asked, testing him.

"Explore," said David, pouring coffee into his cup. Gus screwed up his nose. "It's a ruin. There might even be ghosts."

"Really!" gasped Storm.

"Don't be silly. Ghosts don't exist," said Gus.

"We'll see," added their father. "Mummy, put a chilled bottle of wine in the bag, will you."

"Good idea," she replied, trying not to show her surprise. *This is what family life is supposed to be like*, she thought contentedly, laying rashers of bacon on the grill.

"Did I hear someone say 'chilled bottle of wine?' " Blythe entered the room in a red cashmere sweater and tight black jeans tucked into leather boots. Her face was immaculately made up and her hair washed and shiny, falling in thick waves down her back. Miranda looked at her enviously. She had barely had time to moisturize her face. Blythe pulled out the chair beside David and sat down, enveloping him in tuberose. "Morning, my love," she said to her son. She didn't look at David, but she could feel his eyes on her. She basked in his attention like a cat in sunshine. She raked red nails through her hair and smiled at her son. "The country air is doing you good," she said. "Your cheeks are pink."

"Those boots are more suited to Knightsbridge than castle creeping," said David, running his eyes over her appreciatively.

"Are we castle creeping?"

"We are. We're taking a picnic."

"That's so quaint. I shall sit on the rug drinking chablis while you do the creeping!"

Hartington Castle was built on a natural hill overlooking the town. The central structure, now a ruin, dated back to the thirteenth century. Sadly, the castle had burned down in the late eighteenth century, killing all those inside. It had never been rebuilt. However, as a ruin it held great allure. There were walls and towers still standing, though without roofs, and a grand stone staircase leading up to a landing where the great queen would surely have set foot. Windows gave the ruins an eerie air, for they stared vacantly out from nowhere, and the wind whistled through them like spirits of the dead.

They parked the car at the bottom of the hill and walked the well-trodden path up to the castle. The children ran about excitedly, chasing each other up the grassy slope. Blythe made sure she walked ahead of David so he could get a steady view of her bottom, while Miranda walked behind, carrying the cool bag. A few families were already there, settling their rugs on the grass, nestled against the old stone walls out of the wind. An old couple walked slowly through the ruins with their dog, which scurried about like a large rat with his nose to the ground.

They found a sheltered spot beside a gnarled tree, which some claimed had once given Elizabeth I shelter. Blythe, who had carried the rugs, threw them onto the grass, then positioned herself, wrapping her coat around her to keep warm. Miranda poured them all a glass of wine and gave the children each a carton of apple juice. Gus took his father's hand. Miranda noticed, but said nothing, not wanting to draw attention to this rare moment, in case she jinxed it. "Daddy, will you come and look around with us?" he asked. To Gus's surprise, his father agreed. Ruined castles had always fascinated David. Miranda watched the three of them wandering among the large stones that remained embedded in the soil, touched by the tenderness of the sight.

By midday, the castle was busy. It was a hot May day, an optimistic prelude to summer. Blythe took off her coat and sweated in her cashmere. Miranda sat in her T-shirt, feeling the sun tan her skin. They both wore oversized sunglasses and spent considerable time comparing them. They opened the second bottle of wine and laughed over shared memories and London gossip. The children ate their sandwiches hungrily, having run about all morning, chasing each other up the stone steps and jumping off the landing. After lunch they discovered a few school friends and formed a pack, tearing through the ruins like wild dogs. Rafael had long forgotten his fear of Gus and followed him devotedly. David lay back and let the rays warm his face. He closed his eyes and drifted off to sleep.

Blythe watched him while he slept. She wondered when they were going to find a moment to be alone. Here he was playing the happy family man. Where did she fit in? He had hardly paid her any attention since she arrived. She shuffled uncomfortably in her cashmere and felt her face burning in the sunshine. It was even hot in the shade. By contrast, Miranda looked serene and cool in her white T-shirt. She wore no makeup to sweat under and her hair was tied up in a ponytail. Blythe envied her. She might look glamorous but her jeans were too tight, her boots too hot and her foundation was melting like wax.

Miranda saw a couple of people in Elizabethan fancy dress and remembered Troy pointing to Jack and Mary Tinton in Cate's Cake Shop and mentioning that they dressed up at weekends to parade about the castle. The sight was hilarious and she wished Etta and Troy were there to laugh with. Such local trivia was something Blythe wouldn't understand. "I've got to get the children," she told Blythe, standing up. "They have to see those two dressed up. Do you want to come?"

Blythe declined. "I'm already too hot," she said. "Take off your boots."

"I think I will. Sadly, I've got nothing on beneath my sweater except my bra."

"David's asleep."

"He might wake up."

"I doubt it. He's drunk too much. We'll have to carry him home!" Miranda chuckled and wandered off to find the children.

Blythe waited until she was out of sight then reached across and stroked David's cheek. He stirred a little, but slept on. She ran her finger across his lips, then, in an act of extreme rashness, bent down and kissed him. He opened his eyes, saw it was Blythe and sat up, casting a quick glance around him to check that they weren't being watched. "Are you insane?" he snapped, wiping off her lipstick with the back of his hand.

"I couldn't resist," she replied smoothly. "You looked so adorable asleep."

"Don't be stupid. Most of these people are probably Miranda's friends. Do you want to get caught?"

"I want to be alone with you."

"Not here."

"Then where?"

"Look, this is madness."

"Okay, so not here. Can I see you in London? We've had fun, haven't we?"

"Yes," he conceded grudgingly. "But, Blythe . . ." He looked at her, and was suddenly gripped with fear. If he finished the affair now she could be dangerous in her fury. He had to be careful.

"I don't expect to be the second Mrs. Claybourne. Though I wouldn't pass on the house and your kids are very sweet." She laughed and delved inside her bag for her cigarettes and lighter. She pulled out the packet, tapped it with her finger to release a cigarette, and placed it between her lips. Sheltering it from the breeze she flicked her lighter and inhaled. It was a well-practiced ritual that had once caused David's loins to stir with desire. Blythe had beautiful lips. She exhaled, shaking her head so that her hair fell across her cheeks like shiny curtains, and fixed him with her steady green eyes. "I just want to fuck you," she said simply. "You're a good fuck, David. Is that so wrong?"

Miranda was no longer suspicious that David was having an affair, least of all with Blythe. She felt ashamed for having imagined it. It had been the best weekend they had had together since moving in. David had played with the children. The happy look on Gus's face was better than any present from Theo Fennell. They were a family again.

That night they decided to skip the party at the town hall and have dinner at home. The children ragged around until late, then David read them *Peter and the Wolf*, putting on voices that made them laugh. He had trouble settling them because they were overexcited, jumping on the beds, hiding under their duvets then running from room to room when his back was turned. Miranda left him to it, enjoying a glass of wine with Blythe at the kitchen table. She had lit a couple of candles and made an effort to make the room look pretty with a clean tablecloth and matching napkins. She had enjoyed a long bath, chatting to David about the day, sharing stories about the children, laughing at Blythe's imprudent choice of clothes.

At dinner, her mood was buoyant and optimistic, until Blythe did something that caught her attention. It was a minor gesture; if she hadn't already harbored a grain of doubt she would not have dwelt on it. As it was, it caused her throat to constrict and her happiness to evaporate. When she was at the Aga, pulling out the fish pie, something made her turn her eyes to the table. With a feeling of foreboding, she saw Blythe reach out and take David's wineglass. She put it to her lips, quite naturally, and took a sip. She was so nonchalant, as if she barely noticed what she was doing. Miranda doubted she would have been so forward had *she* been at the table. She froze in horror, reeling from the intimacy of the gesture. David listened to Blythe's story as if it was the most normal thing in the world for her to drink from his glass, then picked it up and took a sip himself. When Miranda returned to the table she noticed that Blythe's own glass was full.

This time she did not dismiss it. When David held her hand across the table and complimented her cooking, she smiled at him, masking the fear that had punctured her heart. Had Blythe's gesture been an isolated one, she wouldn't have given it so much weight. But it was one of many small things that, added together, made an uncomfortably heavy package.

• • •

Jeremy arrived late at the town hall. The party was well under way by the time he entered in a pair of brown trousers and blue open-necked shirt. He had bathed and shaved, shut the dogs in the kitchen and driven into town with the intention of arriving on time. However, half a mile out of town the car began to wobble, then limp and finally grind to a halt on the side of the road. He swore and hit the steering wheel in fury, but there was nothing he could do. The tire was flat. Instead of dropping to his knees in the mud and changing it, he left it there and proceeded to walk instead. He was damned if he was going to ruin his chances with Henrietta by turning up covered in mud and sweat.

Henrietta arrived, in a pair of wide black trousers and a long ivory jacket with sharp shoulders and nipped-in waist. She had read *What Not to Wear* and gone shopping in Blandford with Troy. They had chosen the outfit together. "Monochrome is very in, darling," Troy had said, helping her slip into the jacket. "It's a size four-teen." Henrietta was thrilled. She had always believed she was a sixteen. She scanned the room for Troy, longing to show her new look off. But before she had time to step into the room, she was grabbed by Cate, demanding to know why she hadn't dropped in for her coffee recently. "I've been so busy," she lied.

"Rubbish!" Cate snapped. "You're never busy in

427

that shop of yours. What have you done? You've done something." She narrowed her eyes and studied her from top to toe. "Have you lost weight?"

Henrietta smiled secretively. "I don't think so."

"Yes, you have. It's a good start," she said. "Well done." She made the words sound like a rebuke.

"Have you seen Troy?"

"No." Cate looked sour. "I don't see much of him either. It's a conspiracy."

"It really isn't, Cate."

"If you're worried about getting fat, you don't have to gorge yourself on cakes. Why don't you just come in for a black coffee?"

"I will," she conceded weakly, wishing Troy were there to support her.

"That's a new jacket. It's nice. Better not get it dirty."

"I'll do my best."

"Wouldn't want to eat chocolate cake in that." Henrietta felt uncomfortable. Cate always made her feel inadequate.

She gazed around the room, longing to be rescued. The vicar was talking to Colonel Pike, her voice rising with indignation. He had clearly said something to offend her. Mary and Jack Tinton were back in contemporary clothes, drinking glasses of warm wine, smiling smugly at the amount of money they had made hassling tourists to take their photographs for a fiver. Mrs.

Underwood was in her best floral dress, her lips painted scarlet, her large feet squeezed into a pair of white shoes a size too small for her, talking to Derek Heath and his wife Lesley. Nick and Steve were surrounded by a group of excitable girls, all vying for their attention. Both young men were blond and handsome, prizes yet to be won. Nick raised his eyes at Mrs. Underwood and nudged his brother. With her mouth agape and her formidable eyes fixed on their father, she was an astonishing sight for such a sensible woman. They knew their father was too self-effacing to notice. Mr. Underwood was deep in conversation with their uncle Arthur, sharing his views on edible mushrooms. Even Henrietta's sister, Clare, was busy talking to William van den Bos. Henrietta felt very conspicuous.

Then a voice came from behind—like a rope to a stricken vessel just as she was about to sink. She turned to see Jeremy's long, handsome face smiling diffidently at her. His pink cheeks accentuated the blue of his eyes and the indecent length of his feathery blond eyelashes. She wondered why she hadn't noticed them before.

"Jeremy." She greeted him as if he were her oldest, dearest friend. "It's so nice to see you."

She was more beautiful than he remembered. "You look well," he said, wincing at the inadequate words.

She blushed. "Thank you."

"It's the heat," cut in Cate. "You look like you need some fresh air."

"Actually, you're absolutely right," Henrietta replied, gaining strength from Jeremy's presence beside her. "Jeremy, would you come with me? You never know who might be lurking on the green."

Jeremy was thrilled by her forwardness. "It would be my pleasure."

She slipped her hand through his arm, and turned to Cate. "You know, Cate, you could do with a few more cakes. You're in danger of disappearing altogether."

Cate wasn't used to Henrietta speaking to her like that. She cast her eyes around the room, searching for her husband, but even he had made an effort to avoid her.

"My car broke down a mile outside town so I had to walk. It's a lovely evening," Jeremy said, descending the steps to the pavement.

"It's been very warm, hasn't it? Do you think it means we'll have a good summer?"

"We usually have a hot week in May. June might be warm, but I think July will be a scorcher."

"Are you saying that on authority because you're a farmer?"

"No, because I'm an optimist." She giggled and Jeremy's spirits soared.

"I'm an optimist, too," she said.

"It suits you."

"Do you mind walking a little, after you've walked so far already?"

"I can't think of anyone I'd rather walk with."

Henrietta felt her belly fill with bubbles. From the sincerity in his voice, she knew he meant it.

XXXI

White blossom of the may trees and blackthorn in the hedgerows

That night Miranda couldn't sleep. She was convinced that David was indeed having an affair with Blythe. She felt sick with hurt and fury, but had no concrete proof of her suspicions. She wondered how he could make love to her, play so naturally with the children, look upon her with such tenderness, if all the time he was betraying them.

David slept the peaceful sleep of a man without a conscience. Miranda debated silently in the dark. Should she confront him? Should she confront Blythe? Should she telephone Theo Fennell himself and find out what the mystery item was and what was engraved on it? She envisaged the scene. The row. The horrid things they'd both say to each other. The irreparable damage that would shatter their family life forever.

After breakfast the following morning the children ran outside to the hollow tree, leaving Miranda washing up in the kitchen. Blythe linked her arm through David's. "Right, m'lord, show me around your estate."

"Darling, I'm going to take Blythe around the garden. We'll go and watch the children for a while. They might like to join us. Do you want to come?"

"No thanks. I'll finish the dishes then I'd quite like to wash my hair." She winced at the underhand way they had manipulated her in order to spend time alone together. Her instincts told her to go with them, but she remained by the sink. This might be her only opportunity to catch them at it.

Blythe and David walked to the hollow tree where the children resumed the game they had been playing two days before. Jean-Paul was nowhere to be seen. They'd have to make do without the crocodile. Blythe and David stood watching them scamper around the tree like squirrels and then headed off towards the vegetable garden.

"I love greenhouses." Blythe inhaled huskily. "They're hot and humid. They make me feel horny."

"This isn't a good idea," said David weakly.

"Of course it is. We're quite alone. I've missed you."

"It's got to stop," he added, thinking of his children and longing to be with them. "This affair must end. It's been fun, but you deserve better," he said tactfully.

"There is no better than you, David. Every time we part I think it's going to be the last time. I love Miranda, I love your children. I don't want you to jeopardize that, I'm not that kind of girl. But then I see you again and my resolve weakens. I'm afraid I can't resist you. I didn't come here to betray Miranda. She's my oldest friend, for Christ's sake. If you hadn't turned up I wouldn't have minded. Please believe me. I don't *want* to seduce you in your own home. I just can't help myself."

"We haven't done anything wrong this weekend."

"And we won't," Blythe agreed. "It's just a bit of harmless flirting."

"So you agree that it has to come to an end."

"Most definitely."

"It's not because I don't desire you, but because I respect my wife."

"That's okay. I respect her, too. We should never have embarked on an affair in the first place."

They reached the greenhouse and slipped inside. "Wow!" Blythe exclaimed at the neat rows of orchids and tuberoses. The smell was intoxicating. "This is incredible. Your gardener is a wonder!"

"He's pretty good, isn't he?"

"Handsome, too," she said, hoping to make him jealous. "But you're better looking. You're younger for a start." She placed her hand on his fly. "Well, this is a little disappointing. Shall I wake him up?"

"Absolutely not!" David replied, backing away.

She dropped to her knees and unzipped him. He pulled her up. "Blythe! I said no." Then as his face melted with desire he added, "Not here."

A sudden movement in the greenhouse distracted Jean-Paul on his way to the vegetable garden. It didn't take him long to work out what it was. He had been there before, many years ago. He stood rooted to the spot beside a cold frame recently planted with herbs. Instinct told him it was Blythe with David. His heart faltered, thinking of Miranda and those children. The parallels were impossible to ignore. He was allied with Miranda and therefore found himself in Phillip's shoes. It was not a comfortable position.

The sound of the gate alerted him to Miranda's arrival. She could tell from his ashen face that something was horribly wrong. He strode towards her. "Come with me," he said, taking her hand. His tone was firm and masterful as he tried to lead her from the greenhouse.

"What's going on?"

"Just come."

"No. If it's Blythe and David I need to know."

He stopped and looked at her intently. "You already know?"

She began to cry. "I suspected . . . but I couldn't believe . . ." She fell against him.

"I'm sorry." Miranda was too distressed to speak. He held her close and let her cry. "Let's get out of here."

Miranda shook her head. "No." Her face was red with fury. "I want to catch them. Then I want to throw them out. I don't ever want to see either of them again."

"It is not a good idea to talk to him while you're angry. You will only say things you regret."

"This is no time to be wise, Jean-Paul. I don't want them in my life. I'll never trust him again." She pulled away and strode up the path to the greenhouse. Jean-Paul let her go. He had no choice but to watch the drama unfold.

She banged on the door. "Come out!" she shouted. "Come out!" There was a short pause while Blythe ran her hands through her hair. David felt his orderly world fall about his head like the shattered pieces of a beautiful mosaic. He was the first to emerge.

"It's not what you think . . ." he began.

Miranda looked at him scornfully. "Oh really! Admiring the flowers, were you? Then why is your fly undone?" He looked down, rolled his eyes at his stupidity and zipped it up.

"Let me explain."

"Please do." Blythe stepped out. At least she had the decency to look ashamed. "You bought her the watch! You know the shop called me for your office telephone number? I thought you'd bought me something and taken the trouble to have it engraved. Big Pussycat has never been my nickname, though, has it?"

"Darling . . ."

"Oh save it. Doesn't your tart have anything to say or did you swallow her tongue?"

"You can't leave a husband all week and expect him not to look for it elsewhere," said Blythe.

"Clearly not *my* husband. I thought better of you than that, David. I put you on a pedestal. You were my hero. Now I know you're just the same as every other cheating husband. Do you love her?"

"Of course not!" he exclaimed. Blythe's face flushed with rage.

"Then I pity you—losing your family for a shag. If you loved her it might have been worth it. I want you out of the house in ten minutes and I don't want to see either of you again. If you think you've had it bad, Blythe, David's going to have it much worse. I hope you'll stick by him!"

Jean-Paul followed her to the gate where she collapsed in tears. "Come," he said. "Go to my cottage until they leave. I will look after the children. You have to be strong for them. They mustn't know what has happened."

He watched her go, her shoulders hunched, her arms crossed in front of her chest. For a moment she reminded him of Ava and his heart reached out to her.

David ran through the gardens and house calling her name, but she didn't appear. Blythe packed her bag, called Rafael away from the tree and waited impatiently for a taxi. David had no choice but to leave. He kissed the children, his head swimming with the realization that he had risked everything and lost. Only now, as he hugged them, did he fully appreciate what they meant to him.

"Why are you in a hurry?" Gus asked.

"Because I've been called away urgently. Daddy's work."

"You haven't had lunch," said Storm.

"I know. I'll have a sandwich on the train."

"Where's Mummy?"

"In the house," he lied.

"Did you make her cry?" asked Gus, frowning. He had seen her hurry down the path towards the river.

"She's fine." The children looked at him in bewilderment.

Jean-Paul stood some distance away while Blythe and Rafael piled into the taxi. Storm and Gus stood by the tree, silently watching. Then David strode across the grass to talk to Jean-Paul. "Look, I know she likes you. Talk to her, please. This is all a terrible mistake. I don't love Blythe. I love my wife. I just thought I could have it all." He rubbed his forehead in agitation. "I don't want to lose them."

Jean-Paul shrugged in that expressive French way of his. "Of course you don't."

"I'm a fool. I'm a damn, stupid fool."

"So, you can stop being a fool and be a man."

"It wasn't what you think! I had an affair with her, but it was over. I was telling her it was over!"

Jean-Paul didn't know what to say. David turned on his heel and returned to the taxi. In a moment they were gone. The children remained staring into the void he had left behind.

Jean-Paul stepped into the breach of Miranda and David's falling out. "I have seen a warren full of baby rabbits in the wood," he told the children. "Shall we go and take them some carrots?" Gus chewed his cheek. Storm slipped her hand into Jean-Paul's.

"Mummy has some lettuce in the fridge. Do they like lettuce?" she asked.

"They love lettuce, but Mummy might need it for you."

"Daddy made Mummy cry," said Gus quietly, thrusting his hands into his trouser pockets.

"Let me tell you about grown-ups, Gus," Jean-Paul began. He didn't modify his tone but talked as he would to an adult. "They argue and fight just like children. But that doesn't mean they don't love each other. Your mother and father have had a fight, like you and Storm arguing over what game to play. But they will make up and be friends again. I promise you. Do you know why?" The children shook their heads. "Because they are united by one very important thing."

"The garden?" said Gus innocently.

"No," Jean-Paul replied with a smile. "Their love for you and Storm."

Gus took Jean-Paul's other hand and the three of them walked off towards the wood.

Down in the cottage Miranda sat on the sofa and cried. Her instincts had been right. She wondered how long they had been seeing each other. She wished Jean-Paul were there to comfort her. He always had the right words. She stayed there for what seemed a very long time, until she became aware that the children would be wanting lunch. It was midday. The morning had disappeared, swallowed into betrayal and rage. She didn't know what to do with herself. How to react. How to go on.

She dried her eyes, got up and wandered around the cottage. She had not been alone there since he'd moved in and was suddenly drawn by the curiosity that had enflamed her since meeting him. *How lucky for him the bookshelves are full of French books*, she thought as she ran a finger across the bindings. She went into the kitchen and opened the fridge. It was full of vegetables and fish. She stole a carrot and glanced around the room. The kitchen was clean but cluttered with books, newspapers, box files, unopened parcels. A jacket hung over the back of a chair, a sweater lay across another. It was a lived-in room. However, there was something about the files that gave her the feeling that he had another life besides her garden. She peered outside to check he wasn't about to burst in, and lifted the lid of the first box. Inside were official looking papers. All written in French. Her French wasn't very good but it was adequate to understand the frequently repeated words Château les Lucioles.

With a racing heart she flicked through letters addressed to Monsieur de la Grandière of Château les Lucioles. Could Jean-Paul live in a château? She recalled him saying he had grown up on a vineyard. She hadn't imagined he might *own* it. Her curiosity aroused, she went on looking through the papers. There were balance sheets of figures she didn't understand, but she could understand vintages and years and the French word for wine. It didn't take long to convince herself that Jean-Paul de la Grandière owned a vineyard in Bordeaux. That while he was her gardener, he was also a businessman. *There was nothing wrong with that,* she thought. He had never pretended to live in England. The fact that he hadn't told her meant nothing. She had never asked. She had hired him as her gardener and he had done his job beautifully.

As she left the cottage she suddenly got a whiff of orange blossom again. *How strange,* she thought. *As far as I know there are no orange trees in the garden.* She walked over the bridge, her curiosity in no way abated. Jean-Paul was not what he seemed. If he owned a vineyard and lived in a château that would account for his lack of interest in money. He clearly had more than enough. She couldn't help but ask herself why, with a successful business in France, he would want to be a simple gardener in Hartington. What had drawn him to her corner of Dorset and why did he remain?

Summer

XXXII

The orchard filled with wild dandelions. The pale blue spikes of camassias rising above the grass like candles.

Hartington House, 1980

Jean-Paul returned to England and into Ava's welcome embrace. She smelled of France. Of orange blossom and grapes, freshly cut grass and hay. They lay entwined beneath the eaves of the cottage as the midday sun fell over the bed, turning her skin a golden brown. He ran his fingers over her shoulder, down the gentle descent of ribs to the soft curve of her waist and hips. Her body was slight but feminine, with undulations in all the right places. He had pulled out the pencil on top of her head and scrunched her hair in his hands so it tumbled around her face, framing it like Botticelli's Venus. He had come to know her face better than his own. Her sensitive green eyes, her long, intelligent nose, her short upper lip and her large, sensual mouth that smiled so easily and with such charm. When they made love she looked like a girl of twenty. Her cheeks flushed pink, her eyes sparkled, her lips swelled with desire and her skin shimmered with a dewy translucence.

He pushed her gently onto her back and kissed

her stomach where the skin was scarred by the marks of pregnancy. "Your stomach is very sexy," he said, pressing his face to it.

Ava laughed. "You can't find scars attractive?"

"You don't understand. You should wear them like badges of honor."

"They're ugly."

"Not to me, *ma pêche*. They're marks of womanhood. Motherhood. Femininity. The miracle of childbirth. They make you even more beautiful."

"Now I know why I love you," she said, stroking his hair. He rested his head on her belly.

"I would like you to carry *my* child," he said. Ava's fingers stopped a moment. "I wonder what a child of ours would look like."

"We'll never know."

"I would like to see your belly swell with love. A part of you and a part of me." He closed his eyes. "A son to work with me at the vineyard. A daughter to spoil and indulge as I would like to spoil and indulge you, if only I could take you back to France. I want more of you, Ava. More than you can ever give me." He laid his head beside hers on the pillow. With his hand against her cheek, he turned her face and kissed her. "I curse the God that let you meet Phillip before me."

"Don't curse, Jean-Paul. We should thank the God that brought us together, even if . . ."

He put his finger across her lips. "Don't say it. Please don't say it. Those words are like daggers to my heart. *Un arc-en-ciel*," he said softly, smiling in resignation. "Even if He has given us nothing more than a beautiful rainbow."

Ava could not curse the God that gave her Phillip. She couldn't explain to Jean-Paul that she loved her husband. That there are many ways of loving someone, as many shades as there are colors in a spectrum, and that she loved them both, at the same time, in different ways. He would not understand and she hoped he would never ask her. She thanked God for giving her Archie, Angus and Poppy even though they were obstacles to her happiness with Jean-Paul. If she had a wish, it would be for another life where she was free to love him without restraint.

She was aware that her affair jeopardized her marriage but she never imagined that Phillip would find out. They were careful and he was away so much of the time. Besides, it felt so natural working with Jean-Paul in the garden and making love to him in the grass. The two were intertwined: her love for him and her love for the garden. They had grown together and were now forever connected, like birds and berries, rabbits and radishes.

Their love had flowered with the cottage garden, now ablaze with color and humming with bees. A froth of apple blossom quivered in the breeze beside a tumbling pink rose salvaged and cultivated into an archway over the little red gate that formed the entrance to the garden. Viburnum and lilac made a fragrant backdrop to pink foxgloves and lilies, red roses and spreading alchemilla mollis. They spent hours sitting on the bench that surrounded the mountain ash, talking about nothing, taking pleasure from being together, riding that elusive rainbow.

The summer wore on and the vegetables they had planted with the children were grown and ready to pick. The square patches were neatly planted with rows of lettuces, Brussels sprouts, carrots, leeks, onions, cabbages, marrows and rhubarb. The children gathered raspberries and strawberries, rescuing the odd bird who managed to break into the netted enclosures. Sweet peas had begun to climb the arched frames Jean-Paul had erected for them, intertwined with peas. Ava picked them and arranged them all over the house. Every time she smelled them she thought of Jean-Paul. Never in her life had she been so happy. The ancient walls that enclosed the garden were adorned with roses, white wisteria, clematis and honeysuckle. Squirrels scampered playfully and doves sung low and sweet like gentle flutes. Bright yellow senecio billowed out from under the wall, spilling over the gravel path that divided the garden by way of a large cross. She basked in the loveliness of her garden, glorying in the magic they had sown there.

The long summer days of June belonged to them. The children were at school, Phillip was working on his book, locked away in his study or traveling abroad. They weeded with Hector, stealing kisses in the borders and behind bushes, sneaking off to make love under the eaves of the cottage where only the squirrels were likely to invade their privacy. They shared jokes, a language they cultivated with the same creativity and verve with which they had cultivated the gardens, and a growing love for each other and the natural world that surrounded them.

In July the children broke up from school and Jean-Paul and Ava had to take more care not to be caught. As long as they were together, they were content. The smiles they shared said more than words ever could, and the thousand times a day they brushed against each other were as electrifying as those indulgent afternoons in June when they had lain naked together and made love. Their happiness was infectious. The children played around them like bees about a honeypot. When he came home, Phillip recognized the glow of love in his wife's cheeks and wanted her more than ever. She looked like the girl he had taken to Tuscany before Archie was born. She welcomed his advances at night, ashamed of her duplicity, knowing that her marriage was something she would never discuss with Jean-Paul.

• • •

One afternoon, while the children played with Toddy's at Bucksley Farm, Jean-Paul and Ava rode out onto the hills. Purple clouds gathered above them, setting the countryside below in a dusky light. The wind swept in off the sea causing the horses to spring about excitedly. They galloped over the grass, their laughter rising into the air with the distant cry of gulls. At times like this they could imagine they were alone in the world, just the two of them. They could forget the complications down in the valley. Up here they could see for miles, the rolling fields, the silver river snaking down to the sea, the misty horizon where it was already raining, glimpses of a future they could only dream of.

Jean-Paul stopped first. His cheeks were flushed, his brown eyes sparkling happily. "We're going to get very wet," he said, holding out his hand for Ava to take.

"Let's tie the horses up under a tree. We'll never get back before it rains," she suggested.

He squeezed her hand before letting it go. "I love you," he said, smiling. "I don't think I've ever loved you more."

"*Et moi aussi, je t'aime*," she replied, smiling back.

They rode over to a small copse where they dismounted and tied up the horses. No sooner were they under the umbrella of leaves than it started to rain. Jean-Paul held her close, leaning back against the thick trunk. "I'm grateful to the rain," he said with a chuckle. "Today we have the perfect excuse to remain up here all afternoon."

"Toddy can give the children tea."

"And we can steal an hour or two."

"The garden will love this."

"It's been very dry lately. Ian Fitzherbert will love it, too."

"Farmers are a funny lot. They're never completely happy with the weather. It's either too dry or too wet, too hot, too cold. I think if they were able to control it with a remote they'd still be dissatisfied."

"It's the same at the vineyard. They fret about the frost. Oh la la! You wouldn't believe the trouble they go to to keep it away."

"Is it possible to keep it away?"

"Oh yes. They can light braziers to warm the air. It is not unheard of for a rich vineyard to fly helicopters low over the fields to circulate the air."

"That's a great extravagance."

"Not if it saves the grape."

"You love it, don't you?"

"It is my home. But without you it will be soulless."

"Let's not think about that now."

"I'm selfish, Ava. I want you for myself. Exclusively. I want to marry you, have armfuls of children to run up and down the vines as I did. Just think what we can do to the gardens of Les Lucioles. With our magic we can make it the most beautiful château in France."

"Your mother has already done that."

"We will reach even greater heights. Don't you see what a combination we are?"

"Yes. But I am married and I already have children to run around the gardens here. We cannot change what is past; we can only live in the moment. It's all we have."

"Do you still sleep with Phillip?" His question caught her off guard.

She stiffened. She didn't want to lie to him, but neither did she want to hurt him. "Please don't ask me."

"Don't I have a right to know?"

"What difference would it make?"

"Peace of mind."

"It changes nothing between us."

"I want you to belong to me."

"I never will, my darling. I will always be married to Phillip."

"I could bear it if you were his wife in name only."

"Isn't love more important than ownership? Isn't it enough to know that I love you body and soul?"

He kissed her forehead. "It should be."

"It must be. It is all I can give you."

At that moment the clouds parted and the sun beamed through like a torch from Heaven. They walked hand in hand into the rain to watch as a vibrant rainbow straddled the valley. The colors were glorious, from deep red to pale purple.

"That is what we have," said Jean-Paul.

"And look how beautiful it is."

He swung her into his arms and kissed her. "I don't want to lose you. I'm so frightened I will lose you."

"Don't . . ."

"Promise me that you will come to me when your children are grown up and no longer need you?"

"I can't promise."

"Yes, you can. If you love me you will be here when I come back to get you. Your children will be grown up. Phillip will be an old man. You will be free."

"But you will marry and have children of your own."

"I will never love another."

"You can't put your life on hold for me. I love you, but I'm realistic enough to know that life will part us. Like that rainbow, the rain will take us."

"It will not take our love. I will love you forever."

She took his damp face in her hands and gazed at him lovingly. "You won't want me when I'm an old woman. You will still be young and handsome."

"My heart will always belong to you."

"You're too idealistic. Life isn't like that."

"Just promise me."

"Okay. I promise you. When the children no longer need me. When Phillip is an old man. When I'm free, you can come back and get me."

He hugged her fiercely. "Now I can breathe again, because whatever happens I have something to look forward to." Ava leaned against him, certain that one day he'd give his heart to another woman, raise his own children at Les Lucioles and forget the promise they had made.

She stared at the rainbow, willing it to last. "Can you see pink between the green and the blue?"

"You tease me. There is no pink there. It is next to red, no?"

"Look harder."

"I'm looking as hard as I can."

"That is not hard enough."

"I don't believe it exists."

"Of course it does. I can see it. My eyes don't lie."

"Then you have a sense that I lack."

"Look, the rain has stopped."

"We will lose the rainbow."

"But we have one of our own, right here, inside us." She pressed her hand to her heart. "It'll last as long as we want it to."

In August the weather was hot and dry. The children played with Toddy's twins and other friends from school who joined their pack and roamed the gardens like excitable dogs. Toddy noticed Ava's radiance but didn't imagine for a moment it was because of Jean-Paul. Ava wasn't the sort to have an affair. Her marriage to Phillip was the strongest she knew. She watched her friend walk with a bounce in her step, a grin that remained even when her face was in repose and a bubbling laugh that came from deep inside her, like a secret underground spring. She envied Ava's inner contentment. Her life was like a gentle summer breeze.

Phillip congratulated himself on having taken her to France. Ever since that short break Ava had been transformed. He cursed his book, the fact that it took him away from her. Yet, the sound of her voice singing in the bushes outside, humming in the hall as she arranged flowers, playing in the garden with their children, filled him with joy. They held weekend house parties, cramming the house with friends from London: writers, historians, journalists and painters. Mrs. Marley's eyes bulged at the names, having seen them in the papers or heard them on the radio. They stayed up late at night, the men smoking cigars and drinking port, the women chatting in the drawing room, gossiping about their husbands. They were an older crowd of Phillip's friends, but Ava found them stimulating. Phillip knew that she sneaked off to be alone. He loved that about her—one moment vivacious, the next as solitary as a sandpiper. He never suspected that she took herself off to the little cottage to make love to Jean-Paul. He was confident of her devotion.

At the end of August, Jean-Paul received a telephone call from his mother. It was time to come home. "Your father wants you to take over the vineyard," she said. "He is getting older and his health is not as good as it was."

"Is he ill?"

"No, but he's tired and wants to hand it over to you. The truth is, Jean-Paul, he spends so much time in Paris . . ." Her voice trailed off.

"I see."

"He wants you home early September. He insists."

Jean-Paul was winded with panic. He couldn't bear to face the end of their affair. A giant crack was splitting his heart in two. He had to tell someone. "*Maman*, I am in love," he confessed. The tone of his voice told her that the situation wasn't a happy one.

"I am so pleased, darling. Who is she?"

"You know her."

She hesitated, uncomfortable. "I do?"

"She came to Les Lucioles. It is Ava."

There was a long pause while Antoinette struggled with the terrible revelation. "Not Ava Lightly, surely?"

"Yes, *maman*. We are in love."

"But she is married, Jean-Paul."

"I know." His voice wavered, but Antoinette's gained an edge of steel.

"Does Phillip know?"

"No."

"Does anyone know?"

"Just us."

"It must end," she instructed firmly. "It must end at once!"

"I can't."

"You must. She is not available to you, Jean-Paul. She has a husband and children. Not to mention the fact that Phillip is a close friend of your father. You have no idea what you're getting yourself into. It can only bring unhappiness to everyone, including you. You must come home immediately."

"I thought you'd understand."

"Understand? Yes, I understand. I have suffered years as a consequence of your father's continuing adultery. Let's speak no more about it. I don't want to hear her name mentioned ever again."

"But *maman*!"

Her voice softened. "It is because I love you, Jean-Paul. You are my only son. I have high hopes for you; a good marriage, children, a life here at Les Lucioles. Ava Lightly is a dead end."

"Ava Lightly is my life."

"You are young enough to start a new one. You will recover. She is irresponsible to have led you astray."

"I will not hear a word against her. It was I who was irresponsible. I am the guilty one. She would not have yielded had I not pushed and pushed. Be certain of this, *maman*, if I have to leave her, I will never recover."

His mother tut-tutted down the line. "This is nonsense. But it is over. As far as I am concerned, it is in the past. You will come home the first week of September. Let's speak no more about it."

Jean-Paul fumed alone in the cottage. Of course, his mother was right. Ava Lightly was not his to have. He couldn't convince her to leave her children; love and loyalty were two of the qualities he most admired in her. Would she be the Ava he adored if she were capable of leaving her young family for him, if she were capable of such selfishness?

He couldn't remember the last time he had cried. Certainly not since childhood. Yet the thought of leaving her reduced him to sobs. He buried his face in a pillow. He had ridden the rainbow knowing that in the end he'd pay for it with his own blood. For all the pain, he was certain of one thing: it had been worth it—a lifetime of suffering for a summer of joy.

XXXIII

The amber light of dusk, the smell of burning fields, the shortening days of September

As if to reflect their misery, the skies were gray, the rain heavy and unrelenting on the roof of the cottage, and there was not a glimmer of a rainbow in sight. Ava made tea in his small kitchen, trying to retain a sense of normality while her world was collapsing about her. She laid the table. Two teacups, two saucers, a plate of coffee cake and a jug of milk. They sat opposite each other, barely daring to speak, knowing words were superfluous when saying good-bye.

They held hands across the table like prisoners through bars and gazed at each other in despair. They both felt the same pain in their hearts, the same tearing of nerves and flesh, the same irreparable damage to their souls. Ava poured tea and sliced two pieces of cake, but its delicious taste was little consolation.

"It is September. I have to return to France. Even though I would sacrifice the vineyard and my inheritance for you, living here in secret is no life."

"Darling Jean-Paul, I would never ask that of you. We always knew the summer would come to an end."

"Please don't cry," he said when her eyes filled with tears. "If you cry I will never be able to leave."

"Loving you has been my greatest joy and my most dreadful sorrow. You will always be here in my heart. Every day I walk around our garden I will think of you and with every year that passes my love will grow stronger and deeper."

"I will wait for you, *ma pêche*." She so longed for him to mean it. Gratefully she grabbed the life-line he now threw her.

"You promise? Because as soon as my children are older and Phillip doesn't need me I will cut myself free. I'll be ready for you to take me to France. We can grow old together and love without guilt, knowing that I stayed when I had to. That I did my duty."

"I wish you could leave with me now, but you're not that sort of woman and I love you for it. We have got away without hurting anyone. Only our-selves."

She wiped her cheek with the back of her hand. "Everything will be so empty once you're gone. So pointless. There will be no more magic, just soil and plants like every other garden in the world."

He looked at her with fire in his eyes. "The magic is deep in the earth, Ava. It will always be there because we sowed it. Don't ever forget that."

They made love one last time as the rain rattled against the windows. "One day I'll come back to this cottage and reclaim you," he said, kissing her temple. "I'll find you here, waiting for me, and nothing will have changed. The teacups will be on the table, the kettle hot and a fresh coffee cake, your very best, to welcome me home. This is our special place. Leave it as it is. As a shrine to us, so that one day, when I come back, it will be like yesterday. I will walk in as if I have only been away for an hour and we will pick up where we left off. We will look older, a little frayed at the edges, a little wiser, but our love won't have changed. I will take you to France and we will sow our magic in the gardens of Les Lucioles and live out the rest of our days together."

"What a beautiful dream," she sighed, burying her face in his neck.

"If we dream hard enough it might come true. Like your silly pink in between the green and the blue. If we look hard enough we may see it."

"We'll create a rainbow to last," she whispered, no longer able to restrain her tears.

She stood in the doorway and watched him walk away. It was as he wanted, a small bag in his hand, as if he were only going for an hour. She watched until he was out of sight, walking down the river towards the village where he would take a taxi to the station. He hadn't wanted to say good-bye to the children or Phillip; he didn't think he could bear it. Instead, he had kissed the woman he loved and taken her love with him.

No one else seemed in the least surprised that Jean-Paul had gone, though Phillip was a little put out that he hadn't bothered to say good-bye. It was the end of the summer and he had always said he would stay a year. Hector and Ava continued in the gardens as they always had. But Hector missed him, too. Ava wondered whether he knew about their affair; he looked at her with such sympathy in his eyes, as if he understood her pain. The children went back to school and Phillip finished his book. Toddy took Ava riding on the hills and noticed that the bounce had gone from her step and that she had lost her glow. She suspected it had something to do with Jean-Paul, but for once she kept her thoughts to herself. When Ava had told her that Jean-Paul had left, she had tried so hard to mask her pain, but Toddy had seen it behind her eyes and in the way she had averted her gaze. She knew if she pressed her on the subject she would cause her friend terrible suffering. Ava would tell her when she was ready. In the meantime, she stayed close, as an old and trusted friend, giving comfort with her familiar presence.

Ava wandered around the gardens like a specter. Alone at night she sat on the bench beneath the mountain ash, recalling their relationship in painstaking detail, from the day they met to the day they parted, until finally she withdrew to the cottage where she began her scrapbook, sticking in petals from the flowers they had planted together and leaves from trees and shrubs that held a special significance for them. She wrote poems, descriptions of the gardens, lists of the things she loved the most from the morning light on the lawn to snowdrops peeping through frost. She wrote because it was cathartic and because her memories relieved the pain.

Jean-Paul returned to France, his heart bleeding from a wound that would never heal. His life stretched out before him like an eternal sea upon which he would drift, abandoned and alone, like the Flying Dutchman. He had no desire to discuss his feelings, but his father picked him up at the airport and drove him home, and he found himself confiding his hurt. To Jean-Paul's surprise, Henri didn't berate him as his mother had done, but smiled indulgently. "Look," he began when they were on the open road. "Let's talk man to man." Jean-Paul was in no mood for one of his father's lectures. "I make it no secret that I have lived half my life in Paris with Yvette. There is nothing wrong with a man taking a mistress. There's a great deal wrong with a man wanting to *marry* his mistress. Especially if the woman in question is Ava Lightly."

"I didn't plan to fall in love with her, *Papa*."

"I don't question your taste, Jean-Paul. In fact, I admire it. She's a rather fascinating woman. But you have a responsibility at Les Lucioles. You are my only son and I need you to produce an heir to continue after you are gone. Ava has her own family. Nothing will come from a relationship with her. She is as dry as the desert. You need a fertile young filly . . ."

"I don't want anyone else," Jean-Paul interrupted.

"I'm not asking you to fall in love with another woman. I didn't fall in love with your mother. I admired her, respected her. I knew she would be good for me and Les Lucioles and I was right. Look what she has done to the gardens! She created them out of nothing and now they are the envy of France. She is the perfect hostess to my clients. The perfect chatelaine. A good wife and mother. It is a shame she did not bear me more children. *Tant pis!* Marry a lady like I did. Take a mistress. But Ava is the wife of my friend and therefore she is out of bounds. Cut your losses and thank the stars that Phillip never found out."

"I don't want to marry a woman I don't love," Jean-Paul began, but he knew his father wouldn't understand.

"Love," he said dismissively. "Love with your head, not with your heart. That is the advice I give to you." He patted his son's knee and his voice softened. "I admire you for walking away, though. For leaving without causing ripples. Had Ava not been married she would have made the perfect wife for Les Lucioles. You are not far off the mark. Find another Ava."

"There is only one."

Henri shook his head and chuckled. "You are young. You will learn that no woman is unique. But if you marry your mistress, you create a vacancy."

As the car swept up the drive to the château Jean-Paul felt more isolated than ever. Without Ava by his side its beauty was an affront. He wished the sky were gray and the vines less luxuriant. It was indecent that the place should vibrate with such magnificence when his heart was so full of unhappiness. The dogs trotted out to greet him and he patted their heads and rubbed his face into their necks.

"Go and see your mother," said Henri. "She is beside herself. She thinks this is all her fault."

Jean-Paul found his mother on her knees beside the dovecote, pulling out weeds. When she turned to greet him he could see that she had been crying. "*Maman?*" he inquired anxiously, hurrying to her side to embrace her. "I'm so sorry that I've caused you pain."

"It is all my fault," she whispered, taking his hand. "I encouraged her to persuade you to return to England. She must have thought I condoned the affair. But I didn't know. I was only thinking of you. I didn't consider her, not for a moment."

"It's not your fault. I was already in love with her. If she hadn't come I would have returned to her in the end."

Antoinette's voice hardened. She looked at him

steadily. "But you won't ever go back, will you, Jean-Paul?" When he hesitated, she pressed him further. "Your father has made my life a misery because of Yvette. Don't ruin Phillip's life. Think of the children."

"We have both thought of nothing but the children. That is why I am here."

Her shoulders drooped. "Thank God." She pushed herself up. Jean-Paul followed her back through the gate to the château. "You are young. You will love again. You can't see it now, but you will. The heart has a miraculous way of mending. You think it is not strong enough to withstand such pain and yet it survives to love again.

"Find a girl who can make you happy and give you children. Fill Les Lucioles with love and laughter. Don't be like your father. Make her happy in return by remaining faithful to her as your father should have remained loyal to me. Forget the past. Look at this beautiful corner of Bordeaux. It is ripe for a new family and a new beginning. You will promise me, Jean-Paul?"

"I will try."

She stopped on the lawn and turned to him, determined to bring the matter to a close. "No, you will promise me. I'm your mother and I love you. You're all I have. I know what is best for you. Don't contact her again. Leave her in peace with her family. Please, Jean-Paul. If you want to be happy, consign her to the past and let her go."

"I will wait for her children to grow up. When they no longer need her she will come to me."

"*Eh bien*, let us leave it at that," she conceded, certain that he would forget about Ava in time and marry someone else. "Come now, I want to show you what I have planted in the orchard." He let her slip her hand through his arm and walk him back up the garden.

Jean-Paul felt a small spark ignite in the stone chambers of his heart. For the first time since leaving her he felt uplifted. He would nurture the gardens and tend the vineyard, plant more trees and shrubs and expand the land. He would channel his love into Les Lucioles so that when she finally came home she would see what a paradise he had built for her. She would know that he had never stopped loving her.

It was in the cottage that Ava began to feel sick, a continuous nausea that she put down to misery. She didn't want to eat and only Coca-Cola calmed her stomach. She drank it by the can, lying on the bed beneath the eaves, writing her scrapbook in her pretty looped handwriting. The days wore on. If it wasn't for the approaching autumn she noticed in the cooler wind and shorter days and in the gradual fading of color in her garden, all the days would have merged into one long, miserable day. She wanted to write to Jean-Paul, or telephone him just to hear his voice, but she knew it was useless.

Only time would dull the pain of their parting and she had to give herself that. So she wrote the scrapbook with the intention of one day giving it to him so that he would know how much she had missed him. That she had never given up.

"You're looking rather pale, Shrub," said Phillip one evening during dinner. "You're not eating. Are you unwell?"

"I don't think so. I just feel tired and deflated. Must be the weather."

"Nonsense. I think you're pregnant."

Ava was astonished. "Pregnant? Do you think?"

"Absolutely. You're feeling sick. You're tired all the time. You're not eating. There's nothing physically wrong with you. Why don't you get one of those kits they're always advertising and check."

"I hope you're wrong."

"Why? It wasn't so long ago that you yearned for another child." He took her hand. "Perhaps your wish has been granted. Why not, eh? We make such charming children." Ava paled at the thought of another baby. Then a small spark of optimism ignited in her heart. If she was pregnant, it could be Jean-Paul's baby. She put her hand across her lips to hide her smile. Jean-Paul's baby. She barely dared cast the wish.

The following day she drove to the chemist and bought a kit. With trembling fingers she dipped the stick into her urine, then waited. She closed her eyes and wished: *If there is a God please give me*

468

the blessing of Jean-Paul's child so that I may keep a part of him to love. I haven't hurt anyone. I've sacrificed my love for my husband and children. A baby shall be my reward, were I to deserve it. She opened her eyes to see the clear blue stripe of a positive result. She was indeed pregnant.

She rushed to the telephone to tell Jean-Paul that the child he had longed for was growing in her belly. A part of him and a part of her, created with love. She opened the address book to find the number of Les Lucioles, but she didn't dial. She stood staring at the page, her enthusiasm shriveling in the harsh glare of reality. What would it achieve? It would only make their situation even more impossible. He'd have every right to claim their child. He had nothing to lose. She, on the other hand, had everything to lose. If she confessed to Phillip, she would risk her own children and create unhappiness for everyone around her. She would hurt the very people she had sacrificed everything to protect. She closed the book. It would have to be her secret. No one must ever know. Phillip would think it was his and the children would accept their new brother or sister without question. She would take the truth to her grave.

The following spring, when daffodils raised their pretty heads and blossom floated on the breeze like confetti, Ava gave birth to a little girl. She insisted on calling her Peach after Jean-Paul's nickname for her. Verity questioned her daughter's state of mind in choosing such a ridiculous name, but Phillip indulged her. He gazed upon his new daughter with pride. According to him, Peach looked just like her mother. Ava was relieved at the baby's blond hair and fair skin, but she saw Jean-Paul in the beauty of her smile. To Ava, every smile was a gift.

XXXIV

The melancholy light of summer's end fills my soul with wistfulness

London, 2006

David had never felt lonelier. He had lost everything. Miranda refused to answer his calls. He had written to her, hoping she'd take the time to read his lengthy apology and confessions of stupidity and arrogance. Most of all he missed his children. He tried to keep focused at work, yet Gus's and Storm's inquiring little faces surfaced to flood his heart with shame. He hadn't spoken to Blythe since they had parted at Waterloo Station. He had watched her walk through the crowds of commuters holding Rafael by the hand and had suffered a pang of self-loathing. The people who lost the most were the children. Rafael would never again enjoy a weekend in the hollow tree, and Gus and Storm would never again run around the old ruined castle with their father. Just when he was beginning to enjoy them.

He regretted his arrogance. He had believed he had a right to everything because he worked hard and earned lots of money. But Miranda wasn't one of his chattels like his house and his car, to be added to a list that included mistress and pied-à-terre. He loved her. She was the mother of his children. He was a family man. He'd do anything to put back the clock. Anything.

David had many acquaintances, but there was only one friend he could really talk to. Somerled Macdonald, nicknamed Mac, was someone he had known for a very long time. The kind of man he could trust to keep the most shameful of secrets and not think any less of him for it. With honest hazel eyes, the strong, sturdy body of a gifted sportsman, Mac was reliable and consistent, with a sense of humor that always made the best out of the very worst. Mac's wife, Lottie, had grown close to Miranda over the years they had been married. They had enjoyed weekends shooting on Mac's family estate in Yorkshire, and David shared Mac's obsession with rugby and cricket, staying up until the early hours of the morning in Mac's Fulham sitting room to watch the Ashes on the telly. Mac was Gus's godfather and David was godfather to Mac and Lottie's son, Alexander.

Now it was he who needed a godfather's wise counsel.

While Lottie was upstairs putting Alexander to bed, David broke down in front of his old friend. "I've been a total bastard," he said, sitting on the sofa and rubbing his face in his hands. "I've lost everything for what? A meaningless affair!" Mac listened patiently while he recounted his foolishness in a miserable soliloquy. "Miranda's only ever been the perfect wife and look how I've treated her! My mother would say what goes around comes around and I fully deserve to be kicked out." He raised red-rimmed eyes in supplication. "What do I do? Tell me, Mac. How do I get her back?"

Mac sat with his legs crossed, a glass of lager in his hand, one trouser leg raised to reveal a pair of rugby socks. "You'll get her back, Dave. But she'll make you crawl through the mud first. There's no point going over what's done. It's in the past and you can't change it. The first thing to do is write to her."

"I've done that. I bet she threw my letter in the bin." He took a gulp of whisky.

"I doubt it. If she still loves you, as I bet she does, she'll want to hear your apology. She'll want to hear that you wish it had never happened, that you love her and want her back. How much you value her and the children. How much did you grovel?"

"A lot."

Mac shrugged in his laid-back way. "Putting-your-hands-in-the-mud-to-begin-the-long-crawl-back kind of a lot?"

"Yes, I think so."

Mac grinned and took a swig of lager. "Good. That's a start. Send flowers with a note telling her that she's the only woman in your life. I don't mean a small bunch, fill her kitchen with roses. It's only when you lose someone that you realize how much they mean to you. Use that, it's how you feel right now. If you really want her back you're going to have to fight hard. She's hurt and humiliated. Christ, why you didn't choose someone from another world, I can't imagine! Anyway, that's by the by, you're the father of her children and she's not going to want to lose you either. She'll just want you to suffer as much as she's suffering. Prepare to spend the next ten years of marriage eating humble pie."

"I don't want my kids to see me as a monster. I couldn't bear them to think that . . ." He put his head in his hands again. The whisky had made him dizzy.

"She's a sensible woman. She's not going to poison her children against you."

"People do stupid things when they're in a corner." He heaved a sigh and sat back against the cushions. "You know, I've been so one-track minded, thinking about myself and work, I've been

473

a terrible father. I spent weekends watching sports on telly rather than take my kids off to build camps and catch fish. Then I saw the gardener, Jean-Paul, worming his way into my shoes." He laughed bitterly. "I saw him in the vegetable garden with Miranda and the children. The sun was out, the birds chirping in the trees, all they needed was a sodding dog to make it picture-perfect. I realized I was being pushed out of my own family and you know what? It was all my fault. Not Jean-Paul's. God, he was just doing his job, brilliantly. I distanced myself from Blythe, until she turned up at the office in nothing but a fur coat. After that I resolved to finish it with her and spend more time with my family. I was just beginning to enjoy them when Miranda went and asked her down for the weekend. I didn't continue the affair, I tried to finish it as tactfully as I could. I knew if I made her cross she could spill the beans and ruin everything. Miranda thought I was fucking her in the greenhouse. That's what it looked like, but it simply wasn't true. God, I'm stupid."

"Oh, there were plenty of stupid men before you and there'll be plenty of stupid men after you. You're not unique."

"Look at you, Mac," said David admiringly, draining his glass. "You and Lottie are so strong. Really strong. You're not like me. You've always been self-confident. Happy in your skin. Ever since your school days when you shone on the rugby pitches. I envy you. You'd never be so foolish."

Mac shrugged again. "Everyone makes mistakes. She'll forgive you. Look, here comes my lovely wife."

Lottie descended the stairs with the contented smile of a mother whose child is asleep at last. "Would you like another whisky?" she asked David, looking at him sympathetically. She had heard the whole conversation from Alexander's room above.

"You're close to Miranda, Lottie. Can you talk to her? Persuade her to see me at least." Lottie didn't know whether to play ignorant, or admit that she had listened through the wall. She looked to Mac, who nodded encouragement.

"I couldn't help hearing," she said, taking his glass to refill. "I'll call Miranda."

David looked relieved. "Thank you, Lottie. You're an angel."

"I can't promise anything."

"I know. But seeing as she won't speak to me at all, you're the only way I can get a message to her."

"And what do you want me to say?"

"That I love her. I'm sorry. I want her back." He leaned forward to rest his elbows on his knees and rubbed his eyes. "I miss her and I miss the kids. I'm in Hell."

Mac smiled confidently. Lottie would know exactly what to say.

● ● ●

Down at Hartington House, Miranda sat at her desk typing furiously on her laptop. Absorbed by her novel, she was able to block out the horror of her own relationship. Drawing heavily on Ava Lightly's scrapbook, Jean-Paul, and her own misery, she found the words spilled out so fast her fingers were barely able to keep up. She had written one hundred and ten thousand words and to her surprise it was lyrical and passionate, intelligent and gripping. In spite of the collapse of her marriage, she felt optimistic that at least something good would come out of her unhappiness. Notwithstanding her distraction, she was aware once again of the softly pervading scent of orange blossom.

Miranda took consolation in Jean-Paul. He listened as she cried in his sitting room, recounting how she and David had met, courted and married. He encouraged her to dwell on the things she loved about him. The good times they had enjoyed. The reasons they had married in the first place. She agreed that the cracks were already there in London; the distance imposed upon them after they moved to the country had only deepened them. In London she had been so busy with her own life she had barely noticed. Suddenly, at Hartington, they had all settled in without him; she had grown accustomed to being on her own, and a coolness had swept in through those cracks like a silky breeze.

She longed to tell Jean-Paul that she had fallen in love with him, but she was ashamed. He was so dignified, she dared not cause him embarrassment.

Miranda wrote obsessively. She wrote at night once the children were in bed, until the early hours of the morning when the sound of waking birds and the watery light of dawn tumbled into her study to remind her of the time. She wrote until her eyes stung and her eyelids grew heavy. During the day she was able to work because the children were out with Jean-Paul. To them, nothing had changed. They seemed to accept that their father was unable to come down due to work. Gus looked up at her with dark, suspicious eyes, but she was able to convince him that in spite of their argument, Mummy and Daddy were friends again. Jean-Paul took them riding on Jeremy's horses, up onto the hill from where they could see the sea. He gazed on the horizon remembering that enchanted day when it had rained and he and Ava had sought shelter beneath the trees.

Jean-Paul was proud of the gardens. With the help of Mr. Underwood and Miranda, he had brought them back to their former glory. There were still spaces to plant things and some shrubs would take a few seasons to grow to their full promise, but they had recaptured some of the magic. The place no longer felt soulless. He walked up the path that snaked through the cottage garden towards the dovecote and felt Ava there among the roses and lilies. Sometimes, when he sat on the bench that surrounded the mountain ash, he thought he could smell the sweet scent of orange blossom. He could close his eyes and feel her sitting beside him, congratulating him on the garden, admiring the flowers as she had admired his painting when he had first designed it. Those times were bittersweet. He would blink back tears and wonder whether he had wasted his life waiting for her, when he could have moved on, married someone else and had children. He would watch Gus and Storm playing in the garden as Archie, Angus and Poppy had done twenty-six years before, and yearn for what he had never had.

David's letter was five pages long and full of apologies, of how much he missed her and the children. A week later she received a vanload of red roses with a note that said: *It is only through losing you that I realize how much I love you. I was an idiot to take someone so special and so precious for granted.* Then she received a telephone call from Lottie. "David was over the other night with Mac," she told her. "He's devastated. I've never seen him look so tragic."

"He deserves everything he gets. He slept with a friend of mine. He even shagged her in our greenhouse!"

"He said he didn't."

"Well, why was his fly undone?"

"That I can't answer," Lottie conceded. "Look, he's made a terrible mistake and he's very aware of it. He wishes he could turn the clock back. That it had never happened."

"I know. I got a five-page letter."

"He asked Mac for advice. He's desperate to get you back. He misses the children . . ."

"Jean-Paul is a better father than he's ever been."

"Yes, he mentioned Jean-Paul."

"I bet he did. He puts David to shame."

"David's put himself to shame," said Lottie wisely. "Why don't you at least talk to him?"

"Not yet. It's too soon. I've got to clear my head. It's all too hideous. I'm just getting by, you know."

"Let him see the children then," Lottie suggested diplomatically. She was determined to come away with something to give David.

Miranda thought about it for a moment. "You're right," she conceded. "The fight's between me and David. It's got nothing to do with the children."

"That's very big of you, Miranda," she said, relieved. It was a start.

"Tell him he can come down this weekend. I'll come up to London and stay in a hotel. I've promised a friend a day shopping and I don't want to let her down. It'll do me good to get away for a couple of days. I'll book into the Berkeley on Friday night and return Sunday afternoon."

"You're more than welcome to stay with us," Lottie suggested.

"You're sweet, Lottie, thank you. I'll be with my friend Etta. Anyway, the least David can do is pay for a major suite. I'd stay in Kensington if it wasn't for the fact that he's probably shagged Blythe there."

"Good idea. I'll pass all that on, except the last bit, and call you back."

"Thanks, Lottie."

"It's a pleasure. We love you both, Miranda. I hope you can work through this."

"So do I." But Miranda wasn't sure that she wanted to. Her mind turned to Jean-Paul. Until she confronted him, she wasn't sure what she wanted.

Jean-Paul was sitting on the bench beneath the mountain ash. The children were digging a hole among the larches by the dovecote. "Do you mind if I join you?" she asked, opening the little red gate and stepping beneath the arch of pink roses.

"Please. How are you feeling?" he asked.

She sat down beside him and sighed, not knowing where to start. "He's written a long love letter. Apologized, said he regrets everything and wants me back. He's filled my kitchen with red roses."

"That is a good start."

"I've decided to let him see the children this weekend. I'll go up to London with Henrietta and stay in a nice hotel. After all, it's not their fight. Why should they suffer?"

"You are very wise."

"I wish I was. You're wise, Jean-Paul. You're a better father than he is. I guess Gus just needed a dad who took trouble with him. David wasn't that dad. You were." She lowered her eyes. "Thanks to you, Jean-Paul, I've learned to enjoy their company and get my hands dirty. I've grown to love these gardens. I never thought I would. I was such a Londoner. The idea of gumboots made me recoil in horror, now I rarely wear my heels and I don't mind. I've changed. You've changed me."

"It is not me," Jean-Paul said softly. "I wish I could take credit, but I can't. It is the magic in the garden."

"The magic didn't come all by itself. You put it there." She felt herself blush.

"The magic was always there, Miranda, I just brought it back to life."

She took a deep breath. "You're an incredible man, Jean-Paul. You're wise, you're kind, you're adorable with the children. You're there for me, too. I've come to rely on you. In fact, I'm falling in love with you." He didn't reply, but put his arm around her shoulders and held her close.

"Miranda, you're not in love with me. You're confused."

"I'm not. I think I fell in love with you the day Storm brought you home."

He took a moment to find the right words to avoid hurting her. "You know I cannot love you back. Not in the way you want me to," he said at last.

Miranda felt the sudden rise of tears and tried to blink them away. "You can't?"

"I love you as a dear friend. But I will always love another. No one can ever take her place in my heart. She has it for always."

"Who is she?"

"Someone I knew a long time ago. She was married with children. We suffered an impossible love."

"She stayed with her husband?"

"She wouldn't leave her children for me. Her love for them was deeper. It was the right thing to do. It was a long time ago. Another life. I was young. Now I am old." He chuckled at his own foolishness. "I have given her every year of my life since the day we parted almost thirty years ago."

"You never tried to move on?" Miranda was astonished by such devotion. "I didn't think people loved like that in this day and age."

"When you love like that, you cannot move on. No one could compare to her. She spoiled me for anyone else. I had lived a great love affair, nothing less would do."

Miranda felt she had heard this story somewhere before. Suddenly she grew dizzy with the realization that the secret scrapbook that had so captured her imagination had possibly been meant for him. Had Ava Lightly loved Jean-Paul? "How long did your affair last?" she asked carefully.

"A year," he replied. Now she was certain. But what did M.F. stand for? She would have to read through the book again to find the answer.

"What was she like?"

"She was unique, eccentric, funny and sweet. A talented gardener. Someone who appreciated nature. She taught me all I know."

Miranda hurried into the house. The scrapbook was so fat, with so many pages. If Jean-Paul was indeed M.F. then it was no coincidence that he had come to work in her gardens. It was no coincidence that he had resurrected the gardens the way Ava Lightly had planted them. He had known every inch of the estate because he had worked in it with her. He had painted the picture of the cottage garden. He had come back to find Ava, but found Miranda and her family instead. That's why he had looked so sad. Ava hadn't waited for him as she had promised. Then why had she left the scrapbook in the cottage? Why hadn't she simply sent it to him in France?

She flicked through the pages searching for descriptions of M.F. Now she had made the connection it all began to fit into place like a blurred vision moving into focus. At last she found the sentence that gave him away:

Oh, Mr. Frenchman, you took a large slice of my heart with you when you left. The wound will never heal but bleed and bleed until there is nothing left of me. My children are my consolation, without them my heart would be devoid of love.

XXXV

*The comforting silence of midnight.
I always knew heaven was up
there beyond the darkness.*

That night Miranda refrained from writing her own novel and settled into bed with a cup of soup. She wanted to finish the scrapbook. She wanted to know what happened in the end. She turned the pages until she reached the place where she had left off and impatiently resumed.

Jean-Paul sat in his sitting room contemplating the empty château with a sinking heart. He couldn't stay at Hartington forever. He had done what he had set out to do: revive the gardens as Ava would have wanted. He had no idea where she was and a part of him was too afraid to find out. She had left without a word, that was all there was to it. Almost three decades had passed without a murmur of reassurance from her. She had moved on with her life and he had returned to France to take over the vineyard as he had had no choice but to do.

He had gone home to lick his wounds and throw himself into his new life. His mother had dedicated herself to introducing him to all the respectable, beautiful French women she could find, but none impressed him. His heart was numb and there was no one who could rouse it. Antoinette longed for grandchildren, but Jean-Paul was firm in his determination to remain true to Ava, even though Ava was unable to remain true to him. His mother begged and implored him to marry for convenience, in order to leave the château to a child of his blood, but he refused. If he married it would be a betrayal. Ava remained married because she had no choice. He did and he chose not to. He did not remain celibate. He was a man with needs, but they meant nothing; soulless encounters that came and went like shadows in the night.

It was his mother's death that propelled him to return to Hartington. He had looked after her as a devoted son, but once free he did what he had waited twenty-six years to do: find Ava and bring her back. But life is not a storybook with a happy ending. If he expected her to be waiting for him in the cottage, he was disappointed. What good would it do to search the country for her? That chapter was closed.

Miranda began to cry. The end of the book was more tragic than she had imagined. Ava had kept the cottage a shrine. That was why the table was still laid for two; the only way she could prove her loyalty to him was to leave the place exactly as it was. She remained married, raised her children and continued as before, yet the cottage stood as testament of her love for him.

Miranda was surprised to read that Ava had had

another child as she had contemplated before the affair with Jean-Paul began. It was another tie to keep herself from leaving. Peach tied her to the nursery and restrained her from bolting.

Peach is my consolation and my joy. Every day she fills me with wonder and appreciation. I am blessed. Out of the ashes this little soul rises to dry my tears and stroke my wounded heart with her gentle gaze and enchanting smile. I thought that part of me had died the day he left, but I was wrong. It was growing inside me as bright and beautiful as the man himself. Peach came with enough love to bind together the broken pieces of my spirit and mend my shattered world. If it hadn't been for her I would surely have shriveled like an early flower killed by frost. Peach is my everything and she doesn't even know it. One day I'll tell her. God give me that courage . . . God, give me the time . . .

Miranda was stunned. She reread the last paragraph through her tears and realized that Peach was Jean-Paul's child. The child he had longed for. The child he didn't know he had. She was overwhelmed by the gravity of the secret she now held in the palm of her hand. *What am I to do?* She shuddered at the prospect of telling him that she had had the scrapbook all this time. Would he curse her for removing it from the cottage? Would he understand that she couldn't have known it was left there for him? How would he react when she told him of the table laid for two, frozen for twenty-six years, exactly as he had left it? Would he ever forgive her?

The following day Miranda telephoned Henrietta to explain the plans for the weekend. Henrietta was beside herself with excitement. She hadn't told Miranda about Jeremy. They had spent the evening together that Saturday at the fund-raising party in the town hall. Since then he had frequently called in at her shop. Sometimes she had been with Troy, and Clare had reported his visit. "It's him again," she'd say with a wry smile. "Why doesn't he just ask you out?" Henrietta didn't know why he didn't ask her for dinner. Perhaps he was shy. Perhaps he just wanted her friendship. She couldn't imagine someone like Jeremy falling in love with her. Maybe he just felt sorry for her. Clare rolled her eyes. "No wonder you're still single," she said, not intending to be unkind. "You should have more confidence in yourself. Thanks to Susannah and Trinny you're actually looking rather hot these days!"

After Miranda had booked the Berkeley Hotel she set about finding out where Phillip and Ava Lightly had moved to. She contemplated asking Mrs. Underwood or the vicar, but then she was struck with a better idea. She'd call on the post office under the pretext of having received a package for Mrs. Lightly. Surely, when they moved they had left a forwarding address.

The excitement of unraveling the mystery of Jean-Paul and Ava Lightly's secret world distracted her from the ghastliness of her own marriage breakdown. Far from feeling rejected by Jean-Paul, she felt compassion. Her love for him paled beside the blaze of Ava's. She would recover. Ava never did. Her heart bled for them both. If she could bring them together again, after all this time, he would forgive her for having kept the scrapbook.

She marched into the post office that was housed in the shop owned by Fatima's son Jamal.

"How are you, Jamal?" she asked breezily.

"Very well, thank you."

"Your mother's a star."

"I know. She's a good worker, like me."

"I can see that. You run this place all on your own?"

"With a little help from my wife."

"Of course. Get the whole family working. Cheap labor!"

"Indeed." He chuckled. "What can I do for you?"

"I've a favor to ask you."

"Go on."

Miranda tried not to look nervous. She wasn't used to being underhand. "I have received a package for Mrs. Lightly. It has no return address on it and I don't want to open it."

"Of course. Would you like me to send it to her?"

"I thought I'd telephone her, actually, and ask whether she'd like to see what I've done to her gardens. She can pick up the package. It's rather large, too large to post."

"I see. Not a problem. Let me have a look for you."

He turned and searched among a shelf of old gray files all neatly labeled alphabetically. When he found the right one, he pulled it down and opened it. Miranda's heart thudded at the anticipation of getting closer to the woman whose love story had so fascinated her. At last he found it. "She lives in Cornwall, somewhere called Pendrift. Shall I write it down for you?"

"Yes, please."

"There's a telephone number, too. They were a very charming couple. We didn't see much of Mr. Lightly after he fell ill, but Mrs. Lightly came in regularly to send letters and buy the odd thing she'd forgotten at the supermarket."

"I look forward to meeting her," said Miranda, taking the piece of paper.

"Oh, you'll enjoy her, she's very funny."

Miranda couldn't wait to telephone Ava. Suddenly the scrapbook was coming to life, the characters materializing before her like resurrected ghosts, the love story leaping off the page. Once at home she listened to her messages. There was one from Lottie confirming that David was coming down for the weekend to see the children. She wondered what he was going to do with them for two days and decided to book Mrs. Underwood to cook and put Jean-Paul on standby in case he slunk off to watch telly and left them on their own. Fatima was in the hall, cleaning the floor; Mr. Underwood stood in the doorway enjoying a long coffee break, telling her about the sudden plague of moles that was ruining the lawn. The sunshine lit up the terrace and thyme walk like a beautiful stage and Miranda stopped for a moment to admire it as she walked through the hall to her study.

She closed the door and sat at her desk, deliberating what she was going to say. She decided to introduce herself and invite Ava to see the gardens. The plan was to get her to Hartington where she would find Jean-Paul. She would give him the scrapbook and admit that she had taken it without knowing why it had been put there in the first place. Confidently she dialed the number. It rang for a while. Just before she hung up in disappointment, a woman's voice came on the line. "Hello?" Miranda plunged in.

"Hello, am I speaking to Mrs. Lightly?"

There was a long pause. Miranda looked down at the piece of paper and wondered whether, in her excitement, she had dialed the wrong number. "Who's speaking?"

"My name is Miranda Claybourne, I live at Hartington House . . ."

The woman's voice softened. "I'm afraid my mother died two years ago."

Miranda was shocked. "Ava Lightly is dead?"

"Yes."

"And Mr. Lightly?"

"My father's getting on a bit, but he's well, thank you."

"Am I speaking to Poppy?"

"No, I'm her sister, Peach."

Miranda's mouth went dry and she frantically tried to think of something to say. "I'm so sorry about your mother, Peach. I've heard so much about her, I feel I know her. She was so popular here in Hartington. When we moved all anyone could talk about were her incredible gardens."

"They were her passion. It was very hard for her to leave."

"Forgive me for asking, but I've been so curious. Why did she go?"

"Dad had a stroke and couldn't cope with the stairs. She looked after him single-handedly. She had no choice. I think it broke her heart."

"I'm sure it did. You see, I've brought the gardens back to life. I wanted to do that for her. When we moved in they had gone to seed. They needed a lot of work. I felt it was my duty to bring them back to their former glory, for her."

"That's so sweet of you. She'd have loved that."

"I didn't do it on my own. I enlisted the help of this wonderful Frenchman called Jean-Paul de la Grandière." As Ava expected, there was a long pause. "He seemed to know what I wanted. I rather left it to him, actually. Anyway, they're really wonderful now. If you're able I'd love you to see them. You can always come and stay. After all, it was your home."

"It was my home for twenty-three years," she said hesitantly. "I loved it, too."

"Please come."

"I don't know . . ." Miranda heard a man's voice in the background. "That's my dad. I'll tell him you called. He'll be grateful. We all loved Hartington House."

Miranda put down the telephone and sat back in her chair. So, Ava Lightly was dead. She felt as sad as if she had really known Ava. The disappointment was overwhelming. For almost a year she had lived Ava's story while her own had unraveled around her. Ava had kept her going. Now there was nothing left but ashes. Her heart bled for Jean-Paul, blindly groping through those ashes, wondering why they felt so cold.

For surely he didn't know she had died. Why had he returned to Hartington if not to find her as he had promised he would? Perhaps Ava had left the scrapbook there because she knew she was dying. She wanted him to know that she had kept her side of the bargain. Miranda sighed in confusion. It didn't add up. Why didn't she just send it to him? Why didn't she telephone and tell him she was ill? Why didn't she make an effort to see him before she died, rather than leave the scrapbook in the cottage at the mercy of the new family who would come to live there?

Miranda was sad that Ava would never see what she had done to the gardens. All that was left was the scrapbook and the awful truth she was now going to have to tell Jean-Paul. She got up and went out to the cottage garden to sit beneath the mountain ash and think. There was no reason why she had to tell him immediately. She could put it off. Wasn't it kinder to Jean-Paul? While there was life there was hope. She'd pick her moment carefully.

XXXVI

The healing nature of my garden can mend the most broken of hearts

David arrived at Hartington House a few hours after Miranda had left for the station with Henrietta, who had parked her Fiat in their driveway to pick up on their return. Mrs. Underwood was supervising the children in the kitchen, cooking dinner for three. There was no point putting the children to bed the moment their father walked through the door, and besides, it was the weekend; they could all sleep in the following morning.

Mrs. Underwood heard the front door open. Gus and Storm jumped down from the banquette where they had been podding broad beans for tomorrow's lunch, and rushed up the corridor to greet him. She heard squeals of "Daddy" from Storm and David's laughter as he must have picked her up and swung her in the air. It was a happy reunion. She had heard rumors about an affair and Miranda discovering them necking in the greenhouse, but she wasn't one to pry into other people's business. By the sounds of things, David was as happy as a lark out there.

"How's my boy?" he said to Gus, bending down to ruffle his hair. "You've grown!"

"No, I haven't," said Gus. "You need glasses."

"You're right about that. But I've acquired some, metaphorically speaking, and I've never seen you better than I do now." Gus scrunched up his nose. His father sounded different. "Let's go and find out when dinner is." The three of them went back down the corridor to the kitchen where Mrs. Underwood was drying her hands on her apron.

"Good evening, Mr. Claybourne," she said, smiling at the sight of him. She had always found Mr. Claybourne handsome. He had lost weight, she noticed. Could do with a little feeding up. "I've done roast chicken with potatoes," she informed him, wishing she'd added a few more potatoes to the roasting tin.

"Smells delicious! When do you want us to eat?" She looked at her watch strapped tightly around her fleshy wrist. "An hour. Eight-thirty-ish."

"Good. Come on, children, let's go outside before dinner. It's a shame to waste such a glorious evening." Gus looked at his sister and shrugged. He didn't sound like Daddy at all.

They set off down the thyme walk, towards the woods. "What are we going to do, Daddy?" asked Storm.

"I don't know. Let's see what comes up."

"We made a camp in the dovecote with Jean-Paul," said Gus, running ahead to show it off. David winced at the mention of that man's name.

"I bet you did," he said drily, watching Storm follow her brother. He gazed around the gardens, fragrant in the soft evening light, and noticed how beautiful everything was. There was little color now, just different shades of green and white. There was something very soothing about the lack of vibrant hues and he felt the tension that had built up ever since he had been discovered with Blythe ebb slowly away like a gentle tide carrying away debris with every wave.

The children lingered by the dovecote, showing their father the fire they had built to cook on and the hole in the ground where they were going to bury their treasure. David noticed the purple shadows thrown across it, the way the white was turned to pink, and to his surprise he saw a pair of doves fly in through one of the little windows below the roof. He was injected with optimism, his spirit suddenly filled with excitement as if something magical was going to happen.

"Come on! Let's keep going," he said, marching on towards the field. The children ran after him. David felt a hand slip into his and expected to see Storm, skipping along beside him. To his surprise it was Gus. He smiled down at his son. Gus grinned up at him bashfully before lowering his eyes. He didn't feel he deserved Gus's trust. He hadn't yet done the mileage to merit that level of confidence.

They reached the field where Jeremy Fitzherbert kept his cows and climbed over the fence. Charlie the donkey lifted his head and stopped chewing grass at the sight of the little boy. "We should have brought a carrot for Charlie," said David. Gus felt a wave of shame. Storm put out her hand.

"Come on, Charlie," she called, but the donkey didn't move. He watched them warily, his body stiff in anticipation of flight. "Don't be frightened," she continued. "Daddy, why won't he come? He normally does."

"He's not used to me," said David. "Come on, Charlie." David put out his hand and smiled encouragingly. Slowly they approached him. Charlie didn't know what to expect. They seemed friendly enough. Gus withdrew his hand from his father's and delved inside his trouser pocket for a mint. He had started a packet that afternoon. He placed one on the palm of his hand and stretched it towards him.

"Here, Charlie. I'm not going to hurt you." He fixed the donkey with his eyes, hoping to communicate kindness and honesty. He knew the animal was afraid of him and he didn't blame him. He had been unkind, chasing him around the field with a stick. Now he was ashamed of his actions. He had been young then, he thought, young and ignorant. Now he was more grown up he knew not to hurt living creatures, whatever their size. They all deserved respect. Jean-Paul had taught him that. "Don't be frightened, Charlie. I'm not going to hurt you, *ever again*," he added under his breath, hoping his father had not overheard.

Tentatively, the donkey stretched his neck and sniffed Gus's hand with large, velvet nostrils. The scent was too much to resist. He extended his lips and sucked up the mint. Storm wriggled in delight. David put his hands on his hips and watched as Gus pulled out a couple more mints, giving one to his sister so she could feed him, too. Little by little Gus befriended his old target. Charlie let the boy stroke his face and rub grubby fingers across his broad nose. Storm patted his neck and pulled off matted strings of fur that hung off his back like dreadlocks. "He needs a good brush," she said. "I'm going to ask Jeremy if we can take him out and groom him."

"Good idea," Gus agreed. "We can take him for walks on a rope."

"Yes, and feed him. He can be our pet."

"I think he'll like that," said David. "He certainly liked those mints."

Gus pressed his forehead to Charlie's and whispered that he was sorry. Charlie seemed to understand him. He puffed and snorted and pricked his long ears. When they continued up the field to the woods, Charlie followed them right to the gate and stood staring as they disappeared into the trees. Gus felt elated. Now his past mistakes were completely erased. With renewed energy he ran off up the path that cut through the trees, hurdling fallen branches and brambles. Storm walked with her father, keeping an eye out for the fairies who lived among the leaves. David wondered why he had always been too busy for these simple pleasures. He gazed around as the light faded, singeing the tops of the trees, plunging them into shadow, and he realized that here was where he belonged. Here with his family. Whatever happened, he'd fight to save it.

Miranda and Henrietta settled into their suite at the Berkeley Hotel, a light and spacious room overlooking the busy London streets. Harvey Nichols was just a block away and Harrods a little on from that. Miranda should have felt euphoric. She could almost smell the perfume wafting in through the window. Yet she felt subdued. All she could think about was Ava Lightly and Jean-Paul and the hopelessness of it all. She had lived their love story as if it had been her own.

Henrietta was awed by the grandeur of the hotel. She rushed about the suite, marveling at the marble bathroom where little bottles of Molton Brown bath oils stood neatly beside tiny soaps and a miniature sewing kit. She held the fluffy white dressing gown against her and did a twirl as if it were an exquisite ball dress. "They've even provided slippers!" she squealed.

"There's a swimming pool upstairs if you fancy a swim, and a spa. You have to have a massage."

"I've never had a massage," she confessed, blushing. "I don't think I'd be happy to take my clothes off in front of a stranger. Besides, there's an awful lot of me!"

"Don't be silly, Etta. They massage people ten times the size of you. Go on, I insist. Tomorrow at six when we've exhausted ourselves. I'll certainly be having one." Henrietta watched her friend. Although she was smiling, she could not hide her unhappiness. Even her lovely skin looked gray. She didn't like to pry. She longed for Miranda to confide in her so that she could be a proper friend, like Troy, who was always there during the bad times as well as the good. That's what a friend was to Henrietta: someone she could rely on to love her, no matter what. She longed for Miranda to give her that opportunity.

That night they had dinner in their suite, in their dressing gowns. The waiter brought it in on a trolley, the dishes kept warm beneath large silver domes. Henrietta was so enchanted she drank far too much wine and ate everything on her plate including the little red pepper which she hated.

"I'm sorry I've been a terrible friend," said Miranda, fortifying herself with a glass of wine. "I'm sure you've heard the rumors that David and I have separated for the time being. I caught him sleeping with an old friend of mine. A girl I've known since school. He'd been having an affair with her for months."

"I had heard something along those lines. I didn't want to ask . . ."

"I hadn't seen her for years then bumped into her in London. Her son's the same age as Gus."

"You don't expect to be betrayed by a friend like that."

"But she wasn't a real friend, was she? Just because we were close at school. A lot of water's gone under the bridge since then. We're very different people. School bonded us, but besides Gus and Rafael, we don't have anything in common—except David, of course."

"I'm so sorry."

"Thanks. Life's a bummer. I would have told you, but I needed to get it all sorted in my head first. Anyway, he's apologized."

"Do you still love him?"

Miranda took a swig of wine and narrowed her eyes. "I think I do."

"You *think* you do?" Henrietta wondered how it was possible not to know.

"I've been rather distracted lately." Miranda deliberated whether or not to tell her. She had to tell someone, the secret was burning a hole in her heart.

"What could possibly distract you from worrying about your marriage?"

Miranda laughed. "I know, it's silly. I don't really understand it myself. To be honest, I'm glad something's hotter than David. It's Jean-Paul."

"You're not in love with him, are you?"

"No, and that would make two of us," said Miranda, grinning knowingly at her friend. "You're not in love with Jean-Paul either, are you?" Henrietta shook her head. "Who then? There's someone, I can tell by the look on your face." Miranda needed to hear of someone else's happiness like a ray of light through the darkness that now enveloped her.

"I want to hear your story first," said Henrietta.

"I'll only tell you, if you tell me who you're in love with."

"Jeremy Fitzherbert. There, now I've said it."

Miranda was surprised. She sat back in her chair and stared at Henrietta, suddenly seeing her in a completely different light. "Jeremy Fitzherbert. I'd never have put you two together. But now you mention it, I can't believe I never did. How far has it gone?"

"Oh, not very far," she mumbled, lowering her eyes and turning the color of the pepper she had foolishly consumed. "We haven't even kissed. Maybe he doesn't want to."

"Don't be silly. If you're not kissing, what *are* you doing?"

"We've spent some time together. He comes into my shop."

"He must have a shop of his own by now," said Miranda.

"He's sweet."

"He's handsome. I remember the first time I met him, I noticed his eyes. They're very blue."

"Yes, they are, aren't they?"

"Well, get on with it. Why don't you make the first move?"

"Oh, I couldn't."

"Then you have to give him more encourage-ment."

"I'm sure he knows."

"Then why isn't he making a move?"

"Because he's shy."

"No, he isn't. He's not sure you feel the same way."

"Perhaps he just wants to be my friend."

Miranda nearly choked on her wine. "No man is going to go to all that trouble for friendship—unless he's gay."

"Like Troy," said Henrietta, her smile turning wistful. "So, what's *your* secret?"

Miranda drained her glass and poured another. "I'll begin at the very beginning . . ."

"That's always a good place," giggled Henrietta, feeling deliciously light-headed.

". . . with a scrapbook I found in the little cottage on the estate . . ."

Henrietta listened while Miranda told her of Ava Lightly, her affair with a mystery man she called M.F. and the gardens they had planted together. "The man Ava referred to as M.F. is Jean-Paul."

"Oh my God!" Henrietta gasped. "Are you sure?"

"Mr. Frenchman—I thought it was a coincidence when he just happened to saunter into my home and offer his services as gardener. You know, now I think about it, when I asked him what he did, he said 'I garden.' He never said he was a gardener. 'I garden, why not?' It's only now, with hindsight, that it sounds odd. He owns a beautiful vineyard in France. No wonder he never asked about money. He's a rich man. Only love could make a man of his means and status work as a lowly gardener and live in a little cottage! He said he'd bring the gardens back to life and he has. But he can't bring Ava back to life. She's dead."

Henrietta paled. "Dead?"

"I rang her up and spoke to her daughter."

"Have you told Jean-Paul?"

"Not yet. I'm too frightened."

"You have to tell him! You have to give him the scrapbook. It's his by right."

"At least he'll know how much she loved him."

"You have to tell him that you found the cottage as a shrine to their love. The table laid for two, the teapot and cups. The house kept as if they had just gone out for a walk and never returned. It's the most romantic story I've ever heard."

"But there's more, Etta."

"You have to tell me. I can't stand it!"

"Peach, the daughter I spoke to, is his."

"You're sure?"

"I'm certain. She writes it clearly in the book. After Jean-Paul returned to France, Ava realized she was pregnant. She writes that Phillip thought the baby looked just like her, but she saw Jean-Paul's smile. She called her Peach, which is what Jean-Paul called her—*ma pêche*." Miranda began to cry. "Do you know what she said? She said that every smile her daughter gave her was a gift."

The two women sat at the table, tears streaming down their cheeks. The waiter came to take the trolley away, took one look at them, apologized and withdrew like a scalded penguin.

"What must we look like?" said Henrietta, laughing through her tears.

"There's only one thing that doesn't add up. If Ava knew she was dying and wanted him to have the scrapbook, why didn't she just send it?"

Henrietta looked as perplexed as Miranda. "Maybe she only wanted him to have it if he kept his side of the bargain. She couldn't send it out of the blue, just in case he had married and forgotten about her. It had been over twenty years. But if he came back for her, as he promised he would, then he'd find it. He'd deserve it. Do you see?"

"You know, that's possible. I'm amazed you can think clearly with the amount of wine you've drunk."

"It's made me more lucid." Henrietta laughed. "Do you think he'll be hurt that Ava never told him about Peach?"

"Yes, but the M.F. of the book would understand. She couldn't tell him. Can you imagine the complications? The only way she could protect her family was to keep it secret."

"Do you think Phillip ever wondered?"

"I don't know. I doubt it. She never thought that he suspected."

"It's the stuff of a novel."

"I know," said Miranda.

"You could write it," Henrietta suggested.

"I could, but would that be fair?" She didn't dare tell Henrietta that she'd already written it. It suddenly felt wrong, like walking over Ava's grave.

"Artistic license. You could base it on truth, but make it your own."

Miranda leaned forward. "You know, I think Ava would want me to write it." She remembered the smell of orange blossom that filled the room whenever she sat down to work. "Don't ask me how, but I think she would."

The following day Miranda and Henrietta hit the shops. They went to Harvey Nichols, wandered up Sloane Street, then headed to Selfridges after lunch at Le Caprice. The celebrated Pandora awaited them with flutes of champagne and her own confident sense of style. Miranda sat in a comfortable chair in the private room while Pandora pulled dresses and coats, trousers and jackets off the rail she had prepared earlier. Henrietta did as she was told and tried everything on. "I know a lot of these are shapes you've never imagined you'd wear," said Pandora, her perfect teeth pearly white against her summer tan. "But Miranda said she wanted you to have a complete makeover—a Trinny and Susannah makeover." Pandora held up a bra and laughed. "The secret of their success is the bra! Now it's going to be the secret of *your* success."

The bags were too big and too numerous to carry back to the hotel themselves, so Pandora arranged for them to be delivered that evening. Henrietta was overwhelmed by Miranda's generosity. "This is giving me more pleasure than it's giving you," said Miranda, slipping her hand through Henrietta's arm. "I used to live for shopping, now I don't care for it as much. I'm looking forward to my massage though."

"I'm feeling confident today," said Henrietta, taking a breath, feeling renewed. "I'll have one, too."

When Miranda and Henrietta returned to Hartington House, David had already left. Miranda felt a twinge of disappointment. She had enjoyed her weekend away with Henrietta. It had been good to put some distance between herself and her home, given her time to assess what was important. But she would like to have seen him. In spite of his wickedness, she missed him. Home didn't feel complete without him. Before she could dwell on his departure she was distracted by Jeremy and the children walking up the wild garden with Charlie on a lead. Henrietta swept her hand through her new highlights and waved. Jeremy lifted his hat and waved back. The children ran ahead, into their mother's arms.

"Did you buy me a present?" asked Storm.

"Charlie's our pet!" said Gus. "He eats out of our hands and everything. He loves mints!"

She turned to see Mrs. Underwood standing in the doorway. "Henrietta, I'd better go and catch up with Mrs. Underwood. I've so enjoyed myself. Thank you for making it such fun." The two women embraced.

"No, thank *you* for everything. I'm a changed woman." Henrietta laughed, swinging her car keys on her finger. "I certainly look like one!"

"You look great! Now, go get him!"

Henrietta flushed with excitement. "And you do what's right."

"I will. I'll do it now, while Mrs. Underwood is still here to look after the children."

She watched Henrietta walk through the garden gate with Jeremy to return Charlie to his field, then went to talk to Mrs. Underwood. "How's it all been?" she asked. Mrs. Underwood folded her arms.

"They've had a lovely time together. Mr. Claybourne's had more fun, I think, than he's had in years. He loves those children. They'll tell you about it, I'm sure. I know it's none of my business, but for what it's worth, Miranda, I'll give you some advice. The Christian thing to do is forgive. Men do silly things that mean nothing. He needs his wrist slapped, but he's a good man and a good father. Right, now I've said it." She pursed her lips.

"Thank you, Mrs. Underwood. I appreciate your thoughts," Miranda replied humbly. "I've got a favor to ask you. I need to see Jean-Paul this evening. It's quite important. Would you mind staying with the children? I won't be long."

Mrs. Underwood raised her eyebrows. "If it's that important, I can't decline. Tell you what, I need to get Mr. Underwood his tea. I'll nip back now, while you give the children their bath, then come back to babysit. Is that all right?"

"Thank you, Mrs. Underwood. That would be brilliant."

508

• • •

Jeremy looked Henrietta up and down appreciatively. "You're radiant," he said.

"Thank you," she replied, blushing. "I've had a wonderful time."

"It shows."

His eyes lingered on her face longer than normal. She looked away. They walked up the lawn towards the field. The sun was setting, flooding the sky with golden syrup. Dew was already forming on the grass and the birds twittered in the trees as they settled down to roost. The breeze was warm and sweet. She cast her eyes around the gardens, sensing the magic that Ava and Jean-Paul had created there, and was suddenly filled with wistfulness. Those gardens had been watered with their tears.

"Jeremy," she said suddenly, her face blanching as she realized the strength of her feelings for him, and the need to confess them. He stopped walking and looked down at her. "There's something I want to say to you."

"Yes?" His expression grew serious.

"Well, I've been wanting to tell you for some time . . ." She swallowed hard, the doubts suddenly returning to choke her. She shuffled her feet. "Do you have a shop in your home to rival mine?" she stammered, feeling foolish. He grinned. She felt her confidence return. "You see, if you have then I have no choice but to join the two together and make one big shop because I can't take the competition. This is a small town."

Jeremy took off his hat and put his hand on her shoulder. "I've been worrying about it, too," he said. "You're so clever to come up with a solution." Henrietta forgot to breathe. Jeremy leaned down and kissed her. Astonished, she wound her arms around his middle and let him draw her to him. When she realized that she had forgotten to breathe, she took a gulp of air, then laughed.

"I think you should move in with me as quickly as possible in order to capitalize on our union," he said. "There are, however, legal matters to consider."

She frowned at him, uncomprehending. "Legal matters?"

"Marriage, Henrietta. If you knew how long I've waited to find you, you'd understand why I don't want to waste any more time. I love you. I can say that now. I love you and want to share my life with you. I can offer you a couple of soppy dogs and a rambling farmhouse, a herd of milking cows and a big red tractor. Please say yes, or I don't know what I'm going to do with all that soap!"

XXXVII

Nothing remains the same.
Everything moves on in the end.
Even us. Death is nothing more than
another change.

Miranda found Jean-Paul in the kitchen making himself dinner. "That looks good," she said, watching him prepare a poussin with onions and tomatoes.

"Next time I will make it for two." He looked at her curiously. Then his eyes fell on the scrapbook. His face grew suddenly serious as if he could smell Ava's ashes within its pages.

"We need to talk," she said huskily, unsure of how to begin. "May I sit down?"

"Of course." He watched as she placed the book on the table.

"What is this?" he asked. But he knew. He recognized the writing immediately.

"I think this was intended for you," she explained. "It was here when we bought the house. This cottage had been kept as a shrine. This table was still laid for two, as if the people taking tea had just got up and walked out. I confess I have read the book. It broke my heart. I now realize that you are the man Ava Lightly loved but couldn't have. You are her impossible love, the man she called M.F."

511

"Mr. Frenchman," he said, his voice barely audible.

"I've only just worked it out. Now I'm ashamed that I took it and read it and that I erased her memory in renovating this cottage. I think she meant you to see it as it was, as if you had never left. I think she wanted you to see that she had never forgotten you or given up." He picked up the book and ran his hand over the cover, as if the paper was the soft skin of her face. Miranda couldn't bear to look. She gazed out the window instead; it was getting dark. "I telephoned her house, but she wasn't there." She fought through the lump in her throat. "She died a couple of years ago." The words came out in a whisper. She watched him sink into a chair. Miranda got up. She needed to leave the cottage as quickly as possible. It wasn't right that she was there, invading their love. "I'm so sorry," she gasped. "I'm sorry I am the one to tell you." With tears running down her face, she hurried through the door, closing it behind her.

She stood on the stone bridge, her heart pounding against her rib cage. She had wanted to tell him about Peach. But it wasn't her place. He would read the scrapbook and find out for himself. It was bad enough that she had been the person to tell him Ava had died. Nothing in the world was as important as love. She rushed up the path towards the house, desperate to hold her children against her and breathe in a love that was warm and living.

The telephone was ringing as she stumbled through the door. She ran into her study to answer it, but it rang off just before she could reach it. "Damn!" she swore.

Mrs. Underwood appeared at the door. "I've left your supper on the Aga," she said.

"Did you get the phone?" Miranda asked.

"No. I don't like to answer your private line. Besides, there's an answering machine, isn't there?" Miranda nodded and pressed 1571. There was no message. "Are you all right, Miranda?" Mrs. Underwood looked concerned.

"I'm fine. I hoped it would be David."

Mrs. Underwood nodded knowingly. "You can always telephone *him*."

"Yes." She sounded distracted. "You're sweet to have cooked for them this weekend. I can't thank you enough."

"They ate like kings. David needs fattening up, though. He's got very thin recently. Works too hard I should imagine."

"Yes." Miranda felt exhausted and drained. She could barely muster the energy to talk to Mrs. Underwood. "I think I'll eat and go straight to bed," she said.

"I'll be going then," said Mrs. Underwood, untying her apron.

"Thanks again, Mrs. Underwood. I don't know what I'd do without you."

"Better than you think, I'm sure." She smiled sympathetically and left Miranda alone.

After Mrs. Underwood had left, Miranda ran upstairs to kiss the children. They slept contentedly in their cozy rooms, their heads snuggled into their pillows. She inhaled the sleepy scent of them, nuzzling her nose into their hair, and silently thanked God for the gift of children and the blessing of love.

She ate in her bedroom after wallowing in a hot, pine-scented bath. Mrs. Underwood had made her a delicious vegetable soup with butternut squash and sweet potato. She lay in bed watching television, finding a repeat episode of *Seinfeld* that she had seen before. She needed to forget the scrapbook and Jean-Paul and turn her mind to neutral. She finished her soup, watched the end of *Seinfeld* then switched off the light to go to sleep. The telephone rang.

"I love you, Miranda." It was David. Miranda felt a surge of relief.

"I love you, too," she replied huskily. David was taken aback. He had expected a greater battle.

"You do? I don't deserve it."

"Let's start again," she said. "Forget what's done and begin again from here."

"I'll never forgive myself for hurting you."

"But I can forgive you and I will. I want to move on."

"I realize now that only you and the children

514

matter. Nothing should put our family at risk. It's all we have."

"We have to spend more time together, David."

"Well, I've been thinking . . . I'm going to quit the City."

"You are?" Miranda was astonished. She sat up, suddenly wide awake. "What are you going to do?"

"I don't know. Write the life cycle of the flea? The City is a money-spinner, but it's no life. I've done my bit. I've worked hard. It's time to reap my reward, by that I mean you, Gus and Storm. I've had time to think these past few weeks. We should take a long family holiday. I don't want to send the children to boarding school. I want them at home where I can enjoy them. What's the point of having them if all we do is send them away?"

"You *have* done a lot of thinking." Miranda was impressed. "Gus'll be pleased."

"He was. I told him. We had a man to man, you know."

"Did you?" Miranda felt her stomach fizz. David sounded like the old David she had fallen in love with.

"We understand each other now."

"Come home, darling. I've missed you."

He sighed heavily. There was a long pause as he gathered himself together. "Those are the sweetest words I've ever heard."

• • •

The following morning, Miranda awoke with a strange knot in her stomach. She looked out the window. The sky was gray, the clouds thick and heavy, a melancholy light hanging over the gardens. There was no breeze. Something was missing. Something was wrong. Hurriedly she dressed, pulling on a pair of jeans and a cotton sweater. The children were in the kitchen helping themselves to cereal, cheerily making plans for the day. "I'll be back in a minute," she shouted, as she ran through the hall. Gus frowned at his sister, who shrugged in resignation. Their parents were very odd.

Miranda sprinted across the gravel and through the wildflower meadow. It was just beginning to drizzle, light feathery drops that fell softly on her face. To her relief Jean-Paul hadn't left, but was standing on the bridge, gazing into the water. When he saw her, he didn't smile, but looked at her with weary red eyes, his skin gray.

"Are you all right?" she asked, standing beside him, catching her breath.

"I have read the book," he told her.

"The whole book?" Miranda was amazed. It had taken her months.

"I haven't slept." He shook his head and ran a rough hand through his long hair. Miranda noticed the silver stubble on his face. "I had to finish it. I think I always knew in my heart that she was dead. That is why I didn't look for her. I was afraid."

"What are you going to do?" She dreaded his answer, but she knew it before he spoke.

"Return to France."

"What about Peach?" she asked softly.

He shrugged. "I don't know." He seemed confused. "Ava always put her children first. I must do the same."

"You mean, you won't contact her?"

"I cannot. She may not know."

"But you're her father. You said yourself, 'a part of you and a part of me.'" For the first time since she had met Jean-Paul, he seemed unsure of himself.

They both became aware of someone standing on the riverbank. She approached, dressed in pale blue dungarees, white T-shirt, her long curly hair the color of summer hay. Jean-Paul caught his breath. "Ava," he gasped. "It can't be." The young woman smiled and waved tentatively.

"Jean-Paul," muttered Miranda, marveling at how beautifully his smile translated a woman's face. "That's Peach."

She reached them and her smile dissolved into diffidence. "Jean-Paul," she said. "You don't know me but . . ."

"I know you," he said. "I recognize your mother in you."

"And you in me, too," she said with an embarrassed laugh.

"You have your mother's directness," he observed,

running his eyes over her features, impatient to take her all in.

She turned to Miranda. "You must be Miranda."

"Yes. You don't know how good it is to see you." They embraced as if they were old friends.

"I tried to telephone you over the weekend, but no one answered. I hope it's okay that I just turned up." She gazed around. "Nothing's changed. It looks wonderful."

"Come inside," Jean-Paul suggested. "It's about to pour."

"I think I'd better get back to my children," said Miranda, backing away.

"You're welcome to join us," Jean-Paul said. Miranda noticed the color had returned to his face. He looked handsome again, the irresistible twinkle in his eyes restored.

"I'd love to, because I'm curious. But I think it's right that I leave you together. You've got a lot to catch up on. Maybe, when you're done, I can show you the gardens. It's all credit to Jean-Paul, but they're stunning."

"Yes, please," said Peach. "I'd love that. My mother would be so happy to see them resurrected. It was her life's work. I want to thank you, Miranda."

"Whatever for?"

"For making this possible."

Miranda felt her spirits leap. "Did I?"

"Of course, I never thought I'd find Mr.

Frenchman. Thanks to you, I have." She looked at Jean-Paul and grinned. He struggled to find the words. She was so like her mother. So direct, so open; it wasn't as if she were meeting a stranger, but as if she had known him all her life. "Don't be alarmed," she said, sensing his astonishment. "I've had some time to get used to this."

Miranda walked up the garden to the house. Around her the gardens radiated their magic and inside she felt complete. She belonged. She looked forward to playing with the children. Perhaps they'd go to the old castle and have a picnic. Maybe she'd invite a few of their friends for tea. She reached the house. Storm and Gus tumbled out onto the porch as a taxi drew up on the gravel. She turned to see David stepping out with a suitcase. He wasn't in his suit, but in jeans and a green shirt, looking thin but handsome. Miranda smiled back, but she had to wait her turn for he opened his arms and the children flew in. They belonged there, too, she thought contentedly; at last.

Inside the cottage, Jean-Paul put the kettle on. The two of them sat at the kitchen table as Ava and Jean-Paul had done twenty-six years before. But this time it was not to say good-bye but to begin a whole new life together. "There is so much I have to tell you," said Peach, her green eyes glittering with emotion. "I don't know where to begin."

"Tell me about your mother. How did she die?"

"Let's go back a bit further, or I'll lose track. Darling Daddy—Phillip—had a stroke about four years ago and for a while we all continued to live here in spite of his slow recovery. Mummy looked after him like a nurse. She refused to seek help. You know what she's like. It was a full-time job, but he deteriorated. The stairs were a big problem. Everyone told her we had to move. Of course, she was torn between what she knew was right for Phillip, and what was right for her. She loved this place and the gardens, and I know now that the reason for her determination to hold on to them was because of you. She must have hoped that one day you'd come back and get her. We were all grown up. Poppy lives in London, is married with children of her own; Archie married a Chilean and lives in Valparaiso. Angus is a bit of a bohemian. He hasn't married. He's a successful historian. You wouldn't believe it."

"And you?"

"I've never flown the nest. I'm a gardener." She grinned proudly.

"I am not surprised," he mused, shaking his head at the miracle of her. Her fingernails were short and ragged, the palms of her hands rough like bark. He was sure she smelled of damp grass and hay. "Go on with your story," he said, anxious to hear more.

"Well, she stayed on here long after she should have gone. Finally, she was left no choice. She discovered a lump in her stomach. It turned out to be malignant. We moved to Cornwall because Mummy had always loved the sea. She put the house on the market at such an exorbitant price so no one would buy it. It caused her such pain to let it go. Maybe she hoped it wouldn't sell and she could one day move back. While Daddy recovered, Mummy got worse. It all happened very quickly. She didn't have much time. Now I've read the scrapbook, I think the tumor was a manifestation of the heartbreak she suffered after you left. Her grief was so deep it was unspeakable. She kept it secret all those years. She never told me and I was closer to her than the others, being the youngest." She hesitated, then added shyly: "And being yours." They looked at each other as the rain rattled against the windowpanes, and realized that in spite of the fact that they were strangers, the reality of their shared blood and their mutual love for Ava gave them an immediate sense of unity.

"When did she die?" he asked.

"In spring. May the fifth."

"I so hoped to see her again."

"We buried her in a little church overlooking the sea. She should have been buried here, but she said she didn't want that. I think she felt it inappropriate. Tactless, perhaps, considering Daddy."

"She always put her family first."

"She did. But she left me the scrapbook, not in her will, but in a letter of wishes. She had hidden it in the house, beneath a loose floorboard."

"So it was you who put the book in the cottage?"

"Yes. I read it all. I understood why she never told me about you. What good would have come of it? I love Phillip as my father, and he will always be my father. Think how lucky I am to have two."

"She never told you?"

"No. Maybe she felt guilty for not telling us both. Perhaps she couldn't speak of it to anyone, not even to me. But dying people always want to tie up loose ends and I suppose it is my right to know who made me. I decided to put the scrapbook in here so that if you returned you would find it and know that she had never stopped loving you. I didn't know where to find you and I didn't want to ask my father. At that stage I didn't even know whether I wanted to find you. It's not an easy thing to learn that the man you believe is your father is not."

"Does Phillip know?"

"Goodness, no. And he never will. It would be wrong of me to tell him. Besides, my mother gave her life to him. Maybe she would have left had he not fallen ill. He needed her. Who knows?"

"Why did you come today?"

"Because I feel the time is right. It's what Mummy would have wanted. You both longed for a child so badly, it's only right that you should know." She smiled again and Jean-Paul saw his own face mirrored in hers. He felt his stomach lurch at the sight of it. She blushed. "I was also captivated by the scrapbook and the romance of my mother's secret love affair. She never stopped loving you, or hoping that you would one day be reunited. When Miranda telephoned, I knew it was my chance."

"Why didn't she tell me she was dying?"

"I've wondered about that, too. I can only imagine, knowing my mother as I do, that she wouldn't have wanted you to see her like that. Her hair fell out. She aged terribly. She was very sick. I would imagine she wanted you to remember her the way she was."

"But she knew I loved her."

Peach's eyes filled with tears. Once again she could smell the scent of orange blossom. It crept around her like a familiar blanket and invaded her senses, demanding to be noticed. She looked at Jean-Paul. He lifted his chin, aware of it, too.

"Yes, she did," she said, her voice barely a whisper. "You can smell her, too?" Jean-Paul closed his eyes. How often he had dismissed her perfume as wishful dreaming.

The room filled with sunshine. It was bright and twinkling as it caught the little specks of dust and lit them up like fireflies. Father and daughter opened their eyes to see that the clouds had parted to let the sun shine through. Jean-Paul stood up hastily. "Come," he said, taking her hand. Peach followed him outside, into the rain. There, in a dazzling arc above them, stood a magnificent rainbow.

"It's beautiful," she said in wonder. *"Un arc-en-ciel."*

"Un arc-en-ciel," he repeated, knowing that Ava was up there somewhere in the midst of all those colors. Then he laughed, for there, between green and blue, was the most splendid color of all.

"Can you see pink?" He pointed to the vibrating light, the color of a perfect summer rose.

"I see it!" she said, her face wet with tears. "I see it! The elusive pink."

"She's there," said Jean-Paul, squeezing her hand. "She's there. I know she is."

XXXVIII

The day of Henrietta and Jeremy's wedding could not have been more beautiful. The sky dazzled with sunshine, a cold breeze whipped in off the sea, swirling through the red and gold leaves, breathing autumn on the final remains of summer, and yet the sun was warm. Birdsong rang out from the treetops and squirrels paused their nut collecting to watch the baffling human world below them. But love is an instinct understood by all creation and it was as if the whole of nature conspired to make their day magnificent.

Troy sat in the front pew with Henrietta's mother and sister. He had put the bride's hair up in a glossy bun encircled with purple roses and wiped her tears away himself when she had seen how beautiful she looked. On the other side of the aisle Jeremy waited nervously, his large hands trembling as he fidgeted with the service sheet, exchanging looks with David, whom he had asked to be best man. He took a deep breath, barely daring to acknowledge his incredible fortune, in case he jinxed it and Henrietta did not appear.

Miranda sat behind David with Cate and Nigel, whose coldness sat between them like a corpse. She thought of Jean-Paul and Peach: he had lost his lover but gained a daughter. Ava had said that love was all she had to give him, but that was no longer true; she had given him Peach. Miranda thought of them both in France, at Les Lucioles. He would show her the gardens he had cultivated for her mother and together they would share memories, building a bridge to span the years that separated them.

David caught her eye and smiled. She gave him her hand over the pew and he squeezed it. That squeeze said so much. Her eyes began to well. "Don't cry now, darling. She hasn't come in yet!" he whispered and she nodded, dabbing her face with the hanky she had had the foresight to bring with her.

At that moment the large wooden doors creaked open and Dorothy Dipwood began to play the organ. The congregation stood. Miranda leaned into the aisle to see Henrietta in the elegant ivory dress embroidered with pearls that Miranda had helped her choose at Catherine Walker. Her face was veiled, but her grin was visible beneath it. She walked on the arm of her father, his face pink with pride. Miranda's eyes were so filled with tears that she was barely able to distinguish Gus and Storm, who stepped behind her as page and bridesmaid with Clare's two children. Storm held a ball of purple roses hung from a ribbon and Gus held her hand, his face serious with concentration, taking care not to step on Henrietta's train.

Henrietta watched Jeremy, who stood in the aisle to receive her, beaming as he watched his bride walk slowly towards him. He was relieved he wasn't expected to speak because a knot of emotion had lodged itself in his throat. Henrietta's father placed her hand in Jeremy's and they gazed at each other for a long moment, marveling at the magic that had brought them to this point.

Miranda felt a movement beside her and turned to see Nigel take Cate's hand. At first Cate stiffened in surprise, too proud to yield, but then the love that pervaded the church worked its magic on her, too, and she relaxed, finally letting her defenses fall. The congregation sat down and Miranda caught sight of the purple Louboutin shoes she had recently bought in London. She wiggled them, admiring the height and color and the elegant cut of the toe. Some pleasures never fade.

At the end of the service they spilled out of the church into the sunshine. The children ran around the gravestones, jumping from one to the other like silk-clad frogs. Jeremy and Henrietta climbed onto Jeremy's red tractor and waved as they set off to Hartington House where Miranda had organized the reception in a marquee on the lawn. Mrs. Underwood was supervising the food and Mr. Underwood was valet parking with Toby, the new gardener.

David slipped his arm around her waist and pulled her against him. "She looks beautiful," he said. "Clever you."

"Not at all," Miranda replied. "Her beauty is entirely her own."

"Now you've shared Jean-Paul and Ava's story with me, will you let me read your novel?"

Miranda looked at him in surprise. "How did you know I'd written a book?"

"Gus told me."

"How did he know?"

"Children know everything."

"I might."

"Might?"

"Okay, I will. But I won't ever publish it."

"What if it's brilliant?"

"It *is* brilliant, but it wouldn't be right and besides, I don't think I did it all by myself." David frowned at her quizzically. "I had help," she said enigmatically. There was no point explaining.

She raised her eyes to the sky, remembering the persistent scent of orange blossom that had filled the room whenever she had sat down to write. Since finishing the book she hadn't smelled it. Ava's ghost had gone.

"So what are you going to do with it?" he asked.

"Give it to Peach," she said.

"To Peach? Why?"

"Because I know now that I wrote it for her." She took David's hand. "Come on, darling. We'd better gather up the page and bridesmaid, we've a reception to get to."

"Gus! Storm!" David shouted. The children bounded up, their cheeks red with exertion. "Time to go home," he said, ruffling Gus's hair. Miranda sighed with pleasure. Home. How good that sounded.

Epilogue

Can you hear a bird sing
At the top of a chestnut tree?
I am the song she's singing
So sweet a melody.

Can you hear the stream flow
Forever running free?
My laughter's in the ripples
And bubbles eternally.

Can you feel the sunshine
Warm upon your skin?
I am the very sun itself,
The love you feel within.

For Discussion

1. Gus seems to act out violently as a result of his parents' inattentiveness. Do you think his sins are ultimately forgivable, or should he be held responsible to some degree?

2. At first, "the word 'community' made [Miranda's] stomach churn" (page 33). By the end of the year, she has embraced the country and left London behind. What do you think accounts for Miranda's change in attitude about Hartington? How do her new relationships compare to her old ones?

3. Infidelity played a part in the Lightly marriage and in the Claybourne marriage. One affair was revealed, while the other remained secret. What do you see as the benefits and drawbacks of each situation? How can keeping an affair a secret protect a marriage? How can having everything out in the open allow a relationship to grow and mend?

4. Montefiore describes the setting of the novel beautifully. Nearly every chapter comes alive with details of the characters' surroundings. Which images are most memorable for you? Can you picture any of the gardens or buildings described?

5. How do your feelings about Ava's affair differ from your feelings about David's? Is all infidelity equally condemnable? How does the way in which Montefiore wrote the novel affect your opinions about the injured parties in each affair? Can you be sympathetic to both Ava and Philip? Can you find any sympathy for David? How did Jean-Paul's friendship with Miranda help him contextualize how his affair with Ava must have affected Philip (page 436)?

6. Ava thinks about having "a child to stand between her and the door to remind her where her place [is]" (page 321). Do you think havng a baby is an effective way of maintaining connection to a mate? Or is this a selfish decision on Ava's part? Why do you think the pregnancy effectively kept Ava's marriage going, despite its being Jean-Paul's child?

7. Henri says, "Relationships work better when the air is able to circulate between two people" (page 358). Have you experienced this idea playing out in your own life? Can independence and time apart help strengthen a relationship, or drive people apart?

8. Jean-Paul and Ava's love story exists in so many forms—in Ava's scrapbook, in the

novel Miranda writes, and in the novel we have just read. In what ways is their story classic and ripe for retelling and reworking?

9. When Blythe visits Miranda's new country home she discovers that, "the balance of power [in their friendship] had shifted, leaving her at a disadvantage" (page 401). Many of the female friendships in the book are marred by unhealthy power dynamics and competition. What do Cate and Blythe have in common? Which friendships seem mutually supportive? Which seem to be suffering and why?

10. While Ava was great at entertaining a crowd, she very much appreciated time alone "to relax and not have to make an effort" (page 151). How did this preference affect her relationships? Does socializing exhaust or exhilarate you? Does solitude relax you or make you lonely?

11. Henrietta states: "But all the good I have to give is turning sour in my belly. If I don't find someone soon I'll ferment into vinegar and won't be of any worth to anyone" (page 173). In what ways can the lack of an outlet for romantic love "ferment" a person? How does Jean-Paul's single status differ from Henrietta's? Is it, in fact, better to have loved and lost than never to have loved at all?

12. When Jean-Paul meets Miranda and her family he thinks, "I cannot bring the love back but I can create new love. That is how I will remember her" (page 181). In what other ways do both Ava and Jean-Paul keep the memory of each other alive? Do you think their actions are healthy responses to the loss of love? Or has it proven harmful for them to keep the past alive in their hearts?

13. Toddy tells Ava that, "In the old days we died at thirty. Now we live so long it's like two lifetimes. I think one should be able to call it quits halfway through and enjoy another marriage when it starts to grow humdrum" (page 220). Do you support Toddy's claim and think that longer life expectancy contributes to more failed marriages? What other developments in our modern world may be making second and third marriages more and more commonplace?

14. How do you feel about Miranda's decision to forgive David and move forward in their marriage? Has he proven himself to be a changed man?

15. What are your hopes for Jean-Paul's future relationship with Peach? Do you think their mutual affection for Ava will bond them? What struggles do adult children face when

meeting their biological parents for the first time?

Enhance Your Book Club

1. Ava and Jean-Paul periodically compare their relationship to ephemeral phenomena in nature: a rainbow, a sunset. How would you describe some of the relationships in your life using nature as a metaphor? Have you planted strong roots? Is your family tree a weeping willow, an oak tree with a tire swing, or maybe a crab apple tree?

2. Jean-Paul loves to paint, and it is one of the first things that bonds him to Ava. Go through the pages of this novel and attempt to re-create one of the scenes in any artistic medium you're comfortable with; paint, markers, computer, collage.

3. The cottage garden becomes Ava and Jean-Paul's special place, something they built together. Create a mini garden for your book group with an indoor herb garden. Then, two or three book group meetings from now, when the herbs are ready for picking, make like Mrs. Underwood and whip something up for the group. Go to http://www.doityourself.com/stry/indoorherb garden for instructions.

4. Cate's bakery acts as the town center of Hartington. Why not hold your book club meeting in a local establishment that brings people together in your community? Better yet, channel Ava and Jean-Paul and hold the meeting outdoors.

Center Point Publishing
600 Brooks Road ● PO Box 1
Thorndike ME 04986-0001 USA

(207) 568-3717

US & Canada:
1 800 929-9108
www.centerpointlargeprint.com